# ASIAN PUBLIC THEOLOGY

*Critical Concerns in Challenging Times*

# ASIAN PUBLIC THEOLOGY
## *Critical Concerns in Challenging Times*

**Felix Wilfred**

Tercentenary Publication
2010

**Asian Public Theology: Critical Concerns in Challenging Times –** Published by the Rev. Dr. Ashish Amos of the Indian Society for Promoting Christian Knowledge (ISPCK), Post Box 1585, 1654 Madarsa Road, Kashmere Gate, Delhi-110006.

ISBN : 978-81-8465-084-6

*Laser typeset by*
**ISPCK,** Post Box 1585, 1654, Madarsa Road, Kashmere Gate, Delhi-110006.
Tel: 23866322/23
e-mail: *ashish@ispck.org.in* • *ella@ispck.org.in*
website: *www.ispck.org.in*

# Contents

## PART I

## The Subaltern Journey

## PART II

## Pathways to Justice

# PART III
## Theological Crossroads

# PART IV
## Continuing Common Journey

# Preface

Seventy women and children were killed in a stampede in Uttar Pradesh on 4 March, 2010. The mere rumour about a free lunch and distribution of utensils in a nearby ashram was enough to mobilize a mass of destitutes driven by anxiety to barge through a narrow gate.

This tragic event is a metaphor for the Asia of today with its immense masses of people living in abject poverty, destitution and insecurity and waiting for something good to happen to them. But the dream of a different situation eludes them, and they get stampeded and crushed. Their dreams and aspirations are trampled underfoot. Without a safe space to blossom, the buds wither away. Can religions sit idle and watch these things happen? How can religion and theology address public issues affecting the people, especially the poorest of the poor? How can theology respond to the aspirations of the poor? The existing forms of theology need to transform themselves into public theology, and thus find their legitimation today.

This book is not a theorizing on public theology in Asia. Rather, it takes up issues of public concern in Asia, examines them with the help of many disciplines and reflects on them in the light of the humanistic vision and values of Christian message. It is a theology that is open to the humanistic orientation of all religious traditions and secular ideologies. At a time when more and more people are drawn into the null spaces of social insensitivity and seduced by the glitz and glamour of globalization and its consumerism, public theology as a critical intervention, can take on a prophetic role. It can acknowledge the agency of the subalterns, affirm their ethical sense, inspire courage and evoke hope in them. The book is also relevant for the non-subalterns, since it discusses their human and ethical responsibility to empathize with the victims and take up their cause.

For the past three decades I have rarely dealt with "pure" theological questions around doctrinal issues, convinced as I am that people need to validate our theology in terms of how it addresses their questions. Asian theology needs to break loose of doctrinal narcissism. When people ask me about my specialization, I tell them that I have none and that I am a "general practitioner". All that interests me are the dreams and hopes of the people, and I try to study how the humanistic Christian message can reach them and help them imagine alternatives. This re-envisioning can transform them and the world around through their own agency. If theology can be of help, we can be happy about it.

The agenda for this book was set by people who are struggling in Asia to make sense of their lives as individuals and communities, and who believe that the Gospel can be truly salt and leaven for their lives and for the society. The volume brings together the reflections I made on different occasions, and they are held together by the way they are treated as public issues of Asia. My thoughts were shaped by my conversation with peoples of various backgrounds in different countries of Asia. The teaching of a course every year at the East Asian Pastoral Institute, Manila, to students from various countries of Asia-Pacific was a platform to test my thoughts and get immensely enriched. My doctoral students closer at home provided also a lot of stimuli to leave the trodden path and explore new horizons.

In a special way I would like to mention the contribution of my doctoral student Kochurani who twice read through the entire manuscript in its first draft and in the final version, and made perceptive comments and suggestions to improve the text. I wish to thank her most sincerely S. Nesamony took a lot of interest in this volume, patiently read through the chapters and also carefully checked the references, for all of which I thank him. My sincere thanks go as well to Francis Gonsalves, a former student of mine, who found time to read the volume even while it was in the press for further corrections.

Pramila was very enthusiastic about the idea of this book and helped me in the early stages of its production. At a later stage she also helped with the index. I appreciate her contribution and express my sincere thanks to her. Martina helped me in preparing the final version of the text and also brought to completion the work of index. Mary John and A. Kulandaisamy read through the proofs and did the corrections. I thank them sincerely for their help. With a lot of dedication, Flora assisted me everyday and at every stage of the work. She helped me in all possible ways, so that I could write the various chapters of the work unhindered, and also get it ready for publication. I express to her my warm appreciation and thanks.

My friends at ISPCK have been instrumental, under the direction of Rev. Dr. Ashish Amos, to see this work through the press. In a very special way I wish to thank Ella for getting the work printed and doing the final corrections with her characteristic attention to details.

I hope that this modest work will contribute to promote Public Theology in different contexts of Asia, and help live the Gospel in depth in these challenging times.

*Felix Wilfred*
*Asian Centre for Cross-Cultural Studies*
*Chennai*

# Introduction

A sian Public Theology is one in which the accent will be stronger on the "public" than on theology. The focus will be the issues and questions that affect the people and societies of Asia and which need to be addressed urgently.[1] The theology envisaged here is not the kind that will confine itself within the Christian community, but one which will have an import for all the actors in public life.[2] It does not mean that we impose a Christian theology on others which, obviously, will be counterproductive. Rather, Asian Public Theology will be one that will be inherently interreligious in nature.[3]

---

[1] It may be of interest to note that a similar development is taking place in the field of sociology. In the context of a mere theoretical and academic study of society, there emerged public sociology which engaged itself with the study of social processes as also processes of values. It is an attempt to move from mere instrumental knowledge viewed as means to reflexive knowledge focused on ends. Emmanuel Wallerstein is of the view that public sociology cannot be separate from the rest of sociology, and he summarizes the spirit of public sociology when he notes, "all sociologists - living, dead, or yet to be born - are, and cannot be other than, public sociologists. The only distinction is between those who are willing to avow the mantle and those who are not". Quoted in Dan Clawson et al. (eds), *Public Sociology*, University of California Press, Berkeley, 2007, p. 16.

[2] Cf. Bertelsmann Stiftung (ed.), *What the World Believes. Analyses and Commentary on the Religion Monitor 2008*, Verlag Bertelsmann Stiftung, Bielefeld, 2009. This is a very helpful reference work that surveys the state of religion in various countries. It provides empirical data on the social effects of religion and the perception of it by individuals and it covers a quantitative survey among 21000 people from different religious traditions.

[3] Cf. Jose Kuttianimattathil, *Practice of Interreligious Dialogue*, Kristu Jyoti Publications, Bangalore 1995; Michael Amaladoss, "Dialogue Between Religions in Asia Today", *East Asian Pastoral Review*, 42 (2005), pp. 45-60.

The meeting of various religious perspectives and worldviews happens in the process of addressing jointly public issues concerning everyone in a society. It is a challenge to Christian theology in as much as its new task is to contribute in a dialogical process, the resources and insights that will help address matters of public interest while attentively listening to other voices. While we have many models and precedents for a theology of public life, there are no such points of reference for Public Theology in Asia, which needs to be evolved.

## THE NEED FOR AN ASIAN PUBLIC THEOLOGY

We begin by enquiring what is the public context - political, social, cultural, economic etc. - in Asia that calls for a Public Theology. I see at least four crucial areas that need to be considered. They will also pave the way in shaping a distinctly Asian Public Theology.

In the first place, Asia stands in need of *defence of freedom against state despotism of various kinds and grades*.[4] It is a fact that in many Asian countries, despotism and political authoritarianism and militarism continue to affect the lives of the people. China, for example, has made a mark today as a considerable economic power. However, its economic achievements rest on political feet of clay. The liberal economy co-exists with traditional

---

[4] Cf. Stephen C. Angle, *Human Rights and Chinese Thought. A Cross-Cultural Study*, Cambridge University Press 2002; Joanne R. Bauer and Daniel A. Bell (eds.), *The East Asian Challenge for Human Rights*, Cambridge University Press 1999; Charles F. Keyes et al. (eds.), *Asian Visions of Authority. Religion and the Modern States of East and Southeast Asia*, University of Hawaii Press, Honolulu, 1994; Michael Jacobsen - Ole Bruun (eds.), *Human Rights and Asian Values. Contesting National Identities and Cultural Representations in Asia*, Cruzon, Richmond, 2000; Philip Wickeri, *Seeking the Common Ground. Protestant Christianity, and Three-Self Movement and China's United Front*, Orbis Books, New York, 1988; Donald E. MacInnis, *Religion in China Today. Policy and Practice*, Orbis Books, New York, 1988; *Dangerous Meditation. China's Campaign against Falungong*, Human Rights Watch, New York, 2002; Theo Nichols, Surhan Cam, Wen-chi Grace Chou, Soonok Chun, Wei Zhao, and Tongqing Feng, "Factory Regimes and the Dismantling of Established Labour in Asia: A Review of Cases from Large Manufacturing Plants in China, South Korea and Taiwan" in *Work, Employment & Society*, 18 (Dec 2004), pp. 663 – 685; Peter Zarrow, "Anti-Despotism and "Rights Talk": The Intellectual Origins of Modern Human Rights Thinking in the Late Qing" in *Modern China*, 34, (Apr 2008), pp. 179 - 209; "China's Place in the World. The People's Republic at 60" special issue of *The Economist*, October 3 – 9, 2009. "Communist China at 60. A harmonious and Stable Crackdown" in *The Economist*, September 5 – 11, 2009, pp. 32 – 33. "Tension in Xinjiang" in *The Economist*, September 12 – 18, 2009, p. 30.

socialist political centralization and autocracy.[5] The situation is very similar in North Korea, Myanmar, and Vietnam. Even in countries where democracy is the form of government, in practice, there is a lack of true freedom. Expressions of dissent and protest by the marginalized and subaltern groups are suppressed. Religious freedom is heavily controlled in the socialist countries of Asia and in countries where a particular religion is the state religion, or state-favoured religion. Even in a democratic country like India with the constitutional guarantee of religious freedom, there are cases of serious violation of human rights.

The second area of public concern is the *defence of the poor from the tyranny of the market*.[6] The penetration of the liberal market has resulted in an unprecedented gulf between the poor and the rich, growing unemployment, pauperization of the peasantry, suppression of the rights of workers, starvation-deaths – all these co-existing with a growing culture of middle class consumerism and commercialization of every realm of life. In a situation of market-economy in which the cause of the poor is seriously compromised, Asia needs a Public Theology in defence of the last and the least.

The third important public concern is the *creation of harmonious and non-exclusive communities*. Two related issues are implied here. It is well known that in Asia there has been increasing violence and conflict among various ethnic and religious groups, and among linguistic and regional communities.[7]

---

[5] Cf. Willy Lam, "China's Political Feet of Clay", *Far Eastern Economic Review*, 172, 8 (2009), pp. 10-14; Ching Kwan Lee and Mark Selden, "Inequality and Its Enemies in Revolutionary and Reform China", in *EPW*, 43, 52 (27 December 2008), pp. 27-35; Robert Weil, "A House Divided: China after 30 Years of 'Reforms'", in *EPW*, 43, 52 (27 December 2008), pp. 61-69; Min Qi Li, "Socialism, Capitalism, and Class Struggle: The Political Economy of Modern China", in *EPW*, 43, 52 (27 December 2008), pp. 77-85; Dic Lo and Yu Zhang, "Globalisation Meets Its Match: Lessons from China's Economic Transformation", in *EPW*, 43, 52 (27 December 2008), pp. 97-102.

[6] Cf. Jon Sobrino - Felix Wilfred (eds.) Globalization and its Victims, *Concilium* 2001/5; See also Joseph Stiglitz, *Globalization and Its Discontents*, Penguin Books, London, 2002; Id., *The Roaring Nineties*, Penguin Books, London, 2003; Ajay Gudavarthy, "Human Rights Movement in India: State, Civil Society and Beyond", in *Contributions to Indian Sociology* (NS), 42, 1 (2008), pp. 29-57; Saskia Sassen, *Globalization and Its Discontents*, The New Press, New York, 1998.

[7] Cf. Amartya Sen, *Identity and Violence. The Illusion of Destiny*, Penguin Books, London, 2006; Mark Juergensmeyer, *Terror in the Mind of God. The Global Rise of Religious Viol*ence, Oxford University Press, Delhi, 2000; T.N. Madan, *Modern*

One may recall here the situation in Pakistan, Sri Lanka, India, China, Malaysia, Myanmar and so on. In this regard, we need to pay attention to growing religious fundamentalism in many Asian countries. In recent times, India has witnessed the effects of Hindu fascism in the states of Gujarat where Muslims were targeted and in Orissa where Christian tribals have been victimized. Well-known are the Islamic fundamentalism operative in Pakistan, Indonesia, Malaysia, etc. Conflictual situation arises also from the fact that some people and groups (as for example the Dalits in India and tribals all over Asia) are excluded from full and equal participation in the community and its affairs. We need to also recall here the exclusion of women in which both traditional and modern forces converge. Therefore, the creation of a communion of communities among the various groups remains one of the important public issues in the continent.

The fourth concern is that of *protecting the environment*. Asia is the home of great biodiversity. The accelerated mode of development propelled by technology and market has created an environmental crisis in Asian countries. The natural resources are exploited, stretching them beyond their regenerative capacity. Commercial interests denude the

---

*Myths, Locked Minds: Secularism and Fundamentalism in India*, Oxford University Press, Delhi, 1998; R. Puniyani, *Communal Politics. Facts Versus Myths*, Sage Publications, New Delhi, 2003; L. Stanislaus and Alwyn D'Souza (eds.), *Prophetic Dialogue. Challenges and Prospects in India*, Ishvani Kendra/ISPCK, Pune/Delhi, 2003; Augustine Thottakkara (ed.), *Dialogical Dynamics of Religions*, CIIS, Rome, 1993; Anto Akkara, *Kandhamal a Blot to Indian Secularism*, Media House, Delhi, 2009. K.N. Panikkar, *Before the Night Falls. Forebearings of Fascism in India*, Books for Change, Bangalore, 2002. Id (ed.), *The Concerned Indian's Guide to Communalism*, Viking, 1999; Neera Chandhoke, "Civil Society in Conflict Cities", in *Economic and Political Weekly (EPW)*, 44, 44 (31 October 2009), pp. 99-108; Neil Devotta, "Sri Lanka at Sixty: A Legacy of Ethnocentrism and Degeneration", in *EPW*, 44, 5 (31 January-6 February 2009), pp. 46-53; Giles Ji Ungpakorn, "Class War for Democracy in Thailand", in *EPW*, 44, 12 (21 March 2009), pp. 21-24; Irfan Ahmad, "The Secular State and the Geography of Radicalism", in *EPW*, 44, 23 (6 June 2009), pp. 33-38; Sadia M. Malik, "Horizontal Inequalities and Violent Conflict in Pakistan: Is There a Link?", in *EPW*, 44, 34 (22 August 2009), pp. 21-24; Vibhanshu Shekhar, "Malay Majoritarianism and Marginalised Indians", in *EPW*, 43, 8 (23 February 2008) pp. 22-25; Denis J. Burke, "Tibetans in Exile in a Changing Global Political Climate", *EPW*, 43,15 (12 April 2008) pp. 79-85; Pasuk Phongpaichit and Chris Baker, "Thailand: Fighting over Democracy", in *EPW*, 43, 50 (13 December 2008), pp. 18-21; Harish S. Wankhede, "The Political Context of Religious Conversion in Orissa", in *EPW*, 44, 15 (11 April 2009), pp. 33-38.

forests depriving the indigenous people of their land and livelihood. States encourage the setting up of many hazardous industries by multinationals putting into serious peril the lives of the poor who work in these industries and who live in the immediate vicinity. In Asia, it is becoming clear that the defence of the natural resources is to defend the poor, and defending the poor is the most effective way of protecting the continent from environmental degradation and crisis.[8]

These four major areas which are manifestly public issues need to become the object of concern for Asian Public Theology. In responding jointly to this situation will this theology emerge, and it will be necessarily interreligious in character. In its various chapters, this book addresses the above outlined four major concerns, and indeed from an inter-religious perspective.

## The Wider Context of Asian Public Theology – Western and Asian

In the West we may identify three important factors for the emergence of Public Theology. First of all there is a felt need to bring faith and its significance into public affairs of the world after a long self-isolation of

---

[8] Cf. Vandana Shiva, "Farmers' Rights, Biodiversity and International Treatises", in *EPW*, 28, 4 (3 April 1993), pp. 555-560; Vandana Shiva and Holla Bhar R., "Intellectual Piracy and the Neem Tree", in *The Ecologist*, 23, 6 (1993), 223-227; Ignacy Sachs, "From Poverty Trap to Inclusive Development in LDC'S", in *EPW*, 39, 18 (1 May 2004), pp. 1802-1811; Sam P. Mathew and Chandran Paul Martin (eds.), *Waters of Life and Death. Ethical and Theological Responses to Contemporary Water Crisis*, UELCI/ISPCK, Delhi 2005; John Hanningan, *Environmental Sociology*, Routledge, First Indian Reprint 2008; E.F. Schumacher, *Small is Beautiful. A Study of Economics as if People Mattered*, Radha Krishna, New Delhi 1977; Sebastian Kochupurackal, *Eco-Mission: A Paradigm Shift in Missiology*, Asian Trading Corporation, Bangalore 2007. See also Felix Wilfred, "Toward an Interreligious Eco-theology" in *Concilium* 2009/3, pp. 43-54; Vaclav Smill, "Finding Mutual Interests in Nature", in *Far Eastern Economic Review*, 172, 8 (2009), pp. 44-47; Ashish Aggarwal, "Indigenous Institutions for Natural Resource Management: Potential and Threats", in *EPW* 43, 23 (7 June 2008), pp. 21-24; Milind Wani and Ashish Kothari, "Globalisation vs India's Forests", in *EPW* 43, 37 (13 September 2008), pp. 19-22; Bidhan Kanti Das, "Flood Disasters and Forest Villagers in Sub-Himalayan Bengal" in *EPW*, 44, 4 (24 January 2009), pp. 71-76; Mukul Sharma, "Passages from Nature to Nationalism: Sundarlal Bahuguna and Tehri Dam Opposition in Garwal", in *EPW*, 44, 8 (21 February 2009), pp. 35-42; Tejal Kanitkar and others, "How Much 'Carbon Space' Do We Have? Physical Constraints on India's Climate Policy and Its Implications", in *EPW*, 44, 41 (10 October 2009), pp. 35-40, 44-46; "India's Water Crisis" in *The Economist*, September 12 – 18, 2009, pp. 27-29.

faith and theology which coincided with the secular movement that privatized religion. It is the context of the post-secular. Secondly, there is a need for revising the concept of autonomy of earthly realities. This cannot be interpreted to mean that religion and public life are two water-tight compartments. Today, there is a growing realization of their mutuality and interdependence. Thirdly, there has come about a crisis of the Enlightenment paradigm, variously described. It has its repercussions for re-conceiving the relationship of religion and public life.[9] Finally, there is the awareness of the role religions and religious groups have played in public life in challenging the authoritarian political order in the erstwhile socialist regimes of Europe.

Asia presents another scene with a different set of actors. Politically the influence of Christianity in Asia has been marginal and sporadic. Culturally, Christianity has been a medium to transmit Western education, and it was welcomed in many circles. Economically, efforts have been made in the form of promoting charitable, welfare and developmental works. But even this has been hampered in some countries, especially those under socialist regime or Islamic religious tradition. By and large, what we note is the isolation of Christianity from public life of society. Even the many works pursued in favour of society suffer isolation as it is managed a parallel to the public efforts, without a real encounter and conversation with all those involved in the issues of common concern. Christianity and Christian theology have little influence on the political life of the Asian countries, and on their economic policies. However, there are groups at the margins of Christianity who distance themselves from institutional Christianity but draw inspiration from the Gospel and try to engage in action in public life by participating in various movements.

Why has Christianity not been able to act prophetically in public sphere? Many reasons could be adduced. One reason among them is that the theology it has developed over the years has not prompted it for public intervention. For example, Theology of Public Life would tell Christians

---

[9] Cf. Peter Berger (ed.), *The Desecularisation of the World: Resurgent Religion and World Politics*, Ethics and Public Policy Centre, Washington DC, 1999; Lawrence Cahoone (ed.), *From Modernism to Postmodernism. An Anthology*, Blackwell Publishers, Oxford 1996; John D. Caputo, *On Religion*, Routledge, London, 2001; Paul Heelas (ed.), *Religion, Modernity and Postmodernity*, Blackwell Publishers, London, 1998; Peter Beyer, *Religion and Globalization*, Sage Publications, Delhi, 2000; Robert Bellah, *Habits of the Heart. Individualism and Commitment in American Life*, University of California Press, Berkley,1985.

why they need to involve themselves in politics and how they could do that. Theology of Public Life has a role, therefore, in relation to the Christian community. Where there is a practical overlap of Christian community with the public society, much could be achieved by this theology of public life. In fact, liberation theology as it appeared in Latin America, could be considered as a form of Theology of Public life as it provided the biblical and theological reasoning for commitment to the political and economic realms, and called the community to praxis of faith in these fields.[10]

## Locating Public Theology in the Asian Theological Context

One of the great contributions of Vatican Council II has been to impel the Church to relate to the realities and experiences of the modern world in a spirit of openness.[11] But in the course of last few decades we have become aware that the local Churches, finding themselves in different contexts, are challenged by situations vastly different from each other. Consequently, the theology that is required for the relationship of the Church to the Asian world is also different because of different cultural social and political situations in the context. The theological reflections in Asia including the reflections within the Federation of Asian Bishops' Conferences and the Christian Conference of Asia tried to relate to the Asian situation.[12] The efforts of Vatican II, and the efforts that have been done hitherto in Asia were supported by a Theology of Public Life. This theology provides the justification and motivation for the Christian community to engage itself with the affairs of the world.

To be able to realize the specificity and innovative character of Asian Public Theology, we need to briefly recall here other forms of theology

[10] Cf. Gustavo Gutierrez, *A Theology of Liberation. History, Politics and Salvation*, Orbis Books, New York, 1993; Juan Luis Segundo, *The Liberation of Theology*, Orbis Books, New York, 1985; Ignacio Ellacuria and Jon Sobrino (eds.), *Mysterium Liberationis. Fundamental Concepts of Liberation Theology*, Orbis Books, New York, 1995; Alfred T. Hennelly (ed.), *Liberation Theology. A Documentary History*, Orbis Books, New York, 1990; Deane William Fern (ed.), *Third World Liberation Theologies. A Reader*, Orbis Books, New York, 1987.

[11] Cf. *Gaudium et Spes*, nos 1, 43, 71, 86; Cf. also East Asian Pastoral Institute, *40 Years of Vatican II and the Churches of Asia and the Pacific. Looking Back and Moving Forward*, Quezon City, 2005.

[12] Cf. Vimal Tirimanna (ed.), *Sprouts of Theology from Asian Soil, Collection of TAC & OTC Documents, Federation of Asian Bishops' Conference*, Office of Theological Concerns (OTC), Claretian Publications, Bangalore 2007; Philip L. Wickeri (ed.), *The People of God Among All God's Peoples: Frontiers in Christian Mission*, CCA & CWC, Hong Kong, 2008.

that have been and continue to be pursued in Asia. The theology of the
era of mission expansion in the continent was simply an extrapolation of
the traditional Western theology according to Roman Catholic or Protestant
traditions. This trend can be observed in some of the Asian countries in
which instead of moving towards original theological thinking, one is
engaged in translating into Chinese, Korean, Japanese etc. the works of
Western theologians. When the indigenous movement set in, efforts were
made to adapt and accommodate the Western theological concepts into
local languages and modes of thought.[13] When Asia began to develop its
own version of theology of religions, it was mainly to make sense of other
religious traditions, their beliefs and practices starting from Christian faith.
It was more a self-clarification within the Christian community, even
though it was open to the ways of God manifest in the religions of the
neighbours. Asian liberation theology on its part provided inspiration and
motivation for Asian Christians to engage themselves in the social and
political realities of the continent, and in the process availed also of Asian
cultural and religious resources.[14]

Now, none of these models of theology could adequately respond to
the demands of Asian public life. Liberation theology tried to reinterpret
faith in countries and situations whose history, tradition, culture, etc., have

---

[13] Cf. John C. England et al. (eds.), *Asian Christian Theologies. A Research Guide
to Authors, Movements, Sources*, 3 Vols, ISPCK/Claretian Publications/Orbis
Books, Delhi/Quezon City/New York, 2002-2004; Georg Evers, *The Churches in
Asia*, ISPCK, Delhi, 2005; Michael Amaladoss, *Making Harmony. Living in a
Pluralist World*, IDCR, Chennai, 2003; Sebastian C.H. Kim (ed.), *Christian Theology
in Asia*, Cambridge University Press, 2008; Dayanandan T. Francis - Franklin J.
Balasundaram (eds.), *Asian Expressions of Christian Commitment: A Reader in
Asian Theology*, CLS, Madras, 1992; Peter Chen-Main Wang (ed.), *Contextualization
of Christianity in China. An Evaluation in Modern Perspective*, Institut Monumenta
Serica, Germany, 2007; Joseph Mitsuo Kitagawa, *The Christian Tradition beyond
European Captivity*, Trinity Press International, Philadelphia, 1992; Peter C. Phan,
*In Our Own Tongues: Perspectives from Asia on Mission and Inculturation*, Orbis
Books, New York, 2003; Aloysius B. Ch'shen Chang, *The Catholic Church in
Mainland China. Pastoral and Theological Reflections*, Wisdom Press, Taipei, 1998.
[14] Cf. Felix Wilfred, *Margins. Site of Asian Theologies*, ISPCK, Delhi, 2008;
Aloysius Pieris, *Asian Theology of Liberation*, T & T Clark, London, 1988; Michael
Amaladoss, *Life in Freedom. Liberation Theologies from Asia*, Orbis Books, New
York, 1997; R.S. Sugirtharajah (ed.), *Frontiers in Asian Christian Theology. Emerging
Trends*, Orbis Books, New York, 1994; Virginia Fabella - Sun Ai Lee Park, *We
Dare to Dream. Doing Theology as Asian Women*, Asian Women's Centre for Culture
and Theology, Hong Kong, 1989.

been Christian. By reinterpreting faith, liberation theology could bring out the political significance of faith in public life and contribute to change.

The Asian Public Theology we envisage is different from all these various forms of theologies. It addresses the public concerns and in the process constitutes itself as interreligious. It is involved also in a transformative praxis with movements and ideologies committed to the public cause. In this way, Asian Public Theology ceases to be sectarian, and becomes inclusive. The addressees of Asian Public Theology are not Christians or Christian communities in the first place, but the larger public. It brings in new perspectives and stimuli for the engagement of all for the questions and causes that affect everyone.

Interestingly, Public Theology in Asia was initiated by thinkers who do not belong institutionally to the Christian fold.[15] We may recall here, for example, how Gandhi read and interpreted the Gospels and the Sermon on the Mount in such way that it was for him an ally in his engagement for a non-violent society.[16] Reformers like Jyotirao Phule and others in India could turn the Gospels into a Public Theology in their struggles against casteism and oppression of women.[17] This kind of Public Theology originating from the engagement of non-Christians in the field could, perhaps, make the Christian Gospel more relevant and meaningful to the larger public than what hundreds of years of preaching by Christians and Christian missionaries have succeeded to do.

In these introductory pages we shall try to explore further some of the characteristics of an Asian Interreligious Public Theology.

## From Civil Society to "Political Society"

We begin making a distinction between Public Theology and the intervention of religion in the public sphere. The public sphere or civil society is but one aspect of public life and the role of Public Theology is not limited to this arena. Civil society as a critical space between the individual/family and the state, provides the citizens a platform for

---

[15] Cf. M.M. Thomas, *The Acknowledged Christ of Indian Renaissance*, CLS, Madras 1970; Id., *The Secular Ideologies and the Secular Meaning of Christ*, CLS, Madras, 1976.

[16] Cf. Robert Ellsberg (ed.), *Gandhi on Christianity*, Orbis Books, New York, 1991; M.K. Gandhi, *Christian Missions: Their Place in India*, Navajivan Press, Ahmedabad, 1941.

[17] Cf. Dhananjay Keer, *Mahatma Jotirao Phooley: Father of Indian Social Revolution*, Popular Prakashan, Bombay, 1964.

exchange, debate and expression of their views and for common action. But then in Asia, the public sphere is mostly occupied by the bourgeois and the rising middle-class. The poor and the marginalized groups of Asia are at a different level than being citizens of a bourgeois society. Hence, if Asian Public Theology were to deal only with public sphere, it may not touch upon the burning questions and issues affecting the poor of Asia. That is why it makes sense to speak of *"political society"*[18] in the case of India and other regions of the continent. Political society is where the poor and the subaltern grapple with their life-issues, waging struggles and protests, and thus exercise their agency. Asian Public Theology will respond to this situation rather than address the questions of public sphere.[19]

## Religions Blending into the Secular Space

There is one important difference as regards Public Theology in Asia and in the West. The relationship of religion to society is viewed differently in the Asian continent. This means that religion and society are not connected in terms of sacred and profane, religious and secular. Rather, public life includes also a place for religion. Religion is also in the market-place.[20] Therefore it is part of Public Theology to explain how religions relate among themselves in a harmonious way, so that peace and concord result.

The inter-relationship of religions itself is a public issue in Asia. It seems to me that due to secularization in the West, one is not able to see the relationship of religions as a public issue. Today with many Muslim and other religious migrants, the relationship of religions in Europe has become a public issue closely resembling the traditional Asian situation. Contrary to the general impression, Europe is coming closer to the Asian situation than Asia turning from religion and becoming secular in the European Enlightenment way. It is not only the religions which are to be tolerant; equally important today is that the secular be tolerant of the plurality of religions and their impact on public life of society. In this sense,

---

[18] "Political" here stands for negotiation of power.

[19] Cf. Felix Wilfred, "Asian Religious Pluralism and Higher Education", in *East Asian Pastoral Review*, 46 (2009), pp. 33-45.

[20] To be able to understand this we need to look at the Asian history on how religion and public culture interacted in the past in each society. For South India, for example, see Keith E. Yandell - John J. Paul (eds.), *Religion and Public Culture*, Curzon, Richmond, 2000.

Asian Public Theology which we qualified as inherently interreligious in Asia, could also be helpful for the present-day European situation.

## Ethical in Nature

The demands and challenges of the Asian situation tell us that the theology of public life needs to have a strong ethical component.[21] In the midst of complex, contradictory and ambiguous realities and experiences, developing a moral and ethical outlook is a very challenging task, which once again underlines the importance of conversation and dialogue with other religious traditions and also movements at the grassroots level. In the present-day context, all the religions will need to rethink their traditional ethical approach and outlook, and shape through mutual sharing and exchange a new ethical vision for public life. We have such issues as the massive poverty that is still a dominant characteristic of the life of Asia. Herein live the overwhelming majority of the poor in the world.

There is a growing disparity between the rich and the poor in every Asian country. The middle and upper classes are benefiting from the liberal economy while the poor masses are struggling for survival. Further there are deeply entrenched societal issues as caste and exclusion of different kinds, especially of women, Dalits and tribals. To these we need to add the increasing violence and communal divisions. The scientific and technological developments, on their part, have thrown open new ethical and moral questions in everyday life which remain unanswered. These developments combined with market economy have created problems of immigration, displacement of peoples, trafficking of children and women, commercialization of human organs, etc.[22] To develop the ethical dimension of Public Theology means to take up issues of this kind, and to respond them critically, taking 'life for all' as the criteria of judgment. In each of the five parts of the book the question of ethics figures and is

[21] Cf. Felix Wilfred, "Ethics in a Changing Asia" in *Gurukul Journal of Theological Studies* (in print).

[22] Amit Bhaduri and Medha Patkar, "Industrialization for the People, by the People, of the People, in *EPW*, 44, 1 (1 January 2009), pp. 10-12; Jomo Kwame Sundaram, "Export-Oriented Industrialisation, Female Employment and Gender Wage Equity in East Asia", in *EPW*, 44, 1 (1 January 2009), pp. 41-49; Amit Bhaduri, "Predatory Growth", in *EPW*, 43, 16 (19 April 2008), pp. 10-14; Rohini Sahni and V. Kalyan Shankar, "What Has Economics Got to Do With It? Cultures of Consumption in Global Markets", in *EPW*, 44, 1 (1 January 2009), pp. 50-58; Manoj Kumar Sanyal et al. (eds.), *Post-Reform Development in Asia: Essays for Amiya Kumar Bagchi*, Orient BlackSwan, Hyderabad, 2009.

developed from different perspectives and concerns. The ethical, in a way is the thread that runs through the whole book.

## Organic and Interdisciplinary

Asian Public Theology will be truly an "organic" theology different from traditional theology - to adopt the categories of Antonio Gramsci.[23] Traditional theology explains the truths of faith for the Christian community and elucidates at the most their relevance for society. It tends to maintain the existing order of the society and the Church. On the other hand, Asian theology as organic Public Theology will be innovative, constantly in dialogue with the new questions and issues as they emerge in the continent. The pursuit of Public Theology calls for organic intellectuals and theologians who would give a transformative impetus.

Inter-disciplinarity is another important characteristic of the Asian Public Theology that we envisage. Since Public Theology begins from the concrete realities of life and directs itself to its transformation, it needs to study, analyze and interpret the situation and facts for which the assistance of other disciplines is indispensable. Thus Asian Public Theology will be in dialogue and conversation with disciplines studying Asian societies, its history, its dynamics; so also it will be attentive to what critical studies have to say on the economic and political processes taking place in Asia, and the various struggles Asian societies are going through. All these facts, data, analyses and interpretation will be woven into a Public Theology, so that it could respond more adequately to the developing Asian situation.

### Some Presuppositions

Let me make clear some presuppositions on which Asian Public Theology rests. First of all it assumes that religions do have a role in public life.[24] This point needs some elaboration. Whereas in the West, the role of religion in public life is re-thought in the context of a post-secular society, and the Public Theology there reflects this new situation, in Asia, the relationship of religion and society has a different history and orientation. This is true of the past as well of present times.

---

[23] Cf. Antonio Gramsci, *Selections from the Prison Notebooks*, Lawrence and Wishart, London, 1991.

[24] Cf. Felix Wilfred (ed.), *Transforming Religion. Prospects for a New Society*, ISPCK, Delhi, 2009.

The second assumption is that in Asia, all theology will be inherently Public Theology. This means that whatever belief the Christians profess, it needs to be viewed from its public significance and its power to address matters that concern everybody in a society. Once we admit that faith has a public function, we are confronted with the question of the nature of this relationship. On one extreme is the viewpoint that sees faith as having its influence on the *individual* Christian believer regarding his or her political options and choices. Therefore, the public role of faith is something indirect in as much as the individual is shaped by his or her belief-system and by faith-based reasons to affect the public life. Faith-based reasons do not go to affect public life, rather they become motivating forces for the agents of performance in public life whereas theology remains at the level of rehearsal preparing the individual actors for the performance. A second position is one that would rule out any public role to faith. What we are concerned about is rather that there be public reasons that should justify public policies; and the contribution of a Public Theology, would be to contribute to enhance the public reason.

Moreover, in Public Theology we address and interpret the truths of faith in such a way that they become meaningful to people around us. Even Christology could be so interpreted and explained that a person who is not a Christian by religious belonging will find the discourse meaningful. It concerns the relationship of Christian faith, worldview, ethics, etc., with the present society, its problems, and questions. This needs to be done in a way that does not undermine the autonomy of temporal realities. This problem in the West was addressed by secularization which dismissed any role for religion in public life. Against a threatening religious intervention, secular ideology turned out to be a true defence of earthly realities and their autonomy. Secularism did not ask the question as to what kind of religion or God who should not intervene and undermine autonomy. In Asia we live in a situation in which the chief problem is not of intervention in the public life. Here the question is that of peace and harmony which can be disturbed by a religion that is divorced from the society and its concerns.

Another assumption is that religions have resources in order to play an ethical role in public life, by bringing rational cognition and moral evaluation together. Splitting the two had become one of the root-causes of the present crisis of humanity faced with many ethical dilemmas.

A final assumption is that religions do have a performative role, besides the functional one. Functional role relates to the belief-system, rituals, moral injunctions, etc., that a religion presents and continues to maintain and celebrate for its believers. On the other hand, the performative role is what religion is and what it becomes in relation to society, its questions, and its concerns. Asian Public Theology will focus on the performative role of religions.

The book is conceived in the form of a journey. It starts with the subalterns and moves into the path of justice and in its journey comes to theological crossroads, and then moves on to the future in a common journey with the subalterns and all those who are in solidarity with them.

### Subalterns – the Starting Point of a Journey

Asian Public Theology which this book addresses has as its starting point the subalterns. Therefore, the first part of the book deals with issues that concern the subalterns. It deals with the need to overcome various forms of exclusion in the global world which are experienced as well in the Asian continent in terms of caste, class, gender, ethnicity, physical disabilities and so on. The reflections in this part deal in particular with two most affected groups of subalterns – Dalits and women. Dalits represent the hope for the future because in their aspirations and dreams we already see the shape of the things to come for a just and egalitarian society. Women as subalterns suffer from many oppressive forces, chief among them are the religious ones. However, women do negotiate religious power and build their own agency. This part includes also reflections on affirmative action or reservation, and ethical auditing which are important in the journey of the subalterns so that they are watchful about unrestrained powers blocking their path towards justice and liberation.

### On the Path of Justice

For the subalterns, moving on the path of justice and affirming their agency presuppose that appropriate structures are put in place. Asian societies are today struggling for good governance, which mostly seems to elude them. Obviously, good governance creates the necessary conditions for the practice of justice in a society. History and experience teach us that there is no ideal form of governance, and of all the options available to humanity, democracy seems to be most promising. Religious traditions need to contribute today to democratic forms of governance. In this connection one of the chapters in this part reflects on Christianity and democratic process. Another crucial issue on the path of justice is that of economy. It is the linchpin of justice today. Asian societies underwent a serious economic crisis in 1997, and the recession that affected world-economy in recent times has its serious repercussions on the economy of Asian countries, and it weighs heavily on the poor of Asia. That necessitates a serious theological reflection on this public issue. Social and economic justice may not be separated from the relationship and attitudes of the humans to the Earth. For, the plight of the poor and the degradation of nature are intertwined. I have made an attempt therefore to expand the concept of justice to include also the way humans go about nature. Hence our reflections take us to consider eco-justice. The final chapter in this part reflects on two diametrically opposed social attitudes, namely anger and compassion. However, both converge in terms of responding to the experience of evil.

## Crossroads

The journey takes us to crossroads. We note for example, how Christianity on the one hand seems to be in decline to the extent of creating a discourse of "Post-Christianity" in one part of the world, while it is finding great echo and resurgence in other parts of the world. How could Asian Christianity contribute to the public life of the society and thus become resurgent is an important question to be addressed. Asian Public Theology could contribute to the life of the society by bringing the social message of Christianity. This message has been reflected upon by the Churches in relation to various issues and questions. This is true of the World Council of Churches as well as the social teachings of the Roman Catholic Church. By way of example we study critically how the social message of Christianity has been interpreted by the Roman Catholic Church and to what extent it responds to the public concerns of Asian peoples. These considerations are followed by wider reflections on Christian ethics. An important aspect of ethics in today's Asia is the theory and practice of tolerance. We therefore go into the struggle Asian societies are going through to become tolerant. The next chapter goes into the implication of all this for theological education and the method to be adopted for the same in Asia. The wider experiences of Asian realities prompt us also to develop a new historiography of Christianity in the continent which will be sensitive to the perception of our neigbhours and take into account the common tradition, history, and social conditions we share. Most of the things said in the chapter on Indian Christian historiography are applicable also to other parts of Asia.

## Continuing Common Journey

The fourth and final part of the book reflects on how we can move together towards the future in conversation with other religious traditions, worldviews, value-systems, etc. It starts with a rethinking on the spirit of universality. The next chapter takes us to critical consideration of the dominant Christian narrations of God, and studies how perspectives of other religious traditions could help us for a deeper conception of the divine mystery. Inter-religious understanding will bear upon also on the way Asians relate to nature and environment. Therefore we need to develop an interreligious ecotheology. The concluding chapter deals with the implications of religious pluralism for religious traditions to jointly address public issues and questions. The journey is never ending because God comes to us in ever new ways, and humanity is confronted with ever new problems and dilemmas. That makes the journey exciting.

# Part I

# The Subaltern Journey

# Chapter 1

# Overcoming Exclusions in the Global World

*"No one is born hating another person because of the colour of his skin, or his background, or his religion. People must learn to hate, and if they can learn to hate, they can be taught to love, for love comes more naturally to the human heart than its opposite."*          Nelson Mandela[1]

In 1989 the world celebrated with euphoria the fall of the Berlin wall – a symbol of exclusion, repression and terror. But there is total silence on the walls that have been erected since then. The border between Mexico and United States extends 3141 kms. Poverty and affluence separate the two. To prevent the poor immigrants of Mexico entering into the USA, a wall has been erected. It has become a wall of despair and death. Hundreds of poor immigrants died, or have been killed as they tried to cross over to the other side for survival. Then, there is the wall erected by Israel in the Palestinian territory. It is a network of fences in the Israeli occupied Palestine running to 703 kms. Closer home, a wall that separated the burial ground of the high-caste and low caste in the city of Tiruchirappalli, Tamilnadu, was brought down, even before the fall of the Berlin wall to signify the equality of all children of God. But then this wall was quickly rebuilt – a sign of the hegemony of the upper castes who felt challenged by the audacity of the Dalits. It still stands there unabashedly.

Walls signify exclusion, and they are constructed in the minds before they are executed externally. Exclusions could be on the basis of different grounds: caste, class, gender, ethnicity, religion, language, region, physical

---

[1] *Long Walk to Freedom,* Abacus, London, 1994.

disabilities, etc. We observe the growth of xenophobia[2] in Europe, branding the immigrants and asylum seekers from Africa and Asia as criminals, and blaming them for causing unemployment. Such walls based on racist and caste ideology erected in the minds are more difficult to remove than the physical ones.

We speak about globalization today meaning that the borders are being removed. But in fact, what are not seen are the continuous exclusions that are taking place in our world, in our societies. Exclusions are the breeding grounds of injustice. Any response to injustice will begin by asking what kind of exclusion is involved and how to overcome that particular form of exclusion. I do not want to enter here into any analysis of the different forms of exclusion. Rather, what I intend to do is to reflect upon the various ways in which we could respond to the many exclusions today. Theology needs to address issues of public concern, and become public theology. The experience of exclusion will be one of the central issues on which theology will focus its attention.

## Challenging the Principle and Practice of Competition

Competition is centred on promoting the welfare of a few at the expense of the welfare of all. Elimination of others for the advancement of a few is its dynamics. Competition is something diametrically opposed to the Christian principle of option for the poor – a principle of inclusion of the last and the least. A committed Christian, therefore, cannot but challenge the practice of competition when it is elevated to be the guiding principle in every field. Traditionally, the strategy used for exclusion was the ideology and praxis of purity-pollution. Competition is a 'glorified' version of this traditional criterion of exclusion. Those who can successfully compete are the 'pure', and those who lose out are the 'impure'.

The principle of competition is also close to *social Darwinism* which is at the root of racist ideology. In modern times, the ideology of the survival of the fittest has donned the respectable mantle of 'competition'. It is absurd to apply the same criteria for the able-bodied and to the physically

---

[2] Xenophobia means fear of the stranger. It is part of a civilization how it deals with the "other", the stranger. How traditionally India has been dealing with strangers and the theoretical underpinnings beneath the praxis, see the enlightening pages of Wilhelm Halbfass, "Traditional Indian Xenology" in his *India and Europe: An Essay in Philosophical Understanding*, Motilal Banarsidass, Delhi, 1990, pp. 172-196.

challenged. The otherwise-abled, as the physically challenged are, would require a different set of criteria that would bring out their talents.

Most often the criteria employed in competition are the ones that favour the already powerful and advantaged sections, and exclude the weaker ones. On the contrary, Christian vision begins with what is neglected, excluded and tries to see how they could be included and brought to the fore with dignity and honour.[3] Competition and option for the poor are two polar positions. Option for the poor cannot be reconciled with the philosophy of the survival of the fittest which animates competition.

### From Social Contract to Solidarity

Exclusion originates also from a contractual approach to society. Society is viewed as resulting from the contract individuals make, overcoming the hypothetical state of nature in which one's self-interest is in perpetual war with those of others. Contractual approach, which also inspires modern economy, is based on a negative anthropology.

The contractual approach to society which has heavily influenced today's global political and moral thought, unfortunately, empties all relationships of their subjectivity, and refuses to acknowledge human relationships as having value in themselves. For, every form of relationship cannot be subsumed under contract. It does not allow room for the practice of selfless-love, compassion. The scope of contract ends with what one gains from it. On the other hand, solidarity approach is based on co-existence, mutuality and reciprocity which go beyond contractual obligations. To put it in human terms, the love of a mother cannot be framed within a contractual obligation of her with the child. There is no justification within the contract theory why we should take care of the weaker ones in any society. Consequently, what happens is that the weaker segments of the society get excluded and sidelined.

Solidarity approach is inspired by the social nature of human beings and rests on a positive anthropology. It considers human beings as capable of reaching out to the other without any regard to any benefit

---

[3] Cf. Lk 6:20; see also Pope John Paul II, "Solicitudo Rei Socialis (December 30, 1987)", in *AAS*, 80 (1988), nos 42, 43; Pope John Paul II, "Centesimus Annus (May 1, 1991)", in *AAS*, 83 (1991), nos, 11, 57; Jorge Pixley and Clodovis Boff, *The Bible, The Church and the Poor*, Burns & Oates, Kent, 1989; George M. Soares-Prabhu, "Class in the Bible: The Biblical Poor a Social Class?', in *Vidyajyoti Journal of Theological Reflection*, 49 (1985) pp. 322-346.

to oneself. Challenging the ideology of self-serving contract and its expressions and promoting a solidarity approach in society is a much-needed response to various forms of exclusion in our world. The practice of reservation or affirmative action has been a thorn in the flesh for many 'high' caste or class groups. They see this as opposed to competition in a society of contract.

> The humanness of a society is determined by the degree of protection it provides to its weaker, handicapped and less gifted members. Whereas in a jungle everybody fends for himself and devil takes the hind-most, in a civilized society reasonable constraints are placed on the ambitions and acquisitiveness of its more aggressive members and special safeguards provided to its weaker and more vulnerable sections. These considerations are basic to any scheme of social justice and their neglect will brutalize any human society.[4]

I think the provision of reservation needs to be viewed from a *humanistic perspective* as an expression of solidarity, and not from a legal perspective alone.[5]

## Principle of Diversity and Plurality

A society is made up of peoples and groups with different endowments and capabilities, all of which are important to foster the life of the community. This is what Paul exhorted when he reminded the Corinthians about the charisms and unique gifts of each person. The image of the body with its different organs serves him as the best illustration for the acceptance of plurality and diversity (1Cor 12:12-26; Rom 12:3-8). No part or organ is excluded as each one has its role in the body. The point Paul is trying to make about the non-hierarchization of charisms or functions, has a lot of relevance in the caste and class society of today.

The recognition of plurality in the Christian tradition has its foundation also in the order of creation. Like the biodiversity we find in nature, creation of God is made up of rich human plurality, the cultivation of which is important for the common good of humans and of the entire creation.[6] This is radically opposed to an outlook of homogeneity or uniformity

---

[4] *Reservations for Backward Classes. Mandal Commission Report of the Backward Classes Commission, 1980: Along with Introduction*, Akalank Publications, Delhi, 1991, p. 26.

[5] More about reservation, chapter 4 in this volume.

[6] Cf. David Hollenbach, *The Common Good and Christian Ethics*, Cambridge University Press, Cambridge, 2002.

which does not allow space for diversity. Quantification in terms of majority and minority is a perspective that could jeopardize positive affirmation of plurality, and it could imply – as often it does – that the majority has greater claims than the minorities.

We know what rich talents the Dalits and tribals have. In spite of it, excluding them from their contribution to community in the name of caste or on the basis of purity and pollution ultimately makes the society poor. Often, the exclusion takes place in subtle ways. Dalits are viewed as those capable of doing only menial and impure jobs tradition had assigned to them, and society studiously excludes them from other occupations in which their talents could be of benefit for the common good of all. If such is the case, diversity does not apply only to jobs and positions in the public sector. It is important that the principle of diversity be applied also in the private sector, which contrary to the general impression, excludes Dalits and weaker sections in the society.[7] The various social movements besides empowering the Dalits, also function as a pressure factor in restraining the dominant castes in their strategic exclusion of the Dalits and tribals.

## Promotion of "Subjugated Knowledge"

Humanity is today in a deep crisis, because the paradigms for forging just human relationships in society and the relationship of humans to nature have proved ineffective.[8] Importance of "subjugated knowledge"[9] derives from the fact that it provides an alternative vision of reality, of human

---

[7] Cf. Sukhadeo Thorat, Aryama, Prashant Negi (eds.), *Reservation and Private Sector: Quest for Equal Opportunity and Growth*, Indian Institute of Dalit Studies, New Delhi and Rawat Publications, Jaipur, 2005; G. Thimmaiah, "Implications of Reservations in Private Sector", in *EPW*, 40, 8 (February 19, 2005), pp. 745-750.

[8] See Felix Wilfred, "Eco-Justice. Widening the Horizons", in *Jeevadhara*, January, 2010; Id., "Toward an Interreligious Eco-theology", in *Concilium* 2009/3, pp. 43-54.

[9] "... a sort of general feeling that the ground was crumbling beneath our feet, especially in places where it seemed most familiar, most solid, and closest to us, to our bodies, to our everyday gestures. But alongside this crumbling and the astonishing efficacy of discontinuous, particular, and local critiques, the facts were also revealing something... beneath this whole thematic, through it and even within it, we have seen what might be called the insurrection of subjugated knowledges." M. Foucault, *Society Must be Defended*, (transl. David Macey) Bertani, Mauro & Fontana, Alessandro (eds.), Picador, New York, 2003, pp. 6-7.

interrelationship and of the human-earth bonding.[10] The knowledge available to us only from the vantage point of view of the dominant does not ensure a secure future for humanity and for the Earth. The opening to the knowledge of excluded peoples may help overcome the crisis humanity and the nature is going through. In particular, the indigenous knowledge regarding biodiversity and conservation of nature and its riches are of paramount importance today not only for the survival and health care of the poor in any part of the world, but for the wellbeing of the entire human family.

Through their keen observations the subordinated peoples have developed deep knowledge about nature and its functioning. Think of the Kayapo people of Amazon who have studied the flora and fauna of the region and have made a detailed classification. It is the indigenous knowledge of nature which has provided also insights for the development of modern pharmaceutics.[11] Moreover, the excluded people like the Dalits, the tribals and ethnic minorities and other indigenous people have developed amazing skills through centuries of their hard labour. Unfortunately, in a world of globalization this heritage is neglected and devalued, and there is danger of this precious fund of knowledge and skills disappearing. Nation states are hindering the livelihood of indigenous peoples on the basis of their traditional knowledge by imposing a West-inspired model of development. Ironically, while the dominant sysem discriminates against indigenous knowledge, the market forces are appropriating this knowledge by excluding the local communities who have produced this heritage.

Such being the case, the practice of inclusion should operate at different levels. First of all the subjugated knowledge requires affirmation and inclusion in the fund of existing knowledge. The dominant knowledge is also the one that supports the status quo. Indigenous knowledge, on the other hand, may challenge the existing systems of knowledge. Moreover, the epistemological premises of subjugated knowledge are important to create a mindset of inclusion and challenge the many dualisms of modern knowledge system which contribute to the practice of exclusion.

---

[10] Cf. Clifford Geertz, *Local Knowledge*, Fontana Press, London 1993.
[11] Cf. Madhulika Banerjee, "Local Knowledge for World Market: Globalising Ayurveda", in *EPW*, 39, 1 (January 3, 2004), pp. 89-93.

### Change of Language and Vocabulary

One of the ways of overcoming the deeply entrenched attitudes of exclusion is to try to change the use of language and vocabulary. A classical example is the struggle the Dalit people have taken to reject the derogatory terms with which they were referred to for so long. From *'Untouchable'* to *'Dalit'* expresses the journey of a people from humiliation to dignity and self-confidence.[12] "Untouchables" evokes the feeling of exclusion on the basis of the ideology of purity and pollution.[13] It creates a mental block towards the excluded people, and it even reinforces this exclusion. On the other hand, "Dalits" evokes the experience of an oppressed people and their suffering. It invites inclusion. With the change of terminology it is possible that at least some layers of prejudice could be shed, though the struggle to eradicate it completely must continue.

Further, think of the term *"illegal immigrants"* used in the West, mostly, referring to people from Africa and Asia. The phrase itself is ideologically loaded. Here is a segment of people who are branded in a particular way, without reference to their actual social and human situation. What dominates in this phraseology is the "illegality" and that leads easily to the claim that they could be punished. But if we change it into *"undocumented immigrants"* – it has a very different connotation. Innumerable examples could be brought from different parts of the world, where change of language and vocabulary could imply a long journey from exclusion to inclusion. Let me cite two more examples. There is a world of difference when we drop the expression *"handicapped"* and use instead *"differently-abled"*. The latter expression immediately tells us that they are part of the community contributing to it with their different abilities, whereas the former creates a mindset of exclusion. When we use the expression *complementary* to indicate the relationship of man and woman, it could be very limiting and disadvantageous to women who are expected to do their under-valued, stereotyped roles, and in this way complement men. On the other hand, the language of *"partnership"* brings out the ideal of true equality in gender relationships.

---

[12] Cf. Eleanor Zelliot, *From Untouchable to Dalit: Essays on the Ambedkar Movement*, Manohar, Delhi, 2005.

[13] Cf. Oliver Mendelsohn and Marika Vicziany, *The Untouchables: Subordination, Poverty and the State in Modern India*, Cambridge University Press, Cambridge, 1998; Robert Deliège, The *World of the 'Untouchables': Paraiyars of Tamilnadu*, Oxford University Press, Delhi, 1997.

## Strengthening Substantive Democracy and Promoting Justice

Process of inclusion calls for appropriate institutional structuring. Substantive democracy involving the effective participation of the people could provide such a framework. It is a means that is based on equality of all without any discrimination on the basis of language, ethnicity, religion, etc.[14] Arundhati Roy observes:

> Planners in India boast that India consumes twenty times more electricity today than it did fifty years ago. They use it as an index of progress. They usually omit to mention that seventy per cent of rural households still have no electricity. In the poorest states, Bihar, Uttar Pradesh, Orissa, and Rajasthan, more than eighty-five per cent of the poorest people, mostly Dalit and Adivasi households, have no electricity. What a shameful, shocking record for the world's biggest democracy.[15]

The democratization process is a process of inclusion. Exclusion and undemocratic ways go together. In developing countries, especially in South Asia, it is important that democracy is so practiced as to make room for the inclusion of social and regional diversities for which appropriate mechanisms too are required.[16] These mechanisms need to ensure that various minorities and identities have their representation and voice in what touches matters of common concern. This is different from a bourgeois approach to democracy with its focus on procedural issues. Substantive questions are not always settled by individual votes. It is important that all groups in a society are represented in the democratic exercise.[17] Democracy becomes a platform for sharing of power in which no group or identity is left out.

---

[14] Cf. Zoya Hasan, *Politics of Inclusion: Caste, Minorities and Affirmative Action*, Oxford University Press, New Delhi, 2009; Neera Chandhoke, "Global Civil Society and Global Justice", in *EPW*, 42,29 (July 21, 2007), pp. 3016-3022; B.S. Baviskar and George Mathew (eds.), *Inclusion and Exclusion in Local Governance: Field Studies from Rural India*, Sage Publications, Los Angeles, London, New Deli, 2009; Parvathi Menon, "Success Stories, Some Setbacks", in *Frontline* 25,11 (June 6, 2008) pp. 12-20.

[15] Arundhati Roy, *The Algebra of Infinite Justice*, Penguin Books, New Delhi, 2002, p. 168.

[16] Cf. *State of Democracy in South Asia. A Report*, Oxford University Press, Delhi, 2008.

[17] Cf. Gyanendra Pandey, "The Subaltern as Subaltern Citizen", in *EPW*, 41,46 (November 18, 2006), pp. 4735-4741; Cf. also Ranjita Mohanty and Rajesh Tandon (eds.), *Participatory Citizenship: Identity, Exclusion and Inclusion*, Sage Publications, New Delhi, 2006.

Promotion of justice ensures that people are not excluded and ignored and become victims of human rights violation;[18] it ensures that there are no development projects and plans that exclude the vulnerable - the tribals and the indigenous people, for example. Where displacement has taken place in violation of human rights, or due to ethnic conflicts, or development projects, the victims are to be integrated at the earliest into community, and are to be ensured basic necessities of life.[19] This is a concrete way of practicing justice.

Finally, we need to go beyond structural and institutional means for the promotion of justice. For, in spite of best structural means, there is no guarantee that the behavioural patterns will correspond to the spirit of these structural means. A typical example is the case of caste in this country. There are more than enough legislations and structural means to obliterate this social evil. But the crucial question is whether they can withstand the power of deeply embedded caste and racial prejudices. For, as Amartya Sen rightly points out in his critique of Rawl's, idea of justice:

> Indeed, we have good reasons for recognizing that the pursuit of justice is partly a matter of the gradual formation of behaviour patterns – there is no immediate jump from the acceptance of some principles of justice and a total redesign of everyone's actual behaviour in line with the political conception of justice. In general, the institutions have to be chosen not only in line with the nature of the society in question, but also co-dependently on the actual behaviour patterns that can be expected even if – and even after – a political conception of justice is accepted by all.[20]

In other words, the practice of inclusion implies more than a theoretical approach; it involves "formation of behaviour" and a mindset that is inclusive and integrating. That leads us to view critically some of the misconceptions of justice. For example, in the Indian tradition, the concept of *svadharma* which is supposed to signify justice becomes a matter of doing one's duty within the hierarchical order of society.[21] It may be recalled here that when Rajagopalachari was the chief-minister of Tamilnadu, he

---

[18] Cf. Oliver Mendelsohn and Upendra Baxi (eds.), *The Rights of the Subordinated Peoples*, Oxford University Press, New Delhi, 1996.

[19] Cf. Anupam Hazra, "The Ignored Indians" in *Man & Development*, vol. 31, 3 (September 2009), pp. 73-86.

[20] Amartya Sen, *The Idea of Justice*, Penguin Books, London, 2009, pp. 68-69.

[21] Cf. Wilhelm Halbfass, *India and Europe: An Essay in Philosophical Understanding*, Motilal Banarsidass, Delhi, 1990, pp. 334-348.

tried to introduce in 1953 a bill for elementary education, according to which children would learn in the morning together and follow a common syllabus, and in the afternoon, each one would learn the trade of his or her forefathers. It means then, that children of scavengers would learn scavenging, of dhobi would learn to clean clothes, and a Brahmin child would learn to do pooja. The very fact that something of this could be thought of is symptomatic of a deep-seated mind-set of exclusion, and a misconception of what is just and fair. That most 'high caste' people would not find anything wrong in this only reveals the deeply embedded attitude of confining the 'lower castes' and Dalits to where they are and excluding them from anything higher.[22] Principle of inclusion challenges this hierarchical order of society and its understanding of justice. So too, it challenges the liberal understanding of justice as fairness, and points to a society in which the fundamental equality of all is ensured.

In a democratic set-up, oriented towards the promotion of justice, it is important to avail of the Constitutional and legal provisions against exclusion. For this, the judiciary needs to come closer to the life-realities of the excluded people; hence the importance of judicial activism to challenge all forms of exclusion. Where there is no adequate legislation, there is need for strong advocacy programmes for the enactment of appropriate legislative measures.[23] But as a matter of fact, there are numerous legislations which can serve as shot in the arm to abolish exclusionary practices, and make various forms of exclusions punishable. By way of example, we may cite the SC/ST Atrocity Prevention Act which should serve as a powerful legal instrument to protect the weaker communities. The purpose of this Act is the social inclusion of these oppressed communities.

### Affirming the Universal Destiny of Natural Resources

Exclusionary practices prejudicial to minority groups and ethnicities are widely practiced in the economic sphere. Whether African-Americans,

---

[22] Cf. Kancha Ilaiah, *Why I am not a Hindu: A Sudra Critique of Hindutva Philosophy, Culture and Political Economy*, Samya Publications, Calcutta, 1996; Id., "Productive Labour, Consciousness and History: The Dalitbahujan Alternative", in Shahid Amin and Dipesh Chakrabarthy (eds.), *Subaltern Studies IX. Writings of South Asian History and Society*, Oxford University Press, New Delhi, 1996, pp. 165-200.

[23] Cf. Marc Galanter, *Law and Society in Modern India*, Oxford University Press, Delhi, 1997.

the indigenous peoples, Dalits, tribals, minorities or people belonging to religious groups other than the state-favoured one – they all experience overt and covert forms of discrimination that deny equal opportunities for their economic advancement. Innumerable are the ways in which discriminated groups and communities are prevented from pursuing commercial activities and other economic enterprises. A Dalit cannot prosper as a milk-vendor, for example. There are millions and millions in this country who would studiously avoid buying milk from Dalits for fear of defilement. A Dalit may not easily get a loan to set-up milk-vending business. This is but the tip of deep prejudices against the Dalits and their economic advancement. In America, people assiduously ensure that an African-American family does not move to the neighbourhood for fear that this may bring down the land-price in that area. There is something like a strategic exclusion from the control of natural resources.

The land of the discriminated peoples and groups are encroached upon, and they are excluded even from developing a concept of ownership, as has been the case with the Dalits. Exclusion is not simply withdrawing resources but strategically excluding others from power and from the concept of land-ownership and land-control. Exclusionary ideology adopts certain strategies. For example, the upper castes give food, and claim to offer protection; even they give land to build houses – *enam lands* in exchange of village labour. However, the lower castes and the Dalits must do the caste-assigned jobs. Even where the Dalits happen to own small tracts of land, the village water-tanks benefit the lands of the dominant castes and the lands of the Dalits are excluded or given a step motherly treatment. Colonialism cleverly designed the doctrine of *terra nullius* (no man's land) to legitimize ironically their illegal usurpation of lands from the Indios in Americas or from the Australian aboriginals. But today, Dalits are resisting this long-standing exclusion, as evident in the recent *Chengara* land agitation of Kerala, where landless Dalits claimed land from Harrison Malayalam Rubber plantation after months of strike and struggle and the government was forced to intervene on their behalf and satisfy their demands even to some extent.[24]

Against this background, it makes sense today to affirm more than ever before the universal destiny of natural resources. From a Christian perspective, participation and sharing in the goods of creation confirms

---

[24] Cf. K.T. Rammohan, "Caste and Landlessness in Kerala: Signals from Chengara", in *EPW*, 43, 37 (September 13, 2008), pp. 14-16.

that all human beings are sons and daughters of God.[25] If all land belongs
to Yahweh, all sons and daughters have a share in a common inheritance.
Land and natural resources are important for the identity of marginal
peoples and their development. This is an important basis for the inclusion
of marginalized communities and ethnic groups into the economic
processes with equal rights. In these times of globalization when neo-liberal
economy excludes the poor,[26] the truth that the goods of the earth are
meant for everybody is a powerful challenge to the accumulation of wealth
that excludes the weaker ones and creates growing disparity between the
rich and the poor. Universal destiny of earthly goods should give rise to
mechanisms and provisions that would check the unbridled quest for
accumulation.

### Promotion of Cultural and Social Capital among the Excluded

Many empirical studies show that even with the best of talents and
qualification, the subordinated peoples do not get included because they
lack cultural and social capital. This happens for example when a Dalit,
a tribal, an African-American or an Aboriginal applies for jobs. Whereas
candidates from upper and privileged groups with lesser talents and
qualification get recruited and continuously promoted because of the
linkages and "godfathers" they have, those at the bottom of the society
are left out for want of patronage, and powerful connections.

The concept of social capital – elaborated by Bourdieu, Putnam and
others[27] - is the network of connections which has an important role to
play in an individual or group's advancement. Social capital is increased
in two ways – either by "bonding" that is by promoting internal
connections and solidarity within a group or by "bridging" that is by
forging connections across to other individuals and groups.[28] Both are
important in increasing productivity and for bringing out the potentialities

---

[25] Cf. Charles Avila, *Ownership: Early Christian Teaching*, Orbis Books, New
York - Sheed and Ward, London, 1983.

[26] Cf. Felix Wilfred, "Church's Commitment to the Poor in the Age of
Globalisation", in *Vidyajyoti Journal of Theological Reflection*, 62 (1998), pp. 79-95.

[27] Bourdieu distinguished between three forms of capital – economic, social
and cultural. Cf. Pierre Bourdieu, "The Forms of Capital", in J. Richardson
(ed.), *Handbook of Theory and Research for the Sociology of Education*, Greenwood,
New York, 1986, pp. 241-258.

[28] Social capital could be looked at positively or negatively. Negatively it
could mean the patronage and high connections through which someone

of individuals and groups. In the case of new immigrants, the recognition and acceptance of ethnic differences could help in the 'bridging process' whereby the social capital of the host country/community gets enhanced along with that of the new entrant and he/she is helped to adapt to new conditions.

Cultural capital means a favourable intellectual environment which facilitates the pursuit of knowledge or profession. Children are endowed with cultural capital when their parents and relatives have higher educational background since a few generations. Where cultural capital is missing as in the case of many Dalits and tribals, we could observe for example high rate of dropouts in schools. Therefore, ways and means are to be devised for enhancing the social and cultural capital of the disadvantaged groups so as to end prevailing exclusions.[29]

Developing an inclusive historiography is another way of increasing the cultural and social capital for the marginalized peoples. How is the history narrated? For example, the local caste-landlord could narrate the history of the relationship between caste and outcaste communities in such a way that it is shown as a history of subservience and dependency on the part of the lower castes without agency and history. On the other hand, the Dalits remember their history as that of suffering and exploitation. There should be readiness on the part of the dominant groups to accept and acknowledge this history of exploitation and allow the voice of the subalterns and marginalized to be heard. This is the first step towards solidarity and inclusion.

### Conclusion: Overcoming Xenophobia

The underdogs of history responded positively to the extraordinary event of Barrack Obama's election to the presidency of United States. Why? It signified a break-through in the racial and ethnic barrier and exclusion. It evoked much hope for the world. This election of an African-American also points to a new dimension of justice. Often the justice issue is focused on the inequality of status or is viewed as a matter of distribution. What

---

achieves what others are not able to. Though social capital in itself is a neutral term, Bourdieu employs it in its negative connotation, whereas R. Putnam sees it in a positive sense in as much as the network of connection be empowering. Cf. Robert Putnam, *Bowling Alone: The Collapse and Revival of American Community*, Simon and Schuster, New York, 2000, pp. 22-23.

[29] Cf. André Béteille, "Access to Education", in *EPW*, 43, 20 (May 17, 2008) pp. 40-48.

is often forgotten is that injustice is involved in the process of including some people and some groups while excluding others; opportunities offered to some while they are denied to others. This aspect of justice requires greater attention today.

The feeling of threat or fear caused by the other, the stranger, is at the root of xenophobia that is escalating in our world. Jesus called as friends those 'strangers' whom the Jews viewed as a threat, and he defended them against the xenophobia of his fellow Jews. The praxis of Jesus has been one of constantly including those whom the society was trying to set aside. In fact, Jesus sees this as part of his mission of the Kingdom of God in which those whom the privileged have excluded will find the first places (Good Samaritan Lk 10:29-37; Labourers in the Vineyard Mt 20:1-16; Rich Man and Lazarus Lk 16:19-31; first and last place in the banquet Lk 14:7-14).

The teaching in Jesus' reversal parables shows the subversion of the worldly standards of exclusion and inclusion. So too the way he deals with the Samaritan woman (Jn 4:1-42), the Syro-Pheonician woman (Mk 7: 24-30), the woman who anointed him (Mk 14: 3-9), the lepers (Mk 1:40-45), etc. show how important a mission it is to care for and include those whom society despises and excludes. In fact, Jesus sees the outbreak of the Kingdom of God in the fact that what was zealously guarded by the rich and powerful as their lot is said to belong to everyone without exclusion: Thus knowledge and wisdom are no more the privilege of a few; freedom is no prerogative of some, but of everyone in the Kingdom of God. Every contribution to create inclusive communities is a step towards the Kingdom of God.

## Chapter 2

# Dalit Future: Future of the Nation

*"The Hindus wanted the Vedas and they sent for Vyasa who was not a caste Hindu. The Hindus wanted an Epic and they sent for Valmiki who was an untouchable. The Hindus wanted a Constitution, and they sent for me."*
                                                                          - Dr B.R. Ambedkar[1]

Dalit liberation needs to be placed in the context of the future of the nation. Envisaging a future that is insensitive to the plight of the Dalits and their suffering is a path that will turn India into a failed nation. The destiny of this country will depend upon the agency of the Dalits and the extent of their participation in all areas of life. The vision of the nation-state on its part needs to be based on the larger perspective of the human. Tagore had a larger view of the human, not constricted by narrow considerations of nation. In his addresses on *Nationalism*, Tagore was highly critical of the idea of nation. Nation as the post-Westphalian arrangement for peace after religious wars, ironically, became a source of wars – including the two World Wars. He does not understand how one could appeal to the ideal of nation and ask people to shed their blood, when they do not allow blood to be mingled through inter-caste union.

> And when we talk of Western Nationality, we forget that the nations there do not have that physical repulsion one for the other, that we have between different castes. Have we an instance in the whole world where a people who are not allowed to mingle their blood shed their blood for one another except by coercion or for mercenary purpose? And can we

---

[1] As quoted in Eleanor Zelliot, *From Untouchable to Dalit. Essays on the Ambedkar Movement*, Manohar, Delhi, 2005, p. 317.

ever hope that these moral barriers against our race amalgamation will
not stand in the way of our political unity?[2]

Another great Indian, Dr Ambedkar, was responsible for drafting the
Constitution of the country, and served also as law minister in the first
cabinet of Nehru. He was, obviously, not opposed to nation. However,
what was important for him was human dignity and social equity, and
these, according to him, cannot be sacrificed on the altar of nation. This
explains his concern that the change of power from the colonial rulers to
the upper caste elites (who fought in the name of nation) was not to become
a matter of replacing one oppression with another. For him, the conception
and agenda of a nation should go hand in hand with humaneness and
social equity.

The vision of Tagore and Ambedkar help us for a sustained critique
of the idea of nation that is placed on a pedestal higher than the human.
This is all the more necessary at a time when the ideology of nation has
become a pretext to impose the *Hindutva* and the perpetuation of caste-
hierarchy.

This chapter is an attempt to highlight in what ways the Dalit cause
could become an important force in shaping the nation, and what concerns
should dominate the Dalit movement towards re-defining the nation. In
other words, what this chapter argues is that, even though the cause of
the Dalits is certainly a cause of a weaker section, there is more to the
struggles of the Dalits. For their struggles go to shape the future destiny
of the nation.[3]

## Dalit Re-definition of Secularism, Democracy and Human Rights

The struggles of the Dalits could help create the spirit of secularism and
strengthen the process of democratization, by re-defining both the secular
and the democratic. It has been customary to distinguish the Indian
understanding of secularism from the Western. Many attempts are made
to define secularism in India, and most of them tend to view it as equal

---

[2] Rabindranath Tagore, *Lectures and Addresses*, edited by Anthony X. Soares,
Macmillan and Co, Limited, London 1962, pp. 116-117. "India has never had a
real sense of nationalism. Even though from childhood I had been taught that
idolatry of Nation is almost better than reverence for God and humanity, I believe
I have outgrown that teaching, and it is my conviction that my countrymen will
truly gain their India by fighting against the education which teaches them that
a country is greater than the ideals of humanity." *Ibid.*, p. 105.

[3] Cf. Felix Wilfred, *Dalit Empowerment*, NBCLC, Bangalore, 2007.

treatment of all religions (*sarvadharma samabhava*).[4] But from a Dalit perspective it says too little. Secularism for Dalits means freedom from the control of religion and its ideology that dehumanizes them and defines their lives; it is a freedom from the hierarchical religious ideology; it is a mode of thought and way of life guided by reason and not by any religious obscurantism. In this sense, there is a lot of similarity between the struggles of the Dalits for the secular and the development of the Western notion of secularization in their struggle against a domineering religious authority and its control.

Understood in this sense, Dalit secular agenda is a challenge to *Hindutva* ideology and its caste-hierarchy. Therefore, from a Dalit perspective the accent *is* not on the equal treatment of all religions but on the *equal treatment of every human being with dignity*, irrespective of any caste consideration. This broader agenda of the secular cannot but necessarily be anti-caste. Anti-casteism should be the crux of Indian secularism. This needs to be insisted upon.

Like secularism, democracy also needs to be redefined. The experience of democracy in South Asia shows how the people have tried to refashion it according to their experience and commonsense.

> The idea of democracy has transformed South Asia as much as South Asia has transformed the idea of democracy itself. The language, the practice and the institutions of democracy have transformed popular commonsense, everyday practices and relations of power. South Asia has reworked the idea of democracy by infusing it with meanings that spill over the received frame of the idea of democracy. These two influences have reinforced each other and helped create South Asian culture of democracy, distinctly modern and specifically South Asian.[5]

The marginalization of the Dalits poses a challenge to how democracy is defined and practiced in a given situation. Democratic process is extremely difficult as we could see from the struggle Dalits are undergoing to have a legitimate place in Panchayat Raj.[6] What is becoming clear is that

---

[4] For an overview of the debates on this point, see Rajeev Barghava, *Secularism and Its Critics*, Oxford University Press, Delhi, 1999. See also Neera Chandhoke, *Beyond Secularism. The Rights of Religious Minorities*, Oxford University Press, Delhi, 1999.

[5] *State of Democracy in South Asia. A Report*, Oxford University Press, Delhi, 2008, p. 6.

[6] Cf. Narendra Kumar – Manoj Rai (eds.), *Dalit Leadership in Panchayats. A Comparative Study of Four States*, Rawat Publications, Jaipur, 2006.

democracy gets redefined when it begins with the concerns of the excluded and the marginalized - something different from bourgeois democracy whose focus is to safeguard the freedom of the individual and promote free enterprises. The re-defining of democracy in India and Asia at large, should have as its focus the weaker sections - Dalits, women, tribals and so on - and not the bourgeois individual. Unfortunately, this does not happen. A clear indication of this is the sad fact that democracy and state have not been able to control violence against Dalits, women, tribals and other subalterns.

One may argue that the vision of democracy inspiring our Constitution has through a special provision taken care of the weaker sections. True as it may be, this vision has not been, unfortunately, translated into practice in such a way that the Dalits and other weaker sections can exercise their agency, and thus make democracy work for their benefit. Moreover, in order to translate this vision into practice, there needs to be the general will of the people to find appropriate ways and means, strategies and mechanisms for implementation in practice. Dalit movements and struggles will reshape democracy in such a way that it would signify defence of the weaker sections from violence, oppression and injustice. Historically in fact, the anti-caste movement has been the real democratic movement in the country.[7] Democratization of the nation is correlated to the strength and extent of anti-caste movements.

Similar reflections can be made also regarding human rights. Like secularism and democracy, human rights will be effective in India when practiced from the perspective of the marginalized. Otherwise, like in the case of democracy, human rights can become simply an instrument to protect the interest of bourgeois individuals. In this sense, human rights with the individual as the focal point could become anti-poor. Dalit consciousness is not individualistic; it is collective consciousness. A more comprehensive understanding of human rights takes place in relation to the particular context of a people. For example, the right to life guaranteed in the Constitution is commonly understood as protection from violent aggression against one's life. But the provision

---

[7] In fact this is, according to Gail Omvedt, the central significance of the contribution of Ambedkar. Cf. Gail Omvedt, *Dalits and the Democratic Revolution. Dr. Ambedkar and the Dalit Movement in Colonial India,* Sage Publications, New Delhi, 1994; see also Eleanor Zelliot, *From Untouchable to Dalit. Essays on the Ambedkar Movement*, Manohar, Delhi, 2005.

of the Constitution appears in a completely new light when it is expanded and interpreted, as Krishna Iyer did, from the perspective of the poor as *right to livelihood*, which means the right for food, shelter, health-care, etc., the depriving of which is tantamount to taking away one's life. In relation to differing contexts, human rights keep developing, and we will be discovering new dimensions of this legal instrumentality. In India, human rights should mean first and foremost the rights of the Dalits, women, tribals and other marginalized groups. These rights which often touch the fundamentals of human life and livelihood, take precedence over a general understanding of human rights centred on the individual.[8]

This redefinition of secularism, democracy and human rights is crucial to come to terms with the *Hindutva* which has become a serious menace to all the three. *Hindutva* can feign to be at home with the conventional and dominant understanding of democracy, secularism and human rights. It gets challenged the moment democracy, secularism and human rights are redefined in the way I have suggested, namely, starting from the suffering and concerns of Dalits and other weaker sections. A redefined conception of these realities are inclusive and open-ended, while *Hindutva* with its caste ideology, remains a closed system and cannot rise up to the challenges posed by the redefinition.

Dalit movements can play a cathartic role by cleansing the polluted mind of a nation and mending its ways. But the path is an arduous one. For, the caste is so essential to Hinduism that, as Arvind Sharma observes, if caste is dissolved, Hinduism will lose the very basis of its tolerance and will become a missionary religion.[9] In fact, the aggressively proselytizing efforts of *Hindutva* among the tribals and other weaker sections only goes to prove that its traditional caste structure is getting challenged and threatened. Therefore, we can note a correlation between the threat to caste system and aggression by the *Hindutva* and Sangh Parivar. But the point is that the Dalits need to be prepared and come to terms with such a reaction of Hindutva.

---

[8] Cf. Felix Wilfred, "Human Rights or the Rights of the Poor? Redeeming Human Rights from Its Contemporary Inversions" in *Vidyajyoti Journal of Theological Reflection*, 62 (1998), pp. 734-752.

[9] Cf. Arvind Sharma, *Hinduism for Our Times,* Oxford University Press, Delhi, 1977. "The dissolution of the traditional caste system will then also be accompanied by the dissolution of the traditional basis of Hindu tolerance. Hinduism will ultimately become a casteless and missionary religion instead of remaining caste-bound and tolerant entity." p. 85.

We need to add that the struggles of Dalits introduce a much needed *critical element* in the nation and in its culture. No nation and no people can progress without self-critique. We know that modernity started by challenging tradition and its authority. Tradition was considered until then as the sole criterion of truth. By challenging tradition, scriptures, practices, etc., and by submitting them to critical scrutiny, Dalits are playing a much needed critical role for the shaping of the nation and its future.

### Redefining the Episteme

The future of the nation requires that knowledge system itself be rethought and redefined. As it is, the whole nation is steered by knowledge system monopolized by a small elite to maximize their advantages.[10] In the dominant knowledge system, Dalits and other marginalized groups do not find a place. And yet we know that Dalits and weaker sections have a deeper understanding and knowledge of realities through their experience of suffering. Was not *dhukka* the beginning of enlightenment, knowledge and wisdom for the great Gautama? Their very being at the margins gives the Dalits an understanding and perspective of realities that elude the centre. Being at the margin they have a larger vision of the human which cannot be encapsulated in a narrow vision of the nation, much less that of caste. Moreover, through their continuous praxis in various areas of daily life Dalit contribute to the development of knowledge. Unfortunately, the knowledge indigenously produced through their hard labour and sweat is neglected.

### A Reappraisal of Growth

There is a lot of euphoria about the fast economic growth India has been experiencing for the past few years. This is attributed mainly to the contribution by information technology. People are led to believe that the growth of the nation is in relation to the growth of information technology and service sector connected with it. But this illusion vanishes into thin air when we look at the actual facts.

As per statistics, information technology is responsible just for 6% of national income. On the other hand, income and wealth which derive from agricultural labour and production amount, by most conservative estimate, to 30% of national income. In actuality it could be even 70%.

---

[10] Cf. Felix Wilfred, "Knowledge-Ethics for Our Times", in *Jeevadhara*, 39 (January, 2009), pp. 5-28.

Now it is a fact that 74.50% of Dalits are involved in agriculture of which 25.44% as cultivators and 49.06% as agricultural labourers.[11] What does it mean? It means that Dalits, though they constitute 16.48% of the population, contribute most to the national wealth through their productive labour in agricultural and other fields. If so, much of national income and wealth are dependent upon agriculture sector in which more than any other group the Dalits are involved; it means that for the future of the nation, it is important to strengthen this productive source.

## A Matter of Concern

The hope the Dalits represent for the future of the nation as a counter-culture as an anti-hegemonic and anti-hierarchical force has been, unfortunately, marred by certain development that have taken place since 1990s. It is a fact that among some sections of Dalits there has been the seduction of the Hindutva, which strangely though, wants to co-opt Ambedkarism for its ends.[12] The question is more than co-optation. We could speak of the encompassment of Dalits by the Hindutva. The investigations have clearly shown that in the riots in Gujarat and in the communal killing of Muslim and others, Dalits were involved. How are we to explain these facts? One may say that the communal riots have been engineered by upper caste Hindutva forces and the Dalits are instrumentalised. Should that be the case, it only shows that Dalits could easily become pawns in the manipulative hands of the upper castes and classes. The inevitable question is: Where is the agency of the Dalits? Do not these incidents show that these sections of Dalits have not really come to their true selfhood, and could therefore become victims of caste manipulation?[13]

---

[11] It has been extremely difficult to get exact data on these points. The figures presented here are collected from various sources, including the Ministry of Agriculture, checked, compared and has been compiled by me.

[12] Cf. Anand Teltumbde (ed.), *Hindutva and Dalits. Perspectives for Understanding Communal Praxis*, Samya, Kolkata, 2005. Today there is almost no political party in India, no matter which ideological colour or hue it belongs to, that does not invoke Ambedkar for its survival.

[13] There is also the question of political pragmatism which led Dalit movements and parties to compromise the long term goal of radical liberation for short-term political gains. For an analysis of this point, see Gail Omvedt, "Ambedkar and After: The Dalit Movement in India", in Ghanshyam Shah (ed.), *Dalit Identity and Politics*, Sage Publications, Delhi, 2001, pp. 143-159. Speaking of the plight of Dalit cultural movement, Gopal Guru observes: "Thus,

### Strategies for the Future

Obviously, the future of the nation will depend upon the values that are imparted in the process of education. Here lie the seeds of a nation's destiny. Such being the importance of education, for a cultural transformation of the nation, it is crucial that right from its beginning, education focus its attention on caste, caste system and its consequence as a social evil. Educational policies and textbooks need to be developed that will enable the struggle against the evils of caste and caste-system. Moreover, the national policy of education should identify the forces of communalism and name them. For example, many textbooks of history simply state that Gandhi was murdered. They fail to mention that Nathuram Godse, who was a member of Hindu extremist organizations, murdered him. A failure to educate against communalism is a weakness that has serious consequence for the present and the future of the nation.

It is highly important that the state functions as welfare state and does not yield to the ruling classes who have unfortunately already eroded the welfare state orientation. For those who reposed their faith in neo-liberal economy, the financial meltdown and recession we experience today should be a salutary warning. This kind of economy not only is harmful to the poor and the subalterns, but is flawed in its own logic of capitalism and neo-liberalism. A secure future of the nation is possible when we challenge the neo-liberal economy that is opposed to the cause of peasants, workers, artisans, and others. It is the sector where Dalits are mostly involved. Therefore, ultimately the Dalit challenge to the liberal economic path of the country is to shape its future.

### Dalit Future and the Future of the Church

Through its commitment to the Dalits, the Church would actually be laying the foundations for a nation of equals. If the Church understands itself as the messenger of the Good News to the poor, its plans and dreams for the future will revolve around the Dalits, and the tribals who are the poorest

---

the Dalit cultural initiative before 1970 had the promise and potential to move away from the familiar to the universal. But such a culturally vibrant Dalit movement came to be colonized by the state and the dominant political forces which subordinated this cultural movement to serve its own political ends." "Ambedkar and the Dalit Cultural Movement in Maharashtra", in Ghanshyam Shah (ed.), *op.cit.*, p. 191. Such being the development, it was easy for the Hindutva to drag in its net a section of the Dalits and dampen the radicality of the Dalit movement inspired by the vision of Dr Ambedkar.

of the poor in this country. They will not be simply one of the many concerns of the Church, but the main focus of its attention. Even more, the future of the Church will be gauged by its commitment to the Dalits and the tribals who also form, even from a numerical point of view, the majority of Christians.

Admittedly, much has been done in terms of welfare works, educational assistance, etc.[14] Simply increasing such measures is not really what is ultimately required. The principal mission of the Church in the decades to come is to cast out the demon of casteism both within and without. The argument that the salvation of the soul is the supreme law, and therefore for the sake of this objective caste should be tolerated has been the greatest misfortune that has happened to the Indian Church.

Moving ahead would mean taking earnest efforts, without compromise, to eradicate caste in the Church which would set an example to the larger society. This is the most significant contribution the Church could make to the shaping of a new nation. It involves an educational practice that would transform first and foremost the mindset of the dominant castes who are prejudiced against the Dalits. This could come about through efforts to create inclusive communities on the basis of justice and inspired by the spirit of participation and sense of equality.

The numerous Church-run educational institutions, on their part, will take it as their mission to impart an education oriented to the abolition of caste. The fascination of success and the thirst for recognition can drive these institutions to push this agenda under the carpet, which is to betray the spirit of Christian faith and message. Instead of bending backwards to fulfill the elitist educational policies of the state and the demands of the market, Christian institutions should be rather in the forefront to influence the state policies of education and steer these towards the cause of the poor and the Dalits. If the cause of the poor and the Dalits are to be sacrificed in our educational institutions for the sake of benefits that may accrue from the state or the elites, the most appropriate thing would be to give up these with no sense of regret.

For an inclusive community, it is plain that there needs to be representation from all sections at the leadership level. This is imperative

---

[14] Cf. S. Lourduswamy, *Towards Empowerment of Dalit Christians. Equal Rights to All Dalits*, Centre for Dalit/Subaltern Studies, Delhi, 2005. For historical background, see John C.B. Webster, *The Dalit Christians. A History*, ISPCK, Delhi, 1994.

in the case of Dalits who have been deprived of leadership positions in the Church on various pretexts. Such a move should not be interpreted as causing division or disunity; quite the contrary, it is an effort to create unity by including the excluded, and thus form inclusive communities. It is an effort to heal the community from the rupture which the forced exclusion of the Dalits has caused. It is high time that adequate representation of Dalit people be ensured at the level of hierarchy – which is at the moment only at a token level. So, too in the Church-run institutions care needs to be taken that Dalits have proportionate representation at the leadership level. We could reasonably hope that there will be, before long, Dalit representation also at the level of College of Cardinals in the Roman Catholic Church – a move that would be symbolic affirmation of the serious engagement of the Church to the cause of a struggling people, matching thus its words with deeds.

## Devising a Dalit Index

One of the lacunas in the Church for the participation and advancement of Dalits is the absence of a monitoring mechanism. As long as paternalistic policies and programmes are accepted by the Dalits, there is no conflict. But when it comes to participation and leadership or appointments in Church-run institutions, anti-Dalit sentiments are leashed out, especially when the Dalits make representation. The Catholic Bishops' Conference of India will do well to set up a Dalit Index Committee which will work out a set of criteria for the various Church-run institutions and religious bodies. The same could be done in other Church bodies. These newly developed criteria will measure the Dalit-sensitiveness of the various bodies in the Church, including diocese, parishes, parish-councils, religious societies, institutions, etc. Together with it there needs to be also a Dalit Monitoring Body which will point out the lapses as well as measure and grade the credibility of various church-related bodies against the Dalit Index.

## Conclusion – Collective Prophecy of the Dalits

The future of the Dalits and of the nation will result from three inter-related struggles. First, there is the struggle to move from ascriptive identity to creative identity. Ascriptive identity is something which one inherits as a member of a caste, a language-group or as a member belonging to a particular religion by birth. If the ascriptive identity becomes the ultimate criterion to define a person, then there is no room for choice and personal responsibility. Ascriptive identity imprisons the Dalits within the cage of caste; stunts their growth and allows their talents to wither. Creative identity blossoms when they break loose of the ascriptive identity and fashion for themselves in freedom a future and determine their own destinies.

Second, Dalits are caught up in a structure in which they could be manipulated and exploited, scattered as they are through the breadth and length of the country and with all odds staked against them. As people without identity of their own and stripped off their selfhood, the future of the Dalits will depend upon the extent they are able to move to gain their agency and selfhood. They will be no more victims of structures but active agents who will create new structures of freedom and justice for themselves and for the whole nation.

Finally, the struggle of the Dalits is to pass on from the conception of a nation as given and as defined by their dominators and the elites to an understanding of nation as a project in which the Dalits have an indispensable and crucial role to play through their participation.

The important thing is that Dalits and Dalit movements do not succumb to ascriptive identity, imposed structures and pre-fabricated image of the nation, but keep alive their vibrant hope and the radicality of their struggles. A revolutionary transformation of this nation we may expect only from Dalits and the tribals. For the upper castes and classes are involved in accumulation of wealth through exploitation, and the Indian middle-class is driven by competition and upward mobility, and change in the existing order of things is the last thing they are interested in.

For Dalits, the situation is different. They yearn for a different future and have other dreams. Until these goals are attained Dalits cannot feel at home. The feeling of not being at home and the practice of non-conformity is what would give them the energy and vibrancy to fashion a future for themselves which will be also the future of the nation. As it appears, it is going to be a long drawn out struggle. But the future the Dalits long for may be nearer than what is projected. For, there are imponderables of history. In India, the Dalit people are no more simply the victims; they are called upon today to actively perform collective prophecy for the transformation of the nation and of the Church. That is a great and challenging task indeed.

# Chapter 3

# Subalterns and Ethical Auditing

*"With all his crimes broad blown, as flush as May; And how his audit stands who knows save heaven?"* — William Shakespeare[1]

*"One is still defending reason when one fights those who mask their abuses of power under the appearance of reason or who use the weapons of reason to consolidate or justify an arbitrary empire."* — Pierre Bourdieu[2]

An eight-year-old little girl from a slum in Bangalore, adjacent to luxurious apartments, steps out early in the morning to answer nature's call. Fourteen dogs pounce upon her and bite her to death.[3] The poor in this country have neither self-contained rooms, nor land of their own for such elementary needs. Tragic and shocking as the incident is, it is disquieting for all those who are concerned about what is happening to this country. Day in and day out we hear the trumpeting of the phenomenal economic growth, scientific feats, new IT corridors and parks, industrial estates and so on. The media portrays with gusto flimsy details about the glamour of Bollywood and Kollywood stars and cricket-heroes, models and beauties. And yet the subalterns – the poor, the Dalits, the tribals, women and children – are becoming more and more insecure. Men and women from the poorest sections migrate from Bihar to Assam just for survival, and they eke out their existence as coolies and unskilled labourers, but they are gunned down brutally by ethnic chauvinists.[4] An

---

[1] William Shakespeare, *Hamlet*, Act 3, sc. 3, 1.80.

[2] Pierre Bourdieu, *Acts of Resistance*, The New Press, New York, 1998, p. 20.

[3] Reported in *Dinamoni* {Tamil Daily}, January 6, 2007, p.10.

[4] Cf. Sushanta Talukdar, "Migrants' Massacre", in *Frontline*, January 26, 2007, pp.32-35; Prabhakara, "Assam after the ULFA Strikes." *The Hindu*, (Chennai Edition), January 13, 2007, p. 15; *The Hindu*, January 8, 2007, p. 14; "No discussion

industrialist wallowing in riches and luxury turns bestial, chops off thirty-eight children after sexually abusing them. They are wrapped up in gunnysacks and buried at the backyard of his home.[5] India has always been a land of contradictions. But the contradictions we are experiencing today should make any thinking Indian hang his or her head in shame.

There is a collective responsibility. How can we exercise our collective responsibility, so that there is a modicum of justice and fairness to the powerless and most vulnerable sections of the people? The strange combination of obscurantist caste and liberal capitalism, and the present model of development push the high castes and classes to the pinnacle of scandalous wealth and throw the subalterns to the bottomless pit of misery. If labour is the source of wealth, it is not explainable how some people in the country could accumulate so much wealth within a lifetime. Looking at a similar situation in his time, an early Christian writer noted that either the man with such riches must be a robber; if not at least his father![6] If on the other hand, the earth and its resources belong to all people, how can we explain that the poor farmers are driven to desperation and suicide because they are in huge debts, and do not have the basic minimum for a dignified human life?

Both these situations present the need for a check and auditing, so that there is no undue accumulation of wealth at the cost of the poor and the subalterns, and no lack of basic means to conduct a dignified human life. It is here we realize the paramount importance of ethical auditing as a concrete means for sustaining a society in justice and equity.

---

on Sovereignty, says Jaiswal", *Indian Express*, January 8, 2007, p. 1; *Sunday Times*, January 7, 207, p. 1; *Deccan Chronicle*, January 11, 2007, p. 3; Sanjib Baruah, "January To Nowhere", *The Times of India*, January 16, 2007, p. 14.

[5] What makes the whole thing very chilling is that almost all these children belong to the Dalit community. When complaint was lodged with the police, it was ignored. Cf. *The Hindu*, January 20, 2007, p. 9. It is suspected that there was connivance of the police with the killer. Cf. Ajay Uprety & Payal Saxena, "The Bone Collectors", *The Week*, Vol. 25, no.7, January 14, 2007, p. 14-16; Sandeep Unnithan and Shyamlal Yadav, "Butchers of Suburbia", *India Today*, Delhi, January 15, 2007, p. 60-66; *The Times of India*, January 1, 2007, p. 1; Manas Dasgupta, "Noida Case Accused Likely to be Taken to Delhi Today", *The Hindu*, January 11, 2007, p.11; Amita Verma, "Noida 'curse' keeps Mulayam away", *Deccan Chronicle*, January 7, 2007, p. 3.

[6] Cf. Charles Avila, *Ownership. Early Christian Tradition*, Orbis Books, New York, 1983.

### Three Cover-Ups and Their Ethical Unmasking

Ethical auditing has become complex and very challenging, because the people and institutions that should come under public scrutiny and ethical auditing succeed to cover-up the situation. It requires special efforts to strip it and make people see the reality in all its nakedness. Unmasking of the reality is the first and foundational act of ethical auditing. The awareness that nothing that is of public interest could be concealed and covered up will have a salutary ethical check on all those who thrive by exploiting the subalterns and their labour.

### *Hypocritical Silence on Caste*

The first cover-up is caste. Nothing seems to move in this country without the engine of caste. And yet, ironically, caste is something which the elites in the country do not want to talk about, and even more, do not want to be seen talking about. The hypocrisy of the whole matter is that caste is something the elites and upper castes even now observe scrupulously. It is entrenched deep down in the mindset of the upper castes, not withstanding all modern developments. Even when they travel abroad, to U.S. or U.K., the upper castes and elites carry under their armpit also their castes - something evidenced by the ingenious ways in which they look for marriage-alliances within the same caste and *gotra*. Modernity with all its IT revolution and with high profile entrepreneurial and managerial mantras has not changed an iota in the frame of mind that is soaked in caste-consciousness. To find what is locked in the minds of the upper castes, it may be useful to recall what P.V. Jagadis Aiyar wrote in the early decades of the twentieth century:

> The Indian custom of observing distance pollution, etc., has hygienic and sanitary considerations in view. In general the so called pious and religious people are generally most scrupulously clean and hence contact with people of uncleanly habits is nauseating to them....[P]eople living on unwholesome food such as rotten fish, garlic, etc., as well as people of filthy and unclean habits throw out of their bodies coarse and unhealthy magnetism. This affects the religious people of pure habits and diet injuriously. So they keep themselves at a safe distance, which has been fixed by the sages of old after sufficient experience and experiment.[7]

---

[7] As quoted in M.S.S. Pandian, "One Step Outside Modernity. Caste, Identity Politics and Public Sphere" in *EPW*, May 4, 2002, p.1737.

Like the proverbial cat that has nine lives,[8] caste takes on ever-new avatars which make it difficult to censure and bring under ethical auditing. Just like its avatars, covering up of castes also takes on many forms. There are high caste people who would enter into abstruse philosophical discourses to show that there is no distinction between the Brahmin and Shudra, since the entire reality is one, and all of us form part of Brahman. The cover-up could take on a devotional tone, when it is said that before God all devotees are the same, and there is no caste-distinction; what matters is the love and devotion with which one approaches the Lord. Stories of Nandanar and Chokkamela are narrated by the upper castes as illustrations to prove the point.

They do not realize that such ideological fig leaves may not succeed to cover up the violence and indignity heaped upon the subalterns, especially the Dalits in this country. After making a detailed study of *"The Untouchables of India"*, Robert Deliége notes how there has taken place a lot of change in the way the Dalits view caste, whereas, as for as the upper castes are concerned "in effect, little in their basic conception of untouchability seems to have changed... Untouchability persists, and one might even say that, from a certain point of view, it is thriving in spite of modern ideologies".[9] It is difficult to grasp how some people could derive pleasure and see themselves pure and superior while considering other human beings as impure, inferior and small, as the so-called high castes do. If this is the general ethos, we are in a seriously sick society. The gravity of the matter eludes us because we get used to this kind of reality as everyday experience. This moral illness needs a proper diagnosing and a sustained ethical auditing at all levels.

Modernized upper caste intellectuals prefer, as I noted earlier, to keep silence over caste than attempt to hide it under any ideological cloak. This silence could be explained probably from the fact that caste is considered as the remnant of a pre-modern society, and it is embarrassing to talk about this social reality. To speak of it is not becoming of a modern man, a secular citizen. I have been struck how in the writings of a well-known thinker like Amartya Sen who expatiates on Indian society, there is hardly anything on caste, and much less it is employed by him as an analytical

---

[8] This is an analogy used in the Mandal Commission Report. See *Reservations for Backward Classes. Mandal Commission Report of the Backward Classes Commission*, 1980, Akalank Publications, Delhi, 1991, p. 23.

[9] Robert Deliége, *The Untouchables of India*, Berg, Oxford, 1999, p. 199.

category to interpret Indian society.[10] Is it not the case of the proverbial ostrich burying its head in the sand to delude itself that the world does not exist?

The silence on caste which the upper castes and their intellectuals observe needs to be broken. Caste should become a matter of public discourse and debate. Curiously, it is the Dalits and other subalterns who are often accused, because they talk of caste constructions and inequalities loudly. The implication is that talking about it is unethical, anti-secular and not becoming of a modern citizen. What it really hides is the fact that every aspect of life in the nation is managed and controlled by caste-considerations. If the Dalits speak openly and loudly about caste, it is not to reinforce it – far from it. If there is a group that is most affected by caste-consciousness, it is the Dalits. It is they who are the first ones to drive away caste, because they know the oppression, suffering and humiliation it can cause.[11] The Dalits speak about caste without inhibition, because they want to exorcise this demon. On the other hand, upper castes want to be silent on caste in public and derive all the benefits and power through it.

### Concealment of Equity

Ethical auditing has to take into account a second cover-up and it relates to the issue of social equity. The growing disparity between the rich and the poor globally and nationally is too evident. Today, corporations and multinationals increase their profit manifold by reducing the multitude to poverty and elevating a few to the heights of riches. Even liberal planners, inspired by a sense of pragmatism, are concerned about this situation, and admit that it is not possible to have a sustainable development with such disparity.

What is strange is the effort to justify and cover up these indefensible disparities. Liberal gurus like John Rawls enter, akin to the traditional elites covering up caste, into abstruse theories and fictitious situations to show that inequality need not mean that it is bad for the disadvantaged. Inequality, according to him, could be permitted as long as it brings advantages to everyone – the rich and the poor. Ultimately, this window-

---

[10] Even in his latest book on the question of identities, he turns philosophical, and has but one or two cursory and tangential remarks on the social reality of caste. See Amartya Sen, *Identity and Violence. The Illusion of Destiny*, Penguin Books, London, 2006.

[11] Cf. Felix Wilfred, *Dalit Empowerment*, NBCLC, Bangalore, 2007.

dressing of liberal capitalism is meant to demonstrate that, after all, liberalism is also concerned about justice which is "fairness".[12]

The attempt to conceal and even theoretically justify inequalities is accompanied by the praxis of generous philanthropic works. Think of the philanthropic works in the field of HIV/AIDS promoted by one of the richest men on the globe – Bill Gates, or McDonald's campaign for cleanliness and hygiene of the surroundings or Infosys' development work, or Tata's adoption of development blocks, and so on. To cap it all, Margaret Thatcher, the mother of liberal capitalism and former prime minister of England, is supposed to have drawn out an important lesson for the world from the parable of the Good Samaritan. The moral of the story is that you should produce wealth. For, how could the Good Samaritan help the person he found on the wayside, if he did not have the money and the means? Curious as it may sound, this seems to be the logic of many liberals on whose aprons hang also our Indian elites and upper castes.

*"Corporate Social Responsibility"* is a fashionable phrase under which the cover-up of equity takes place. It is supposed to be something voluntary by which a company or a corporate positions itself socially. The philosophy behind the concept of corporate social responsibility is that a corporate benefits from society. Therefore, it feels obliged to give back some of its profits by way of beneficial activities to the public and society. The equity question, on the other hand, is a challenging and disquieting one. For, it uncovers the weak foundation, fades and frail structures. At bottom, individuals and institutions benefiting from modern market and globalization at the cost of the subalterns and the poor, want to be enthroned as Good Samaritans by throwing away some pittance.

### Hiding of Knowledge – Ignorance and Secrecy
Hiding of knowledge is a third cover-up that makes ethical auditing very challenging. It is an age-old stratagem: If people are kept in ignorance, they can be easily controlled. Therefore, as we know, all dominators have tried to prevent the subjugated people from knowledge and education, from access to information and truth. This is true also of the casteist society which proscribed education to the shudra and the Dalits with strict punishments.

---

[12] Cf. John Rawls, *A Theory of Justice*, Revised Edition, Harvard University Press, Cambridge, 2003; see also Quentin Skinner (ed), *The Return of Grand Theory in the Human Sciences,* Cambridge University Press, Cambridge, 1997, pp.101-119.

Today people are kept in ignorance about the very things that touch upon their lives and are of immense importance to their safety and survival. Decisions are made over their heads. There is the clan of all-knowing experts who keep the people at bay. For example, information should be available to people regarding the environment in which they live – one of the principles formulated by 1992 Rio Declaration on Environment and Development. The poor of Bhopal knew nothing of the way Union Carbide was working until the tragedy struck them, killing thousands and crippling for life many more. Keeping people in ignorance is to be viewed as a criminal act, and that is why it should be brought under ethical censuring. Moreover, hiding knowledge from the people prevents them from exercising their agency. Today development planners and corporates do this hiding.

*Secrecy* is the way in which knowledge and information are withheld from the public. History and experience tell us that secrecy is the weapon of the powerful and the dominators. It is a veil to cover up the actual messy realities, and keep the people subjugated. The subalterns do not have secrets. Their emotions are openly expressed without inhibition, and no information is withheld under the shroud of secrecy. They are like an open book. Their very way of life has a public character – even regarding matters which the upper castes consider taboos. They do not lock themselves up in their homes, nor isolate themselves in the cocoon of their world of the self. In other words, in the life of the subalterns, there is a conflation of the public and the private. Dalits and other subalterns have nothing to hide. On the other hand, what we note is that upper castes and the elites in the society have many things to hide, guard against and cover-up. For, if those truths are known, if those informations are divulged, their positions could become very shaky; could have serious consequences for their power and privileges, and undercut their ambitions.

## Some Means and Parameters for Ethical Auditing

In the light of what we said on the three cover-ups and their ethical unmasking, we could reflect now on some of the ways in which ethical auditing could be practiced and on the criteria and principles implied in this.

Let me state at the outset, what we are envisaging is something that goes beyond the deployment of ethics in the entrepreneurial and managerial world. In this environment, social and ethical auditing is today much talked about. What we really find here is that ethics itself is turned into a technology in the hope that it will bring in its dividends. Like other means, ethics is made use of for better production, output efficient management and for more competitive marketing. No wonder that this kind of ethical and social auditing discoursed in managerial jargons is often nothing but a pale reflection, not to say travesty, of a foundational ethics and ethical auditing required today for the creation of a just and equitable society – a society in which the subalterns will have the means for their livelihood and necessary security.

If we analyse deeply the values inherent in the discourses of ethical and social auditing in the corporate world, they are *self-referential*. The goal of ethics is the self, the organization, enterprise, and their success and credibility. Instead, the ethics that we propose and which should underlie all genuine ethical auditing is one in which the point of reference is *the other*, distinct from the self. Ethics and ethical auditing are deeply human and humanistic issues. One has to take a stand vis-à-vis the other, especially in favour of the weak and the vulnerable. This kind of ethical auditing is highly challenging, and we can only surmise that entrepreneurs and managers will conveniently set them aside. This ethical language is for them quite disturbing. For it threatens to bring to the fore the subalterns as the point of reference for any genuine ethical and social auditing – be it the state, any institution, organization or corporate. The subalterns are the litmus test on whether an institution or enterprise is ethically oriented or not.

## The Presuppositions

It is of immense importance today that the state, its bureaucracy and the private sector provide the public and the subalterns with all informations. This calls for, as I noted, a different way of looking at ethics and ethical accountability, inspired ultimately by a new conception of power. Let me explain. Traditionally power was considered in terms of *possession*. One possessed power by way of appointment, inheritance, through sacred rituals, etc. This is a strongly legal conception of power.

When power is considered as a matter of possession, hierarchy is built up. Hierarchy is nothing but the slot or position of power one occupies in a given society, which becomes the point of reference for the relationship with others in that particular society or organization. The accountability and auditing took place within this frame of power and hierarchy. Accordingly, the lower officials are accountable to those who have more power in the hierarchy. Subaltern approach to accountability and ethical auditing revolutionizes this stand: It is those who have more power in the traditional sense who are accountable to those who are in the lower rungs and to the general public. Ethical auditing is complete when power at various levels becomes accountable to the marginalized in the society. To hold any power or organization accountable is a right of the subalterns. It is an empowering mechanism. Besides, the practice of giving account to the public, has a cathartic effect on any institution.

### Enabling Conditions for Ethical Auditing

For ethical auditing to take place, first and foremost there should be a basic *shift in the mindset of the subalterns.* For too long they have been subjected to a dependent mode of thought and praxis. Imagining themselves at a low position, they look up to authorities, institutions and leaders for favours, concessions, gifts, development etc. In such a frame of mind, ethical auditing, transparency and accountability do not make any sense. Their thoughts and attitudes will be one of subservience, loyalty, gratitude, adulation, etc. Ethical auditing demands that this mindset of the subalterns vis-à-vis the state, public authorities and institutions as one of ruled vs. the rulers, change. If, for example, the government is really perceived as something by the people, for the people and of the people, then there will be truly a revolutionary change in relationships. The people are the masters; and the state, its officials and bureaucracy are there to serve the people. Is it anything strange if the master calls for accounts from the servants? People as masters have to hold pubic servants and institutions accountable. Here the accountability is not from bottom up, but from top to bottom. This revolutionary change of mindset is the beginning for any serious thought on ethical auditing and accountability.

There needs to emerge a general conviction that a society's healthy functioning depends on its accountability to the weaker sections. Here is a crucial point. The subalterns on their part have the important task of demanding from the state, public authorities and private entrepreneurs that their actions and decisions are ethically sound and transparent. Precisely because this demand is often missing, the state, public authorities and corporates feel emboldened to behave as masters and as if they are above accountability.

### The Subalterns and Right to Information

The present political situation dominated by the elites and upper castes have created a weak state that is eager to fulfill the demands of this group of people. They take refuge in a colonial-style bureaucracy. It is not a political atmosphere conducive to the cause of the subalterns. In the economic realm, the new economic policy, market and globalization have created a world where decisions are made keeping the people and affected groups in ignorance. The subalterns are losing control of their lives, and are more and more at the mercy of these market forces with whom the state and politicians are hands in glove.

It is part of ethical auditing that people demand information pertaining to their daily lives. Is it not the right of the poor to ask how much supply is made to the ration-shops in their area when they observe that officials and middlemen divert the supply meant for them through corrupt practices? Is it not the right of the subalterns to demand how the provisions are distributed to the ration-card holders? Should the subalterns not demand from local panchayat bodies how accounts are maintained? Precisely to vindicate the right of the people and to hold the public servants accountable, from October 2005, there has come about, as a shot in the arm, the new *Right to Information Act.*

The significance of this Act is that it has replaced the archaic *Official Secrecy Act of 1935*, enacted during the colonial period. According to this latter Act, state officials and bureaucrats are not to give out information. The legacy of this Act continued even after Independence. Under the influence of this Act, officials have claimed their right to withhold information from the public. It is clear that the Act was meant to protect the interest of the state and facilitate unchallenged governance. The new Act has, at least in theory, reversed the situation. While officials felt that they were acting legally and ethically when refusing information because they were bound by secrecy, today, if they refuse to part with information to the public it is unethical and illegal, and therefore becomes a punishable offence. Through this Right to Information Act, the conditions are created for corruption-free and transparent governance. But this could remain a reform on paper unless the subalterns demand for information at every level. But the information and truth need not come out only under pressure from the public. It is desirable that a culture of governance is created in which the state *suo motu* will provide all the necessary informations to the public.

The ethical auditing regarding information needs to be applied also to the private sector. For, with the entry of private sector and multinationals in a massive way, the economic scene in the country has changed. The subalterns are often spectators before the imposing structures, economic zones and other business and entrepreneurial activities taking place around them. The poor are kept completely in ignorance of what is going on around them, as these production units and service centres with international connections are operating insulated from the local population – exploiting their land, their water and their electricity. It is important then that the subalterns challenge these institutions and enterprises and demand information about them. The private sector cannot set itself above accountability to the public and refuse to supply information about what is being transacted in those high-rise glass buildings. Bringing the private sector under ethical auditing and accountability will be an important task of the subalterns.

**Catalysts for Ethical Auditing – Civil Society and Social Movements**
The public, especially the subalterns, will be the principal agents who will do the ethical auditing. It cannot be reduced to a task of experts, who could at the most assist in this matter. Civil society will have an important role to play in ethical auditing of the state, its bureaucracy and its institutions. It is also the civil society which can effectively raise the issue of public auditing of private enterprises.

Since the very concept and institution of civil society has come under serious questioning, we need to specify what is intended here by civil society in relation to ethical auditing. In fact, there could be a form of civil society dependent upon the state; it promotes the goals and programmes put forward by the state. Obviously, no one can trust these forms of civil society to do the ethical auditing, since they will be biased in favour of the state or the market. We mean here another kind of civil society – one in which issues touching upon the good of the society is brought up for public discussion and debate. This kind of civil society presents the space for promoting the cause of ethical auditing both in the public and in the private sectors. It will be the task of the civil society to scrutinize whether in this regard, opportunities are offered, especially to the subalterns and weaker sections.[13]

---

[13] Speaking of opportunities I am reminded of an episode the great statesman of Africa, Nelson Mandela narrates in his autobiography. He speaks of his classmate Mathona, a highly gifted and brilliant girl. Nothing was heard about her later. We can surmise that she ended up probably as a simple woman labourer doing hard physical work, because Mandela says her parents did not have the means to send her for higher education. Mandela concludes his narrative with a lapidary statement. "It was not lack of ability that limited my people, but lack of opportunity". Nelson Mandela, *Long Walk to freedom*, Abacus, London, 1994, p. 42.

Given the resistance by authorities, organizations and institutions to submit themselves to ethical checking, there is need for strong social movements which will play a critical and challenging role. All segments of society are to be made aware of the need for ethical auditing. Social movements could challenge the authorities and institutions to shift from the traditional mode of secretive practices to a culture of transparency and accountability.

The existing social movements could incorporate these aspects of ethical auditing as part of their important agenda. And if they are not able to effectively promote it, new social movements could be created with specific focus on social and ethical auditing. For example, if there are discriminatory practices against Dalits in the market (restriction on space, sale and purchase of goods and services, etc.) on the basis of caste and untouchability or in hiring and employment practices, these could be censured effectively by a vibrant civil society or a social movement. A common effort by civil society and social movements could put in place a general legal mechanism of "Equal Employment Opportunity Act", which will prevent any discrimination in the field of economy, education, etc.

### Ethical Auditing in the Church

We lack a culture of social and ethical auditing in this country. The basically hierarchical model of society bolstered up by the deeply entrenched caste-mentality, uncritical approach to tradition, self-demeaning loyalty to authority, the feudal and semi-feudal value-system conditioning the minds of even the educated ones – all these make the practice of ethical auditing extremely challenging.

What we experience in society is sadly reflected also in the Church. The general social situation of absence of ethical auditing should spur the Church on to act as a catalyst for public accountability. Instead, the Church itself is lacking in ethical censure, checks and balances in its decisions and praxis.

If the ministers are servants according to the best of Christian tradition, and if the highest authority in the Church is *"servant of servants"*, then ministers and leaders at every level including religious superiors – minor ones and major ones – are accountable. Unfortunately, the model of master-slave in the feudal spirit, with focus on obedience and uncritical loyalty, has replaced this tradition of holding the leaders and ministers accountable; those at the lower rungs are to obey and give account. But the truth is that, in the spirit of Christian Gospel, the higher the office, more severe is the obligation to give account to those being served.

If we examine the present structure, we will not fail to note how present legal provisions in the Church aim ultimately to protect the leaders at all costs, even when they blatantly and scandalously violate moral and ethical accountability. The trend of ethical amnesty for leaders and ministers does not fit into the demands of our present-day awakened public consciousness about ethical accountability. An indication of a general lack of transparency and accountability is the way secrecy in the Church is conferred an aura of sacredness. As we noted, secrecy is the weapon of the powerful, and the more authorities take protection under it and shield themselves from public scrutiny, their credibility also becomes, unfortunately, suspect. At the global level, the issue has come up in recent times with several cases connected with the sexual abuse of children by the clergy in different parts of the world.[14] The question is raised, how come that refusing communion to divorced couples is justified on basis of the public scandal, while the scandals of the ministers in the Church are covered up and they are allowed to continue in public ministry.

We cannot sufficiently underline the importance of ethical auditing for the Church, and its long-term fruits. This auditing will go into the management of institutions, properties, and relationship with personnel, etc. In what ways the resources – material and human – are utilized? This is an important question to be faced. Religious congregations and dioceses may have to account for wasting of human and financial resources; for uncalled for duplication and triplication of structures and institutions; and for dolling out resources on pet-project of the leaders and superiors who refuse to submit themselves to an ethical auditing and accountability.

If in the political world there could be a legislation to provide transparent governance, there could be no valid reason why the Church also cannot have legislations to this effect. There is a justified expectation that the Church as a moral force will readily submit itself to ethical auditing by the people. It implies that information should be available to the people in the Church regarding the rationale of the decisions taken and about the administration and policies of Church-run institutions of every kind. If

---

[14] Cf. Special issue of *Concilium* 2004/3 on "Structural Betrayal of Trust" edited by Regina Ammicht-Quinn, Hille Haker and Maureen Junker-Kenny; see also Jeff Israely and Howard Chua-Eoan, "The Trial of benedict XVI" in *Time*, vol. 175, no. 22, June 7, 2010, pp. 16-23.

the Church is the people of God, it is not clear why the people cannot have a deliberative role also in what concerns all. The distinction between "deliberative" and "consultative" is but a fig leaf to cover the lack of proper rationale and foundation for decisions in the Church. In a world that considers access to information as a basic human right, it is important for credibility of the Church that the decision-making process is not shrouded under the veil of secrecy. It could only reinforce the image of the Church as an authoritarian institution.

Ethical auditing in the Church becomes all the more important since overwhelming majority of Christians happen to be from Dalit and tribal communities and from other subaltern groups. For example, when there is legitimate pressure on the part of Dalits and tribals for their representation in various bodies in the Church, or for taking up their cause in education, welfare, etc., it is strongly resented by authorities. They want to be free from pressure and negatively react when it is exerted. But is it a virtue not to yield when facts, reason and faith tell us the truth? Greater transparency and dialogue will contribute to a more positive ethical auditing of the Church.

We know that the Church has a lot to give to the world and to society. What is often not realized is that the Church has also a lot to *learn from the world and society.* One important lesson it could learn today is the need for submitting itself to ethical auditing, and thus become more transparent and credible.

## Conclusion

There are other values in human life than economy and technology; market and competition, profit and consumption. At the same time, ethical questions cannot follow a trajectory of its own, and form a discourse divorced from these realities of everyday experience. The crucial question is how to integrate and co-relate in a way that technology, economy etc. are imbued with the ethical dimension, and are conducted in a socially and ethically responsible manner. It is here we realize the importance of ethical auditing as a practice that should accompany the pursuit of goals of any institution or organization – public or private. Even more, in the light of ethical auditing, the goals and objectives of institutions and organizations should be constantly revised. For example, today the profile of a company or institution is measured ultimately on the basis of the increase in the profit it has made, or the "success" it has achieved. By introducing new criteria in evaluating and assessing the performance of any organization or institution, foundation is laid for a sustainable and holistic development. The Church should feel obliged to undergo such an ethical auditing which will ultimately increase the credibility of its mission in society.

Ethical auditing begins by unmasking and exposing the actual position of the state, organization, institution, bureaucracy, etc., since they all tend to conceal and keep the people in ignorance. The process of ethical auditing is done effectively when civil society and social movements involve themselves in this issue. In particular, there is the need to create awareness among the general public about their right to information. Moreover structures and mechanism are required to monitor and implement the inherent ethics in the provisions as reservation for the weaker sections. In short, ethical auditing is an important means today for the creation of an egalitarian society and for the achievement of social justice.

# Chapter 4

# Competition and Affirmative Action

*"But freedom is not enough. You do not wipe away the scars of centuries by saying: Now you are free to go where you want, do as you desire, choose the leaders you please. You do not take a person who for years has been hobbled by chains and liberate him, bring him up to the starting line of a race and then say, 'You are free to compete with all the others', and still justly believe you have been completely fair."* — Lyndon Johnson[1]

While the Indian Constitution (1950) adopted a secular approach transcending caste, creed, language, ethnicity, etc., it had to face, nevertheless, the actual reality of discrimination practiced in the name of caste, socially, culturally and economically. Dalits did not figure as a legal category in the Constitution, which adopted a terminology that was in vogue since 1936 when the Government of India Act was passed: The Constitutional term to refer to Dalits is "scheduled castes" and this expression goes back to a list of castes attached to a schedule to the Government of India Act. Since the British times, the "untouchables" were referred to also as "Depressed Classes".[2]

The so-called untouchables are a heterogeneous group scattered all over India, speaking different tongues, and following a wide variety of customs.[3] There is nothing common among them except the sharing of

---

[1] Speech at Howard University, June 1965, in the context of the issue of affirmative action in favour of African-Americans.

[2] A similar schedule with list of various tribes of India were attached to the Act, and hence this grouping of tribals are referred to as "Scheduled Tribes" (ST).

[3] The following are some of the more recent and significant works on the untouchables of India. Robert Deliége, *The Untouchables of India*, Oxford, Berg,

similar experiences of discrimination and untouchability, poverty and misery. They accepted the term "scheduled castes" which had a secular slant, and were averse to the condescending expression "*Harijan*" (people of God), employed by Gandhi. Dr. B.R. Ambedkar, the supreme leader of the Dalits of modern India, not only adopted this constitutional term but also formed a party for scheduled castes in 1942. In the last few decades, this subaltern group of India has preferred the term *Dalits* to refer to themselves and this term is semiologically rich referring to a situation of being oppressed, ground, divided, broken, etc.

## Reservation Circumevented

Reservation has been a bone of contention. It has found spirited opponents among the elites and the upper castes.[4] In recent decades this opposition

---

1999; Id., *The World of the "Untouchables": Paraiyars of Tamilnadu*, Oxford University Press, Oxford, Delhi, 1997. To know the inner world of the Untouchables of India, in their struggles for dignity and social equality, see the writings of B.R. Ambedkar. In particular one may refer to his following works. *What Congress and Gandhi Have Done to the Untouchables*, Thacker, Bombay, 1945; *The Untouchables: Who Are They and Why They Have Become Untouchables?*, Bheem Patrika Publications, Jalandhar, 1988; *Annihilation of Caste*, Arnold Publishers, Delhi, 1990; Louis Dumont, *Homo Hierarchicus. Caste System and Its Implications*, Oxford University Press, Delhi, 1998; Hugo Gorringe, *Untouchables Citizens. Dalit Movements and Democratization in Tamilnadu*, Sage Publications, Delhi, 2005. This is a work based on field-study. Michel Moffat, *An Untouchable Community in South India. Structure and Consensus*, Princeton University Press, Princeton, 1979; Gail Omvedt, *Dalits and the Democratic Revolution. Dr Ambedkar and the Dalit Movement in Colonial India*, Sage Publications, Delhi, 1994; Ghanshyam Shah (ed.), *Dalit Identity and Politics*, Sage Publications, Delhi, 2001; Ghanshyam Shah et al. (eds.), *Untouchability in Rural India*, Sage Publications, Delhi, 2006; Eleanor Zelliot, *From Untouchable to Dalit. Essays on the Ambedkar Movement*, Manohar Publications, Delhi, 1996; Jaffrelot Christopher, *Ambedkar and Untouchability*, Permanent Black, Delhi, 2004.

[4] Cf. We need to pay attention to some of the important contributions that have appeared in *Economic and Political Weekly* (*EPW*): Surinder S. Jodhka and Katherine Newman, "In the Name of Globalisation: Meritocracy, Productivity and the Hidden Language of Caste", in *EPW*, 42,41 (October 13, 2007), pp. 4125-4132; Ashwini Deshpande and Katherine Newman, "Where the Path Leads: The Role of Caste in Post-University Employment Expectations", in *EPW*, 42,41 (October 13, 2007), pp. 4133-4140; Sukhadeo Thorat and Paul Attewell, "The Legacy of Social Exclusion: A Correspondence Study of Job Discrimination in India", in *EPW*, 42,41 (October 13, 2007), pp. 4141-4145; Sukhadeo Thorat and Katherine Newman, "Caste and Economic Discrimination: Causes, Consequences

has intensified and is orchestrated by right wing religious fundamentalists and liberals following the laws of market and the spirit of globalization. Time has come now to underline that reservation is not only a constitutional right of the subalterns, but is also a *matter of ethics*. And as such, the practice of reservation should be brought under ethical scrutiny and needs to be constantly monitored. There are many reasons to ethically uphold and monitor the practice of reservation: First of all, it provides opportunities in various areas to people who were denied basic rights during the millennial history of India. Thus from an ethical perspective it is a legitimate compensatory measure. Secondly, it contributes to the promotion of equality in a widely unequal society. Thirdly, it creates a culture for the just distribution of resources, and serves as a process of social education for all the citizens. Finally, reservation creates self-respect among the victims and gives them self-confidence.

In spite of this importance of reservation, what the Dalits and other subalterns experience are unethical practices. The provision of reservation is hijacked by vested interests. To cite some examples, middle and upper caste people manage to get, with the connivance of state officials, "false certificates" in order to grab government jobs and other privileges intended for the Scheduled Castes. Besides, there is reluctance to fill up the vacancies reserved for the weaker sections as a result of which thousands of posts lie vacant and unfilled for many years.

All this reveals the unethical and casteist attitude and mindset which is given vent in the systematically organized anti-reservation agitations. An analysis of these agitations will bring out the deeply entrenched discriminatory attitudes of the upper castes and classes. Illustrative in this context is the incident Uma Chakarvarthi narrates. She refers to placards carried by women students of Delhi during the anti-Mandal agitation.

---

and Remedies", in *EPW*, 42,41 (October 13, 2007), pp. 4121-4124; Carol Upadhya, "Employment, Exclusion and 'Merit' in the Indian IT Industry", in *EPW*, 42,20 (May 19, 2007), pp. 1863-1868; Satish Deshpande, "Exclusive Inequalities: Merit, Caste and Discrimination in Indian Higher Education Today", in *EPW*, 41,24 (June 17, 2007), pp. 2438-2444; Amman Madan, "Sociologising Merit", in *EPW*, 42,29 (July 21, 2007), pp. 3044-3050; T.K. Rajalakshmi, "Lesser Citizens", in *Frontline*, 26,12 (June 19,2009), pp. 124-126. See also T.K. Rajalakshmi and Purnima S. Tripathi, "For and Against, with Reservations", in *Frontline*, 25,9 (May 9, 2008) pp. 16-19; V. Venkatesan, "How Long the Inequalities", in *Frontline*, 25,9 (May 9, 2008), pp. 20-24; V. Venkatesan, "Unequal Race", in *Frontline*, 24,7 (April 20, 2007), pp. 4-9.

They read: *"We don't want unemployed husbands"* Interpreting the implications of these words, she writes:

> What these placards were saying was that these girls would be deprived of upper caste IAS husbands. But what they were also saying was that the OBCs and Dalits who would not occupy these positions in the IAS could *never* be their potential husbands. But who had told them that they could not marry the new entrants into the IAS drawn from the "backward" or Dalit castes, I wondered.[5]

This is another example that shows how caste-discrimination and endogamy hide themselves behind the mask of secularism, justice and merit.

As regards the private sector, it is again a matter of ethics when systematically candidates from Dalit or lower caste backgrounds are left out in the hiring practices of private enterprises.[6] The ethical principle of positive discrimination could function fully, only if reservation is extended to companies and private enterprises.[7] The implementation of reservation in the private sector calls for new state policies.

**Reservation for Scheduled Classes, Tribes and for Backward Classes**

At the time of the framing of the modern Indian Constitution, there was a heated debate regarding how the social question of inequality and asymmetry of power experienced by the discriminated groups is to be addressed. It is in this context that the idea of reservation or affirmative action in favour of the scheduled castes and tribes was proposed.[8] It was

---

[5] Uma Chakravarti, *Gendering Caste Through Feminist Lens,* Stree, Calcutta, 2006, pp. 1-2.

[6] For a very enlightening presentation of the various aspects of the question of reservation in private sector, see Sukhadeo Thorat – Aryama – Prashant Negi (eds.), *Reservation and Private Sector. Quest for Equal Opportunity and Growth.* Indian Institute of Dalit Studies, Rawat Publications, Delhi-Jaipur, 2005.

[7] The state of Maharashtra was the first one to realize this by enacting a law. Cf. P.G. Jogdand, "Reservation in the Private Sector. Legislation in Maharashtra", in Sukhadeo Thorat et al., *op.cit.,* pp. 160-171.

[8] On the question of affirmative action in India since Independence, see Chalam K.S., *Caste Based Reservations and Human Development in India,* Sage Publications, Delhi, 2007; Padhy K.S. and Jayashree Mahapatra, *Reservation Policy in India,* Ashish Publishing House, Delhi, 1988; Parmanand Singh, *Equality Reservation and Discrimination in India,* Deep & Deep Publications, Delhi, 1982; Vakil A.K., *Reservation Policy and Scheduled Caste in India,* Ashish Publishing House, Delhi,

opposed by some members of the Constituent Assembly who argued that in a modern polity, the principal of equality, going beyond traditional identities such as caste, religion, language, must be upheld. There were others who did not oppose it, however were skeptic whether such a policy instrument will really address the problem of social inequality. They were of the view that one needed to pursue the matter of equality from a class perspective, rather than from a caste perspective. Finally, there were others, the foremost among whom was Dr. Ambedkar, who welcomed and supported the policy of reservation as an important means to overcome inequality and discrimination the subalterns were suffering for millennia. This reservation policy has been practiced in public sector.[9]

Besides the Dalits and the tribals, also other groups found themselves in a situation of social and economic disadvantage due to caste discrimination. Therefore, pressure was mounting to extend affirmative action also in regard to other backward castes and classes (OBCs).[10] A

---

1985; Sharma B.A.V. and Madhusudhan Reddy, *Reservation Policy in India*, Light and Life Publication, Delhi, 1982; Ishwari Prasad, *Reservation Action for Social Equity*, Criterion publications, Delhi, 1986; Gaikwad S.L., *Protective Discrimination Policy and Social Change*, Rawat Publications, Jaipur-Delhi, 1999; Aroobhai Metha and Hasmukh Patel (ed.), *Dynamics of Reservation Policy*, Patriot Publishers, Delhi, 1985; Aravind Sharma, *Reservation and Affirmative Action*, Sage Publications, Delhi, 2005. In this work the author enquires what could be the foundation for reservation. The work reveals the anti-reservation prejudice of the author in spite of his efforts to present the matter in an impartial way; J. Prabhash, *Affirmative Action and Social Change. Social Mobility of Dalits*, Anmol Publications, Delhi, 2001.

[9] The beginnings of reservation go back to the non-Brahmin movements in the erstwhile Madras Presidency and Maharashtra. These movements had an impact on  the order the Maharaja of Kolhapur (1902) issued for reserving half of government jobs for people of non-Brahmin origin, and a similar practice was followed subsequently also in the princely state of Mysore. This was taken up by the British government as a regular policy in 1921, on the basis of the recommendation of the Miller Committee (1918).

[10] Whereas in the decades after Independence, the constitutional provision of reservation was applied to the Dalits (Scheduled Castes or SCs) and tribes (Scheduled Tribes or STs), and those who did not benefit reservation were referred to as *"others"*, a new division was introduced from 1980s, namely those who are neither SCs and STs nor belonging to the Forward Castes (FCs). These new groupings made up of lower castes - but not untouchables - are called *Other Backward Classes* (OBCs). On the identity of OBCs, see André Béteille, *The Backward Classes in Contemporary India*, Oxford University Press, Delhi, 1992;

commission was set up to study the issue under the headship of B.P. Mandal.[11] The report was submitted in December 1980. The policy of reservation was subjected to a fresh debate as a result of the Mandal Commission Report which advocated that 27% reservation should be extended also to other backward castes in the country.[12] When Prime Minister V.P. Singh tried to implement the recommendations of the Mandal Commission, there was such a vehement opposition on the part of upper castes and classes, that it led even to the fall of his government.

The debate has been further accentuated in recent years after Indian economy opted for economic liberalisation policies, and began to rely for its development on capital, market and competition. The policy of reservation in this new context has been questioned as a retrograde measure and not in keeping with economic modernization and globalization.

We need to look at the actual reality of the Dalits and backward classes, confronted by neo-liberalism with competition and market as its driving force.

## Some Theoretical Perspectives

The upper caste intelligentsia argue that caste should not be the criterion for reservation. If at all there is an affirmative action, it should be fixed on the basis of economic criterion, with no regard to caste. Those who argue that class should be the point of reference and criterion for the

---

Marc Galanter, *Competing Equalities: Law and the Backward Classes in India,* Oxford University Press, Delhi, 1984; Government of India, *Report of the Backward Classes Commission,* 3 vols, Government of India Press, Delhi, 1955. Backward classes have been also an important political force in modern India. A formidable backward class movement was built up in the early decades of twentieth century, especially in South India, which promoted their advancement. The backward class movement, obviously, challenged the Brahminic hegemony at all levels and fought for representation of backward classes. The movement was characterized in its ideological, cultural and political orientation as decisively anti-Brahminic.

[11] B.P. Mandal was former Chief Minister of the State of Bihar.

[12] The Mandal Commission Report occasioned a heated debate between reservationists and non-reservationists. It also widened the discussion by re-assessing caste in contemporary India. In this latter sense, one may refer to the following work of the well-known Indian anthropologist. M.N. Srinivas (ed.), *Caste. Its Twentieth Century Avatar,* Viking, Delhi, 1996.

distribution of goods and services, forget that the disadvantages suffered by certain groups of people such as the Dalits during centuries and millennia is the cause of their present plight. Therefore, a general policy that wants to fix economic criteria for affirmative action does not take into account the historical wrongs done to particular groups which need to be compensated. In other words, affirmative action bases itself primarily on social and economic disabilities inherited from the past. On the other hand, a redistributive approach is concerned with the elimination of present inequalities, whereas compensating for the historical wrongs is the quintessence of the policy of reservation.[13] In view of the historical reality and social conditions prevailing in a particular society, principles such as equality before law and equality of opportunities stand modified. When one takes recourse to these principles – as the higher castes in India do – it gives a semblance of justice, but in fact by failing to respond to concrete situation in a particular context, justice is negated.

If the basis for reservation is the enduring discrimination experienced by the Dalits, the elites of the upper castes stoutly oppose this argument. For them, discrimination of the past should not serve as a criterion to determine the beneficiaries of reservation today. For, it would imply that the present high caste people who did not have any role in past discrimination are punished for something for which they are not responsible. In this context, one speaks of *"reverse discrimination"*.

Reservation, it is further argued, would reinforce the caste social order by allocating quotas for certain caste groups. In this way, so goes the reasoning, caste will get reinforced, rather than eliminated. How true are these assertions? The question, I think, needs to be viewed from both global and local perspectives.

From a global perspective identity-politics is something we are witnessing in different parts of the world. There is a certain ambiguity inherent in identity. It can both empower as well as lead to violence.[14] Having said that, we need to make an important distinction between the identity-assertion of dominant groups in society and the identity- assertion of the disadvantaged groups. It is unethical to place on the same balance and to measure by the same standards the identity-assertion of the upper

---

[13] Cf. Sheela Rai, *"Social and Conceptual Background to the Policy of Reservation"* in *EPW*, October 19, 2002, p. 4309.

[14] Cf. Amartya Sen, *Identity and Violence. The Illusion of Destiny*, W&W Norton, New York, 2006.

caste Brahmins as a group and the identity-assertion of the Dalits, or the identity-assertion of Anglo-Saxon whites and the African Americans. In the former case, identity serves the agenda of power domination, and in the latter case it empowers those who are deprived of power.

If we look at the issue from the contextual perspective, the assertion by Dalits and the lower castes of their identity is not with the intention of maintaining this highly discriminatory social system of caste,[15] but rather to abolish it.

## Realpolitik and the Issue of Reservation

The question of reservation for the Dalits and other backward castes has to be understood also against the political developments that have taken place. The Congress Party which dominated the Indian politics and held power in the decades following Indian independence (1947) provided an umbrella unity for all the disadvantaged groups – the Dalits, backward castes, tribals etc., and claimed to represent their cause. But subsequent developments in the country went in the direction of identity-politics. The assertion of various groups and castes through their distinct political movements and parties led to a culture of securing vote-banks among the Dalits and backward castes and classes by the dominant parties. It was necessary to ensure the support of these groups – a strong electorate – to be able to come to power. The other backward classes of India (OBC) alone constitute 52% of the population – no negligible group of voters. They can tilt the scales of power. If not by force of conviction, at least for practical political expediency, all the major parties, including the right wing Bharathiya Janata Party (BJP) today support reservation. This is clearly seen also in the reaction to the April 10, 2008 verdict of the Supreme Court of India regarding the "creamy layer". Barring the Communist Party of India (CPI), all other parties were critical of the verdict which set aside the "creamy layer" of the backward classes from obtaining the benefits of reservation in the elite educational institutions of India such as Indian

---

[15] On the political assertion of Dalit identity, see the various contributions in Ghanshyam Shah, (ed.), *Dalit Identity and Politics*, sage Publications, New Delhi, 2001; Narender Kumar - Manoj Rai (eds.), *Dalit Leadership in Panchayats*, Rawat Publications, Jaipur-Delhi, 2006; Oliver Mendelsohn - Maarika Vicziany, *The Untouchables. Subordination, Poverty and the State in Modern India*, Cambridge University Press, Cambridge, 1998; Felix Wilfred, *Dalit Empowerment*, ISPCK, Delhi, 2007, pp. 31-58.

Institute of Technology, (IIT) and Indian Institute of Management Studies (IIMS).

## Recent Developments on Reservation to the Other Backward Classes (OBC)

When in April 2006 the United Progressive Alliance (UPA) government sought to implement reservation in the elite educational institutions of the central government such as prestigious Indian Institute of Technology (IIT), Indian Institute of Management Studies (IIMS) and Indian Institute of Medical Sciences, it gave rise to violent protests on the part of students, faculty members from the upper castes. This protest was meant, as they claimed, to uphold the principle of equality. It was spearheaded, ironically, by a newly formed organization called "Youth for Equality" (YFE). The two-judge bench of the Supreme Court stayed the government order of admitting 27% of backward castes in the central government educational institutions after admitting the plea by the petitioners that their fundamental right to equality was violated by the practice of reservation.

Reservation has been a matter also of conflict between the Union of India and the Supreme Court of the country. In 1992, in the case of Indra Sawhney vs Union of India, nine judge bench upheld reservation of 27% in central government services. In the well-known case of T.M.A. Pai vs Union of India, the Supreme Court prohibited the application of reservation for backward classes in privately-run educational institutions without government aid. This led to the 93rd amendment of Indian Constitution which introduced a new clause - article 15 (5) - in the Constitution. It empowers the state to enact special provisions through law so as to promote the educational and social advancement of backward classes and groups.

## The Issue of Exclusion, Inclusion and Time-boundedness of Reservation

It has been often stated that reservation is a provisional and transitory measure in a situation of historically inherited social inequality. But the question is how long should reservation be practiced. There have been attempts to fix a time-schedule. Initially it was thought of for a limited period. But facts proved that the situation of scheduled castes and tribes is far from achieving the objectives of reservation. Therefore, the provision of reservation needs to continue. This is true also in the case of other backward classes.

One may raise the question whether some of the castes who have been benefiting from reservation have not reached a stage of advancement that they cannot anymore be included in the list of those who benefit from affirmative action. Here again the fact is that there are many sub-groups both among the Dalits and among other backward castes. It is a fact that of the many groups, only a few of them have availed the benefits of reservation to the maximum. Could not these groups be excluded from the list of reservation? This is a point brought out repeatedly by the opponents of reservation. Even the Supreme Court advocated the need to review the list periodically. But the truth is that even in these cases, the Dalits and other weaker sections have not reached a stage where reservation can be dispensed with.

A most intriguing issue in the current debate on reservation is connected with the basic question of identifying which groups belong to other backwards classes (OBC). According to one view, it would comprise a large spectrum of the caste-hierarchy covering all the castes and groups below Brahmin and Kshatrya (priestly, and warrior castes) and above the outcastes. For others, the criterion for backward classes should not be only caste, but also the economic condition of a particular community. The list complied by Mandal in his report, is far from being satisfactory. Strangely, many communities claim to be low in status to be included in the list of scheduled castes, and avail the privileges of reservation. Suhas Palshikar thus describes the difficulties involved:

> The category of other backward classes (OBCs) is a porous one. The Constitution gives limited assistance in defining this category; the Constituent Assembly debates less so. Therefore, one has to agree that the boundaries of the OBCs will evolve through deliberations and contestations. To put it crudely, the supporters of quotas, policy planners and social scientists have very inadequate answers to this complex issue.[16]

There is, as of now, no reliable census data which could help identify backward classes. A more clear data-base remains an important task, and the creation of it will enhance the policy and practice of affirmative action. Supreme Court precisely directed the central government to provide such a database.

---

[16] Suhas Palshikar, "Challenges before the Reservation Discourse" in *EPW*, 43, 17 (April 26, 2008), pp. 8-11.

## The Question of "Creamy Layer"

What proved to be highly provocative for the higher castes is the fact that the government, in introducing reservation for the other backward castes in educational institutions through its 2006 Act, did not exempt the "creamy layer", that is those from the backward castes who have already advanced economically. This could be inferred from the Act's silence on the issue of exclusion. But then, in its judgment on 10 April, 2008, the Supreme Court has ruled that the creamy layer are not to be given the privilege of reservation, and it made the validity of the Act dependent on this exclusion on the part of the state. This has once again opened up the debate regarding the criteria for reservation. While the higher castes harp on the economic criteria, so that reservation benefits also the poor from the upper castes, those who are familiar with ground-realities highlight that, in spite of economic advancement of some individuals among the backward castes, they, as a group still suffer social discrimination. Therefore, individuals belonging to backward castes, need to be looked at not simply as individuals, but as part of communities which continue to be discriminated.

The exclusion of "creamy layer" undermines the spirit of reservation which was meant for the social and economic advancement of the discriminated groups and communities. If this is to happen, then, people of dalit and lower caste origin need to be participants at every level – economic, educational, social, cultural, etc. Excluding reservation at higher levels of education and allowing the field to be dominated by the forces of market and competition, would mean that opportunities at a higher level are barred for Dalits and lower castes.

One school of thought proposes that reservation in the educational field should be limited to high school level, while higher education should be on competitive basis. This is meant as a device to exclude the creamy layer. But as a matter of fact, it is only few Dalits and people from lower castes who have made it to higher level of education. If this "creamy layer" is excluded, there is little chance of Dalits and other backward castes benefiting from the quotas of reservation. The truth is that, in the public sector among the quotas reserved for SC/ST it is mostly jobs of lower grades - "C" and "D" which are filled up, whereas often there are no qualified candidates to fill higher level of employment at "A" and "B" levels.[17] If the creamy layer is excluded, it would mean that job-reservation

---

[17] Cf. Felix Wilfred, *Dalit Empowerment*, ISPCK, Delhi, 2007 (2nd edition).

for the Dalits and backward castes will be confined to low-paying jobs, whereas they will not be able to reach the higher levels of employment.

It is argued by the opponents of reservation, that educational opportunities for Dalits and disadvantaged groups, should concentrate on primary and secondary education. But then as Thomas Weisskopf notes,

> The fact that reservation policies in admissions to higher educational institutions tend to benefit a creamy layer of SC and ST students is often taken by critics as prima facie evidence that these policies are failing to achieve their objective. Such an inference would be warranted, however, only if the primary objective of these policies were to improve the distribution of educational opportunities within the SC and ST communities...Positive discrimination policies in admission to higher educational institutions should instead be understood as an effort to promote the integration of the upper strata of the society – by increasing the access of members of highly disadvantaged and under-represented communities to elite occupations and decision-making positions.[18]

In the hearings and arguments preceding the landmark judgment of the Supreme Court of India on 10 April, 2008, it was argued on behalf of the Union of India that unless one is in economically sound and in stable position it is difficult to arrive at the level of higher education or attend competitive examinations. This is possible only if the Dalits and backwards castes are enabled with the legal provision of quotas. Though the Supreme Court judgment excluded the "creamy layer" from benefiting from reservation in elite institutions of central government, nevertheless the judgment was highly significant because the Supreme Court thereby once again underlined the *legitimacy of reservation* for disadvantaged groups amidst growing opposition by forward castes to this provision.

## Comparison with Other Countries

At the international level, the principle of affirmative action has been accepted as a means to undo the historic wrongs inflicted on minorities and weaker sections of people.

> Special measures for the sole purpose of securing adequate advancement of certain racial and ethnic groups of individuals requiring such

---

[18] Thomas Weisskopf, "Impact of Reservation on Admission to Higher Education in India", in *EPW*, September 25, 2004, p. 4347; see also Pradipta Chaudhury, "The Creamy Layer. Political Economy of Reservations", in *EPW*, May 15, 2004, pp. 1989-1991.

protection as may be necessary in order to ensure such groups or individuals equal enjoyment or exercise of human rights or fundamental freedoms shall not be deemed racial discrimination.[19]

The Indian system of reservation can learn also from the international experience, from the U.S., Malaysia and other countries.[20] Affirmative action is practiced in the US in regard to African Americans, Hispanics and other minority groups.[21] The various systems and provisions made have to be understood against the background of the history of a particular country. In the case of United States, the rationalization of affirmative action is based on the importance of reflecting the *diversity* of a community at various levels of its life through proper representation. This is considered important for the healthy growth of any national community. When affirmative action is advocated in the private sphere, it is again the principle of diversity that dominates. Further it is underlined that only with representation from all groups can a community reach advancement in any sphere, including market and capital.

On the other hand, in the Indian debate what dominates is the question *of social equity* and providing of opportunities to the disadvantaged section. But then it is important today to add to the concerns of social equity also the argument on the basis of diversity. A second difference is that whereas in US affirmative action is *voluntary*, in India it is *a provision protected by law*. The deeply entrenched caste-system and hierarchical mindset are factors which dissuade a voluntary measure. Legal protection of reservation is necessary to ensure that the upper castes do not exclude the Dalits and lower castes from the avenues of education, employment, etc. There is also another difference. In India, affirmative action is practiced only in employment at the state-run public sectors and in the educational field. On the other hand in US, affirmative action covers both the state and private business and enterprises.[22]

---

[19] *International Convention on the Elimination of All Forms of Racial Discrimination (1969).*

[20] Cf. S.P. Pathe, "Patterns of Affirmative Action: The American, Malaysian and Indian Experiences", in *Journal of Indian School of Political Economy,* vol. (1997) pp. 754-765; "Affirmative Action and Caste Dilemmas" in *Frontline,* June 14, 2006, pp. 27-31.

[21] Cf. Thomas Weisskopf, *Affirmative Action in United States and India: A Comparative Perspective,* Routledge, New York, 2004.

[22] Cf. Ashwini Deshpande-Katherine Newman, "Where the Path Leads. The Role of Caste in Post-University Employment Expectations, in *EPW,* 42, 41 (October 13, 2007), pp. 4133-4140.

## Market Discriminations

For the sake of a fair and just competition it is indispensable that conditions for empowerment are created and resources are invested, so that the Dalits could compete with other middle and upper caste groups. But the ground-realities narrate a different story. It is true, as M.N. Panini observes, "liberalization opens up a genuine possibility of breaking the stranglehold of caste over the economy".[23] This is based on the fact that market-economy replaces traditional forms of patron-client relationships and allows the mixing and mingling of different groups and peoples in productive relationships,[24] which implies that the various caste groups transcending their identity could become players in a new economic field. However, in the actual functioning of liberalization and market, the plain truth is that there is strong caste undercurrent. For, the same kind of discrimination experienced by Dalits and lower castes in relation to ownership of land, traditional occupations and other means, is carried over also to the modern field of business, market and in access to capital and credit. More and more studies are pointing out with clear empirical evidence that people from upper castes do not want to do business with Dalits and lower castes.

There is also discrimination in the labour market.[25] Though equally qualified and competent, there is a clear wage-difference between the upper castes on the one hand and Dalits and other backward castes on the other in the urban labour market. It was found, for example, in many states that Dalits are not allowed to be construction-workers for upper caste people.[26] This is due to the traditional purity-pollution mental-frame. It is feared that the very touch of the Dalits – even if it is for construction – renders their homes impure.

Besides the traditional prejudices and discrimination, Dalits and lower castes suffer also many disabilities in the world of business and market. Many of them are new entrants in the world of business and they lack a "track record". Contrast this with the century and millennia old

---

[23] Cf. M.N. Panini, "The Political Economy of Caste", in M.N. Srinivas, op.cit., p. 63.

[24] Cf. Lal Deepak, *The Hindu Equilibrium vol. I: Cultural Stability and Economic Stagnation 1500 B.C–AD 1980*, Clarendon Press, Oxford, 1988.

[25] Cf. The various contributions and studies in Sukhadeo Thorat – Aryama – Prashant Negi (eds.), *Reservation and Private Sector. Quest for Equal Opportunity and Growth*, Rawat Publications, Delhi, 2005.

[26] *Ibid.*

commercial traditions among certain castes like the Chettiars of Tamilnadu or the Marwaris of Rajasthan or the commercial castes of the state of Gujarat.[27]

What Indian neo-liberal position fails to see is that market and competition take place in a particular historically, culturally and socially determined environment. The liberal argument may appear modern, because everything is measured on the basis of productivity and competition going beyond class, caste and religion. However, it is fallacious. This is for two reasons. First, market and competition are abstracted from the concrete social realities and conditionings and the social interplay between traditional identity groups. Secondly, there is a gap between what is professed in theory, (the claim of equality and fairness) and actuality.

The anti-reservationists argue that in these times of globalization and competitive market, promoting incompetent candidates from lower castes into various jobs and business will bring down the image of the country and would serve as a factor restraining foreign investment, and thus national interests will be compromised. Such, apparently noble sentiments for the development and modernization of the nation mask the traditional discrimination against the Dalits and lower castes, which continues in spite of modernization and globalization.

### Ground-Realities
Empirical evidence shows that things do not function on the basis of presumed equality and competition. The fact is, that there exists in effect, serious discrimination against the Dalits. The candidates from the lower castes are discriminated in practice because of the absence of social networks and cultural capital. In the case of upper castes, acquaintances, family connections, well off relatives - all exert unfair influence in their favour which advantages Dalit candidates do not have.

---

[27] We could draw a certain parallel with the situation of African Americans and ethnic minorities in USA. The discrimination to which they are subjected has rendered it that, though the African Americans form 12.1% of the population, their share in business is only 3.1%. Similarly in the case of Hispanics, they represent just 3.1% of American business, quite disproportionate to the 9% population they represent.

> Dalit students from comparable degree programs as their high caste counterparts have lower expectations and see themselves as disadvantaged because of their caste and family background...Our study so far suggests that social and cultural capital (the complex and overlapping categories of caste, family background, network and contacts) play a huge role in urban, formal sector labor markets, where hiring practices are less transparent than appear at first sight.[28]

Moreover, given the fact that Dalits and other backward castes have been doing menial jobs and works connected with pollution, they lack the sophistication of the family background which candidates from the upper castes enjoy. Empirical studies show how human resource managers during the interview question about the candidates', family background by which they are able to differentiate those from the upper and lower castes. Candidates from upper castes with fluency of language, urban manners and influential connections are selected, while equally competent candidates from the weaker sections are eliminated. To this we should add the many ways through which the Dalits are excluded – through deliberate interventions or subtle discrimination–from participation in the market and from access to capital, which again raises serious question about the fairness of competition. S. Thorat and Paul Attewell after reporting the results of their field-study regarding job discrimination, conclude:

> The field experiment study of job applications observed statistically significant pattern by which, on average, college educated lower-caste and Muslim job applicants fare less well than equivalently-qualified applicants with high caste names when applying by mail for employment in modern private–enterprise sector. The only aspect of family background that was communicated in these applications was the applicant's name, yet this was enough to generate a different pattern of response to applications from Muslims and Dalits, compared to high caste Hindu names. These were highly-educated and appropriately qualified applicants attempting to enter the modern private sector, yet even in this sector, caste and religion proved influential in determining one's job chances.[29]

---

[28] Ashwini Deshpande – Katherine Newman, "Where the Path Leads. The Role of Caste in Post-University Employment Expectations", in *EPW*, 42, 41 (October 13, 2007), p. 4140.

[29] Sukhadeo Thorat – Paul Attewell, "The Legacy of Social Exclusion. A Correspondence Study of Job Discrimination in India", in *EPW*, 42, 41 (October 13, 2007), p. 4144.

One of the arguments to oppose affirmative action in the private sector is that when people on the basis of reservation or quota are promoted to tasks to which they are not capable, efficiency and productivity will suffer. On the face of it, the contention seems to be convincing. But if we dig deeper, we will note that reality is much more complex. First of all it is not a question of promoting incompetent people. The point is that, given the same qualification for admission into educational institutions or for employment, a certain percentage is reserved for the socially disadvantaged group so as to ensure that these groups have equal opportunity. This point is important, for some in the upper castes like many private entrepreneurs think that the best way to help the lower castes is to provide training for them and provide capital for candidates from lower castes to do business. But when the representatives of the corporate sector advocate these measures for the amelioration in education and business of the lower castes, they refer to educational institutions. This is often a way to exclude the lower caste candidates and eliminate them as if they are in need of special training.

We need to probe more deeply into the issue and ask how true is the assumption that candidates from high castes are competent and efficient. As everyday experience in India shows, many incompetent and inefficient candidates from upper castes manage to get into prime educational institutions and into highly remunerative labour markets through the social network they have and influential relatives and connections they foster, and not in few cases by paying "facilitation costs" – not to call it greasing the palms – and capitation fees. In sum, what is presented as competence and efficiency is often the result of the social capital the upper castes have at their disposal and the power they wield.

### A Restraining Mechanism

The foregoing description of the background and analysis of the situation makes one thing clear. Competition and market need to be restrained, so that human development becomes integral and inclusive. Without adequate policy orientation and remedial measures, the law of market and competition becomes a matter of the survival of the fittest. For, the initial conditions in the race are vastly different, with some having a disproportionate advantage over others, ethically invalidating the end-result of the competition. Hence we realize the place of reservation as a restraining mechanism, so that the market does not become exclusive and competition unfair. Obviously, reservation policy is only one measure which is ethically sound and socially expedient. We need to think of other remedial measures. This will include for example the economic empowerment by making resources and capital available to the Dalits and other lower castes.

**Affirmative Action - A *sine qua non* for a Sound Indian Economy**
Affirmative action is generally viewed as a matter of social equity. It certainly is. However, what is less known and needs highlighting is that discrimination in market will adversely affect economic growth. This interconnection between discrimination and economy needs to be explored. As S. Thorat observes,

> In case of implications of discrimination on economic growth, the standard mainstream theoretical analysis indicates clearly the adverse impact on profits, wages, and efficiency in the allocation of labour. Economic theory implies that the economic discrimination will slow down economic growth by reducing efficiency due to less than optimal allocation of labour among firms and economy (employing fewer than optimal number of labour who are discriminated as they received lower wage than their marginal product), by reducing job commitment and efforts of workers who perceive themselves to be victims of discrimination, and by reducing the magnitude of investment in human capital by discriminated group and return on this investment.[30]

To understand the caste-discrimination practiced in the market today, we could refer to an excellent study by George Akerlof, who notes that "the behaviours of one member of society towards another is predicted by their respective caste statuses".[31] This has serious economic consequences. For example, if the behaviour of Dalit candidates are predicted on the assumption that all the members of the group have the same defects and weaknesses without regard to the merits and abilities of the individual, it is clear then that not only discrimination is practiced, but also that possibly some of the best candidates for a particular job or service are not enrolled, which shows that it is an inefficient economy.

In his time, Dr. Ambedkar addressed the economic inefficiency caused by caste system. Traditionally the caste system operated with segmentation

---

[30] S. Thorat, "Remedies against Market Discrimination" in S. Thorat (ed.), *Reservation and Private Sector Quest for Equal Opportunity and Growth.* Indian Institute of Dalit Studies, Rawat Publications, Delhi-Jaipur, 2005, pp. 326-327.

[31] George Akerlof, "The Economies of Caste and of the Rat Race and Other Woeful Tales", in *Quarterly Journal of Development Economics*, 90 (1976), pp. 600-617.

of labour. Occupations were fixed rigidly for various caste-groupings, and these were not to be transgressed. For fear of reprisal and ostracism that could befall, people stuck to their caste-bound and inherited labour. This meant, for example, a Dalit has to deal with impurities like cleaning human excreta, disposing of dead-cattle, etc. He or she could never think of being even a cook in a Brahmin home. For, that would be a shocking defilement, and the upper castes would not permit an "untouchable" as cook. This is true in the past as much as today. To put in modern terms, given the immobility in the labour market due to caste rigidities, again economy gets affected and the market does not function optimally. For, here again the system does not permit movement of labour which would enable to enlist the best of human resources. Similarly access to capital is also fixed by the caste-system in such a way that some castes are, for example owners of the land, while others do not have any right to ownership. In other words, there is inequality in economic rights, depending on which position one occupies in the caste-hierarchy. When this deeply entrenched caste-matrix is at work in present-day market, it is natural that it continues to breed the traditional discriminations in new ways affecting the economic growth of the society.

## Conclusion

In these times of globalization, market and competition, ways and strategies must be devised that will provide equal opportunities for the disadvantaged groups. One such important means is affirmative action or reservation.[32] Reservation has social and economic consequences. The most significant social effect of reservation is that it challenges the caste by breaking the identification of occupation and caste. There is a de-linking of jobs from castes. When Dalits change their traditional occupations - facilitated by reservation - which were once considered the privilege of the upper castes, there takes place social change. Fear of social change is at bottom the deeper reason for the vehement opposition to affirmative action on the part of the upper castes.

---

[32] Speaking of the overriding importance of the means of reservation among all others, Jayati Gosh notes, "[W]hile reservations have been inadequate and relatively rigid instruments of affirmative action, they do have certain advantages which explain why they are still preferred. They are transparent, inexpensive to implement and monitor and therefore easily enforceable. Any other system of affirmative action must have these attributes in order to be practical" in *People's Democracy*, April 17-23, 2006, p.10.

The present chapter has argued that, due to discrimination in the market place and because of difference in social and cultural capital, it is unethical to rely on competition as the sole criterion for development and human advancement. Even from the market perspective social discrimination and absence of equal opportunities will only negatively impact on production or output. Given the fact that there is no level playing field and differential social and cultural economic conditions, a social engineering is indispensable, as a means of creating economic empowerment and equal opportunity, especially for the weaker sections.

Reservation or affirmative action or protective discrimination is a policy instrument to restrain the market and de-absolutize competition. The policy of reservation already in vogue in the public sector needs to be extended also to the private sector. The shrinking of opportunities in the public sector on the one hand and the phenomenal expansion of the private sector in India since 1990's makes it imperative, for the sake of equity and for the optimal functioning of the market, that private sector also practice reservation. Given the deeply entrenched caste-mentality and social customs and practices of discrimination, the reservation in private sector cannot be left to voluntary action by entrepreneurs. It should be legislated, so that the intention of social equity finds a legal anchor.

## Chapter 5

# Religious Power and Women's Negotiations

*"Religious initiatives in the cause of unsettling patriarchy are far more effective in those contexts where scripture is being constantly quoted to refuse women their rights...By bringing their own piety and interested re-readings of scripture to bear upon their concerns, women succeed in interrogating male claims of scriptural authority."* – V. Geetha[1]

As in most other realms, religions are ambiguous also in the realm of power. This ambiguity is most evident in the case of women. The power that envelops religion in the name of the sacred is overwhelming, and it informs every sphere of life. As a result, cultural forms, social behaviours and everyday practices are under the pervasive influence of religious ideology and legitimisation. The most important means of oppression of women is patriarchy, which receives much of its ideological ammunition from religion, its beliefs, injunctions, customs and rituals.[2]

In this chapter we shall study how women are confronted with different forms of power, often religiously sanctioned, and how they go about negotiating it, and what strategies they deploy to challenge, to scuttle, to undermine and to circumvent oppressive forms of power, and how they succeed to channel other aspects of religious power to change and

---

[1] V. Geetha, *Patriarchy*, Stree, Calcutta, 2007, p. 160.

[2] On the nexus between gender and religion in the Indian context, see Julia Leslie – Mary McGee, *Invented Identities. The Interplay of Gender, Religion and Politics in India*, Oxford University Press, Delhi, 2000.

transform themselves, others and society in a given context. This is what is meant here by "negotiations". The power of patriarchy over them is so repressive, and the structures of the society and the force of tradition so rigid, that women cannot in every instance resist the religiously sustained patriarchy and its power.

It is remarkable that women find ingenious ways to go about power, and are able to invent new spaces and avenues to exercise their subjecthood and agency. Moreover, in everyday practice, women navigate deftly the interstices between defiance and acquiescence to the existing order, which, though does not bring about full freedom, nevertheless bring into their lives a modicum of autonomy and respect. By negotiating power, women are able to benefit the people around them and the entire community. They are also able to create a new awareness. The negotiation of power by women is happening everyday to which patriarchy is blind. Moreover, in women's negotiation of power, nobody is belittled. This is different from the patriarchal mode of exercise of power in which some are winners and others are losers. Patriarchy reproduces the existent system and reinforces hierarchy. As a result, some benefit through their domination, and others loose. This is true also of the realm of religion, on which this chapter is focused. We shall begin our reflections by analysing some basic conceptions of power.

**Forms of Power – An Analysis**

Given the importance of power in every domain of life, there has taken place a lot of theorizing on its understanding and the way it operates. The most widespread understanding of power views it as *"power over"* which creates a relationship of domination and subjugation. Hierarchy is a system of power of this kind. This form of power as dominion has its own cultural and social mechanisms of functioning and institutions which sustain it. In other words, it is a practice that is bound up with our social and cultural practices of everyday and the entire society is involved in it.

Quite different is a second conception of power which can be characterized as *"power to"*. This means that a person or a group is able to act without coercion. This understanding of power has a positive connotation, since it enables people to act autonomously, make their choices and achieve the goals they have chosen freely. This is the power that is necessary for every person to live and flourish by bringing out the inherent potentialities. A third conception of power views it as *"power with"*. It highlights the collective dimension of power. Power is not what an individual possesses or looses; it is something that derives from being together. In this sense, solidarity is an expression of power. The subalterns and other weaker sections do not possess power individually, and yet could be powerful as a collective entity. The fourth understanding of power is *"power within"*. It refers to the kind of power that a person has within oneself, no matter what the external circumstances are. As Manju Kar, an ordinary Bengali woman put it,

> Power is not necessarily what we experience in our social and professional status. It has also much to do with what I feel inwardly. Divine mother is reflected in me, as such; power is in me.[3]

It is a power that is connected with the subjecthood and agency of a person. It gives self-confidence to a person to face the external situation. As we shall see below in this chapter, this form of power is highly significant for women and for their well-being.

Women's approach to power is much broader than the patriarchal understanding and practice of it. The only conception of power in patriarchy is "power over", whereas feminist approach to power is one which values the other three forms of power, and on that basis is able to challenge the patriarchal power of domination. In this sense, as Foucault rightly points out, power circulates in the capillaries of the social body where every one exercises it according to his or her capability.

## Caste and Patriarchy

All religious traditions, in varying degrees, subject women to patriarchal power. Patriarchy is strongly entrenched also in the exercise of religious authority. In India, the "brahminical patriarchy", upheld by religious scriptures and ideologies, is embedded in the caste system. Just like the religious legitimation of caste, patriarchy also gets ideological sanction. What we need to particularly note – and which is absent in most studies of women till recently – is the nexus between caste and gender. If feminine is a social and cultural construct, this construction is buttressed and maintained by the caste-system. Women as guardians of tradition become also those who uphold the purity of caste by scrupulously observing its rules and injunctions of the caste. This is one more way in which the space of women within the private realm is circumscribed.[4] The mutual shaping

---

[3] As quoted in Lina Gupta, "A Hindu Woman's Journey", in *Concilium* 2006/3, p. 95.

[4] In this connection, it is interesting to note that in the nineteenth century colonial India, nationalists and social reformers highlighted the inner and

of caste and gender is sealed by endogamy which restricts the exchange
of women within the same caste or clan. As Uma Chakravarti points out,

> The term 'brahminical patriarchy' is a useful way to isolate this unique
> structure of patriarchy, by now dominant in many parts of India. It is
> a set of rules and institutions in which caste and gender are linked, each
> shaping the other and where women are crucial in maintaining the
> boundaries between castes…[C]aste hierarchy and gender inequality are
> maintained through both the production of consent and the application
> of coercion.[5]

Given the importance of maintaining the purity of caste for which women
are crucial, it follows that 'brahminical patriarchy' tried to control women
by controlling their sexuality, and consequently creating a cultural and
social mores that is intolerant of the subjecthood, free choice and autonomy
of woman. The control of the sexuality of woman takes on the subtle form
of *pativrata* ideal. It eulogizes loyal submission to the husband and extols
motherhood with which being woman is sought to be identified.[6] This is
done with the ideological aid of religious beliefs and narratives in epics
and puranas. The proscription of *varnasamkara* (mixing of castes) was
particularly stringent with regard to women, whose defilement in this
way was viewed as a portent of the times of cataclysmic disasters or
*kaliyuga*.

## Virgins – "Female Men of God"

Besides Hinduism, we could study in detail also other religious traditions
and see how all of them have contributed to reinforce patriarchy. Here we
limit ourselves to examine the Christian tradition by way of example.

---

spiritual superiority of India in contrast to the material West. As for the
colonialism, it was maintained that, though India is materially subjected to the
West, the West could not conquer the inner and spiritual self of the nation.
Now, the inner realm untainted by the external developments was represented
by women. They were the unconquered territory of the colonizers. To maintain
women in that status was to tie them down to the millennial traditions.
Therefore, in spite of the reforms advocated in favour of women, there were
not many who thought of the subjecthood of women, their identity and
autonomy.

[5] Uma Chakravarti, *Gendering Caste. Through a Feminist Lens*, Stree, Calcutta,
2006, p. 34; see also Id., *Rewriting History. The Life and Times of Pandita Ramabai*,
Kali for Women, Delhi, 2000.

[6] Cf. V. Geetha, *Patriarchy*, Stree, Calcutta, 2007.

In spite of the fact that Christianity proved attractive to women in its origins, since it provided alternative ways of life for them and for their self-expression, it has also contributed its share to the patriarchal domination of women in various ways. To recall some of the aspects, a misinterpreted anthropology, under the influence of certain Christian tradition, saw woman inferior to man (cf. 1Cor 11:8-11). Even an otherwise highly enlightened figure like Thomas Aquinas could see in woman nothing but a defective male. Misogyny became part of spirituality and asceticism. Again, a false interpretation of original sin, made women the source of evil and moral deprivation. Since women were identified with body, sensual association and sexual relation with them was viewed as a compromise with the soul and its salvation. As for women, salvation meant renouncing to their nature so bound up with body. Virginity became the supreme ideal for women, precisely because through sexual renunciation they rise above their nature and become truly "men of God". As Mary T. Malone observes,

> Virginal women have become male and have learnt to practice 'manly virtues'. In this way, they assure their eternal salvation because, in the next life, all will be male. Besides, having a virgin in the family guaranteed the salvation of all. The consecrated virgin is an example to all of the human being as she came from God's hands. Her body remains intact, without penetration of any kind.[7]

It is easy to see how the devaluation of sexuality meant in the Christian tradition also depreciation of woman, unless they took on the life of virginity and continence.

Medieval Christianity presents contrasting pictures of valiant and unconventional women on the one hand, and the effort to control any expression of women's independence, on the other. The infamous witch-hunting illustrates how women who sought to be themselves could easily be labeled as "witches" and burnt at stakes. What transpires from Christian history is that the preoccupation with orthodoxy and its defence did not aid the cause of women. On the contrary, it meant often the development of anti-woman attitudes and practices. The emergence and consolidation of clericalism sealed the fate of women as obedient subjects – without

---

[7] Mary T. Malone, *Women and Christianity*, Orbis Books, New York, 2001, p. 150; see also Elizabeth A. Clark, *Women in the Early Church,* Michael Glazier, Wilmington, 1983; Peter Brown, *The Body and Society. Men, Women, and Sexual Renunciation in Early Christianity*, Columbia University Press, New York, 1988.

identity and selfhood of their own - to be deployed for whatever purpose
or service the religious patriarchy thought them fit to be.

## Examples from the Past

I have tried to present some glimpses of religious patriarchy from two
traditions – Hinduism and Christianity – by way of example. What is
important to note is that religious traditions have developed ideologies,
institutions, rituals, customs and practices which all serve to disempower
women. But then, women have found, as I noted earlier, ways and
strategies to negotiate the power exercised over them by the patriarchal
control of religions. We could make a study of this from a historical
perspective which is not my intention here. Nevertheless, let me recall
here two towering women of nineteenth century who were able to
negotiate the power-hold of religion over women – Pandita Ramabai and
Elizabeth Cady Stanton. Ramabai was equally critical of brahminical
patriarchy and Christian clericalism, and Stanton produced the celebrated
"Women's Bible" to enhance the negotiating power of women in the
Christian religious sphere.

Instead of going into history, what I propose here is to present some
of the ways in which women today negotiate power in the religious realm
and how they invent alternative spaces of power.

## Re-reading of Religious Sources

Since patriarchy has recourse to religious scriptures to legitimise the control
of women and their subjugation, women in all religions are re-reading
these sources from a feminist perspective, resulting in a challenge to the
patriarchal interpretation of these sources. In this way, women strike at
the very root of ideological validation of dominion over them. Let me
highlight here the process that has taken place in Christianity by way of
women's negotiation of power.

The Bible – the Old Testament and the New Testament – forms the
basis of Christian beliefs and practices. This is true also in what touches
upon women. We could distinguish three orientations in the re-reading
of scriptures. There are women who think that the scriptures are so
dominated by patriarchy that they will not serve the cause of women.
They turn to other sources for their liberation. A second orientation is
represented by those who highlight the women characters and their stories
in the Bible, and these are amply made use of in the context of Christian

worship. This way of approaching scriptures does not go into any analysis of the way women are presented and the social and cultural conditionings behind the sacred texts in what concerns them. A third orientation is espoused by feminists who go into deeper explorations of the scriptural statements and narrations. They take a critical approach to the scriptures and begin their interpretation by applying the hermeneutics of suspicion. When tradition and interpretation in the past have worked against women's cause, it is legitimate that their approach to scriptural resources begins with hermeneutics of suspicion. By delving into the Christian origins, they highlight the historical agency of women. They sift the patriarchal elements and cultural conditionings inherent in the texts and narrations. A re-reading of the scriptures from the perspective of women, their concerns and experiences bring out an empowering and challenging message that breaks the patriarchal interpretation and control of the Bible.[8]

One of the strategies employed to break loose of patriarchal control is imagination. By this is not meant any "subjective' and arbitrary interpretation by women. The traditional interpretation of the role of woman and her identity as highlighted in the patriarchal understanding of feminity, is resisted and challenged by feminist imagination. It explore new ways to interpret and bring out the identity and agency of women. Rereading the texts and narrations with imagination helps them to see how women in the Bible have negotiated power, which in turn helps them negotiate power in their daily lives.

Let me illustrate this with few examples from the Old and New Testaments. In the Biblical tradition we have several examples of women who emerged as powerful leaders by employing strategies of inversion with the purpose of ensuring justice for the marginalized groups they represented. Esther is someone who did not keep quiet in the face of the calamities that fell on the Jewish people in exile, but used her beauty to ably negotiate and argue with the king to save her people (Esther 1-4). She wins a beauty-contest and gets into the centre of power by not disclosing her Jewish identity to a king who was bent on their destruction.

---

[8] Cf. Elisabeth Schüssler Fiorenza, *In Memory of Her. A Feminist Theological Reconstruction of Christian Origins*, Crossroad, New York, 1994; See also Kwok Pui-Lan and Elisabeth Schüssler Fiorenza, "Women's Sacred Scriptures" *Concilium* 1998/3; on the cultural conditioning of patriarchal domination in Christian scriptures, see, Esther Fuchs, *Sexual Politics in the Biblical Narrative. Reading the Hebrew Bible as a Woman*, Sheffield Academic Press, Sheffield, 2000.

Crowned as queen, she was able to deal with the king with courage and boldness.[9]

Another striking case is that of the Canaanite woman in the New Testament and her negotiation of power (cf. Mk 7:24-30; Mt 15:21-28). Being a gentile woman and not a Jew, she was in a very disadvantageous position. She argues with Jesus when he showed reluctance to respond to what she wanted for her child. Two things happen in her dealing with Jesus and argumentation with him. She makes Jesus aware of his bias as a Jew towards the gentiles to whom she belonged (cf. Mk 7:27). Secondly, as a result of her negotiation, she was able to get what she needed – the healing of her daughter.

In interpreting the scriptural resources, feminist scholars depart from the understanding of power and authority as dominion over. In feminist interpretation, power and authority are centred on community, and understood in terms of partnership. As Letty Russell notes,

> The emerging feminist paradigm trying to make sense of biblical and theological truth claims is that of authority as partnership. In this view, reality is interpreted in the form of a circle of interdependence. Ordering is explored through inclusion of diversity in a rainbow spectrum that does not require that persons submit to the "top", but rather, that they participate in the common task of creating an interdependent community of humanity and nature. Authority is exercised in community and tends

---

[9] Another significant figure in the story is queen Vashti. King Ahasuerus, who ruled over the entire region between India and Ethiopia, arranged for a sumptuous banquet for all the officials, nobles and governors from his entire kingdom. This was an occasion for him to exhibit all his fabulous riches. Not satisfied, he wanted to show to the guests something very precious he possessed – the beauty of his queen Vashti. He commands her to appear before his guests and show off her beauty. According to some commentators, it is to be inferred that she was to appear naked. But the queen refused the king's bidding, for she wanted to be herself and not an object of beauty or show-piece to be exposed to the ravenous eyes of the males. Her principled defiance led to her being deposed as queen. For the interpretation of the story of Esther and queen Vashti, see Andre Lacocque, *The Feminine Unconventional*, Fortress Press, Minneapolis, 1990, pp. 50-83; see also James W.G. Williams, *Women Recounted. Narrative Thinking and the God of Israel*, The Almond Press, Sheffield, 1982; Letty M. Russell (ed.), *Feminist Interpretation of the Bible*, Basil Blackwell, Oxford, 1985.

to reinforce ideas of cooperation, with contribution from a wide diversity of persons enriching the whole.[10]

## Re-interpreting Religious Tenets

The negotiation of power by women could be seen also in the way they go about traditional religious tenets and perspectives, starting from the image of the Divine. If "the symbol of God functions as the primary symbol of the whole religious system, the ultimate point of reference for understanding experience, life and the world",[11] it is of utmost importance in what way God is imagined and presented. The fact is that the dominant image of God in the Judeo-Christian tradition and in daily practice is androcentric; divine mystery is masculanized and named with male designations. It is often argued that naming God in male terms, is not to be taken literally. If that is the case, it is not understandable why there should be objections when God is referred with female designations. It only shows that God-talk has deeper ideological implications. Speaking of God in male terms often implies that it is the male who is representative of God, and therefore is the holder of power; he is master and ruler over women. The masculine image of God has led also to the monopoly of leadership by men in Christian tradition and practice up to our day. As Anne Carr observes,

> The idol of male divinity in heaven issues in a divinising male authority, responsibility, power, and holiness on earth, despite pious avowals of religious leaders about women's equality. For the symbolism is so deeply embedded in Christian theology, church structure, and liturgical practice that the Christian imagination unconsciously absorbs its destructive and exclusionary message from childhood on.[12]

How justified is this male discourse of God with all its ideological implications and ethical consequences? Even if one speaks about divine mystery, when women who are created equally in God's image (Gen 1:27) are left out, it is sinful sexism. Rosemary Ruether calls it "idolatry" – the

---

[10] Letty M. Russell, "Authority and the Challenge of Feminist Interpretation", in Letty M. Russell (ed.), *Feminist Interpretation of the Bible*, Basil Blackwell, Oxford, 1985, p. 144.

[11] Cf. Elizabeth  A. Johnson, *She Who Is. The Mystery of God in Feminist Theological Discourse*, The Crossroad Publishing Company, New York, 2002, p. 4.

[12] Anne E. Carr, *Transforming Grace*, Continuum, New York, 1998, pp. 138-139.

most detestable sin in the Semitic religious traditions.[13] How else could the exclusion of women and their experience from the approach and understanding of the divine be characterized? The attempt to name the unnamable divine mystery through the experience of woman is basically a recognition of their dignity as human persons and affirmation of their distinctive experience.

Obviously, the presentation of the divine mystery as male has served to consolidate patriarchal system and its claims. For women, negotiation of power means to challenge the very approach to the divine exclusively through male experience and symbols. Some of them show how the male image of God is to be complemented by images in the scriptures which speak of the maternal traits of God (cf. Is 66:13). This is seen as an attempt to carve out some small space for women in what is dominantly a male image of God. Others go a step further and show that in the divine ontological reality itself there is the feminine – the Spirit. In this way, "we end up with two clear masculine images and an amorphous feminine third".[14] These two approaches are found not adequate to really negotiate the dominant andocentric images and approaches to God. Hence, other feminists have highlighted the mystery of God as that of Sophia or wisdom.

As for Hinduism, the reality of male and female is reflected in the divine realm with male deities and female goddesses. Even more, there is no border between the world of the human and the divine; on the contrary, both these realms interpenetrate each other. Even though, more than any other religion, Hinduism is attentive to the feminine in the divine, with innumerable goddess figures, however, when it comes to negotiation of power by women, these very images of goddesses could inspire subordination under patriarchal ideology. In fact, in the mainline Sanskritic tradition, female deities like Sita, Lakshmi, Parvathi are consorts of male deities, and the virtues and ideals surrounding these female deities are not very different from what are projected patriarchally as ideals for a woman or for a wife. What we observe, then, is that the mere acknowledgement of goddesses does not contribute to empower women.

However, there is another stream of Hinduism in which village goddesses (*gramadevata*) are associated with subaltern people. Here goddesses are not consorts of male divinities, but are independent; they

---

[13] Rosemary Radford-Ruether, *Sexism and God-Talk. Toward a Feminist Theology,* Beacon Press, Boston, 1983.

[14] Elizabeth A. Johnson, *op.cit.,* p. 50.

exude power and compassion, and have agency of their own. A goddess is deeply rooted in the village; even more, she is seen as married to the village whose protector and guardian she becomes.[15] Obviously, highlighting of this image of goddesses has great potential for women to negotiate the issue of power in daily lives against the strongly entrenched patriarchal system.

### Life-cycle Rituals and Negotiation of Power

We have seen the opening of women's negotiation of power in areas like the scriptures, the image of the Divine, etc. Now, rituals also have strong symbolic overtones and are repository of sacred as well as social power. If it is the general experience of women that they are excluded from this symbolic realm, on the other hand, women from the lower strata are the central figures in some areas of religio-cultural practices. One such realm is that of life-cycle rituals. In South India, an event like menstruation is not something that is hidden from the eyes of the public; rather something that is celebrated. In this as well as in rituals connected with pregnancy, Dalit women, for example, play important ritual roles. The negotiation of power does not consist merely in women being ritual agents. There are other noteable dimensions to these rituals. In spite of the many ambiguities surrounding them, these rituals succeed to give women at least momentarily a sense of power, respect and attention. These rituals are significant, because through them, the entire family of the girl or woman gains "*mathippu*" or self-esteem in the society.[16]

Secondly, the bodies of women are affirmed and celebrated in these rituals – bodies which otherwise are debased and often humiliated as source of pollution and as object of shame. The way women's bodies are dressed and ornated during menstrual and pregnancy rituals and the way they are fed on these occasions bring to expression the worth of their bodies. Life-cycle rituals, stand out as sites where women negotiate power, especially if we contrast this with the daily drudgery of life in which their bodies are exploited and humiliated. Thirdly, these life-cycle rituals provide women a sense of well-being and auspiciousness. Celebrating the

---

[15] Cf. David Kinsley, *Hindu Goddesses. Vision of the Divine Feminine in the Hindu Religious Traditions*, Motilal Banarsidass, Delhi-Varanasi, 1986, pp. 197 ff.

[16] Cf. Theresiamma Thomas, *Women and Rituals. A Critical Inquiry into the Religious-Cultural Practices of Catholic Women of Dalit Origin in Tiruvallur District, Tamilnadu* (Unpublished doctoral dissertation written under my guidance at the University of Madras, Chennai, 2007).

puberty rituals highlights the generative power of woman as the one who has the potential to bring forth new life, and in this she is viewed akin to the Divine in its mysterious creative power. While the affirmation of the generative potential of women is celebrated in the feminist discourse,[17] these life-cycle rituals create in lower caste women an empowering inner state of mind. This subjective basis of power could be present even in conditions of the absence of objective basis of power such as economic means, legal entitlements, etc.

To these life-cycle rituals we need to add explicit religious rituals women – especially women from the lower castes and classes – perform. Empirical data show that the religious rituals at home are performed mostly by women. The religious practices they do, prove to be a source of inner power in the case of many women who, thanks to their religious rituals, have shown the ability to negotiate power in the external realm. The fasting they do, the vow they take and the pilgrimage they go to, become means for them to negotiate the realm of power that weighs in every sphere of life against them.

> Females are also becoming religious specialists and conduct life-cycle rituals, even though males are temple-priests and leaders of most public rituals. Hindu women have considerable religious involvement. Women alone perform a large number of calendrical rituals; women's participation in the life-cycle rituals is definitely a part of the little tradition. The sexual segregation of Hindu society also articulates with the role that religion plays in drawing women together. Female solidarity is continuously reinforced through religious practices.[18]

Obviously, we do not conclude that religious practices bring a solution to the powerlessness of women. This could only lend substance to the claim that religion alienates women from the material realities of life and power.

---

[17] Obviously, one may view these rituals as reducing the role of women to reproduction or see them as events heightening the honour of men. Certainly, these rituals do not challenge the patriarchal system *in toto* or its dominance in ritual realm. That is why some women play down traditional puberty rituals which give the false notion of women's bodies being identified with fertility and procreation. What these life-cycle rituals highlight are flashes of power that women gain and they could be viewed as strategies to negotiate power in a world and society in which the ritual realm is controlled almost entirely by men, and more specifically by the priestly caste or class.

[18] Madhavi D. Renavikar, *Women and Religion*, Rawat Publications, Delhi, 2003, p. 31.

But it is undeniable from the perspective of the subjecthood of women, that these practices, of which they themselves are actors, contribute to heighten their inner power. Barbara Holdrege analysing the Phenomenology of Power distinguishes four dimensions of power - ontological, existential, material and socio-political.[19] The power of religious rituals in which women are involved invests them with a power with which they are able to often negotiate and even resist other forms of power imposed on them. The very power that is exercised as domination over them in which traditional and institutional ritualization consolidates the existing order – is subverted by other forms.

## Women's Transgression of 'Sacred' Spaces

Yet another way in which women negotiate power is to circumvent the patriarchal boundaries. Traditionally, the space of woman was highly restricted. First of all, according to patriarchal injunctions, her movements are to be inside home, performing those stereotyped construct of gender roles. Movements outside home, in the open and public spaces were considered highly dangerous.[20] This is due to various reasons within the caste framework. The chastity of woman was crucially important for the status and good name of the family which will be exposed to danger by letting women to have access to the public space.

Secondly, there is a strong prejudice, especially in the Indian tradition, that women's sexuality is insatiable, erratic and uncontrollable. This is supported by many religious myths and narratives. This view is at the origin of many customs, traditions and structures that control women and their mobility. Paradigmatic is the proverbial "*lakhsmana rekha*" – the line drawn by Lakhsmanan, the brother of Rama, which Sita was not to cross. The space within the lines drawn by patriarchy is safe, while any trespassing of the boundaries meant danger. In everyday life, all this could be seen in such practices as women being married off quite early; women not being allowed to undertake any job that exposes them in the public realm; while going out, they are accompanied by family members. There

---

[19] Cf. Barbara A. Holdrege, "Towards a Phenomenology of Power", in *Journal of Ritual Studies* 4/2 (Summer 1990), pp. 5-35.

[20] Seemanthini Niranja argues the importance of analysis of women in terms of *body-space*, and her field-study evidences this. See Seemanthini Niranja, *Gender and Space. Feminity, Sexualization and the Female Body*, Sage Publications, Delhi, 2001; see also Liana Borgh–Braidotti, *Thinking Differently*, Zed Books, London, 2002, pp. 83-96.

have been religious myths created to say that if women go out at night, especially to secluded places, they will be attacked by spirits or by ghosts!

Through different practices and strategies, Indian feminist movements challenge these customs and traditions by which patriarchal power is exercised. For one thing, the sheer necessity of survival, pushes women, especially women of lower castes and classes, to transgress the patriarchal boundaries. Unless they move out of the traditionally restricted spaces to the open fields, to new spaces of work, their families cannot survive, and their children will starve. This mobility women claim has become an important means for their empowerment. While responding to the needs of livelihood, the breaking of boundaries infuses them with a new power and confidence that is able to challenge patriarchy.

One important source for women's challenge to patriarchal religious power and its ideological legitimation, derives, as far as South India is concerned, from the Self-respect movement. The Self-respect movement of 1930s, and 1940s, initiated by E.V.R. Periyar challenged the Brahminical religious orthodoxy, and one of its important contributions was to liberate women from obscurantism and taboos wrapped up in religious ideology. It was characteristic of the women of Self-respect movement to break all the religiously sanctioned customs and transgress 'sacred' spaces. Its radical critique of caste was at the same time a challenge to the oppression of women and their subjugation in a hierarchical society. For example, among Self-respecters, marriages did away with the traditional rituals that called for the presence of Brahmin priest. They challenged the dyad of private and public spaces, and they opted out of the identification of women's space as "inside" home, which devalued their labour and public visibility. Defying in many different and ingenious ways the control of patriarchy, women enlarged their spaces - physical and mental - which is highly important today for their well-being and full humanity.

Given the paradoxical nature of religion which can cause wounds as much as it can heal them, women draw from religious resources – through a feminist re-interpretation – the power as well as strategies to challenge their confinement within patriarchally defined spaces. I may recall here from the Christian tradition two examples. In the story of Martha and Mary (cf. Lk 10:38-42), one sister is engrossed in a traditional gender role – she is busy preparing food, while the younger sister crosses the boundaries to enter into new spaces. She does what was forbidden for a woman in Jewish society. She becomes a student in the school of the Rabbi

Jesus. The realm of learning that expands the horizons of the mind and intellect – which was proscribed for women – is precisely where Maria dares to enter, and this transgression invites praise and appreciation from Jesus. "Martha, Martha, you are worried and distracted by many things; there is need of only one thing. Mary has chosen the better part, which will not be taken away from her" (Lk 10:42). The other story is that of the Samaritan woman (cf. Jn 4). She does something that was unconventional, and looked down upon by the society. She enters into intense conversation with a man at the well. Jesus' own disciples were taken aback by the audacity of the woman as much as by the sight of Jesus engaged alone in conversation with a woman - and that too with a 'low caste' woman - who spoke to him her thoughts. The significance of this event is all the greater, since the Samaritan woman breaks the boundary of ethnic division (almost like caste division) erected between the two endogamous groups, the Jews considering the Samaritans as low and impure. Among Jews and Samaritans there was little exchange. By venturing to break the conventional barriers, she challenges the patriarchal power defining "caste" and gender. This breaking of boundaries leads her to new vistas of reality and to understand her own self in a new light.

## Women Interrogate Priestly Power

Since in most cultures, patriarchy enjoys the blessings of the priestly class or caste, it is of crucial importance for women to challenge the power wielded by these religious agents in the name of God. The ideological mechanism and structures of religious establishment prove often impregnable for women and feminist movements. And yet, here again women have found ways of negotiating with this form of power. The task is all the more challenging, since misogyny seems to be widespread among the priestly class, for various reasons, including historical and doctrinal ones. Clericalism does exactly in the religious sphere what patriarchy does in general to women. Clericalism, that is the undue domination of the priestly class over women, is at the root of women's marginalization in the domain of religion.

To begin with, one way in which most religions subjugate women is to ascribe impurity to them, which becomes the basis for their exclusion from sacred spaces and roles. Such a view is being contested by increasing number of women, who challenge the myths underlying such prejudices among religious agents. Studies show that increasing number of women do not consider themselves impure, unless they have internalised the patriarchal ideology.[21]

Everyday experience shows that women are the ones who are very much attached to religious practices and devotions. Their visibility is much more evident in the religious sphere than in the civic realm. They visit temples, churches, gurudwaras and mosques frequently. And yet, they are relegated to the margins when it comes to leadership or decision-making in religious establishments and performing public rituals and ceremonies. In recent times, women's voices have been growing louder clamouring against discrimination in religious leadership, participation in decision-making, etc.

Evidently, the priestly class and its religious establishments want women to participate in religious rituals and other programmes. But their idea of participation is narrowly conceived and in a way that is protective of priestly power, clerical authority and privileges. This narrow understanding rests on a false premise of complementarity. Invoking the idea that men and women complement each other in the religious sphere some secondary roles are assigned to women, and roles that involve power are firmly retained by the priestly establishment. The idea of complementarity is valid as long as the partners are viewed and treated as equals. As it is, there is an asymmetry of power. In a situation wherein there is a serious imbalance of power between men and women, acting on the principle of complementarity goes to the disadvantage of women. Complementarity means, for example, excluding women from being performers of official rituals, since, it is argued, that women have other roles.

But feminist movements continue to challenge such arrangements of power-sharing. The issue became a serious one in Christian Churches, when feminists and women movements challenged the view that certain ministries were reserved only for men, and women are debarred from them. This resulted in some Christian Churches admitting women to become ordained ministers; however, not without serious conflicts. The debate has been raging in the Christian Churches and has caused also serious polarization and division wherever women were admitted to ordained ministry. In Churches where this has not happened, feminists

---

[21] Cf Metti Amirtham, "*Socio-Cultural Perceptions of Female Body. A Critical Study with Reference to the Women of Dindigul District, Tamilnadu*" (Ph.D. dissertation written under my guidance), University of Madras, Chennai, 2007.

are fielding very persuasive arguments challenging their exclusion from priestly functions. They view it as a "politics of power".[22] Even in Churches where these functions are admitted, as empirical studies show, women experience discrimination, as for example when they do not find postings commensurate to their capacity and qualification, which does not seem to be the case with ordained men.[23]

Since "brahminical patriarchy", clericalism, etc., do not permit public performance of rituals by women, they have found ways and strategies to invent new spaces. Let me cite two examples. The phenomenon of shamanism in which mostly women are the actors, calls into question a situation in which the power of mediation between heaven and earth, the natural and the supernatural is retained by men. Shamans are also intermediaries between human beings on earth and the world of the spirits. The practice of shamanism and spirit-possession has given women a sense of freedom and agency, which otherwise they do not enjoy. The fact that they are the medium of the spirits and that the deities speak through them evokes awe and respect towards them. No wonder then, in many cultures, patriarchal guardians of religious authority and orthodoxy have felt threatened by shamanistic practices through which women express their religious agency.

The second case is that of mosques for women. The *jamaats* are attached to mosques and they sit in judgement on many issues directly affecting them, including dowry harassment, *talaq*, settling of domestic disputes, domestic violence etc. The *jamaats* are dominated by men with no representation of women. Women could hardly hope for any fairness in the religiously dominated patriarchal mode of functioning. This experience led a group of women inspired by Daud Sharifa of Pudukottai, Tamilnadu, to form their own *jamaat*, and what is more, to have, perhaps, for the first time in history, a mosque for women. As Sharifa observed,

> The male jamaats are unlawful kangaroo courts that play with the lives of women. A mosque-jamaat axis is power centre that controls the community. When women are refused representation here, we have no

---

[22] Cf. Elisabeth Schüssler Fiorenza – Hermann Häring (eds.) "The Non-Ordination of Women and the Politics of Power" *Concilium* 1999/3.

[23] Cf. Dean R. Hoge, "Religious Leadership/Clergy", in Helen Rose Ebugh (ed.), *Handbook of Religion and Social Institutions*, Springer, New York, 2000, pp. 373-387.

choice but to have our own jamaat. And since a jamaat is attached to a
mosque, we have to build our own mosque.[24]

The *jamaat* of women functions today with forty members meeting
regularly every month discussing in their meetings issues affecting women.
Obviously such a daring initiative to challenge the Muslim cleric's
authority and power has brought about virulent opposition and threats.

### Reappraisal of Female Body and Negotiation of Power

The issue of negotiation of power in relation to women's body is crucial
for the following reasons: First, body is so inextricably bound up with the
self and identity of a woman and her agency. Second, the power of
patriarchy is most dominating over the realm of women's body and
sexuality. Third, religious traditions have contributed in varying measure
to the devaluation of women's bodies through their doctrines and practices
– a point which is so evident from history and present practices, that it
does not require elaboration. Fourth, if - as Erving Goffmann notes - body
is crucial to identify the nexus between the self and social identity,[25] this
is all the more true in the case of women. By the way a woman bears her
body, positions it, dresses, decorates and makes it appear, and by the
manner she gesticulates and expresses emotions, there takes place a non-
verbal communication which is most important in public behaviour and
for the mediation of her self-identity and social identity.

Culture under religious inspiration, has created mechanisms to control
the space and movement of the body of woman and discipline it right
from childhood, especially from the time a girl attains maturity and reaches
the stage of reproduction. Researching on the perception about their bodies
among the women of Dindigul district, Tamilnadu, Metti Amirtham
observes,

It was also obvious that woman's body is subjected to a still finer
discipline while sitting or waiting for a train or bus. They take as little

---

[24] Quoted in S. Anand, "Getting Ready for World's First Women's-only
Mosque", in *Outlook*, 2 September, 2004. There is a growing pressure on the
part of self-assertive women who challenge the patriarchal power that prevents
them from prayer in mosques. This was felt strongly among Afghan women
whose initiative has recently led to the creation of a mosque for women in
Kabul.
[25] Cf. Erving Goffmann, *The Presentation of Self in Everyday Life*, Penguin,
Harmondsworth, 1969.

space as possible with arms close to the bodies, hands folded together on their laps, toes pointing straight ahead or turned inward, and legs pressed together. Even while sleeping woman mostly lie towards one side and not on their back.[26]

Feminists assert that women's body is not a mere biological reality; there is an inherent element of agency in woman's body. It implies that in women's assertion, resistance and in their critical consciousness, etc., their bodies are also a part. Women negotiate with ideological power of religion and patriarchal domination in their quest of autonomy in making decisions in what concerns their bodies, and its needs, and thus give expression to their agency. There is then something like the "politics of the female body".[27]

For the early feminists of twentieth century like Simone de Beauvoir, the affirmation of the dignity and agency of woman called for a flight from the body. For, in a culture that identified woman with her biological and reproductive function, feminist response was negation of body, since it was seen as the sole site of women, and patriarchy had complete control over it. Further developments in feminist thought has led to a reappraisal of women's body and its affirmation, while at the same time refusing to identify woman with patriarchally constructed gender roles. Against this background we need to reflect on the ways women today negotiate power over their bodies sanctioned by religions.

Women resist the control of their bodies in different ways and claim their own agency. Whereas the Indian tradition in general, and Tamil tradition in particular, has laid emphasis on motherhood, women in the organized sector, under the influence of urbanization and economic independence and other factors, refuse to identify their selves with motherhood as the only or supreme value for women. Again, the stringent traditional dress-codes – under the pervasive influence of culture and religion - meant to control women are increasingly challenged by them. In the case of Muslim women's dress-code, religious injunctions play a most important role. Non-conformity to religiously and culturally sanctioned dress-code is symbolic of the autonomy women claim in what

---

[26] Metti Amirtham, *op.cit.*,  pp. 84-85.

[27] Cf. V. Geetha, "Gender and the Logic of Brahminism: Periyar and the Politics of the Female Body", in Kumkum Sangari and Uma Chakravarti (eds.), *From Myths to Markets: Essays on Gender*, Manohar Publishers, Delhi, 1999, pp. 198-233.

concerns their bodies. Most importantly women question the double-standards in sexual morality which have far too long put women in a disadvantageous and unfair position.[28] For 'brahminical patriarchy', the bodies of upper caste women and their chastity became the site for the inscription of tradition and religious orthodoxy, whereas lower caste women's bodies were allowed to be exploited through the "devadasi" system or so-called "temple-prostitution".

Another form in which women negotiate power relates to the emerging new attitude towards barrenness. In the past, religious ideology made barren women low in front of society and prevented them from performing auspicious functions. Today, not a few transcend these traditional strictures and value women for what they are, irrespective of their fertility and motherhood, as is clear from the growing trend among Indian women who choose to remain single and not wanting to sacrifice their career at the altar of the family.

Closely related to these negotiations of power, is the attitude of increasing number of women about beauty. In the past, women cultivated beauty as a response to male expectations ("the male gaze"), which is largely true even today. The beauty-myth with its colour-consciousness, internalised by women, is a subtle power exercised by patriarchy with the support of media; its consequences are disastrous for the life of a lot of women. Today, more and more women, setting aside the patriarchal parameters, would like to care for and feel good about their bodies. It gives them a sense of truly being themselves. In the lives of these women, beauty becomes part of their agency, self-assertion and legitimate pride about their bodies.

## Conclusion: Inventing New Spaces

The patriarchal power-structures and regimes of social regulations deeply entrenched in culture and religion present formidable challenges to women and for their project of claiming their dignity and full humanity. Especially the hold religions have over the lives of people and their consciousness are at the root of patriarchal power. However, feminist movements have found strategies and mechanisms to negotiate this kind of power.

---

[28] Once again we must underline the contribution of E.V.R. Periyar for challenging the duplicity of "brahminical patriarchy" in what concerns sexual morality. See V. Geetha, "Gender and the Logic of Brahminism: Periyar and the Politics of the Female Body", art. cit.

The very scriptures which have been used for millennia to tighten the chains of oppression are loosened and women are set free through a re-interpretation of the same sources. Feminist hermeneutics of religious scriptures and doctrines, besides serving the cause of women's liberation, also enrich the religious traditions. Feminist re-readings correspond to the new insights in modern hermeneutics. What is important to note is that feminist hermeneutics of religious scriptures do not remain simply at the level of notional knowledge; this hermeneutics needs to be deployed to transform reality by challenging the patriarchal modes of interpretation that have been dominant in all religious traditions.

Those who control the symbols, as it is said, control the society. If religion is a symbolic system invested with power, ritualization becomes the foremost expression of power. It serves to reinforce existing power-structures. But women have, again, found ways to circumvent the ritual control. Through their agency in life-cycle rituals and by creating alternative liturgy or worship forms, women are negotiating the patriarchal control of rituals. In the same spirit, they also transgress "sacred" spaces and enclosures zealously guarded from women by religious establishments.

Finally, the very bodies of women on the control of which hinges the patriarchal power are today endowed with a different meaning for women. In their perception, their bodies are no more to be subjected to patriarchal control; for women, their bodies are today a site of new power, the basis to claim their dignity and agency.

The task of challenging the religious powers by women has just begun. There is a long way to go. What is promising is that women today are inventing new spaces and alternative paradigms which help not only their cause but contribute to the emergence of a different world and humanity.

# Part II

# Pathways to Justice

# Chapter 6

# Good Governance –
# The Struggle of Asian Societies

*"...as we all know, infrastructure is not just a matter of roads, schools and power grids. It is equally a question of strengthening democratic governance and the rule of law. Without accountability, not only of the government to its people but of the people to each other, there is no hope for a viable democratic state"* — UN Secretary General, Ban Ki-moon[1]

*"I don't think they [people] will really thirst for vengeance once they have been given access to the truth. But the fact that they are denied access to the truth simply stokes the anger and hatred in them. That their sufferings have not been acknowledged makes people angry... We do not think that there is anything wrong with saying we made a mistake and that we are sorry."* — Aung San Suu Kyi[2]

How well did Britain govern its colonies? Speaking of colonial times, it is often argued that the British were good at governance, and there was rule of law, order, fairness, etc. The implication is that disorder and corruption followed, because the "natives" were incapable of governance. In fact the colonial ideology held that power could not be transferred to the natives because they had not reached a stage of self-rule. Yet, the fact is that when faced with the short-supply of cotton from America due to slave-labour abolition, Britain cultivated more intensely cash-crops in India to such an extent that it increased by 85%, whereas food production saw a decline of 7%.[3] The result was that millions perished by famine. We may think of the ghastly Bengal famine (1769–1773) that

---

[1] Remarks to the Security Council on Timor-Leste, 19 February, 2009.

[2] Aung San Suu Kyi, *The Voice of Hope*, Rider, London, 2008, p. 38.

[3] Cf. P. Sainath, in *The Hindu*, 20 August 2005.

caused the death of fifteen million people in Gangatic plain. How could we name something good governance when millions are allowed to die of hunger and famine? And yet, Warren Hastings, the Governor General, had good tidings for his East India Company, which did not suffer, notwithstanding the famine, any loss of tax,[4] which was as much as before[5] – at least in his estimation, a sign of good governance!

Let us take the example of the visit of General Musharraf of Pakistan to the West for damage-control after those tumultuous months of unrest and assassination of Benazir Bhuto. In a BBC interview, he presented his performance as the best possible governance, and among other things he pointed out how the stock-market was booming in his country, and how press enjoys freedom as perhaps in no other part of the world.

Claims of good governance as this, is not anything new. If we take any country in our parts of Asia, the rulers – be it Myanmar, Vietnam, China, Singapore, Sri Lanka – all of them are convinced that they do the best of governance. The understanding of governance behind such claims is grossly at variance with the experience of the common man and woman in these countries. We have international bodies such as World Bank and International Monetary Fund who have suddenly become apostles of "good governance", and they never cease to advise the developing countries on what that means. For them, good governance means following the prescriptions they give; refusal to do so is equal to mis-governance.[6] As the rulers, so too such international bodies have their own understanding of what governance means.

---

[4] The East India company raised the land-tax from the earlier 10% to 50% - a fivefold increase, causing severe burden on the people. At the height of the catastrophic famine, the British East India Company raised the taxes to another 10%.

[5] It is instructive that one of the worst famines in human history – the Irish famine – took place during the British rule over that country. See, *The Irish Famine*, Thames & Hudson, London, 1995.

[6] Critical questions could be raised regarding the governance of these institutions themselves. Since they purportedly serve the welfare especially of developing countries, it is only proper that these bodies be also governed by representatives from the countries they intend to serve.

## Promoting Good Governance – Asian History

Governance is such a basic reality in the life of any society. No wonder then, that the cultures and civilizations of Asia, each one in its own way inspires us with examples of good governance, and provide us with a lot of insights into its understanding. For example, in the Indic civilization, governance is indissolubly related to *Dharma* or *Dhamma*, a concept so rich with many layers of meanings that it is difficult to translate. As shorthand we could render it as righteousness.

In the Indic tradition, a whole science of governance was developed and it was known as *arthasastra*. Kautilya wrote an entire classical work on this topic. He tells us that "in the happiness of his subjects lies the king's happiness, in their welfare, his welfare. He shall not consider as good only that which pleases him but treat as beneficial to him whatever pleases his subject".[7] In almost all classical literature we could find the basic thought that the primary responsibility of the king is to protect *dharma*, and the Brihadharanya Upanishads tells us that when a ruler follows *dharma*, justice is done to the weaker ones, and that they are not exploited, and overpowered by the strong. In the Tamil tradition of India, this *dharma* or righteousness was not only viewed as the goal of governance, but as something which protects the ruler himself. In other words, it is in protecting the people, the king is best protected; in following *dharma*, the king finds his own security.[8]

To interpret in terms of our experiences of today, the rule of law understood as *dharma* or righteousness should be above the rulers. Abiding by the rule of law would mean that in governance nobody is discriminated against or disadvantaged, and that everyone is treated equally.

There are a lot of insights in the Confucian tradition which we can draw for governance today. Deeply embedded in the Confucian tradition is the conviction that exercising responsibility towards society is an inalienable part of being ethical. Just as in the Indic tradition, a ruler should abide by *dharma*, in the Confucian tradition the ruler should practice *ren,* that is humaneness. It is the foundation of the Confucian political theory. The very legitimacy for governing (deriving from the "mandate of Heaven") lies in the exercise of humaneness. As we could see, the Indic

---

[7] *Praja sukhe sukham  rajyaha prajanamcha hitehitam natma priyam hitam rajnaha prajanam cha hita priyam.*

[8] This is what the great Tamil poet, Tiruvalluvar said in one of his couplets: *Irai kakkum vayayakam ellam avanai murai kakkum muttacheyn.*

and Confucian tradition placed important checks on governance and these were centred on high ideals and basic ethical principles.

We could note a convergence between the Asian thought on governance and the classical Western thought. To cite just one example, Plato in his work *The Republic,* projects philosopher-king as ideal ruler.[9] One may wonder about the viability of this proposal as the philosophers are supposed to be impractical theoreticians, whereas politics and governance require the art of negotiating power and practical sense. But that is to misunderstand the point Plato wants to make. Philosopher is someone detached from the desire for wealth; he is a renouncer. Plato means to say that good governance is possible when a person of detachment, endowed with wisdom, governs and conducts the affairs of the city. As in the case of the Asian tradition we mentioned, here too there is no conflict between the personal interests of the ruler and those of the people. For, the very welfare of the people becomes the welfare of the rulers, precisely because the latter has no other desires or interests to cultivate.

Another important point of convergence is the fact that, in spite of historical experiences of despotism, tyranny and other unjust forms of government, both Asia and the West have continuously nurtured the dream of an ideal governance.[10] This aspiration and idealism can function as fuel for reforming the concrete modes of governance and envisioning a different future for governance.[11]

---

[9] Cf. Plato, *Republic*, Wordsworth Classics, Hertfordshire, 1997.

[10] There has been critique about idealization of governance in the name of practicability and empirical experience. This is true both of the East and the West. To cite one instance from the West, Tacitus as a historian preferred to draw lessons for good governance from the experiences of history, rather than from the ideals of city and governance proposed by Plato, Cicero and others. In fact, Tacitus has this to say in his *Annales*: "Indeed, a nation or city is ruled by the people, or by an upper class, or by a monarch. A government system that is invented from a choice of these same components is sooner idealized than realized; and even if realized, there will be no future for it." (*Annales* IV, 33).

[11] Speaking of the peoples of Asia, the Theological Advisory Commission of FABC (later renamed Office of Theological Concerns) in its document on "Asian Theological Perspectives on Church and Politics" noted the following: "The aspirations and hopes of our poor and oppressed sisters and brothers do not remain simply a pious wish or a pie in the sky, but are embodied in concrete struggles and political actions to overcome the situations and structures that

## Stemming the Practice of Corruption

There are several parameters against which good governance can be assessed. In general, the quality of governance can be said to be proportionate to the degree of the absence of corruption in any society. When we look at the present-day realities all around, they are far from the civilizational ideals of governance I just sketched. Sometimes some serious measures are taken to stem the tide of corruption, as for example when China recently went to the extent of executing Zheng Xizoyu, the former head of its State Food and Drug Administration, for having received bribes from eight drug companies to the tune of U.S. $ 850, 000.[12] Such measures with demonstrative effect, do not help much when millions of citizens suffer as a result of corrupt practices by the various agents of the state. In spite of the efforts of the central government in China, corruption thrives with authorities at the local level and severely affects the daily lives of millions of people in that country. Corruption finds its way among the military junta of Myanmar. Every Asian country has its own cup of woes in this regard.

I need not go into any description of the rampant corruption and graft in Asian societies. It is well-known to us through our experiences in our countries and societies. At this point, we could, perhaps, recall the extent of corruption which is very striking, since some of the Asian countries are among the most corrupt in the world. Transparency International has been conducting survey of the situation of corruption in the world, and it provides tables for every year. For example, Myanmar is the most corrupt country in the world (179th place) with a score of 1.4, measured against a scale of 10, and it is closely followed by Bangladesh and Cambodia, both of which are in 162nd place. India and China are both in the 72 position for corruption and their score is an average of 3.5 during the period of 2002 – 2007. In India the corruption has grown from the position of 3.5 in 2002 to 2.7 in 2007.[13]

---

dehumanize them. There is a general disaffection with the present mode of governance and the prevailing political culture, which has set in motion a serious search for alternatives which respond to the yearnings of the people for equality and participation." Vimal Tirimanna (ed.), *Sprouts of Theology from the Asian Soil. Collection TAC and OTC Documents (1987–2007),* Claretian Publications, Bangalore, 2007, pp. 72-73.

[12] Cf. *Business Daily* from The Hindu group of Publications, Monday, 6 August 2007.

[13] See the *Corruption Perception Index* of Transparency International for the year 2007. *www.transparency.org*, accessed on 8 September, 2008.

Corruption operates at various levels. It thrives among the elites and critical media often makes sensational revelations of corruption in high places. There is a flourishing of bribery in weapon procurement as for example, the Bofors case in India, in awarding contracts for public services, granting licenses and permits, etc. Where there is martial rule or dominance of military, corruption enters into every segment of economy like construction, manufacturing, agriculture insurance, road-building, etc. People are confronted with corrupt practices in everyday life when they have to deal with government offices, with the army and police-force, health-services, permissions of different kinds, etc. The services which the state and its agencies are to offer freely or for a nominal fee have become a matter of sale and shady dealings. Public servants make a private gain abusing their office and power. In many countries from top to bottom corruption circulates corroding every organ of the society and perverting every segment of life.

Most preoccupying is the corrupt practices that have entered into the judiciary. When confronted with injustice, for many people, the last resort to vindicate their cause are the courts. But when the judges themselves are corrupt, and pronounce judgments for a price, then even the last hope the people nurture begins to wane. In many Asian countries, the courts from the lower level to the highest level, have been found seriously wanting in integrity.[14] Let me recall here one widely publicized case in Indonesia. Judge Syafiuddin Kartasasmita was assassinated through the instigation of Jutomo Tommy Mandala Putra Suharto, a son of the former president Suharto. This is because, the judge, though promised a favourable judgment taking bribe, did not keep his word.[15] Even the Indian judiciary which enjoyed credibility and good reputation until recently, appears to be tainted as more and more cases reported in the media reveal how several judges are allured by money and other benefits.[16] Justice Dinakaran of India was accused of

---

[14] In a widely publicized case of the crushing of six people to death by a youth from high class (known as BMW case), speeding in his vehicle, two lawyers were found guilty of bribing a witness in a bid to acquit the perpetrator of the crime. See *Times of India*, 23 August 2008.

[15] The same Tommy siphoned off an estimated fortune of U.S. $ 800 million, and when summoned to the court, for formal inquiry, refused to attend, pleading ill-health.

[16] Recently the police of Uttar Pradesh, one of the states of India, has identified 34 sitting judges as involved in corruption. See *The Times of India*, 10 September, 2008.

alienating a large area of common land and his elevation as supreme court judge was stalled, thanks to the activism of public spirited persons.

## Corruption in Broader Context

The issue of corruption cannot and should not be treated as an isolated issue. Nor should it be approached simply as a moral issue. It should be viewed as part of the mode of governance and political praxis in any society. In many Asian countries there are quasi dictatorships. Genuine democracy creates condition for peace, justice and the attainment of common good. In Asia, political centralization and authoritarianism are often justified in the name of "harmony" as an Asian value, whereas often it serves as a means for circumventing the demands of justice.

Corruption is embedded in the functioning of a society and its roots go deep. Moral exhortations and prescriptions cannot claim to offer any viable solution to an ill of which corruption is but a symptom. The very air we breathe in the society and the environment we create – for which the entire society is responsible in various grades and degrees – contribute to the thriving of graft and corruption. Uprooting corruption, then, calls, first of all, for a more radical approach. It involves the active agency of the people themselves who have to deploy appropriate measures to stem the tide of growing corruption in our societies. Secondly, at the structural level, there should be a separation of the judiciary from the executive power, represented by the state and its organs. In many countries in Asia, this is precisely the problem. The state has turned the judiciary as one of its own organs. In this way, it ensures a practical immunity from indictment of any corruption or malpractice. A most glaring example in recent times is the suspension of the Chief Justice Muhammad Chaudhry, by the president of Pakistan.[17] It led to a constitutional crisis in that country for about four months with lawyers, politicians, journalists and public-spirited people agitating and demonstrating. This event demonstrated how crucial the independence of judiciary is for good governance.

---

[17] It is instructive to note that the chief justice acted in an independent manner and challenged the privatization of Pakistan Steel Mills to the benefits of business interests close to the government officials. He also took up the cases of "missing people" under the military rule, all of which drew the wrath of the president and state authorities.

### Corporate Governance – Ethical Issues

Till recent times, under governance was understood invariably and almost exclusively, the political governance and the main actor was the state, its bureaucracy and its various arms of execution. But with globalization and the proliferation of private enterprises, we speak today of corporate governance. Given the generally recognized crucial role of economy and political processes, it is of paramount importance to study the form of governance in the private and corporate sector that would contribute to the general welfare and common good.

If not out of conviction, at least out of external factors and pressures, there is increasing consciousness in the corporate world about ethical standards and the need for proper governance. These business enterprises claim to follow strict ethical practices in their governance. This is one way of protecting themselves from what they fear as the external interventions. But as a matter of fact, in the corporate world, corruption is deeply entrenched, contrary to its claim and the general impression.

Corporate governance should, in the first place, be checked by the state as to whether the pattern of governance in these companies and enterprises respond to ethical standards – in terms of the mode of investment (whether the investments made are ethically justifiable), in what concerns the mode of operation, in the treatment of the labour force, and finally as to what contribution they make to the society, especially to those who are in the immediate environment of the particular company or enterprise.

But as it happens, often, the public governance colludes with corporate governance, and that is when the environment is ripe for corrupt practices for mutual benefit at the cost of the public good and general welfare. That is reason enough why corporate governance cannot be left off the hook – so to say. Private enterprises can seduce the guardians of public good and welfare and cause public damage. It is possible that corrupt officials in public governance get hand in glove with the greedy in the corporate governance. As such the corporate governance cannot be viewed as simply a private affair, exempted from any outward intervention. That is why we my not today rely on the state to play any restraining or censuring role on the multinational companies and other national business enterprises.

Today, the corporate world of Asia should be brought under the scrutiny of the public. This has become increasingly important with growing privatization in Asian countries and with the flow and investment of foreign capitals. In most Asian countries, the aspiration to attract foreign investment and the fear that flight of capital may take place, leads the states to exempt these enterprises and companies from conforming to accepted ethical standards. Those in charge of public governance are supposed to be the guardians of public good. But *quis custodiet custodes*? (Who would guard the guards?).

## The Role of Media and General Public

One of the effective checks for governance is media which is said to be the fourth pillar of democracy (the others being the legislature, executive and judiciary). The same media today could play a very constructive role by exposing instances of corrupt practices of the politicians, bureaucrats and all those who form part of the governance. In a functioning democracy with the freedom of press, this has proved very helpful as many experiences show.[18] It is a fact that the centralized and authoritarian states of Asia happen to be also the most corrupt ones, the people being powerless to resist and at the mercy of the state and its organs. The process of democratization with the possibility for the people to check the functioning of the legislators, rulers, bureaucrats, police-force, and other constituents of the state is a force that can restrain the practice of corruption. A vigilant press and media that exposes corrupt practices and does investigative journalism could also be an important force in the fight against corruption.

But then we are in a situation in which we need to free the media itself for it to be able to play a positive role in terms of good governance. It often happens, as for example in Malaysia, that the media is controlled by a group of companies close to the political power as a result of which the instances and issues critical of the state or of the corporate world are covered-up, scuttling the possibility of public discussion and debate in the civil society. In fact, the Constitution and laws of many states have placed restrictions on the media on the plea of internal security, public order, morality, etc. Such a situation is an invitation for the citizens to fight for a free media as a control mechanism that will help create a good governance. Individual citizens are often powerless to challenge the state and its control of media. That is why strong social movements centred on particular issues affecting the people are required which will also embolden the media to bring into the open the mis-governance and corruption.

---

[18] For example, in India the corruption involved in defence deal was exposed by Telhelka.com on 13 March, 2001.

## Enactment of Legislations and Abolition of Laws

Another important means to check the mode of governance is to ensure that the elected legislators who make laws do not turn to be the violators of laws. In several democracies in Asia, as perhaps elsewhere in the world, there is a "criminalization of politics". The criminal elements with the power of money get elected as representative of the people and being in a position of governance means opportunity to accumulate wealth by bestowing favours against all laws and regulations. Therefore, it is crucial that there be a screening process before someone presents himself or herself as candidate to be elected.[19]And this screening would imply checking the assets of the candidate, and to see whether the person has any criminal background. It is also essential to have a ceiling on the money that could be spent for election campaign and to monitor whether it is observed. Such monitoring processes should be accompanied by continuous revision and when necessary abrogation of obsolete laws. For, every law becomes also an opportunity for personal gain and corrupt practices. The more these laws, like dead-woods, are shed off, the opportunities and chances for corruption also get reduced.

## Some Hurdles for People-Centred Governance

First of all with globalization and expansion of the corporate world, there is a tendency to adopt techno-managerial approach to the issues and problems of the society with the result that the political process is undermined. It is by participation and active involvement in a political process that people are able to challenge and check the state and its various executive arms.

A second issue is that of progressive marketisation of the state, by which is meant the fact that political governance is manipulated by the business interests to deflect it from its primary goal of attaining common good. With globalization and adoption of liberal capitalist economy in many states of Asia, including those which profess officially a socialist ideology (China, Vietnam, Myanmar, etc.), the efforts to bring about good governance becomes more complex and challenging.

Closely related to the above is the excessive reliance on experts. It may be true that matters of economy require expertise in the field. At the same time, the nature of economy and the way it functions is the concern

---

[19] This is one of the measures the Election Commission of India has taken to check on corruption.

of all the people. The claim that experts know better does not hold good here. The ill-effects of bad economy are best known to the ordinary people in everyday life; it pinches them. Therefore, it is only proper that the views and experience of the people are seriously taken into account in economic planning, without which there cannot be any good governance.

There is yet another hurdle which bears the traces of the past. Though the bureaucracy is supposed to be an advancement over the traditional "disorder" of society in that it brings order through rationality and application of standardized procedures,[20] in effect, bureaucracy in Asian societies has been transformed by the traditional patterns of behaviour. As a result, in many of our countries the relationship of the administrator or bureaucrats to the people is modeled on patron-client relationship. People are given the impression that they are passive recipients of the munificence of the bureaucrats who don the mantle of benefactors. The bureaucrats take refuge in anonymity which helps the thriving of corruption and nepotism.

Even when the elected representative would like to take up the cause of the people and the common welfare, a degenerated bureaucracy could stand in the way. With more information at their disposal, than what the peoples' representative may have, the bureaucrats can scuttle policies and programmes meant for the welfare of the people whom it is supposed to serve.

## Christianity and Good Governance in Asia
After our analysis and reflections on governance and corruption, we now turn to our Christian faith and ask what inspiration and praxis it could possibly offer to face the struggle of Asian societies for good and corruption-free governance.

Speaking of Christian contribution to good governance in Asia, we need to take note of two significant facts: First of all, most Asian countries were directly or indirectly ruled by colonial powers from the Christian West. Secondly, there is the fact that numerically Christians are a minority. Both these facts impinge upon any intervention of Christians in the political realm today. The first fact raises suspicion in the minds of our compatriots and a sense of fear about unwarranted political intervention, since Christians are often seen as "agents" and "stooges" of Western political powers, continuing the colonial legacy. A clear example is the case of China

---

[20] This is the view developed by Max Weber.

in its relationship to the Christian communities and to Vatican.[21] The fact of being a minority leaves the Christians with little influence on the political realm, in these days when numbers count in the political process. It also creates among the Christians a minority complex and a siege mentality.

Given this background, to what extent could the Christians participate and intervene in Asian societies for good and corrupt-free governance? In the first place, there are internal reasons that call for good governance. For many Christians good governance often amounts to a political situation where *religious freedom* is guaranteed, so that the Christian community could profess and practice its faith. But unfortunately, the situation in several countries is one of severe restriction on religious freedom. Sometimes, it goes to such an extent as in Vietnam that a bishop has to obtain permission from the state even to make a pastoral visit to any Christian community. There are discriminatory laws against minorities seriously affecting the Christian community. In other countries, there are cases of violent attack on the Christian mission-centres and institutions – as it happened recently in the state of Orissa in India – when the state was apathetic and did not respond adequately to protect the Christians. These are, obviously, matters of serious concern and are no sign of good governance. Necessary steps and strategies are to be devised to respond to such critical situations.

I think Christians should, however, go beyond these concerns and judge good and bad governance in terms of what it means to the larger community, and how this community, and especially its weaker ones, are affected. The denial of religious freedom is a clear sign of lack of democratic practice, which is a matter of general concern affecting every one, and not only an issue touching upon the Christian community. Taking such a broad outlook on governance is to give expression to the understanding of the Church as a sacrament in service of the entire humanity, and in our case to the peoples of Asia.

It is natural that one is bound to those who share the same faith, and have close affinity and tend to care for them. But the Gospel beckons us to act in surprising and unconventional ways; to go beyond the immediate circle and to reach out to the concerns of those who are beyond this circle. A Church oriented along these lines will take the sufferings caused to the people by undemocratic governance as its own. Intervention in the public

---

[21] Cf. Felix Wilfred – Edmond Tong – Georg Evers, "China and Christianity" *Concilium* 2009/2.

sphere from this perspective will lead to forging of solidarity with all the people in a society or in a country. Bishop Tutu or Bishop Belo (remarkably both Nobel prize winners for peace), were viewed as intervening in the public sphere in the name of peace and good governance, not primarily motivated by the plight of Christian community. They viewed the political situation in their respective countries as affecting the entire people. They acted as concerned citizens moved by the suffering of the people and inspired by faith and Christian vision. It is that which gave credibility to them and their political involvement. Again the struggle of the Korean people against authoritarian rule in 1980s was for the restoration of democracy for all the people of the country, and it was not motivated by what happened to Christians and Christian community. In short, I mean to say that the understanding of Christian faith and identity in Asia should be such that it enables the believers to act and intervene in the political processes, institutions and spaces for the cause of the common good, and good governance.

Asian Christians involving themselves in the struggle for good governance will find rich resources and inspiration in the Christian Scriptures and in numerous examples throughout Christian history.

### Checking the Governance – The Role of Prophets

Governance and kingship among the people of Israel in the Old Testament were different from the rest of the neighbouring peoples. The most distinctive character was precisely in that the governance in Israel was under censure and check, so that it does not go to excesses and betray the cause of the people whom the kingship in the name of God was to serve. Against the self-deception of the kings of Israel about their good governance, prophets raised their voice to tell about their miserable failure. To the despotic ways of the royalty and its presumption of a rule without end, Jeremiah responded saying that it is God who "builds, tears down and plucks up" (Jer 1:10). His prophetic vision did not permit him to get reconciled with the governance as it was; he instead, called for the projection of a different beginning and alternatives. Translating his prophetic vision into political terms, Jeremiah could warn about the threat from Babylon to the present rulers and their mis-governance. We could cite also many other examples from the other Old Testament prophets like Elijah who confronted the political powers of the kings of Israel.

Jesus' own attitude to the governance of his times was, obviously, not one of compliance to the existing order. He was both critical of the Jewish rulers (calling Herod a "fox"), and the gentile lords. He was aware of domination and misrule. "The kings of gentiles lord over them and those in authority over them are called benefactors" (Lk 22: 25-27). He took a distance from the Roman imperial rule, which, for him, could claim no absolute authority to rule. "Render to Caesar the things that are Caesar's, and to God, the things that are God's" (Mt 22: 17-21). He was very critical of the corrupt practices found in religious governance centred on the temple, which he also denounced (Mt 21: 10-17; Jn 2: 13-22). It is this Christian vision and heritage that inspired St John Chrysostom to challenge the misrule of his times and become a spokesperson of those who were unjustly dominated and oppressed. He paid the price by being sent into exile by the empress Eudoxia.

**Christian Foundation for Intervention in Favour of Good Governance**
In the Catholic tradition, the state is recognized as a divinely ordained and necessary institution since it offers the possibility to forge the kind of social ties and bonding necessary for the full development of human beings.[22] State and political governance are good in themselves as they have in their scope the wellbeing of the society and human beings, and they relate to the goodness of God's creation. This is something striking compared to the Lutheran conception of the state and governance where the perspective of sin and death dominate. The state is viewed as an institution that has more a preventive role – it is there so as to ensure that

---

[22] Cf. *Gaudium et Spes* no. 25. We need to take note of the fact that in Catholic social teaching there has taken place an important shift in the understanding of the state and its role. The earlier teachings by Leo XIII and Pius XI spoke of the state, using the metaphor of human body. The individuals play different roles in the organic body; so too the employer and employee in the world of labour contributing to the wellbeing of the body. But *Gaudium et Spes* moves away from this analogy and views society more as a *community* in which individuals with all their potentialities participate and interact freely for the common good. This orientation is taken further in *Octogesima Adveniens*. "Political power... is the natural and necessary link for insuring the cohesion of the social body...To take politics seriously...is to affirm the duty of the individual, of every individual, to recognize the concrete reality and the value of the freedom of choice that is offered to the human being to seek to bring about both the good of the city and of the nation and of humankind...The passing to the political dimension also expressed a demand made by the people of today: a greater sharing in responsibility and in decision making" (*Octogesima Adveniens* nos. 46-47).

sinful human beings do not kill one another. In short it is a coercive power meant to create order, and prevent chaos.

The positive Catholic outlook on state acknowledges many important roles for it, as for example the defence of justice, and providing of all the necessary means for human wellbeing such as education, health-care, etc. Equally important is that the political governance is directed to the attainment of common good. If common good is basically the goal of governance, then, this cannot be attained by the state alone. For, the good of the society does not overlap with the goals of the state, which is at once an affirmation of the role of other actors for the wellbeing of the society as well as recognition of the limits of the state.[23] Therefore, it is extremely important that, the state be constantly in dialogue with other bodies and institutions (cultural, religious, non-governmental organizations, social movements, etc.) which attend to those dimensions of life that go beyond the confines of the state and its operation.[24] In this way, governance becomes a dialogical praxis, which also guards against any totalitarian trend that annuls the space for the various actors – civil society, non-governmental organizations, media, etc. These too have important roles to play for common good.

In Asia we need to go even beyond the common good approach which presupposes that all citizens are endowed with equal rights. That is not

---

[23] In Catholic teaching, this concern has been expressed through the "principle of subsidiarity". In *Quadragesimo Anno*, Pius XI explained it this way: "One should not withdraw from individuals and commit to the community what they can accomplish by their own enterprise and industry. So, too, it is an injustice and at the same time a grave evil and a disturbance of right order to transfer to the larger and higher collectivity functions which can be performed and provided for by lesser and subordinate bodies" (no, 79).

[24] In fact in the definition of *Commission on Global Governance*, Oxford University Press, Oxford, 1995, this aspect of dialogue is expressed when it states: "Governance is the sum of many ways individuals and institutions, public and private, manage their common affairs. It is a continuing process through which conflicting and diverse interests may be accommodated, and cooperative action may be taken. It includes formal regimes empowered to enforce compliance, as well as informal arrangements that people and institutions either have agreed to, or have perceived to be in their interest". See also *Governance for Sustainable Human Development*, UNDP, New York, 1997; OECD, *Participatory Development and Good Governance*, Paris, 1995; Haq Mehbub ul, *Human Development in South Asia: The Crisis of Governance*, Human Development Centre, Oxford University Press, Oxford, 1999.

always the case. In a situation in which a lot of migrants, refugees, and stateless people are marginalized; the minorities – religious, linguistic, ethnic etc. – are denied full rights; many groups such as the Dalits do not have equal citizenship, we need to take an approach that will render justice and equality to all these groups as an important responsibility of the state. This needs to be reflected in the policies and programmes of its governance. In this case, a mere citizen's approach to governance is inadequate. At this point, the Christians will find a convergence of the demand of their faith to opt for the poor and the responsibility of the state to render justice to the disfranchised and subaltern groups, through policy and programmes of inclusion. Viewing the role of the state and governance in this way is to go beyond the liberal view of the state as simply the protector of the autonomy of the individual and as guardian of the public order. In this context, we may recall here that *Rerum Novarum* had already underlined the responsibility of the state, going beyond political liberalism. Leo XIII noted that, "Whenever the general interest of any particular class suffers, or is threatened with evils which can in no other way be met, the public authority must step in to meet them".[25]

A further important aspect derives from the economic liberal policies of most Asian countries today. Under neo-liberal economic policies, many Asian states are withdrawing from several areas (education, health-care, subsidies for the poor, etc.) of public life for which they felt responsible. This leaves the workers for example at the mercy of the employers who can at will hire and fire. But the state cannot exempt itself from responsibility towards the workers. For, as John Paul II observed, there is something like "indirect employer" of which the state is an important factor. This applies as well in the question of unemployment.[26] The relationship in the world of labour is to be viewed from a larger perspective involving serious responsibility on the part of the state.

---

[25] *Rerum Novarum* no. 28.

[26] "In order to meet the danger of unemployment and to insure employment for all, the agents defined here as "indirect employer" must make provision for overall planning with regard to the different kinds of work by which not only the economic life, but also the cultural life of a given society is shaped: they must also give attention to organizing that work in a correct and rational way"

## Christian Pedagogy and Governance

In these times when through globalization and neo-liberal economic domination, more and more techno-managerial approach is being adopted, it is highly important that we emphasize the role of political processes for the welfare of society in justice and without exclusion. We can understand the difficulty of putting this into practice especially in countries under centralized rules and with repression of religious liberty. However, it appears to me that this is the direction we need to move. In fact recent history tells us that believers motivated for the public cause and who help the society organize itself have been one of the important forces in challenging the claims of totalitarianism and dehumanizing governance. These experiences should serve as inspiration for interventions on the part of Christians who require appropriate political education.

The immense importance of good governance and political intervention calls for imparting a new orientation to the various activities of the Asian Churches. A culture of participation in political processes should be inculcated among the believers right from the beginning of their Christian formation. The fact that in several Asian countries, the local Churches run educational institutions at all levels, offers unique opportunities for imparting education for political participation and critical approach to governance. A proper political education of Christians will be a great contribution to good governance and a bulwark against the creeping of corruption in public life. It would appear, not much has been done in this direction. One reason is that, with its minority complex, the local Churches prefer to act all by themselves, and do not feel the need to interact with the public sphere – something which contributes to even greater alienation of the Christian community from the context.

## Conclusion: The Witnessing Value of Governance in the Church

We may produce in the Church excellent ideas regarding governance and fight against corruption. But the litmus test of these ideas is in the self-critique the Church makes on this point, which has a lot more witnessing potential than all the ideas it has generated and its moral prescriptions to society.

In a world of corruption and misrule, the most effective witness the Asian Churches could give is to subject themselves to critical scrutiny. The Church cannot exempt itself from such a scrutiny under the pretext that what applies to the larger society does not apply to itself. It is something like saying that the general principles of hermeneutics does not apply to the Bible, a position that could easily land in fundamentalism. Failure to subject its practices and mode of governance for public scrutiny is against basic principles of ethics and will only foster authoritarianism and arbitrariness in the Church. The Asian Churches have to rid off the many inherited Western feudal traces of governance to be found in its institutions, laws and practices, and become an engaged participant in the political histories of Asian societies.

# Chapter 7

# Christianity and Global Democratic Process

*"I am not the evangelizer of democracy: I am the evangelizer of the Gospel. To the Gospel message, of course, belong all the problems of human rights; and if democracy means human rights, it also belongs to the message of the Church."*
- John Paul II [1]

**D**emocracy has established itself in the general consciousness of humanity as an irrefutable standard of human conduct to such an extent that even the most authoritarian regimes wear a democratic mask, and the barbarous dictators love to march beneath the banner of democracy. However, the truth is that we are in a period in which less than half of the world is on the democratic path, and even where democracy seems to exist, it is in deep crisis.

There are many signs that point to a critical situation of democracy as a mode of governance. To name a few, people have become political spectators than active participants, a sign of which is the dwindling number of people exercising their franchise in different parts of the world; the elected representatives betray the cause of the people they claim to represent, through scandalous corruption and graft; there is then the sinister intervention of global power structures and rapacious economic interests which render democracy in many cases a sham. And finally there has taken place "A Structural Transformation of the Public Sphere"[2] - the

---

[1] At a press conference on his flight to South America in 1987.
[2] Jürgen Habermas, *The Structural Transformation of the Public Sphere,* The MIT Press, Cambridge, 1989.

public sphere or civil society so very crucial for sustaining democracy. The public sphere is hijacked by the state; the market and media offer the people the palliative of consumerism to anesthetize them from active political participation.[3] To wrap it up, think of the new generations of 300 million Chinese between 20 – 29 years whose income has increased 34% in the last three years; democracy is, perhaps, the last thing that can warm up their hearts![4]

We also need to take note of the fact that in the post 9/11 world of today, democracy is converted into an ideological weapon in the battle against terrorism. While terrorism continues to spread its tentacles all over the world, the most important point is that democracy as a system of governance is bound to fail unless it is accompanied by a democratic vision and spirit. A system imbued by the spirit and vision of democracy will attend first and foremost to the creation of a just order, the precondition for sustaining democracy. Democracy in its turn will be an instrument for the establishment of justice, and not a coercive means (ironical enough!) in the hands of the empire.

The importance of religious roots for democratization comes out in one of the major insights of Alexis de Tocqueville. In the mid-nineteenth century he made an interesting point of comparison between the French and American tradition of democracy. Whereas, the French revolution ended up in terror, counter-revolution and establishment of despotism, the American revolution, according to him, succeeded establishing democracy because, it still retained the religious foundation for human equality while this had disappeared in the case of French revolution.[5] This connection to religious tradition – in this case Christianity – could be

---

[3] There is, of course, an idealization of European bourgeois public sphere of eighteenth and nineteenth centuries in the thought of Habermas. It has little to say about plebeian forms of debate, nor women's forms of discourses, not to say about the absence of the way public sphere has been experienced and lived among non-western peoples. It only confirms the male euro-centric view of the public sphere in Habermas' thought. Nevertheless there is a general point of validity, that is, the importance of debate, discourses and discussions, which, however, may not be exaggerated.

[4] Simon Elegant, "China's Me Generation. The New Middle Class - Young, Rich and Happy - Just Don't Mention Politics", in *Time*, August 6, 2007, pp. 22-27.

[5] Cf. Alexis de Tocqueville, *Democracy in America*, Wordsworth Edition, Hertfordshire, 1998 (original French edition appeared in 1835).

revisited in the new democratic wave experienced in different countries of the world.

## Christian Influence on Modern Political Process

Modern political ordering mirrors the nature of a machine. The democratic machinery has routine elections, representation, formation of political parties, etc. "The booth in which we deposit our ballots is unquestionably too small, for this booth has room for only one".[6] With this incisive statement Hannah Arendt underlined the limits of a mechanical type of representative democracy. What is lacking today is the spirit of democracy and the conditions necessary for sustaining it. Like in the case of revolution, democracy by itself does not constitute an answer to the question of human governance, unless it is accompanied by participation by the people facilitated through various structures and means at the grassroots.

Could Christianity and religion in general contribute to the sustaining of democracy and peoples' participation? In what ways could Christianity be participant in the present-day democratic process, and contribute to the creation of democratic structures and to democratic spirit? Where does Christianity stand vis-à-vis the challenges of democracy today, and what has it to offer to the process of democratization?

Such questions are to be raised in the global context today. For skeptics and hard-core secularists what happened in recent decades in Spain, Brazil, Chile, South Africa, Malawi, Nicaragua, Poland, Lithuania, Philippines, South Korea, East Timor, etc., could not but evoke disbelief. Religion, specifically Christianity, seems to have played a crucial role in creating some of the conditions for the emergence of democracy. More specifically, Samuel Huntington points out that, out of the thirty countries that have transited to the democratic path between 1974-1990, three-quarters were predominantly Catholic.[7]

What is proving a great support to democratization is the way Christianity is lived at grassroots level. The model of Basic Christian Communities and groups, for example, has significance not only for promoting a participatory and vibrant Christian living; it has also larger political import. We need to take into account the fact that many Christian grassroots groups refuse to uncritically conform to the state and its goals.

---

[6] Hannah Arendt, *Crises of the Republic*, Harcourt Brace Jovanovich, New York, 1972, p. 232.

[7] Cf. Samuel Huntington, *The Third Wave: Democratization in the Late Twentieth Century*, University of Oklahoma Press, Norman, 1991, p. 76.

They engage themselves for the defence of human rights. The Basic Christian Communities and groups could serve as an important means for the practice of democracy at grassroots level and could become a means to check the abuse of power. In fact, wherever there has been a prophetic challenge by Christians to the abuse of power, we could identify grassroots Christian activism. Here in fact Christianity would find firmer roots of a Gospel-approach to democracy than what liberal democracy has to offer. In fact, one of the crises of democracy is that the roots of democracy in liberalism, the dominant ideology that associates democracy with itself, are too weak to sustain it, calling for firmer foundations.

### Ambiguity of Christianity vis-à-vis Democracy

In re-conceptualizing the connection between Christianity and democracy we can learn a lot from history. On the one hand, history of Christianity shows that its practices were, by and large, against the spirit of democracy as it was deeply entrenched in the hierarchical mode of thinking. On the other hand, the spirit of democracy, participation, solidarity, etc, especially as it was lived in early centuries, energize Christian message. There is then an ambiguity that surrounds Christianity regarding its position towards democracy. In spite of the many seeds and resources of democracy enshrined in the Christian vision, it is the hierarchical and centralized mode of governance that has dominated Christian history. Christianity in its spirit, vision and inspiration is truly democratic. Unfortunately, this lofty ideal so intimately connected with Christianity was lost during the Enlightenment, which, while extolling democracy, created an antithetical position between Christianity and democracy. This was possible because the historical praxis of Christianity went more in support of monarchy, hierarchy and other modes of governance than democracy. Small wonder, then, that emperors and dictators from Constantine to Salazar and Franco could invoke Christianity in support of their regimes; and Catholic Christianity in modern times could sign with ease concordats with fascist governments in Italy and Germany.

At the ideological level, one could see at work political Augustinianism – the subjugation of the earthly city to the City of God, which has contributed to the development of theocratic tendencies in the Christian history – tendencies that served as a reactionary force in the face of the emergence of sovereign states and democracy in the secular realm.[8] In

---

[8] We should acknowledge the contribution of dissenting thinkers like Marsilio of Padua who foresaw the importance of Church-state separation, which has

short, Christianity is a confusing signal: its one hand is stretched in the direction of democracy, while the other hand is raised towards hierarchy, centralization and authoritarianism. This contradiction will get enacted throughout history including in the Reformation tradition. For, while Luther tried to establish that common person is sovereign in the religious realm that cannot be controlled by religious mediators and alleged representatives of God, ironically, he could ally himself with despotic princes against the people and the peasants, and these princes he thought, were not accountable to people but only to God.

To put forth the matter differently, we could identify two broad streams in the relationship of Christianity to democracy: First of all there is the early Christian democratic surge. We have here a conception of society based on diversity of talents, charisms, and working together for the welfare of the community. This conception of society is basically democratic in nature and spirit. Secondly, there has also been an authoritarian and centralized scheme of spiritual totalitarianism. It has been a force against the development of democracy. This has taken place through a misrepresentation of the idea of representation. The claim of office-holders in the Church that they are representatives of God, Christ, etc. has led to absolutization of power, whereas this should have precisely done the opposite – relativization of power. In other words, the sovereignty of God which should remind us about the relativity of all human enterprises, paradoxically, is exploited to claim absolute power as invested in human representatives. This is what has happened in the course of Christian history. Such a position was philosophically challenged through the Enlightenment and the political theory of democracy. What resulted was a false conflict between a theological orientation based on the idea of divine representation and a philosophical conception of democracy – representation of the people.

## Democratization as De-absolutization of Every Power
Today we need to challenge the conception of representation as a means of absolutization on the one hand, and to imbue democracy with spiritual

---

proved important for a healthy functioning of democracy. On the other hand, Pope Innocent X condemned in the strongest terms the system of sovereign states resulting from 1648 Peace of Westphalia. This settlement was for him "null, void, invalid, iniquitous, unjust, damnable, reprobate, inane, empty of meaning and effect of all time". As quoted in Daniel Philipott, "*The Catholic Wave*", in Larry Diamond et al. (eds), *World Religions and Democracy*, The John Hopkins University Press, Baltimore-London, 2005, p.103.

élan, on the other. In fact what democracy does is to say that the idea of representation is relative to the people. But democracy could produce the opposite effect if it absolutizes the conception of representation. Then it would cease to be democracy. In the Christian vision, the democratic impulse is ingrained in the fact that all powers are relativized in relation to the sovereignty of God on the one hand, and in relation to the creation of human community in freedom and fellowship, on the other.

Relativization of power that should be inherent in every form of human governance, is, at least in principle, ensured in the democratic system. Foremost example is the means democracy offers for the transfer of power. In other systems, transfer of power does not voluntarily take place (as in the case of totalitarianism, dictatorship, etc.), or is limited to the family or clan as in the case of monarchy, or could take place only through violent revolution with disastrous consequences. Democracy affirms the truth that power is relative, time-bound and that no human being can hold on to power without limits in terms of extent of power and the period of holding power. In other words, democracy is a challenge to stagnation of power and stands for its circularity. The time-bound character of office of governance brings out the fact that power returns through circularity back to the people who put it into effect by choosing anew those who would represent them. In this way, democracy creates a system which reflects Christian vision of power that has transcendent roots. "You have authority only because it was given to you by God" (Jn 19: 11); the representatives have power in a democracy only because the people gave it – and the voice of the people is the voice of God (*vox populi vox Dei*).

Relativization of power, which democracy ideally represents, also finds expression in the division of power exercised by different agents: legislative, executive and judicial power. It is authoritarianism when all these are conflated and is vested with a single agent. This separation of power which is absent in every absolutist form of power is a very central feature of governance in democracy. In these ways, checks and balances are built into the democratic system that can prevent abuse of power and exploitation of the people. The original Christian vision and practice was greatly attuned to division of power in as much as the various services in the Church-community in the early period of Christianity were exercised by a variety of offices – something which kept the community healthy. (1Cor 12:4ff). One of the most important form of power was the power to govern and organize community (Ex 18:13-27; Deut 1:9-18) which was not identified with the power of teaching which had its own distinctive features and autonomy. Unfortunately, in the course of time there came about a concentration of power in one single office which paved the way also to de-democratization in the Church.

A Christian ideal that has immense consequence for the democratic mode of governance is the thought that any form of authority is *service* to the community. In the same vein, as servants those who govern the community representing the people in a democracy have the obligation to render account to the people; the people on their part are to demand that their representatives are transparent and they provide them all necessary knowledge and informations. The right of the people for information in all the things that concern them, is an indispensable means today to hold in check any abuse of power.

**Tall Platonic Claims**

"The democratic impulse bursts forth as a temporal manifestation of the inspiration of the Gospel".[9] This is how Jacques Maritain relates Christianity to democracy. His approach suffers from a certain Platonic idealism in that he relates both these realities in their ideal forms and does not pay attention to the interplay of these two realities in the course of history. What he has to say about historical realization remains on the level of idealism: The failure of democracy is attributed to the departure from faith and the teachings of the Church.[10] He tends to attribute to Christianity a credit that history defies to support in the manner he presents. It may not be correct to say that Maritain makes any identification between democracy and Christianity – something difficult to maintain in the light of his overall thought that Christianity cannot be subsumed under any one particular political form, since it transcends all of them. What he endeavours to say is that democracy is the form of governance to which Christianity has closest affinity, which dovetails with his vision of a Christian humanism. However, the reasons he adduces for this are far from satisfactory today, and this point needs to be rethought.

At any rate, Maritain's position cannot be invoked today in support of right-wing conservative Christian posture which maintains that

---

[9] Jacques Maritain, *Christianity and Democracy*, The Centenary Press, London, 1945, p. 38. "Not only does the democratic state of mind proceed from the inspiration of the Gospel, but it cannot exit without it", *Ibid*. p. 39.

[10] The importance of Maritain's thoughts derives also because of the great influence of his thought on Pope Paul VI and John Paul II.

democracy needs Christianity.[11] We could sense here a nostalgia for the medieval Christendom. Today, the connection between Christianity and democracy should be re-conceptualized and worked out along different lines than what such neo-conservative positions seem to maintain. Let us take the example of post-communist Poland. In this country where almost the entire population is Catholic, there did not come into existence any Christian Democratic party. For the conditions under which Christian democratic parties appeared in Western Europe have vastly changed, and they do not apply to post-socialist Poland. However, the Church played in Poland and in many parts of the world the role of civil society, since it was absent in these countries. Christianity could stand up to totalitarian and apartheid regimes in the erstwhile East Germany and South Africa, and trigger democratic waves. The witness of the Church and its support to democracy will be greater, and the impact stronger if such interventions of the Church were to challenge the undemocratic regimes and power in the name of a different set of values than motivations connected with the survival of the Church.

### Christianity and Global Roots of Democracy

There are two myths making the round in the world: the first is that rationality is the monopoly of the Western tradition, and the second myth is that democracy is the creation of the Western culture. There is no need to go into the Euro-centrism of such views. What I am concerned here is the danger of making the connection of Christianity to democracy through the Greek tradition. There is hardly a book written in the West on democracy that does not speak of democracy as originating from the Greeks, in spite of the blatant fact that the Greek city-states where "democracy" is supposed to have originated, practiced slavery, and women were excluded from participation and deliberations for the common good. My suggestion is that with such exclusion, the political governance the Greeks practiced be called by some other name than democracy.

We rather begin the connection between Christianity and democracy by referring to the global roots of democracy. Freed from the Greek straight jacket, Christianity will be open to enter into dialogue and interaction with the rich democratic traditions among the different peoples of the earth and will contribute to strengthen and promote the local democratic practices

---

[11] Such seems to be the position of George Weigel, Joseph Weber and others.

and traditions. These traditions can be identified in Asia, Africa and among the indigenous peoples of America, Oceania, and elsewhere.

Moreover, ethnic, gender and cultural differences have introduced new dimensions to democracy which can redeem it from homogenization and from the danger of universalizing a cultural specific Western form of democracy. For example, the *Sangha*[12] (the Buddhist local community) is much more radical and closer to present-day ideal of democracy than the Athenian "democracy" (which, as we saw, forbade women and slaves from participation), since *Sangha* made no distinction between gender, class or race – women as much as men, "Untouchables" as much as Brahmins, peasants as much as princes  could participate and contribute to common deliberation  in the *Sangha* on equal basis. This, as His Holiness Dalai Lama explains, is due to the equality of all human beings Buddhism recognizes.

> As a Buddhist monk, I do not find alien the concept and practice of democracy. At the heart of Buddhism lies the idea that the potential for awakening and perfection is present in every human being and that realizing this potential is a matter of personal effort. The Buddha proclaimed that each individual is a master of his or her own destiny, highlighting the capacity that each person has to attain enlightenment. Like Buddhism, modern democracy is based on the principle that all human beings are essentially equal ...[13]

As what concerns democratic procedures, we have the examples of Buddhist councils through the centuries which stand as a symbol for consensus-building and resolving disputes through discussions and deliberations.

### Democracy, Totalitarianism and Capitalism – Closure and Openness to the Future

An important connection between democracy and Christianity is given in the fact that democracy, unlike totalitarianism, is open to the future. Totalitarianism represents a closure. Contemporary interpretations of capitalism seem to have assumed the ideological closure similar to that of

---

[12] Cf. Kirti Bunchua, "Buddhism and Democracy", in Waang Miao Yang et al. (eds.), *Civil Society in a Chinese Context*, The Council for Research in Values and Philosophy, Washington, 1997, pp. 95-103.

[13] His Holiness the Dalai Lama, "Buddhism, Asian Values and Democracy", in Larry Diamond et al. (eds.), *op.cit.*, pp. 70-71.

totalitarianism.[14] It is not becoming of the spirit of democracy to claim that it could answer all human problems the way totalitarianism and capitalism do. In this sense, capitalism is in reality closer to totalitarianism than to democracy. Democracy is the creation of an environment or climate in which the flourishing of the individual and of groups is enabled by keeping open alternatives and hitherto unexplored future possibilities. It is precisely here we are able to find affinity between the spirit of Christianity and of democracy.

To put it differently, democracy would represent the secular version of what is intended by the "eschatological reserve" that is not exhausted in any single form of human organization or arrangement as the ultimate. One of the deeply embedded human instincts is to seek security in something definite for which people are often ready to surrender their freedom, and that explains the allurement of totalitarianism. But Christianity has often raised its voice against such an impulse in the name of God and God's absolute sovereignty pointing to the Kingdom of God which cannot be embodied in any particular historical realization. It is closely allied to Jesus' programme of de-divinizing Caesar and relativizing all powers: "Give unto Caesar what is Caesar's and to God what is God's..." (Mt 22:21). There is a realm of life that goes beyond the confines of Caesar's empire. Following the path of Jesus closely, early Christianity challenged the divinity of the ruler and the absolute sovereignty of the state. The concept of sovereignty of God has a deconstructing and prophetic impact: It de-absolutizes any claim of power and shows that human power and its exercise is relative.

A second area of affinity between the ideals of Christianity and Democracy could be identified in the promotion of pluralism as the guarantee for a secure-human-future. Even though a liberal interpretation of democracy may make us doubt how in practice democracy stands for pluralism, at least in principle, this mode of governance is attuned to fostering pluralism than all other modes of governance. Whereas in certain regimes of governance as for example the imperial mode, plurality has been tolerated,[15] in democracy, pluralism becomes a legitimate right and not a concession for the sake of political expediency or for other considerations.

---

[14] Cf. Francis Fukuyama, *The End of History and the Last Man*, Avon Books, New York, 1997.

[15] Cf. Michael Walzer, *On Toleration*, Yale University, New York, 1997.

Speaking of pluralism, one of the important concerns of democracy should be to safeguard the interest of minorities. In these times when minorities have become a sensitive global issue, it will be the Christian contribution to give such a turn to democracy that it becomes an instrument for the protection of minorities. For, there is a certain weakness in the democratic system, which was very well formulated by Rousseau:

> It may be asked how a man can be at once free and forced to conform to wills which are not his own. How can the opposing minority be both free and subject to laws to which they have not consented?[16]

If majoritarianism is democracy, then, Christianity would be totally alien to democracy. For, Christianity understands its task as the protection of the small, the weaker one, and the powerless minority groups. Hence it would be the Christian task to challenge the "tyranny of majority". The issue becomes even more serious in the case of permanent minorities as are small ethnic groups and identities in a nation-state. There is the need to respond in a concrete way at the local level to the protection of the powerless minority groups and their legitimate political expressions. This has a lot of relevance for Asian societies.

It is easy to see why today Christianity in its contribution to democracy should attend to the representation of minorities. This reflects the need of the hour in a world where the demographic composition of societies, as in Asia, is made up of many ethnic groups, cultural groups, etc., due to fast mobility, migration, etc. In fact, the crisis and failure of democracy has much to do with the approach to the question of minorities.

The principle of pluralism could be safeguarded by overcoming the trivialization of democracy into the rule of the majority and perpetual subjugation of ethnic and linguistic minorities to the will of the majority. The limitation of majority and minority categories was brought out in a lighter vein by Annadurai. Responding to the argument that Hindi should be the national language because it is spoken by the majority, he said that it is like arguing that crow is to be our national bird and rat our national animal, because they are in majority compared to peacock or tiger![17] Majoritarian argument contradicts the spirit of democracy.[18] Ultimately,

[16] Jean Jacques Rousseau, *The Social Contract*, Penguin Books, Harmondsworth, 1968, p. 153.

[17] Cf R. Kannan, *Anna: Life and Times of Anna*, C.N. Annadurai, Penguin, Delhi, 2010.

[18] Cf. Neera Chandhoke, *Beyond Secularism. The Rights of Religious Minorities*, Oxford University Press, Delhi, 1999.

the spirit of unity in plurality should inspire true democratic way of life in any society. Here, early Christianity offers rich resources to legitimate and support democracy as a symbol of life together in the spirit of unity in diversity (1Cor 12: 4-6; 10:17). "There is neither Jew, nor Greek, male or female ..." (Gal 3:28). We also notice in early Christianity there was a principled openness to share material resources with other communities at the time of need. Unfortunately, not enough has been done to develop this theological motive in relation to contemporary global democratic struggles.

### Reshaping Democracy as the Way to Justice

What is not often sufficiently realized is that inequality undermines democracy. As Charles Tilly notes with reference to South Africa,

> Social inequality impedes democratization and undermines democracy under two conditions: first, the crystallization of continuous differences (such as those that distinguish you from your neighbour) into everyday categorical differences by race, gender, class, ethnicity, religion, and similar broad groupings; second, the direct translation of these categorical differences into public policies. Before the 1990s, the South African regime not only fostered crystallization of everyday differences by what is treated as "race" into massive material inequalities, but it also built those distinctions directly into political rights and obligations.[19]

Liberalism promises freedom and political choices. But what does that mean in the face of persisting race and gender inequalities? Capitalism is able to create the impression that it is allied to democracy by making it appear that it enables freedom. In fact, it creates inequalities that ultimately threaten democratic governance, in which case capitalism takes refuge and thrives under the wings of dictatorship and authoritarianism – which is probably its real place.

Democratization is not a linear process, but has ups and downs, and the movement with greater democratization is inevitably related to creation of the conditions for social and economic equality, whereas de-democratization process is bound up with the absence of such conditions. One such crucial condition is the access to economic and cultural resources and distribution of opportunities across ethnic, cultural and gender divide. In the present circumstances, a chief contribution of Christianity for the

---

[19] Charles Tilly, *Democracy*, Cambridge University Press, Cambridge, 2007, p. 110.

democratic process will be to create such conditions for the emergence and nurturing of democracy. Reshaping democracy as a means of justice would imply that the representatives in democratic governance will not represent the people in a neutral way. All of them, independently from which constituency or group they are elected, ought to represent the poor by foregrounding the welfare of the weaker and marginalized ones. Christian approach to democracy cannot but be consonant with the heart of the Gospel – God's love and concern for the poor. The spirit of the Gospel can inspire and help us in transforming democracy from a mechanical representation, to a mode of governance in which all the representatives become representatives of the poor and of the weaker ones in society.

History attests to the fact that the poor are not the cause for authoritarianism and de-democratization; quite the contrary. De-democratization has resulted through the manipulation of the elites, the powerful and the affluent. Today, those who are most passionately concerned about democracy are the Dalits ("Untouchables") of India,[20] the masses of the rural China, the excluded and powerless ethnic minorities, the indigenous peoples in different parts of the globe. In the case of India and China,

> pressures for democratization understood to mean voice and demand for expanded power and rights for rural producers, and changing social structure, including class, caste, ethnic and gender relations...[T]he specific gravity of population in both nations remains the countryside, as evident in rural unrest and discontent, because the problems of development and democracy are most intractable there and because we discern important changes underway there that affect national as well as global dynamics.[21]

Therefore, Christian stance with the poor and their aspirations is also a stance for democracy; and alliance with the elites in whichever form, risks Christianity and exposes it to be supporter of authoritarian regimes.

---

[20] Cf. Felix Wilfred, *Dalit Empowerment*, ISPCK, Delhi, 2007 (2nd edition); Jeffrey N. Wasserstrom – Elizabeth J. Perry (eds.), *Popular Protest and Political Culture in Modern China*, Westview Press, Boulder – San Francisco – Oxford, 1994 (2nd edition).

[21] Manoranjan Mohanty – Mark Selden, "Reconceptualising Local Democracy. Reflections on Democracy, Power and Resistance in Indian and Chinese Countryside", in Manoranjan Mohanty et al. (eds.), *Grassroots Democracy in India and China*, Sage Publications, Delhi, 2007, pp. 459-477.

Option for the poor has then a democratic implication. Justice and the cause of the poor are defended more effectively through enabling their participation in the specific local context.

## For a Culture of Democracy

The importance of a culture of democracy derives from the fact that it is not always smooth sailing. Often it is a sailing in rough waters. Therefore, unless there is a culture anchored in democracy, it can easily fall prey to authoritarianism.

> The prospects of a stable democracy in a country are improved, if its citizens and leaders strongly support democratic ideas, and practices. The most reliable support comes when these beliefs and predispositions are embedded in the country's culture and get transmitted, in large part, from one generation to the next. In other words, the country possesses a democratic political culture.[22]

What Christianity could do is to create a culture, an ambience where democracy could bloom. It could make alive the spiritual vision of the prophets of the Old Testament who were the most passionate critics of a political order (monarchy and theocracy) that fed on the people and forgot their interests. Jesus' own vision is a powerful stimulus for the ideals democracy stands for. The Council of Jerusalem (Acts 15) and councils of early Church were participatory processes of decision-making and resolving conflicts. Historically, it is the prophetic vision and Jesus' life - not the Athenian democracy, nor the Renaissance city-states - that inspired Christians of dissenting tradition (Marsilius of Padua, Savonarola, Arnold of Brescia, Anabaptists, Quakers and others) to challenge powers and dominations, and stimulate the lower strata of the society to struggle for democratic revolution.[23]

Infusing the democratic system with such ideals is an arduous task. It calls for the cultivation of a spirituality of democracy. For in depth the struggle for democracy is a spiritual struggle. It implies the acceptance of the other – individual and collective – as participants in the same journey, the practice of just relationships and placing of the common good over the allurement of selfishness. The democratic path is an arduous one because a person has to be constantly politically active and vigilant,

---

[22] Robert Dhal, *Democracy*, Yale University Press, 1998, p. 157.

[23] Cf. John de Gruchy, *Christianity and Democracy: A Theology for a Just World Order*, Cambridge University Press, Cambridge, 1995, pp. 57 ff.

compared to the easy path of surrendering one's will and freedom to the will of a despot who could claim authority even in the name of God. When Churches live in the spirit of participation at the level of local communities, they create democratic vibration in the society, and are able to contribute for the transformation of society along democratic lines.

## Vulnerability of Democracy and the Spectre of Reversals

We need a culture and spirituality of democracy also because history teaches us how vulnerable democracy is, and how it is constantly under threat of reversals. Monarchy, theocracy, dictatorship, and other similar forms of governance appear to give a sense of security, resoluteness and stability. Compared to the impression these evoke, democracy is a poor competitor. Instead of robustness, democracy exhibits grievous vulnerability. The leftist or rightist forces could take it over easily, as the pre-War Weimar experiment of democracy in Germany showed. In such situations, Churches too, in order to defend their interests, easily toe the line of dictatorship instead of supporting democracy in spite of its vulnerability. There have been so many examples of this kind not only in Europe but also in Latin America.

The likelihood of stable democracy in the developing world is thought to be less compared to the West – which, because it is developed, has to be necessarily also democratic – so it is assumed. When there have been Fascism and Nazism not too long ago in the European continent, what guarantee is there that democracy will be stable in the West and not in other places? Ultimately, what underlies such a view is the connection between market and democracy. Because market has found success in the West, it is assumed that democracy is stable. For many, success is the unexpressed criterion for the triumph of democracy. To rely on market as the guarantor of democracy is tantamount to appoint a burglar as the night watch of one's home! If Christianity wants to free itself from its traditional euro-centrism, the approach to democracy should reflect the universal character the Church claims. It should, as I noted earlier, build on global roots of democracy.

We should get rid of the static picture of democracy as something achieved once and for all, and not divide the world and its nations on this presupposition. A more dynamic and realistic view would be to consider that there are both processes of democratization and de-democratization in every nation and society in varying degrees. How could a country be considered democratic when it refuses citizenship to immigrants, flouting all international norms, and takes only narrow chauvinistic ethnic-national considerations into account? These nations of the West through their brazen anti-humanistic immigration policies miserably fail against an important criterion of democracy, namely inclusion. Here we have a trend of de-democratization. Therefore, there is always a mixture of both democratic aspirations on the one hand and forces of de-democratization in every society.[24] It is the duty of every Christian to augment the democratic process in one's nation while fighting against the process of de-democratization. All this has rich lessons for Christians involving themselves in the Asian public sphere.

The history of a country like France illustrates very clearly, how the path of democracy is full of reversals. Democracy is a continuous struggle, and there is no guarantee that it is not reversible. The spectre of reversal threatens every democracy and dangers could develop from within with changes in social and economic conditions. We may recall here that the German experiment with democracy ended with the economic crisis clearing the way for Hitler and the establishment of Nazist ideology. What this history tells us is that democracy needs to be continuously sustained, cultivated by promoting the sovereignty of the people and their participation. It is this which will make democracy a radical political option, which liberal democracy is not.

Moreover, any equation of the sovereignty of the people with the sovereignty of narrowly defined nation-state is to be avoided. Christian understanding of democracy, while affirming identity, plurality and diversity, will challenge any conflation of the sovereignty of the people with the idolatry of the nation that is at the root of many wars and violence. The sovereignty of the people has meaning in relation to the universal community of humankind. By sovereignty of the people is meant here the creation of self-governance that facilitates expansion of freedom of a people through self-determination in which they are involved either directly through participation or through representation.[25]

---

[24] Cf. Charles Tilly, *op.cit.*

[25] Analysing the French Revolution, Hannah Arendt noted that it failed because it did not pay attention to the participation of the people even though it was engaged with the social question.

## Conclusion

We uphold democracy because it is a form of government in which human flourishing could take place, and this is a central concern of Christianity. Democracy lends itself, in spite of its many failings, for the realization of human ideals and their blossoming. Democracy is not something ready-made. There is no single form of democracy so ideal as to become a model. It is an incomplete project. To think of democracy as ready-made and to be only imported is too much of a mechanistic conception of democracy.

True to the universal character it claims, Christianity should seek the roots of democracy in the various cultures and traditions of the people all over the world, and not get ensconced in the Greek and Western tradition and legacy. In the Asian cultures and civilizations there are many resources and examples which are capable of sustaining democracy today.

Christianity could set aside its past ambiguous history vis-à-vis democracy and turn on a new leaf by its support in resolving some of the thorny issues and challenges of our times. They relate to the protection of the weaker sections and minorities, defence of social and cultural pluralism, equitable sharing of resources, engaged participation of the people in what concerns the common good and their control and check over any abuse of power. These are today the crucial pillars necessary to uphold democracy as a mode of governance and way of life. What Christianity could signify for democracy could be gauged by its (Christianity's) contribution to these questions and issues. Another important contribution Christianity could make is to promote a culture and spirituality of democracy. These need to be supported theologically by a participatory conception of power and ultimately relativization of all forms of power.

Why is it that in some cases Christianity has been effective in the democratic process, whereas in other contexts it has not been? I think the answer lies in the effectiveness with which the message of social justice and human rights and pluralism has been carried out in different contexts. Where the engagement of the Church for justice and human rights has been strong, the democratic impulse has also been significant and effective. It has enabled the people to critically challenge anti-democratic and authoritarian forces, and hold accountable those who are invested with authority to serve the public good. Secondly, the differentiation between the political power and religious sphere (unlike the model of Christendom) has ultimately helped a proactive and critical role of the Church vis-à-vis the state and enabled a democratic process through support to popular protests and participation.

While liberal democracy may have played a role in breaking down power structures of the past, it has not ensured the democratic participation of the people. There is a groundswell of democratic upsurge among the poor of Asia. Their democratic participation is the means for equality, dignity and survival, and it comes to expression in many local social movements. It is the passion of the poor that propel democracy today and not the diktats of the empire. In this context, Christianity through its vision, praxis and spiritual resources can challenge anti-democratic forces and throw its lot with the democratic aspirations of the people.

The future of Christianity as an advocate of democracy in Asia will depend on the extent it is able to challenge the apparent connection of capitalism and market with democracy. In a situation in which capitalism and market seek democracy as an ally to create strategic positions and conditions for their success, Christianity is challenged to expose their anti-democratic orientations and practices and project a vision of democracy that will be centred on the spirit of solidarity. Democracy is a way of life in which we become partners and sharers with others in a common destiny.

## Chapter 8

# Political Economy and Christian Engagement

*"The love of money is the root of all evil"* (I Tim 6:10)

*"You cannot consume beyond your appetite. The other half of the loaf belongs to the other person, and there should remain a little bread for the chance guest."*
– Kahlil Gibran[1]

Economy is a matter of common concern. It affects everyone, though in different ways: for some it is a matter of livelihood, and for others a matter of profit and accumulation. There are, then, two economies in Asia – the economy of survival and the economy of profit. Both these economies are bound to be in conflict, and indeed they are. Today, in Asia the economy of survival seems to be losing out to the economy of profit, thanks also to the role played by the state. We are dealing with matters of life and death for millions of people.

A theology sensitive to the plight of the poor and of the earth will occupy itself with the question of economy as a matter of urgency. However, the present chapter does not go into the question of why political economy is to be considered as a theological question. Here I do not aim at providing any justification for a theological reflection on political economy, something which I take for granted. For, economy dealing with the very material basis of human life and flourishing, goes to define our theological understanding of human beings, God, the world and the nature around. What is intended here is to reflect on how economy could be

---

[1] *The Greatest Works of Kahlil Gibran*, Book Three, Jaico Publishing House, Mumbai, 2008, p. 33.

transformed into a humanizing enterprise with due responsibility to the weaker sections and to the earth. A truly contextual theology could contribute significantly to a responsible and earth-sensitive political economy today, especially in favour of the poor and the marginalized in Asian societies.

## A.  THE CONTEXT OF OUR THEOLOGICAL REFLECTIONS

### The Consequences of a Shift

It is reported that 182,936 farmers committed suicide since 1997 in the country.[2] Poverty, and indebtedness and bleak prospects for the future crushed their will to live. It is an irony that these suicides have taken place when the country was proclaiming proudly about its eight percent growth and forecasting double-digit growth.[3] The contradiction here is too glaring to ignore.

Our reflections begin from the situation of an economy in the country that took a clear neo-liberal orientation in the 1990s, with the intention of becoming part of the global capital and market. It was a remarkable turn around from the times when economy was oriented towards the goal of independence and self-sufficiency. This rupture has brought about changes in every field of life in the country. There have been changes in terms of economic actors, priorities, allocation of funds, etc., as well as in the economic and fiscal policies of the country. The consequences of these changes have been no less than the upheavals colonial economy created in the Indian traditional economy.[4]

The resistance to colonial economy is symbolized by the expression "*swadeshi*" – the indigenous.  The salt march and the dumping into large

---

[2]  Cf. Bhaskar Goswami, "The Problem" in *Seminar* 595, p. 12. The whole issue deals with "Agrarian Transitions. A Symposium on the Growing Distress in Agriculture".

[3] The obsession with the percentage of growth has led to the neglect of Human Development Index (HDI) which would give us the real measurement of the growth of the country.

[4] For an overview of Indian economy, especially since Independence, see Anne O. Krueger (ed.), *Economic Policy Reforms and Indian Economy*, Oxford University Pres, Delhi, 2002. It gives a historical overview of Indian economy since 1940s. Francine R. Frankel, *India's Political Economy 1947 – 2004. The Gradual Revolution*, Oxford University Press, Delhi, 2005; see also Dharma Kumar, *The Cambridge Economic History of India*, Orient Longman, Hyderabad, 1991.

fire imported Manchester  clothes processed out of Indian cotton stirred the minds of the people on the necessity of protecting the economy of the country, by protecting the farmers, the weavers, the artisans, etc. whose livelihood was seriously challenged. Boycott of foreign goods and wearing of Indian-made coarse handloom clothes fired the minds of the people with pride, and made them aware of the local economic potential.

The colonial economy was imposed; the neo-colonial liberal economy, on the other hand, is embraced by the state and the upper and middle castes and classes. Here is the difference. The opting for liberalization and the integration of Indian economy with global market has upset the traditional livelihood of millions of people in the country. Various forms of traditional economy in the country, including subsistence economy and informal economy, have been all brought under the sway of capital and market, and they have been progressively loosing their autonomy and identity. One example would be the invasion of technology and creation of genetically modified food and seeds which seem to cause devastation of the productive forces of the earth. It can cause pauperization of the peasants by making them more and more dependent on market forces.

Added to this is the fact that the new economy has led to the progressive withdrawal of the state from its responsibility to provide the basic needs of the people precisely at a time when those involved in subsistence and informal economy are led to a crisis through the onslaught of the neo-liberal economy.[5] We need to point out here the difference between these two forms of economy. While the subsistence and informal economy (non-corporate economy) are oriented towards providing the means for the survival, the corporate economy operates for maximization of profit.

### Vulnerable Areas

If we take the overall situation in the country, "a little more than three-fourths of the Indian people are poor and vulnerable in 2004-2005, based on a value that is double the official poverty line".[6] But we need to point

---

[5] Cf. *Report on Definition and Statistical Issues Relating to Informal Economy*, National Commission for Enterprises in the Unorganized Sector, Delhi, 2008.

[6] Arjun Sengupta - K.P. Kannan - G. Raveendran, "India's Common People: Who Are They. How Many Are They and How Do They Live?", in *EPW*, March 15, 2008, p.59. This article is revealing for its detailed statistical information on the economic life of the common people of the country.

out a few vulnerable areas which affect the livelihood of the weaker sections in our society.[7] In a country in which almost two thirds of the population depend upon land and agriculture related occupations, on fishing and forestry, what happens in these sectors is, obviously, of utmost importance. The present economic policies affect adversely the agricultural and unorganized labourers. On the other hand, it is this agricultural field which contributes at least 19% of national income. What is worse is the general apathy to the agrarian issues and the tendency to evade them. The whole agriculture sector is brought under the logic of capital and market with all its social consequences, and there is almost a total black-out of news from the agricultural field in our media which does not fail to blow up even the least tremors in the stock market.

Another area that affects the livelihood of the poor is retail trade. It is part of the informal economy of the country which is as large as, if not more than, the formal economic transactions. Millions of people depend upon retail trade with their petty shops and street-vending carts. Foreign direct investment (FDI) in this field could be most disastrous as this move could – and already signs are there – wipe off the livelihood of large masses of people. Public anger burst out when some corporate business tried to invade the retail trade.

A third important area of concern is that of state-subsidies in favour of the poor. Though the state has not succumbed fully to the pressure of

---

[7] The various economic surveys bring out a lot of details and statistical table which throw light on the actual situation, especially the surveys made by the groups for an alternative economy. See *India. Social Development Report 2008*, Council for Social Development, Oxford University Press, Delhi, 2008; *Alternative Economic Survey India, 2007–2008. Decline of the Development State*, Danish Books, Delhi, 2008; *Social Development Report*, Council for Social Development, Oxford University Press, Delhi, 2006; *Alternative Economic Survey (2002 – 2003) Liberalisation sans Social Justice*, Rainbow Publisher, Noida, 2003; Kirit S. Parikh - R. Radhakrishna (eds), *India Development Report 2002*, Oxford University Press, Delhi, 2002; see also Jackie Assayag - C.J. Fuller (eds.), *Globalizing India. Perspectives from Below*, Anthem Press, London, 2005; Kaushik Basu (ed.), *The Oxford Companion to Economics in India*, Oxford University Press, Delhi, 2007. This is a very helpful volume from A-Z on all aspects of Indian economy. Jean Drèze - Amartya Sen, *India Development and Participation*, Oxford University Press, Delhi, 2003. The work investigates critically various aspects of India's economy – education, health, gender inequality, etc.

international monetary and trade bodies (IMF, World Bank and WTO)[8] and domestic business interests to withdraw from this field, nevertheless, there is a slackening of involvement. Instead of furthering the support to the poor and the weaker sections, the resources of the state are increasingly diverted to business interests that benefit only a small elite.

Women are one of the groups most affected by liberalization. It may be true that women have entered into new areas of modern economic life. However, they remain discriminated in terms of wages, nature of work, promotion, etc. The present crisis has struck them even more severely because it is women who have to maintain the household and attend to food, fuel, fodder, etc. at a time when the means are diminishing. In short, *"feminization of poverty"* is a reality in this country.

Finally, the process of privatization of public sector enterprises has affected the life of the masses of people who depended on the state and its service institutions. This happens in spite of the resistance by the general public. There is a wrong assumption that public enterprises and services do not function efficiently and are corrupt - myths propagated by business interests negatively disposed towards any state-intervention.

Any economic system is located in a particular social and historical context. When the context is marked by longstanding patterns of discrimination, as in the caste-society, then, the economic system should be such that it has inbuilt measures and mechanisms to effect compensatory justice in terms of enabling groups and communities for adequate economic activities. It means concretely that ways and means be found to stimulate the economic agency of Dalits, tribals and women in our country.

## B.  HUMANISTIC AND THEOLOGICAL UNDERPINNINGS FOR A DIFFERENT SYSTEM OF ECONOMY

### Biblical Insights

With the risk of oversimplification, let me now highlight some major biblical insights that could inspire us to respond critically to the present economic system and help explore more humane and ethically sensitive economy.

---

[8] These three bodies are referred to as 'Bad Samaritans" in a recent work by a Cambridge economic historian. See Ha-Joon Chang, *Bad Samaritans. The Myth of Free Trade and the Secret History of Capitalism,* Bloomsbury Press, New York, 2008.

The Old Testament sees riches as God's blessings, something that has lent substance to the "prosperity Gospel" (Prov 3:9-10).[9] However, this appreciation of wealth goes along with laws and injunctions of restraint (Ex 21:1-11; 22:2-23; Deut 24-25; 15:1-18). Sabbatical year and jubilee were an invitation to halt material accumulation and to rectify, by redistribution, the injustices that had crept in (Ex 23:11; Lev 25:2-7; Ex. 21:2-6). All this was to help the people acknowledge and confess that ultimately the ownership of the land and all the riches of creation derive from God (Ps 24:1; Deut 10:14), and therefore, all have a claim on these riches. They cannot become the exclusive possession of any one individual (the King) or an affluent class. These values were embedded in the tribal structure of the Israelite society before the advent of monarchy.[10] The laws of the covenant were precisely intended to enable a community in reciprocal responsibility and they contained provisions to take care of the last and the least.

It is one of the deepest moral intuitions of the Bible that the quality of a community is measured by the way it takes care of the weaker ones who are vulnerable and lacking protection. This runs through the entire corpus of Biblical tradition.[11] The prophets represent God's spokesperson for justice for all and as critics of accumulation that excludes people and leaves them in want and penury. Against the economic background of their times we understand the prophetic critique of the society and their defence of the poor (Amos 4:1; 8:4-5; 5:11-12; Is. 3:14-15).[12] We find the prophets making a double condemnation – idolatry and injustice. Both these are inextricably interlinked. For the dereliction of Yahweh caused practice of injustice in the society. Reversely social injustice led one away from Yahweh to the idols.[13] The Wisdom literature on its part sees wealth

---

[9] Proverbs only reflect the general theme on riches in the Old Testament. "Honour the Lord with your wealth, with the first-fruits of all your crops: then your barns will be filled to overflowing and your vats will brim over with new wine" (Prov 3:9-10).

[10] Norman K. Gottwald, *The Tribes of Yahweh. A Sociology of the Religion of Liberated Israel, 1250 – 1050 BCE,* Sheffield Academic Press, Sheffield, 1999.

[11] Craig L. Blomberg, *Neither Poverty nor Riches. A Biblical Theology of Possessions.* Intervarsity Press, Downers Grove, 1999; see also Julio de Santa Ana, *Good News to the Poor,* WCC, Geneva, 1977.

[12] Cf. Walter Brueggemann, *The Prophetic Imagination,* Fortress Press, Minneapolis, 1978; Id., *Hopeful Imagination. Prophetic Voices in Exile,* Fortress Press, Philadelphia, 1986.

[13] Cf. Franz J. Hinkelammert, *The Ideological Weapons of Death. A Theological Critique of Capitalism,* Orbis Books, New York, 1986.

as God's gift for a life of righteousness and fidelity, but is at the same time critical of wealth accumulated through unjust means. It also warns about relying on wealth. "Cast but a glance at riches, and they are gone..." (Prov 23:4-5). We find in the book of Psalms the same concerns of the poor as in Deuteronomy. "Defend the cause of the weak and fatherless; maintain the rights of the poor and oppressed. Rescue the weak and needy; deliver them from the hand of the wicked" (Ps 82:3-4).

In the teachings of Jesus we find practically no trace of wealth as sign of blessing but a concentration on the poor as beneficiaries of God's gifts. There are serious warnings to the rich and on the dangers of riches and the thirst for accumulation. Even more, in Jesus' teaching there is a clear contrast between God and the mammon and the impossibility of reconciling the two, as they represent two different poles. "You cannot serve God and Mammon" (Lk 16:13; Mt 6:24; Lk 16:13; Mk 10: 25). The riches turn a person godless and heartless (arrogant) and they are an obstacle to the Kingdom of God.  Precisely because the poor are not arrogant and haughty, blinded by wealth, they are open to God's gifts and sensitive to the needs of their neighbours (Lk 6:20-23; Mt 5: 3-12).

There is no condemnation of material possessions as such in Paul, but a transformation of wealth into a means of mutuality and communion, different from patron-client relationship of benefaction as we find in the Greco-Roman culture of the times (2Cor 8-9; Rom 12:18). The Acts presents the picture of an ideal community where possession is relativized and the good of the community takes priority over individual possession. "There was not a needy person among them, for as many as were possessors of lands or houses sold them, and brought the proceeds of what was sold ...and distribution was made to each as any had need" (Acts 4:34-35). Letter of James comes down heavily on the rich and their accumulation of wealth that slights the poor and ignores their needs (Jas 2:1-7; 5:1-6).

The basic biblical perspectives are further illustrated by the life of the early Christians, the teachings of the Fathers of the Church and the many movements of poverty in Christian history.[14] These are so universal, in spite of the particular religious convictions on which they are based, that they provide a common point of dialogue with other religious traditions and with all those who are concerned with the deeper human and ethical issues in today's economy. The interreligious and ethical perspectives lead

---

[14] Charles Avila, *Ownership. Early Christian Teaching,* Orbis Books, New York, 1983.

us to view the deeper human questions involved in economy. In particular they help us identify greed as that which leads to injustice, violence and aggression, and to the neglect of the poor.[15] When a whole economic system is based on greed and self-interest, the contribution of these traditions offer important insights and means to challenge it. Moreover these theological and ethical perspectives offer elements for a framework to respond to the pressing issues the present economy has thrown up.[16] That leads us to the next consideration.

## The Price of Greed and the Struggle for Basic Needs

"The Price of Greed" is how *Time* magazine characterized the present financial crisis.[17] Greed begets more greed and finally the price has to be paid. Unfortunately, it is the poor of the world who are paying the price for the avarice of the rich money-spinners, speculators and business interests. This is shown by the bail-out measures by the state. It is a strange irony that the tax money of the poor are spent to save the greedy rich. It is again the greed that lays off in times of crisis the workers to save costs and maintain its profits.[18] What we do not realize in normal times is that it is the same greed that is at work in the mainline economic system.

---

[15] Cf. Paul Knitter - Chandra Muzzafar (eds.), *Subverting Greed,* Orbis Books, New York, 2002.

[16] For a very interesting reading of the economic world of the Bible in the context of our times, see Roelf Haan, *The Economics of Honour. Biblical Reflections on Money and Prosperity,* William B. Eerdmans, Grand Rapids, 2009.

[17] *Time,* September 29, 2008. See also "The Financial Crisis – Into the Storm", in *The Economist,* Oct. 2008, pp. 11-12; "World economy- Accelerating Downhill", *The Economist,* Jan 2009, pp. 11-12. For an excellent analysis of the downward trend, see Joseph Stiglitz, *The Roaring Nineties. Why We Are Paying the Price for the Greediest Decade in History,* Penguin Books, London, 2003; see also his *Globalization and Its Discontents,* Penguin Books, London, 2002; Taggart Murphy, "Asia and the Meltdown of American Finance" in *EPW,* November 15, 2008, pp. 25-29. For the impact of this crisis on India and Asia, see Ruddar Datt, "Global Meltdown and Its Impact on the Indian Economy", *Mainstream,* Vol. 47,15, (March 28, 2009), pp. 9-13; "China and India, Suddenly Vulnerable", in *The Economist,* Dec. 2008, pp. 13-14.; "Asia's Suffering", *The Economist,* Jan 2009, p. 9. For a historical perspective, see Farshad Araghi, "Political Economy of the Financial Crisis - A World-historical Perspective, in *EPW,* Nov. 8, 2008, pp. 30–31. For a comparative study, see Wang Tseng – David Cowen (eds.), *India's and China's Recent Experience with Reform and Growth,* Palgrave, New York, 2005.

[18] Cf. Ozlem Onaran, "A Crisis of Distribution", in *EPW,* March 28, 2009.

Capitalism is nothing but organized greed with all the evil it produces. We are reminded of the words in the Letter to Timothy which help us to understand what is deeply at work in capitalism: "Love of money is the root of all kinds of evil" (1Tim 6:10). No wonder then that Jesus said that it is easier for the camel to go through the eye of a needle than the rich to enter into the Kingdom of God (Mt 19:24; Mk 10:25; Lk 18:25). The ugly nature of the avarice gets exposed in times of crisis we are living through. How could the well-being of humanity be based on an economic system whose structuring principle is greed?

Freedom from greed and attachment is the cornerstone of Jesus' social teachings. He does not command this only to his close disciples; it is meant for all those who want to follow him. There is even more to his teaching. By enjoining renunciation and detachment, Jesus responds to a basic human and societal issue at large. It rests on a deeper vision of human beings and the society. Jesus commands to his disciples freedom from greed and attachment, because it is something that will make them authentic human beings. For servitude which greed and attachment represent diminish and corrode human and societal life here on earth. Therefore, the exhortation against avarice and attachment are not to be interpreted as something esoteric or fostering otherworldliness. Further, his teachings on the dangers of riches and the need for detachment and renunciation are not meant simply as spiritual principles for individuals. They are principles for the life of the community as well. Absorbing the teachings of Jesus, the early Christians tried to create an ideal community free from greed and accumulation.

Greed is accompanied by violence. For to be able to wrest control of possessions one needs to employ violent means. The imbalance and asymmetry of power to which greed leads is a situation of injustice. It exploits the poor and marginalizes them. The greed that is deeply embedded in the capitalist system of economy continues to generate violence at all levels and in every part of the world. This is something that is obvious. A Buddhist text brings out very lucidly the path of violence greed and exclusive possession lead to:

> Thus from the not giving of property to the needy, poverty became widespread, from the growth of poverty, the taking of what was not given increase, from the increase of theft, the use of weapons increased, from the increased use of weapons, the taking of life increased.[19]

---

[19] As Quoted in *Subverting Greed, op.cit.,* p. 63.

The present capitalist system as the epicentre of greed is also the source of violence. Open and subtle forms of violence of all kinds have become a strategy to safeguard the unjust accumulation of resources and wealth. Capitalism-induced poverty can also be a source of violence. Challenging the unrestrained capitalist economy, then, is a contribution to peace in the world. Capitalism and peace are diametrically opposed to each other.

Religions have, unfortunately, often times contributed to legitimization of accumulation of wealth and have supported practices of greed. A classic example is the position of Christianity vis-à-vis colonialism in its greed, robbery and genocide, in the processes of the appropriation of the "wealth of the nations". On the other hand, we also find that all religions concur in the deep wisdom that attachment to riches is harmful to human beings and society. Greed (*lobha*) and acquisitiveness (*aparigraha*) have been viewed in some streams of Indian religious traditions as contradicting the call of a *dharmic* life. They are to be countered by the generosity of sharing (*dana*) and wisdom (*prajna*) that redeem us from delusion. Buddhism speaks of the insatiable desire (*trsna*) for riches which deviates us and leads us to suffering (*dhukka*), instead of happiness. *Dana* is to be understood not simply as almsgiving; it has a depth of significance which would combine in itself the Christian understanding of social justice and compassion.[20]

Greed operates in two ways. It functions as insatiable desire to make profits without limits. It operates also as the desire to consume ever more. In a country in which about 77% of the people are able to spend nothing but just Rs. 20 per day for all their needs – food, clothing, medicine, etc.[21] we have an economic system in place that permits the greed and consumerism of a few to thrive unrestrained. The growing disparity between the poor and the rich resulting from this greed is inherently unjust. What we require is an economy that will in the first place attend to the basic needs of the millions, and not cater to the accumulative instincts of the upper castes and classes. Starvation of children, suicide of farmers, eviction of tribals, sales of human organs, trafficking of women – these and other human tragedies are what the country is paying for the greed of a few.

---

[20] Cf. Felix Wilfred, "Prophetic Anger and Sapiential Compassion", in *Concilium* 2009/1, pp. 27-38.

[21] This is the data from the Report of the Arjun Sengupta Committee on the Unorganised Sector (2004-2005). 77% would mean in total about 836 million people who live on Rs. 20 per day.

### From Competition to Cooperation and Solidarity

Neo-liberal ideology that animates the mainstream economic system is based on competition as a general law or principle. What happens in the economic realm, it is argued, is nothing but concretization of a general law of nature. It is viewed as the engine that promotes progress and growth. Competition is associated with growth, greater effectiveness and productivity.

It is esential to examine more closely the arguments fielded in favour of competition to be able to unmask the myths behind it.[22] It is said that competition is something that is inherent in human nature and therefore it is inevitable. Human nature is prone to be lazy, greedy and aggressive. In this connection competition is seen, with reference to Darwinian socio-biology, as something that underlies the survival of the fittest as it injects a force of dynamism to overcome what is at the level of nature. Numerous studies have shown that natural tendency to compete, win and distinguish oneself from others is nothing but a socially learned behaviour pattern.[23]

If we are to assume (and not concede) that competitive spirit is natural, we should, on the basis of no less strong evidence, conclude that the spirit of cooperation too is natural. Apart from scientific studies to this effect, even ordinary observation makes it evident that cooperation is ubiquitous without which human species cannot survive. In fact, so many peoples and cultures of the world manifest in their way of life and tradition such a spirit of cooperation that we are forced to question whether the tendency of competing is not peculiar to a few cultures and whether this limited experience is extrapolated as a general principle. Christian vision, on its part, sees human being not as competitors but as members of a family sharing the same origin and striving together for the realization of a common destiny.

A second important argument that seems to lend plausibility for competition is the situation of scarcity. At first sight it may appear normal that precisely because there is want and the means are scarce, the response should take the form of competition. Here we need to distinguish between a scarcity that is engineered and manipulated and actual scarcity. Scarcity created through manipulation is the result of greed and a situation of injustice. On the other hand, actual lack of material resources could be

---

[22] Cf. Mary John, Pottiyinriyum Vetri Peralam (Tamil, Success Without Competition), Vaigarai, Dindigul, 2008.

[23] Cf. Alfie Kohn, *No Contest. The Case Against Competition*, Houghton Mifflin Company, Boston, 1986.

viewed as an environment in which human agency of solidarity and
participation could come into play. Far from the Malthusian prognostics
of doom for humanity because of the geometrical growth of population
and arithmetic production of food, we realize in the light of Christian
faith, that scarcity triggers the spirit of generosity and sharing, especially
as to be seen among the poorest of the poor. Moreover it provokes the
human economic agency as an extension of God's work of ongoing creation
in that it maximizes the use of available resources through a process of
participation and sharing for the sustaining of life.

> Scripture highlights the centrality of justice and love if want and
> destitution are to be avoided or alleviated. Covenant election and
> kingdom discipleship call for personal self-sacrifice in interpersonal
> economic relations. There would be no poor (Dt 15:4) if only humans
> take their obligations to each other seriously. Chronic Malthusian scarcity
> is prima facie evidence of moral failure whether by sins of omission or
> commission.[24]

These considerations on competition lead us to conclude that the present
system of economy is not anything inevitable. The serious consequences
we experience in the form of the suffering of the innocent should trigger
another system of economy that is based on the spirit of cooperation,
solidarity and sharing. Precisely because there are limited resources,
human beings forming one family, should share what is available equitably
and competition is not at all called for. On the contrary, it is counterproductive. The vision of the society the symbol of Kingdom of God evokes
is one of communion, mutuality and reciprocal support. Nowhere does
the Bible tell us to follow the law of competition, which is diametrically
opposed to the Kingdom of God. What transpires through the scriptures
and Christian tradition is a call to cooperation in love and in the spirit of
interdependence.

## Whose Ownership

Christianity shares with Islamic and Jewish tradition the belief that the
earth belongs to God, the creator, and human beings are but God's
representatives and they cannot be owners of the earth. This reference to
creation and to the divine disposition relativizes any human claim of
ownership and possession. The question of ownership had a very
intriguing history in modern Christian tradition. Leo XIII held it as a

---

[24]Albino Barrera, *God and the Evil of Scarcity. Moral Foundations of Economic
Agency,* University of Notre-Dame Press, Notre Dame, 2005, p. 200.

natural right and it served as a weapon against the socialists. He thought in this way he was defending the dignity of human persons. It was viewed by him as an extension of human freedom.

Today in a world of capitalism that stresses the absolute ownership of individuals and private enterprises, it is crucial to assert, in order to save the dignity of the poor and the marginalized, that the right of ownership cannot be without restraint. For as Pope Paul VI stated, "private property does not constitute for anyone an absolute and unconditional right".[25] Implicit in the whole discussion is the question whether private property is a matter of natural right (Leo XIII), or whether it is based on human sinfulness (Thomas Aquinas).

> Aquinas regards the strict right to private property not as an absolute based on human nature but as resulting from human sinfulness. The right is subordinate to and instrumental in the service of the universal destiny of the goods of creation to serve the needs of all. For this reason Aquinas holds that a person in extreme necessity can legitimately take from another the material goods that he or she needs. This action is not theft because in necessity all things are common.[26]

The teachings of Jesus on poverty and riches and the admonitions of some of the early Fathers of the Church and the theological position of St. Thomas Aquinas get reflected in the teachings of Vatican Council II. Harking back to these sources, *Gaudium et Spes* stated:

> God intended the earth and all that it contains for the use of every human being and people. Thus, as all people follow justice and unite in charity, created goods should abound for them on a reasonable basis. Whatever the forms of ownership may be, as adapted to the legitimate institutions of people according to diverse and changeable circumstances, attention must be always paid to the universal purpose for which created goods are meant. In using them, therefore, a person should regard one's lawful possession not merely as one's own but also as common property in the sense that they should accrue to the benefit of not only oneself but of others.[27]

---

[25] Pope Paul VI, *Populorum Progressio*, no. 23.

[26] Charles E. Curran, *Catholic Social Teaching. A Historical, Theological and Ethical Analysis (1891-Present)*, George Town University Press, Washington D.C., 2002, p. 177.

[27] *Gaudium et Spes*, no. 69.

The social mortgage to private ownership and the primacy of the universal destiny of earthly goods offer theological foundations for distributive justice.

Placed in the Indian context, the question assumes yet another dimension. In India it is not a question of private ownership vis-à-vis universal destination of earthly goods. In any case, this is not as important as the question: Whose ownership? In a country where the poorest of the poor are without land, it is crucial to assert the importance of ownership of land by the poor for their survival and for their dignity and self-esteem. This may not be the same thing as the question of private ownership by a bourgeois individual. For example, policies need to be devised that will ensure that the lands are not snatched away from the Dalits and that, through just distribution, they become owners of the land they till. Private property here is a matter of social justice. On the other hand the possession of vast stretches of land by upper castes and classes goes against the universal destiny of earthly goods. *In short, fighting for the ownership by the poor is a matter of social justice; so is fighting against the ownership and accumulation by the rich.*

The argument from creation and from the universal destiny of earthly goods provides the basic foundation for a new economic order. However, the issue requires further expansion in our present circumstances. Today not only are the goods of nature part of economy, but also resources like knowledge, skills, multifarious human endowments. Increasingly, economic life seems to depend upon human creativity and resources. Here we need to postulate another principle like the one of the universal destiny of created goods. I mean to say that whatever human beings produce in terms of knowledge, skills, technological know-how, social capital, etc. cannot be confined to the realm of the individual. These need to serve the common good and should be available for all. This has a lot of practical implications, for example, in terms of sharing technical knowledge especially when many lives can be saved in medical and pharmaceutical fields. It also critically challenges the whole regime of patents and intellectual property-rights which embody privatization of common good for one's profit.[28]

---

[28] Cf. Felix Wilfred, "Knowledge-Ethics for Our Times", in *Jeevadhara*, 39 (January, 2009), pp. 5-28.

## C. CHARTING THE FUTURE COURSE

The following reflections on the future of economy flow from the theological underpinnings we saw in the second part. The present economic crisis is an opportunity for the Christian community to renew its commitment to the poor and the marginalized, especially by thinking ways and means, structures and institutions that will enable a dignified life. The growing gap between the rich and the poor created by the current economic policies need to be overcome by a clear stand in favour of the marginalized and by involving their agency in the economic field.

What is expected of theology is that its contribution be in the line of a humanizing political economy both in its theory and praxis. The position of neutrality would be in this matter as foolish as to assume that the middle of the river is where we begin the construction of a bridge because it is neutral! The bridge needs to begin from the shore of the poor and the marginalized. That would mean a different beginning, and the hope of an alternative economic order.

### Participative Economic Life

In the mainstream global economy and market, some people, some groups, and even some continents (Africa, for example) do not count. The reason is the presumption that they have nothing to contribute to accumulation of wealth, the linchpin of modern economy. They are the excluded. A healthy economy, on the contrary, is one in which there is a dynamic flow of wellbeing throughout the social body. This can take place when all parts of the body are involved in this movement.

Social inequality and other evils derive from the fact that people are excluded from participating as active agents in the economic life of the country. Either economy is viewed as something that is to be directed by the experts in the field, or by a group of elites whose economic activities overlap with the fulfillment of their own self-interest without benefiting the people, claims to the contrary. A primary form of participation takes place when people become active contributors to economy through employment. Therefore, the situation of unemployment is a situation that excludes opportunity to people to be participant in the economic life of the society or of the country, which is also important for their dignity and self-esteem as well as the realization of their needs of life. Therefore any policy that deprives people of employment in the name of increasing profit or accumulation of capital is a process of exclusion, and therefore needs to be challenged.[29] Displacement of millions of people from their traditional means of livelihood in our country, and the lack of opportunities for growing number of young people are symptoms of the deep malaise afflicting the current political economy in the country. It calls for immediate attention.

India is a world-experiment in the complex relationship of democracy and poverty. The experiences in our country show that a formal democratic system could coexist with capital accumulation and exploitation in spite of mass poverty and destitution all around. This is the anomaly we experience in India and in South Asia at large. Participative economy, on the other hand, is of vital importance for sustaining a substantive democracy.[30]

> Continued co-existence of mass democracy and mass poverty is both a challenge and paradox of democracy in South Asia. While the working of democracy has not led to freedom from want, it may have given more space for struggles for securing better economic conditions. A manifold mismatch informs the relationship between democracy and freedom from want: between the objective economic condition of the citizen and their sense of satisfaction, between objective and subjective placement in the economic hierarchy .., and between popular preferences on economic policies and the policies pursued by the state. While this mismatch between the 'objective' and 'subjective' economic conditions of the people creates a space of democratic contestation, it also allows for state inaction on poverty and destitution.[31]

On the other hand, a substantive democracy and participative economy reinforce each other. A close connection between the two was visible in the parliamentary elections of 2004. The new economic policies became the testing ground and the BJP proclaimed the "India shining" slogan. But there was rejection of a democracy associated with a shining India – shining in the homes of a few wealthy. A "shining India" of neo-liberalism could not win the support of the poor, because it did not respond to their

---

[29] A programme called National Rural Employment Guarantee Scheme (NREGS), but it is still to take off seriously.

[30] Cf. Pranab Bardhan, *Scarcity, Conflicts and Cooperation. Essays in the Political and Institutional Economics of Development*, Oxford University Press, Delhi, 2005. This book goes into the external environment of politics and governance required for economics, and appears to be of liberal inspiration.

[31] *State of Democracy in South Asia. A Report*, Oxford University Press, Delhi, 2008.

mass poverty. There can be no lasting solution to mass poverty except when, through a process of economic participation, people take control of their own lives. This is also a matter of dignity and self-esteem.

> The much-hyped story of India's economic growth hides the truth about heightened inequality, the blatant biases against the poor, the hostility of the state toward welfare, and the misery wrought upon the poorest of the poor. Only an alternative path to development that lays stress on dignity and participation of all sections can be an answer to the ravages of predatory growth.[32]

In the immediate post-independent India, a state or a political party was judged in terms of its ability to alleviate the poverty and misery of the people. On the contrary, in the last few decades under the spell of neo-liberalism this substantive ideal was left in oblivion. Fortunately, there has come about the realization that democracy should mean abolition of want and destitution. Humanistic and theological reflections should sustain this trend and support movements and institutions pursuing a political democracy which is at the same time also an economic democracy. It is important to sustain this democratic spirit in that the masses of people who are more and more getting convinced, due to their pauperization, about the adverse economic policies, put continuously pressure on the elected representatives and the state to pursue policies that will respond to their situation and needs. As it is, today, momentous economic decisions affecting the lives of the masses are taken in isolation from them and without taking the public opinion into account. Holding the state accountable for its economic decision will be a significant move in democracy.

As it is, the present system of economy does not incorporate and value the economic contribution of certain segments of people. Most glaring is the exclusion of the household work of women to the maintenance of the family and society. Women's economic contribution to the family in terms of household works like cooking, cleaning and caring remain hidden and invisible. If one were to take into account the economically measurable income that would be generated if women were to do the same work outside the domestic walls, the very understanding of economy is bound to change. The etymology of economy (*oikos* + *nomos*) means the management of the household. At the primary and fundamental level this is done by women. Besides, we need to take into account the role played

---

[32] Amit Bhaduri, "Predatory Growth" in *EPW*, 43, 16 (April 19, 2008), pp. 10 ff.

by women in the administration of the finances of the family especially in times of crisis.

Moreover, in a caste-ridden society where social and economic roles are assigned by birth according to the principle of purity and pollution, the model of an egalitarian society with a participative economy may appear strange. But then we have numerous indigenous and tribal traditions wherein the values of solidarity, equality and sharing are deeply embedded. When we read these values in the light of the egalitarian society the Kingdom of God symbolizes, we may derive a lot of inspiration for the transformation of the present economy in the country.[33] The indigenous and tribal values, very different from the values of the casteist society, reflect the "antipride" and "antigreed" teachings of Jesus and the tribal values of the Bible.[34]

### An Economy of Care and Mutuality

The present economy reduces relationship only to the level of producers, and consumers through the mechanism of market. This is an impoverization of human relationality and a very dangerous reductionism. It leaves out some very significant dimensions of human life. Feminist critique challenges this reductionism where the human dimensions of life get commercialized. It is an irony that 'care', for example, has become a big industry, a commodity that can be bought and sold. In this situation the relationality of the web of human life gets disrupted blocking the mutuality of the flow of life.

The present crisis is basically a consequence of a mechanistic economy that needs to be redeemed today by bringing in relationality, mutuality and care, which were earlier devalued as the 'feminine'. A feminist redeeming of this situation for the wellbeing of humanity and the earth would be to bring back the soul into economy by centring on relationality and mutuality. This ethics of care woven into our way of life is the new

---

[33] George Soares-Prabhu has attempted such a Biblical reading. See George Soares-Prabhu, "Antigreed and Antipride Mark 10: 17-27 and 10: 35-45 in the Light of Tribal Values", in his *Biblical Themes for a Contextual Theology Today*, Jnana-Deepa Vidyapeeth Theology Series, Pune, 1999, pp. 241-259. See also Paulus Kullu, "Tribal Culture and Religion", in *Jeevadhara*, 24 (1994), pp. 89-109.

[34] George Soares-Prabhu, *op.cit.* p. 243; see also Ulrich Duchrow, *Alternatives to Global Capitalism. Drawn from Biblical History, Designed for Political Action*, International Books with Kairos Europa, Utrecht, 1995; "Outside the Market no Salvation" *Concilium 1997/2*.

software by which a new economy should evolve. Part of this software is to forge a new relationship with the earth and all that it implies. The economy of care extends also to the whole of nature. We need to care and sustain the nature which in turn nourishes us and makes life possible for us.

### From Human Rights to the Economic Rights of the Poor

There are serious consequences to the universal destiny of earthly goods on which we reflected in the second part of this chapter. One implication of it is that we need to go beyond a general human rights discourse and address more specific issues. The regime of human rights is often turned into a weapon in the hands of those already powerful to assert their individual rights.[35] One may not compare the claim that 'homosexuality between consenting adults'[36] be declared as basic human right with the right for food of the 16000 children dying everyday of hunger-related causes; nor the rights of the corporates for free trade with the right to a dignified life of almost two lakh indebted farmers in our country forced to commit suicide since 1997.

There was a serious discussion at the UN regarding the formulation of two separate covenants - one covering civil and political rights, and the other economic and social rights. Those who proposed one single covenant argued that economic and social rights are inextricable from civil and political rights. On the other hand, those who held the need for two covenants made a distinction between enforceable or justiciable rights which are civil and political rights, and non-justiciable rights, namely economic and social rights. Moreover, civil and political rights, they noted, can find immediate application, economic and social rights, on the other hand, still remain as programmes to be implemented.[37] Whatever the nuances introduced by the advocates of these two positions, what matters is the consensus on the necessity of including economic and social rights into human rights regime. But the crux of the question is that, in spite of theoretical support to the necessity of economic and social rights, there is

---

[35] Cf. Felix Wilfred, "Human Rights or the Rights of the Poor. Redeeming Human Rights from Contemporary Inversions", in *Vidyajyoti Journal of Theological Reflection*, 62(1998), pp. 734-752.

[36] Cf. Chandra Muzaffar, "Setting Western Standards for Human Freedom", in *Third World Resurgence*, No. 11, July 1991.

[37] Cf. Henry J. Steiner – Philip Alston , *International Human Rights in Context. Law, Politics, Morals*, Clarendon Press, Oxford, 1996, pp. 260 ff.

a vast gap between what is professed and what is practiced. Given the importance of economy for the survival and wellbeing of the poor, we need to focus more and more on their economic rights.

The International Covenant on Economic, Social and Cultural Rights of the UN spells out right for work, right for security, etc. But in view of the developments that have taken place globally in the economic field and in view of the developments within India, this instrument of economic rights appears quite inadequate. Hence we need to develop more sharply the economic rights of the poor in relation to our particular socio-political context.

### Economy and the Political Society of the Dispossessed

It would be utopian to expect that the inequality we experience in society could be made good by the intervention of the state. It is too much hand in glove with neo-liberal corporate interests for this to happen. Could we then pin our hope on civil society for radical economic transformation? That too does not seem to take us far. Though the concept of civil society is about two hundred years old, it could gain wide currency only since the collapse of erstwhile centralized socialist states. There is obviously some space for civil society in the country wherein the citizens claim their civil rights and are able to exchange views, debate, etc. Such a civil society would still serve as an instrument to put into effect some of the ideals enshrined in the Constitution. But we cannot deny the fact that civil society as a liberal conception may not respond adequately to the plight of the poor, their conditions of suffering, negations and marginalization. They are people who struggle to survive and have to constantly exert pressure on local authorities, with the state, with market forces, etc. The dynamics characterizing the endless negotiation these groups of people make is something distinct from the way civil society operates, and this distinctness is maintained when it is referred to as *political society*.[38]

> Indeed, the frequently spectacular quality of actions in political society, including the resort to violence, is a sign of the ability of relatively small groups of people to make their voices heard and to register their claims with governmental agencies. As a matter of fact, it could even be said that the activities of political society represent a continuing critique of the paradoxical reality in all capitalist democracies of equal citizenship

---

[38] Partha Chatterjee has argued strongly for this distinction between civil society and political society.

and majority rule, on the one hand, and the dominance of property and privilege, on the other.[39]

## From Profligacy to Sustainable Way of Life

When the Club of Rome warned in the 1960s about severe limits to growth, it came as a shocking realization. Unfortunately, it has not led to any change in the economic realm; much less to any radical rethinking of the reigning neo-liberal paradigm. For mainstream economy, it is business as usual. If India, China, Brazil, etc., were to follow the logic of mainstream economy and chart for themselves a course of progress as in the developed nations, it is plain that the resources available is far from adequate, and probably two or more earths as the present one will be required to sustain such a model of development. If every Chinese and every Indian were to own a car, our earth will literally turn into a gas chamber choking people to death. What we need is not a sustainable development, but the practicing of a sustainable way of life.

Neo-liberal economy has created, on the other hand, an environment for the flourishing of consumerism – a consumerism by the well-to-do castes and classes at the expense of the poor and of the earth. It is changing the face of India and its traditional ethos. Whereas renunciation, self-restraint and postponement of enjoyment were cultivated in traditional India, consumerism has introduced a culture of instant gratification. In India consumerism is not only a way of life based on instant gratification; it is also coloured by casteism and hierarchy. Consumerism and extravagance are also a way of exhibiting social status and caste-superiority. Such being the case, for the upward mobility of the middle classes, make-belief through their pattern of consumerism is important. In the process, those at the lower rungs of the caste-hierarchy and the poor are trampled upon and crushed.

The fascination of consumerism among our upper and middle class is spreading fast, as a result of media penetration, also into rural areas, along with the values and ideals these classes nurture.[40] The anatomy of consumerism tells us how it leads to the amnesia of the other and especially of the poor.

---

[39] Partha Chatterjee, "Democracy and Economic Transformation in India", in *EPW*, 43, 16 (April 19, 2008), p. 61.

[40] Cf. Pavan K. Varma, *The Great Indian Middle Class*, Penguin Books, New Delhi, 2007.

The concepts of responsibility and responsible choice, which resided before in the semantic field of ethical duty and moral concern for the Other, have shifted or have been moved to the realm of self-fulfillment and the calculation of risks. In the process, the 'Other' as the trigger, the target and the yardstick of responsibility recognized, assumed and fulfilled has all but disappeared from view, elbowed out or overshadowed by the actor's own self. 'Responsibility' now means, first and last, responsibility to oneself...while responsible choices' are first and last, those moves serving the interests and satisfying the desires of the self.[41]

Pavan Varma tells us how the Indian middle-class of the immediate post-independent India lived with the ideals of Gandhi and Nehru and how restraint and moderation characterized their lives. This has undergone today such a change that the middle-class has become a class of competitors with Bill Gates, Ambanis and Mittals as their new icons of success. Instead of restraint and moderation, they are given more and more to exhibitionism and ostentation.

Indians love the spiritual halo ascribed to them by foreigners, but are in truth among the world's most ingenious and resilient entrepreneurs, with their feet on the ground and their eyes on the balance sheet. Indeed, in the world view of Hinduism, Artha, the acquisition of wealth is among the four highest purusharthas or goals of life... there is no biblical injunction in Hinduism to the effect that it is more difficult for a rich man to reach heaven than it is for a camel to go through the eye of a needle. On the contrary, Lakshmi, the goddess of wealth and prosperity, is a ubiquitous presence in homes across the country.[42]

What is most disturbing is the callous indifference of the middle and upper castes to the plight of the poor and absence of any sense of community, except allegiance to one's caste group.

If such is the case, the future course of economy should be one in which the focus will be on the basic needs of the poor and not an economy that will trigger the consumerist instincts of the middle and upper classes. Moreover the future beckons us also to ecologically responsible use of the resources of the earth that is fast depleting. We need to only recall that whereas at the beginning of the 20th century, about 30,000 varieties of rice

---

[41] Zygmunt Bauman, *Consuming Life,* p. 92; see also Id., *Does Ethics Have a Chance in a World of Consumers?* Harvard University Press, Cambridge, Massachusetts, 2008.

[42] Pavan K. Varma, *The Great Indian Middle Class, op.cit.,* p. xxi.

were cultivated by our farmers, today there are practically ten major varieties which account for 75% of rice production.[43] That is an important lesson for the future. Economy and model of development need to sustain the biodiversity. To preserve and foster the diversity of nature is to respect God's creation and make the earth habitable for the future generations. This is part of the moral responsibility of the future economics. There is a lot to learn from indigenous traditions in our own country and from all over Asia.[44]

### Forward to Labour and Employment

The greed capitalism embodies, has brought the world to a situation in which accumulation of wealth has taken absolute priority over labour and employment. With liberalization, India has also fallen into a trap of sacrificing the livelihood and employment of millions for the profit of a small percentage of the rich. In the process, it has thrown to the winds the wellbeing of the workers as exemplified in the case of Special Economic Zones.[45]

There has been also drastic increase of unemployed worldwide in 2007-2008. Moreover, during the past years productivity growth has exceeded wage growth affecting the lives of the labourers, and this is particularly so in the case of women. This trend is glaring in India and Brazil. The world trend, as per the report of International Labour Organization, shows that proportionate share of wages of women has drastically declined. "Income gap between the top and the bottom ten percent of wage earners increased in 70 percent of the countries for which data are available."[46]

---

[43] Cf. *Seminar* 595 (Agrarian Transitions) p. 12.

[44] For a very scholarly presentation of the ecological approach of the indigenous peoples in different parts of the world, see John A. Grim (ed.), *Indigenous Traditions and Ecology*, Harvard University Press, Cambridge, Massachusetts, 2001; see also Roger S. Gottlieb, *The Oxford Handbook of Religion and Ecology*, Oxford University Press, Oxford, 2006; see also Christopher Key Chapple - Mary Evelyn Tucker (eds.), *Hinduism and Ecology*, Harvard University Press, Cambridge, Massachusetts, 2000.

[45] Preeti Sampat, "Special Economic Zones in India" in *EPW*, 43, 28 (July 12, 2008), pp. 25-30.

[46] Quoted in T.K. Rajalakshmi, "Wake-up Call", in *Frontline*, March 13, 2009, pp. 86-87. "For instance in the United States in 2007 the chief executive officers (CEOs) of the fifteen largest companies earned over 500 times more than the average worker" *Ibid*. p. 87.

The health of the employees is not the priority with the government, or with the employers. As a result, employees with low wages are forced sometimes to spend as much as 80% of their wages for health care, leaving little for food and other basic necessities.[47]

Charting a new economic course means bringing the question of labour and employment to the centre-stage. The private sector cannot throw overboard the legacy of over hundred and fifty years of labour movement which has ensured just wages, security, and health-care for the workers and employees. In a situation of crisis, neo-liberal economy and private corporations and enterprises tend to frantically cut wages and other benefits, increase working hours, and also to layoff workers. This trend needs to be arrested. Economic participation of the people will help check such anti-labour practices in future. Besides, state-intervention is important and it should hold the private sector responsible for the violation of the basic norms of social justice. The widely talked-about corporate responsibility is often a matter of make-belief. It does not really address the question of social justice in the field of labour and the common good.

## Freedom and Alternatives

The present economic system is totalitarian in character. It makes everything and everybody into commodities and the network it casts drags the whole world into its sweep. The worst harm it does is to stunt the imagination and foreclose any hope for the victims of the system. It presents itself as the only solution without any alternative. As deregulated economy and market, with no adequate checks and controls, it functions with totalitarian powers over the life of the people. Competition and market need to be restrained, so that human development becomes integral and inclusive. Without adequate policy orientation and remedial measures, the law of market and competition becomes a matter of the survival of the fittest. For, the initial conditions in the race are vastly different, with some having a disproportionate advantage over others, ethically invalidating the end-result of the competition.[48]

Faith and theology that help flourishing of life, cannot subscribe to death-dealing totalitarian economy. Just like political totalitarianism and

---

[47] Cf. T.K. Rajalakshmi, "The Other Half" in *Frontline*, April 24, 2009, pp. 90-92.

[48] Hence we realize the importance of reservation as a restraining mechanism, so that the market does not become exclusive and competition unfair.

empire need to be opposed in the name of faith, so too in the name of the same faith, an economic system that spells suffering and death to the innocent should be resisted. Along with resistance which can take different forms, there needs to be also efforts to devise alternatives. A sign of hope is that in our country and in different parts of the world there have come about significant movements and micro-initiatives that challenge the claim of the inevitability of the present economic order.

### Priorities and Formulation of Policies

In a situation in which the gap between the poor and the rich are widening more and more, there should be ways and means by which the needs of the poor are defended over against the extravagance of middle and higher castes and classes. This could happen if the nation has its economic priorities clear. The turn towards liberal economy and globalization brought about a sea change in this area.

A future course of economy that is sensitive to the needs of the subalterns calls for rethinking priorities and consequent reallocation of resources. In a country where large masses of people are still illiterate and where poverty prevents children from attending school, it is normal that education should be accorded high priority with allocation of adequate funds. Similarly, taxation and fiscal policies should be continuously revalued so as to benefit the poor, and aimed at the advantage of the already rich and well-to-do.

India has one of the worst health-care system in the world, and with liberalization, the state spending on health of the poor has reduced substantially. According to one report, though the UPA government promised to spend 3% of national income for health-care, in actuality what is spent is a meagre 0.3%.[49] While sophisticated five-star health-care for the rich is multiplying, the masses of people, workers, and those in informal sector of economy woefully lack basic medical facilities. What point is there to strive to increase the percentage of growth – *cui bono*? – when there is little spending for the primary health of the people.

> Few subjects can be more important than health as a constitutive element
> of the well-being and freedom of a nation. And yet health care has been
> one of the most neglected aspects of development in India. Despite
> stirring statements in planning documents on the centrality of health

---

[49] Cf. Suhas Borker, "Rapid Inclusive Economic Growth: The Only Way Forward", *Mainstream* Vol. 47, 6 (January 24, 2009), pp. 42-44.

and health care, the field has suffered from persistent neglect in public policy in general and development planning in particular...A direct consequence of inadequate official attention to health matters is that the Indian population continues to be exposed to a high incidence of communicable disease and readily preventable illness.[50]

In short, it is important to see whether the formulation of economic policies really reflect the needs and concerns of the poor and the weaker sections. The extent of commitment to justice on the part of the state will be seen the way these policies are accorded  priority. Above all, the alienation that has come about between the people and economy policy-makers should be overcome with constant interaction of the state, its institutions and agency with the people.

## Challenge to the Discipline of Political Economy

Our foregoing reflections lead us also to ask about the state of the mainline economics of present times and of social sciences in general. Christian theology could make a contribution by provoking the present economy from its claimed neutrality. There is a scandalous superficiality in the present state of these sciences which fail to address the human condition suffered by the weak and the marginalized. Today's economics has become a matter of theories, numbers, equations and models. The self-assurance of present economy is shaken. There seems to be a sudden black-out, and the financial music has come to a halt. With all the sophistication economics vaunted and its claims of prescience and capability for prediction, it is today dumb-found to explain how this financial disaster descended to affect the economies of the entire world, and alas, of the poor and developing nations like those in Asia. Even more, it is clueless today as how to get out of the deep mire into which it has sunk the world. The present discipline of economics and especially its neo-liberal ideology is far from capable of pulling the world out of this situation. There is need for a radical transformation of the science of economics along with other social sciences. The reason is spelt out clearly by the Gulbenkian Commission on the Restructuring of the Social Sciences:

> For, unlike the natural world as defined by the natural sciences, the domain of the social sciences not only is one in which the object of study encompasses the researchers themselves but also one in which the persons they study can enter into dialogue or contests of various kinds with these researchers. Matters of debate in the natural sciences are

---

[50] Jean Drèze – Amartya Sen, *op.cit.* p. 201.

normally solved without recourse to the opinions of the object of study. In contrast the peoples... studied by social scientists have entered increasingly into the discussion, whether or not their opinion was sought by scholars, who, indeed, frequently considered this intrusion unwelcome.[51]

Economics requires constant dialogue with the entire society and its various strata. We need voices from the ground and alternative perspectives that will wake up these sciences from their slumber in the abstruse world of isolation. It would be highly presumptuous to assume that theology could do that. For, we have innumerable varieties of theology, most of which, are unfortunately no less isolated and superficial – and that is even worse since it presume to tell us about the ultimate mystery of God, humans and the world.

An engaged theological critique of dominant political economy can be assisted by the feminist critique of it as well as the theoretical conceptions it has attempted to develop. One important thing theology needs to be aware of is that economy is not gender-neutral. In its critical study and analysis of both macro and micro-economy (which would include the process of production, distribution, consumption, trade, etc.), theology needs to incorporate gender inequality as operative in the very economic structures. The unequal power-relationships patriarchy creates, is at work in all economic processes. The dominant economic system simply reproduces and reinforces the existing unequal gender-relationships of power as well as the caste-hierarchy. All this is important to redesign economics as a discipline that responds to the complexity of the Indian social system.

Theology and economy need to come together today and reinforce each other. We are reminded of what Gandhi had to say about the relationship of religion and economics: "Whereas religion to be worth anything, must be capable of being reduced to terms of economics, economics to be worth anything must also be capable of being reduced to terms of religion and spirituality".[52]

---

[51] Immanuel Wallerstein et al., *Open the Social Sciences. Report of the Gulbenkian Commission on the Restructuring of the Social Scienc, s,* Vistaar Publications, Delhi, 1997.

[52] *Young India,* 15 September, 1927. Quoted in Christopher Key Chapple – Mary Evelyn Tucker, *Hinduism and Ecology,* Harvard Univesity Press, Cambridge Massachusetts, 2000, p. 227.

## Conclusion

There are those who argue that the present global economic system could be modified and shaped so as to avert some of its unfortunate collateral damages. Of capitalism and of its changes it can be verily said... *plus ça change, plus c'est la même chose*. Capitalism is clever and it ceaselessly dons the Good Samaritan's mantle.[53] It is intriguing and deceptive. For the very system itself is so aggressive and damaging to the poor and the earth, that any efforts to tame it could be as successful as taming the tiger to ride on it. Capitalism's promises to alleviate poverty and create a world of prosperity for all are but a mirage. We need to look with hope in a new direction and change course – no mean challenge.

In the face of the catastrophe the present economic system spells for the poor and the earth, theology may not be silent. It has the obligation to defend the threatened life of the poor and of the planet earth, by challenging the reigning economic system. As Enrique Dussel noted, "capital's self-absolutization, its claim to utter singularity, isolation, existence ex se, its denial that it is beholden to anyone or anything, constitutes its character as a false god and an idol".[54] Theology could trigger the imagination for humanizing alternatives that will challenge the rule of the idols and usher in the Kingdom of God. It needs to join in the struggle to drive out the merchants of death from the temple of life (cf. Jn 2:13-18).[55]

On their part, Christian Churches and institutions need to question themselves whether they have not fallen victims to the fascination of capitalism and have adapted themselves to its ways. Millions in this country are steeped in abysmal poverty. Unfortunately, the lifestyle of

---

[53] This is the impression I get going through the work of Jeffrey Sachs. In the whole work the question of poverty is posed as something to be managed by strategies and techniques. There is no questioning of the structures that cause endemic poverty and misery to millions, nor any critique of the capitalist system of economy. See Jeffrey D. Sachs, *Common Wealth. Economics for a Crowded Planet*, The Penguin Press, New York, 2008; see also his other widely-publicized work, *End of Poverty. Economic Possibilities for Our Time*, Penguin Press, London, 2005.

[54] Enrique Dussel, *Ethics and Community*, Orbis Books, New York, 1988, p. 133.

[55] Cf. Ivone Gebara, "Can the Merchants Be Driven Out of the Temple of Life? An Ecological Feminist Reflection from Latin America", in *Concilium* 2007/2, pp. 97-100.

many Christian communities, their leaders and religious orders seem to reflect more and more the plight of the rich young man (Mk 10:17-22), and the accumulating tendency of the rich fool (Lk 12:16-20), and not the economic vision of the "Good News to the Poor". The economic critique of theology, to be credible, should also be a critique of the commissions and omissions of the Churches and their failure to intervene in defence of the poor and of the environment.[56] Much more needs to be done by Christian communities for a radical transformation of the economy of the country, assisted by constant theological reflections. These reflections need to be supported by empirical data, analysis and interpretation.

In general, Indian theology has focused on cultural and interreligious issues. The political and particularly the economic dimensions of the life of the people have found little attention in Indian theology. What I have tried to indicate in this chapter are but some preliminary thoughts to initiate a serious theological discourse on the economy of the country and of Asia at large. There is no Asian public theology without addressing the issue of economy. We need to base our humanistic and theological reflections on empirical facts and contextual factors and also encourage studies, researches and publications emanating from interaction with humane economists, grass-root workers, feminists, and others.

---

[56] On the active role Churches could play by creating ecologically conscious communities, see Jacques Haers, "Environmental Theologies as Processes of Ecclesiogenesis and Common Discernment", in *Concilium* 2009/3, pp. 67-75.

# Chapter 9

# Eco-Justice
## Expanding the Horizons for a Common Future

*"Our ancestors viewed the earth as rich and bountiful, which it is. Many people in the past also saw nature as inexhaustibly sustainable, which we know is the case only if we care for it. It is not difficult to forgive destruction in the past that resulted from ignorance. Today, however, we have access to more information, and it is essential that we re-examine ethically what we have inherited, what we are responsible for, and what we will pass on to coming generations."*
— Dalai Lama[1]

In these initial years of the twenty-first century, we face two great crises: The one relates to the ordering of relationships among the humans in a just and equitable manner; the second one concerns the way human beings relate to nature and Mother Earth. There is a threatening deficit on both these counts, and the crisis assumes ever greater dimensions. The past few millennia have been a struggle to establish justice in the human community, and it is far from being achieved. The second agenda of justice – that of relationship of the humans to the Earth has just begun. Before the night falls, there is the urgency to direct our attention to this crisis and engage in the struggle for justice.

The Copenhagen Summit was a frantic effort to make up for what humans continue to inflict on nature with disastrous consequence for all creatures.[2] Even the measures and strategies projected to be endorsed by

---

[1] Dalai Lama, *My Tibet* (Text by H.H .the Fourteenth Dalai Lama: Photographs and Introduction by Galen Rowell) Thames and Hudson Ltd., London, 1990, p. 80.

[2] Cf. Chitra Ganesh, "Come Let Us Join Hands to Save the Earth", in *The Hindu*, December 20, 2009, p. 18; Raj Chengappa, "Enemies of the Earth", in

the Summit – and which woefully fell short of the minimum - are far from adequate to come to terms with the magnitude of the ecological problems and the convulsion of climate changes. They touch only the surface, and do not seem to address deeper questions underlying the crisis of the relationship of humans to the Earth.

Moving towards the future calls for a change of vision, perspectives, values and human conduct vis-à-vis the Earth. The present chapter wants to be a small contribution by way of reflecting how we need to expand our horizons in understanding justice, so as to comprise Human-Earth relationship. This latter relationship is covered by eco-justice.

## A Limited Understanding of Justice

Let me begin with a reference to a recently published work by Amartya Sen, and entitled *"The Idea of Justice"*.[3] It evokes immediately in our mind another work by an illustrious thinker John Rawls *"A Theory of Justice"*[4] on which Sen builds his own ideas. His emphasis is on the role of public reasoning in the realization of justice. According to him, though perfect justice may elude us, what we can try through public reasoning is to move from less to more justice. He also notes how we need to go beyond a parochial approach to justice to address global issues of justice. The work of Sen, in spite of its ponderous scholarship, has two serious limitations. First of all, his consideration of justice has strong Western philosophical tradition as its background – both classical and modern – and is heavily centred on reason as the point of reference for elaborating the idea of justice.

A second serious limitation will be obvious to anyone who reads it in the light of the present-day situation of humanity and of nature. There are hardly four pages devoted to the environmental issues,[5] and even those

---

*India Today*, December 21, 2009, pp. 30-35; Id., "Warming up to a New Deal", in *India Today*, December 21, 2009, pp. 38-40; Soni Mishra, "Under the Weather: Climate Change Calls for More Actions than Researches and Negotiations", in *The Week*, December 20, 2009, pp. 48-53; T. Jayaraman, "Will It Be a US Endgame at Copenhagen?", in *EPW*, 44, 50 (December 12, 2009), pp. 13-15; Martin Khor, "Copenhagen Battle for Climate Action with Equity", in *EPW*, 44, 48 (November 28, 2009), pp. 25-29; Lavanya Rajamani, "The Copenhagen Agreed Outcome: Form, Shape and Influence", in *EPW*, 44, 48 (November 28, 2009), pp. 30-35.

[3] Cf. Amartya Sen, *The Idea of Justice*, Penguin Books, London, 2009.

[4] Cf. John Rawls, *A Theory of Justice*, Revised Edition, Harvard University Press, Cambridge, 2003.

[5] Cf. Amartya Sen, *op. cit.*, pp. 248-252.

few pages do not address the question with the seriousness they deserve. Nor does he go into the intimate connection of poverty and environmental degradation. In short, one remains with the impression that the issue of ecology and nature is out of the purview of justice, which is an intra-human reality. It is surprising that a book of four hundred and sixty pages could be written on justice today with such scant attention to ecological and environmental questions. Given the inextricable link of social justice to ecological justice, the absence of the latter in the theoretical framework of Sen is highly regrettable.

## Interdependence – The Macro Picture

The awareness of interdependence among humans brought about a sense of solidarity and the realization that common is the destiny of human beings. The tragedy of Hiroshima and Nagasaki brought home powerfully the truth of the unity of humankind, and how destructive powers could wipe out the entire human species. Even as we struggle to give expression to human sustainability through regulating inter-relationships in peace and justice, we are confronted more and more with the truth of how human beings are dependent on the Earth, its products, the biosphere and the ecosystems. However, it has not sunk deep into the consciousness of humanity.

For the practice of eco-justice we need to equip ourselves with a vision of unity of the entire reality.[6] We are assisted in this through important resources. The vision of Hinduism, Buddhism, Daoism and primeval religious traditions show how we human beings are part of a web of intricate relationships constituting the whole universe and how all creatures – biotic and a-biotic – depend on one another for their wellbeing

---

[6] It is important to note that eco-justice is different from *environmental justice*. Whereas eco-justice is something basic challenging the present paradigm of the understanding of justice itself, environmental justice limits itself to the consideration of how the environmental burdens are so distributed that there be equity and that vulnerable peoples, groups, minorities are not affected unequally by pollution, industrial waste, floods, etc. Dalits, the tribals, African Americans, indigenous people, peoples of small islands may be disproportionately affected by the environment and its destruction. Balancing and sharing of these burdens equitably among all peoples and nations would be a process of environmental justice. This is not the concern of the present article; it rather focuses on the fundamental issue of eco-justice.

and flourishing.[7] Secondly, modern scientific discoveries show more and more clearly that the Earth is not an inert material to be acted upon by human beings, but presents itself as a mega-organism with all its parts held through a delicate balancing, and it resembles less and less a machine. As a creative organism the Earth brings forth new species and genera, and dissolves them into itself. This continuous process of creation from the womb of the Earth and its dissolution makes it into a vibrant reality. Human beings are part and parcel of the Earth and its processes.[8] The tragedy of modernity is that it has widened the gap between the humans and nature, and we need to recover a vision that brings them together.

## From Human Community to Earth Community

If such is the intimate relationship between the  humans and the Earth, then the understanding of community requires a widening. Communion and community are no more to be viewed as inter-human realities; they need to be taken as applying to the relationship of humans to the Earth with all biotic and a-biotic realities inhabiting in its womb.[9] Such a communional attitude towards all creatures would contribute to the promotion of eco-justice. There is solidarity among all life-forms on Earth which share many things in common, including the genetic code. Human body shares the power of nature in its composition of water, air and other elements of the Earth. In fact, if the Earth is made of two-thirds of water, the same composition is mirrored in the human body. Eco-justice happens when human communion and solidarity with all living and inanimate nature contributes to the maintenance of the whole Earth in its ecosystem, equilibrium and balance. Eco-injustice creeps in when this balance and interdependence is tilted, and the relationship of the humans to nature is hierarchized.

---

[7] Cf. Roger S. Gottlieb (ed.), *The Oxford Handbook of Religion and Ecology*, Oxford University Press, Oxford, 2006; Christopher Key Chapple and Mary Evelyn Tucker (eds.), *Hinduism and Ecology: The Intersection of Earth, Sky, and Water*, Centre for the Study of World Religions, Harvard University, Cambridge, 2000.

[8] Cf. D.C. Srivastava (ed.), *Readings in Environmental Ethics: Multidisciplinary Perspectives*, Rawat Publications, Jaipur and New Delhi, 2005.

[9] Cf. John A. Grim (ed.), *Indigenous Traditions and Ecology. The Interbeing of Cosmology and Community*, Centre for the Study of World Religions, Harvard University, Cambridge, 2001.

## From Stewardship to Kinship

The ideology that has contributed to ecological crisis today has three streams of praxis flowing from a hierarchical mode of thought. In the Hebrew thought, man is at the helm of the hierarchy, ruling over the family, the women, the slaves, etc. He represents the rule of God in the world by ruling over nature. A second stream of thought is of Greek origin with its dualism of body and soul. The soul finds its true destiny by escaping from nature, creation and the world. A third source is from the Western Enlightenment tradition which makes a stark contrast between nature and history. It is not nature, but history, that is the realm of human beings and their agency, and they affirm their sovereignty over nature by intervening in it through exercise of their freedom.

The confluence of these three streams have created a forceful current in Christian tradition that brushes aside the truth of the communion of human beings with the Earth, its elements and living beings. Foregrounding the reality of Earth-community and placing human beings within it called for a re-interpretation of the Biblical texts, especially of Genesis (cf. Gen 1:26-28). Biblical scholars sensitive to the ecological issues tell us how God's command to Adam needs to be interpreted not as a domineering over nature and creation, but to be read as a call to stewardship.

This clarification is important, but inadequate to respond to the crisis of today. We need to strengthen this interpretation from other insights of the Bible. In this respect we may note how in the creation account, God is portrayed as someone working – creation is the work of God. The truth of this statement stands out when we realize that in ancient societies – both in the East and the West – not working but to be at leisure (the so-called "leisured class") was the mark of superiority, and it belonged to the high classes. God does not assume this high class character but is depicted as someone who works, and God also rests on the seventh day (cf. Gen 2:1-3; cf. also Ex 2:2). This is a pattern that forms part of the entire creation and nature. The Earth works but it also needs to rest, just like human beings. So, then, we have the injunctions that the land be periodically left fallow, so that its regenerative capacity be increased (cf. Ex 23:12; Lev 25:8-55). So, too, human communities get regenerated by overcoming the accumulation of wealth, usurpation of land etc. and by creating a fresh situation for the flourishing of everyone, which is the meaning of the Jubilee. Here we have both eco-justice and social justice, and in both cases, there is a common pattern at work. Eco-justice is practiced when human beings respect the rhythm of nature and its dynamics.

In this way, the Earth-community lives in communion, peace and harmony. This requires that we go beyond mere stewardship approach to nature – which would be still infected by anthropocentrism – and move towards *kinship with the Earth*.[10] Kinship expresses the reality of interdependence of the humans and nature. We need to draw inspiration also from different religious traditions. In the Christian tradition we have the sublime example of St Francis of Assisi who dealt with all creation – with birds, fishes and animals - in a relationship of kinship, and could address the sun as brother and the moon as sister. A nurturing and caring attitude and praxis towards all creatures is an expression of spirituality and spiritual childhood.[11]

## From Common Good to the Good of the Earth

If the chords that bind humans and the Earth in kinship is so strong, it follows that the pursuit of good needs to benefit both human beings and nature. Technology is moving, at an alarming speed in the belief that, in this way, common good of human beings is assured. In the view of the Greek thinker Aristotle, given the fact that people are by nature social and are bound up with the *polis* (city-state), they need to share their lives with others, going beyond the conception of good life each one may have, and this came to signify the common good. The forum for the pursuit of this common good was the public sphere. However, in a city of exclusion – of women, slaves and other weaker sections – the common good had a

---

[10] Cf. John Hart, "Catholicism", in Roger S. Gottlieb (ed.), *The Oxford Handbook of Religion and Ecology*, Oxford University Press, Oxford, 2006, pp. 65-91

[11] We need to keep alive our senses to forge true kinship with the Earth and nature. As people grow old they lose slowly the touch with the Earth as they perceive less and less, whereas children, with their active senses find affinity with the Earth, and with all creatures. Spiritual childhood and rejuvenation could be interpreted as the activation of our senses with which we live our affinity with the entire creation. If spiritual childhood is the experience of our dependence and trust in God, this needs to be re-interpreted today in terms of our dependence on nature and through our intimacy with the Earth through which we experience the divine mystery in a new way. The realization of divine presence in everything – a traditional Christian spiritual theme – needs to be brought today in relation to the Earth and all its creatures.

limited understanding even within the human community. It was basically the good sought and shared by the *males* of the city.

From a theoretical point of view, the concept of common good has widened in modern times with a renewed understanding of justice in an inclusive way. It came to signify the good of everyone irrespective of the class, race, gender, etc. It got further expanded with the emergence of the consciousness that human beings share the same destiny. Consequently, it was argued that common good is to be sought globally across national borders, given the growing interdependence of humanity.[12] It is enabled through a range of networks of communication in today's global world.

These developments on the understanding of common good may facilitate creation of solidarity among human beings. But the point is that the achievement of common good is today dependent upon the good of the Earth. In the past, the Earth and nature never came in the picture in this conceptualization of common good. Today, any understanding or discourse on common good remains woefully inadequate if it is not set in context of the interdependence of the humans and the nature. If we form a wider community with the Earth and all its life-forms, we may not pursue any common good among the humans that does not benefit the Earth. The nature with all its richness and rhythm is a participant in the common good. To the life of the Earth-community about which we mentioned earlier, there corresponds the quest of the good of the Earth indispensable for the good of the human community.

The pursuit of the good of the Earth takes place through a process of relationship –we may call ecological relationship – that maintains a balance between the good of every part of the Earth-community including the humans. One way of understanding the formation of culture is to study what kind of relationships people in different bioregions and in biotic communities have fostered. Cultural differences depend to a large extent on the kind of relationships to nature, as for example in an agricultural community, in an industrial urban society or in a fishing community.

### Beyond "Sustainable Development"
"Sustainable development" is an expression in wide currency today, but also is quite vague in its connotation. Sustainable development resulted

---

[12] Cf. David Hollenbach, *The Common Good and Christian Ethics*, Cambridge University Press, Cambridge, 2002.

from the realization that there are "limits to growth". The fact that many things are technically possible need not mean that they should be actually realized, even if that were to harm human welfare from a long-term perspective. The ideal of sustainable development is still very much tied to an anthropocentric vision of reality. The dominant concern here seems to be the survival of humanity which is not possible when the environment is damaged, or the resources of nature are overexploited.[13] Sustainable development does not focus on the present situation of poverty in a world where 20% of the population consumes 80% resources of nature. Sustainable development seems to be concerned more about *intergenerational equity* by which is meant that the use of natural resources be such that we leave behind for future generations the necessary to fulfil their needs.[14] This is in fact, one of the central points of Brundtland Commission Report entitled *"Our Common Future"*. Hence the restraint on development becomes imperative for human security. In fact, the Brundtland Report notes,

> Sustainable development is development that meets the needs of the present without compromising the ability of future generations to meet their own needs. It contains within it two key concepts: The concept of "needs", in particular the essential needs of the world's poor, to which overriding priority should be given; and the idea of limitations imposed

---

[13] Cf. Herman E. Daly, *Beyond Growth: The Economics of Sustainable Development*, Beacon Press, Boston, 1996; A.K. Sharma and P. Vigneswara Ilawarsan, "Dilemmas of Sustainable Development in India", in D.C. Srivastava (ed.), *Readings in Environmental Ethics: Multidisciplinary Perspectives*, Rawat Publications, Jaipur and New Delhi, 2005, pp. 227-240; Amit Bhaduri and Medha Patkar, "Industrialization for the People, by the People, of the People, in *EPW*, 44,1 (1 January 2009) pp. 10-12; Jomo Kwame Sundaram, "Export-Oriented Industrialisation, Female Employment and Gender Wage Equity in East Asia", in *EPW*, 44,1 (1 January 2009) pp. 41-49; Amit Bhaduri, "Predatory Growth", in *EPW*, 43,16 (19 April 2008) pp. 10-14; Manoj Kumar Sanyal et al. (eds.), *Post-Reform Development in Asia: Essays for Amiya Kumar Bagchi*, Orient BlackSwan, Hyderabad, 2009; Ignacy Sachs, "From Poverty Trap to Inclusive Development in LDC'S", in *EPW*, 39,18 (1 May 2004) pp. 1802-1811.

[14] Human beings are not masters of nature but pilgrims who pass through the Earth as through an inn. We do not take away the bed sheets and blankets from the inn (!), but leave them for those who come after us. This is how St Augustine viewed the relationship of human beings to nature, namely, in the manner of pilgrims.

by the state of technology and social organization on the environment's ability to meet present and future needs.[15]

Such an orientation, however, does not provide us the *vision* for eco-justice. It is possible only when we look at nature not as an instrument for the present and future human wellbeing and progress, but as having *value in itself*. Unfortunately, even in classical Christian thinking, not to speak of Cartesian dualism, the whole reality was hierarchized in such a way that the lower forms in nature are to be of service to the higher ones, while all of them exist for the sake of human beings – a view held also by Thomas Aquinas.[16] On the other hand, poets, artists and mystics view nature and the Earth as endowed with meaning and value in themselves and not in terms of their utility for human beings. This aesthetic perspective needs to percolate in all relationships of human beings to nature, including economic activity, and this would ultimately enhance and heighten the quality of human life which is not to be measured on the basis of the capacity to extract maximum benefit from nature. Such an orientation is conducive to the practice of eco-justice.

## Ecological Economics

The dominant model of market economy and liberal capitalism has failed in promoting social justice and eco-justice. Even more, the reigning paradigm of economy is at the root of social inequality and ecological injustice. Both are two sides of the same coin; you cannot have one without the other.

> Ecological economics does not pretend to be value-free; its preference is evident: the well-being and sustainability of our household, planet Earth. Ecological economics is a human enterprise that seeks to maximize the optimal functioning of the planet's gifts and services for all users. Ecological economics, then, is first of all a vision of how human beings ought to live on planet Earth in light of the perceived reality of where and how we live. We live in, with, and from the Earth.[17]

---

[15] *Our Common Future*, Report of the Brundtland Commission, Oxford University Press, Oxford, 1987.

[16] John Hart, "Catholicism", in Roger S. Gottlieb (ed.), *The Oxford Handbook of Religion and Ecology*, Oxford University Press, Oxford, 2006, p. 68.

[17] Paul F. Knitter – Chandra Muzaffar (eds.), *Subverting Greed. Religious Perspectives on the Global Economy*, Orbis Books, New York, 2002, p. 127.

Liberal economy is driven by the laws of demand and supply, by competition and by profit-considerations all of which have turned out to be prejudicial to the Earth and environment. Ecological economics,[18] on the other hand, will attend to nature and the regenerative capacity of the resources of the Earth, and economic processes of production, distribution and consumption will be directed by these ecological concerns. Ecological economics will go into the study and analysis of the correlation between economic growth processes and eco-systems. More basically it will view both society and economics as subsets of the eco-system which is different from the misconception that they (society and economics) could function independently from the environment.[19] We need to view ecological economics as part of a new vision of reality and choice of different set of values.

### Promotion of Biodiversity – Expression of Eco-Justice

Cultural Darwinism created a hierarchy of cultures, and the progress of humanity was viewed as a movement from the *"savage"* state to the *"civilized"* one by adopting one single superior culture – which, of course, was the Western one. Thanks to the work of many committed anthropologists, it became clear that there are numerous cultures each one with its own specific characteristics, and they all manifest the richness of humankind. Today cultural pluralism is accepted at least in principle, and there are efforts to foster cultural diversity and build intercultural connections.

As a comprehensive term, biodiversity refers to genetic diversity, species diversity and ecosystem diversity. Promotion of biodiversity contributes to the life of the weaker and vulnerable sections of humanity. In fact some of the poorest and vulnerable groups live in areas with a lot of biodiversity and herbs and plants around them are important for their livelihood, for their healthcare, etc. Tribals and indigenous peoples have closer knowledge of the various plants, and are familiar with their nutritional and medicinal values. Destroying biodiversity - fruit of 3.5

---

[18] Ecological economics was initiated through the contribution of such thinkers as Kenneth E. Boulding, Nicholas Georgescu-Roegen, Herman Daly, and Robert Constanza.

[19] Cf. Mark Sagoff, *The Economy of the Earth. Philosophy, Law and the Environment*, Cambridge University Press, Cambridge, 1992; Sallie McFague, "God's Household: Christianity, Economics, and Planetary Living", in Paul F. Knitter and Chandra Muzaffar (eds.), *op.cit.*, pp. 119-136.

billion years of evolution - in the name of development or cultivating monocultural cash-crops spells doom to biodiversity dependent population.[20]

One may recall here the tragic example of Irish famine of 1846 when millions died because only two varieties of potatoes were cultivated, not to mention the agricultural disasters in India and other tropical countries through the colonial practice of monoculture still profitably continued by agri-business. Conservation of the various species of flora and fauna is to defend both social justice and eco-justice. Moreover, given the fact that most of the medicines are created from bio-materials, the failure to conserve biodiversity is bound to reflect on the health care of the poor of the world an overwhelming majority of whom depend upon numerous medicinal plants. Promotion of eco-justice through biodiversity is an important way of bringing justice closer to the poor. The implementation of various conventions relating to conservation of biodiversity require a wider vision in which, as we noted earlier, the heritage of nature is acknowledged as having value in itself.

## Synergy for Eco-Justice

Promotion of eco-justice calls for the convergence of many forces from different quarters. The kind of transformation eco-justice implies, warrant a change of paradigm. The question of the relationship of faith and reason has absorbed the Christian thinking for the past several centuries. It reflects a strong anthropocentrism in which the relationships are twofold, namely, between the individual (or human community) and God and the relationship among the humans. Today Christian faith – for that matter any religious faith – needs to not only add the new dimension of relationship of the *humans and the Earth*, but also make this the focal point from which to understand and define the other two relationships. This

---

[20] Cf. Vandana Shiva, "Farmers' Rights, Biodiversity and International Treatises", in *EPW*, 28, 4 (3 April 1993) pp. 555-560; Vandana Shiva and Holla Bhar R., "Intellectual Piracy and the Neem Tree", in *The Ecologist*, 23, 6 (1993) 223-227; Ashish Aggarwal, "Indigenous Institutions for Natural Resource Management: Potential and Threats", in *Economic and Political Weekly* 43, 23 (7 June 2008) pp. 21-24; Vandana Shiva, *Biopiracy. The Plunder of Nature and Knowledge*, South End Press, Cambridge, 1996; Surender Singh Chauhan, *Biodiversity, Biopiracy and Biopolitics. The Global Perspectives*, Kalinga Publications, Delhi, 2001; Vandana Shiva, *Staying Alive. Women, Ecology and Survival in India*, Kali for Women, New Delhi, 1989.

vision would create the environment and condition for the practice of eco-justice.

The practice of eco-justice is in need of continuous new inputs from science which presents to us even the complexity and intricacies of nature. The data it provides helps us widen our vision and understand the importance of the new paradigm. The present educational systems – both secular and theological – are not attuned to a new ecological vision. It fosters a culture of consumerism that lives on the exploitation of nature beyond its regenerative capacity. We need an education that will create a mindset of valuing nature in itself and nurturing it. A new educational process to be fostered at all levels will foreground the relationship of humans to nature, and the Earth will not be viewed simply as objects of technological exploitation.

Theology, as John Clammer rightly points out, is one of those sciences which has still the potential for an integral approach to reality.[21] Unfortunately, this potential remains untapped. Promoting a new vision of the interrelationship of human beings with nature remains one of the important tasks of theology today. In particular there is an urgent need to rethink the narration of God in her relationship to the Earth and the whole creation in such a way that the mystery of the Divine is experienced immanently as present in nature and in its dynamism.[22] These perspectives will contribute both to social justice and eco-justice, since both are intertwined. Here we need to add also the importance of inter-religious sharing and conversation. One religious vision could be corrective to another one, and there could be mutual enrichment in relating to the environment.[23]

---

[21] Cf. John Clammer, "Learning from the Earth: Reflections on Theological Education and the Ecological Crisis", in *Concilium* 2009/3, pp. 95-101.

[22] The challenge to rethink the traditional Christian approach to God comes from the ecological crisis today as much as from the post-secular situation. On this latter point see Felix Wilfred, "Crisis in the Christian Narration of God and the Encounter of Religions in a Post-metaphysical World", in *Bangalore Theological Forum*, 41, 2 (2009), pp. 15-28 (This is a lecture originally delivered at Pontifical Catholic University, Rio de Janeiro and at the Department of Humanities, UNISINOS University, Porto Alegre, Brazil, respectively on 15th & 17th September, 2009).

[23] Cf. Felix Wilfred, "Toward an Inter-religious Eco-theology" in *Concilium* 2009/3, pp. 43-54.

## Conclusion

One of the things that is becoming more and more evident in today's world is that if we travel the way of social justice we will reach eco-justice; reversely if we promote eco-justice we will land in social justice. To put it differently, the defence of the Earth and its ecosystem is the defence of the poor; and the defence of the poor implies the protection of the environment. For, the people who suffer most from environmental degradation and climate change are the poor ones. *The failure of Copenhagen Summit is precisely in its reluctance to relate the poor to the ecological question and to face the implications of this relationship.*[24]

Our relationship to nature invariably rests on our unexpressed assumptions about our understanding of them, and the perspective from which we view them. The expansion of justice to include eco-justice helps us forge new relationships with the Earth, and it implies that we also widen our understanding of community, common good, development, etc. Basically there is the need to change the mode of our thinking and to acquaint ourselves to a new and different cosmology. It also calls for a shift from an instrumental approach to nature to an approach that would value the Earth and all its beings for what they are in themselves. The development of various disciplines, including theology, needs to rethink some of their foundational conceptions in consonance with the demands of eco-justice which should form part of the educational praxis at all levels.

Let me make one final point. The increasing violence we experience in the world has, of course, its immediate causes. However, if we analyze in depth the escalation of violence and expansion of structures conducive to violence, they have something to do with the whole environment of exploitation both in human communities and in the relationship of humans to nature. The schooling in violence begins from what humans do when they wantonly deal with creation. A non-violent society and world will be a distant dream unless the humans begin to relive in harmony their relationship to the Earth and the entire creation.

---

[24] Cf. John Vidal, "Bolivia Stuns Climate Summit With Target", in *The Hindu*, December 18, 2009, p. 17; "No Hope in Copenhagen", Editorial, *The New Indian Express*, December 21, 2009, p. 8; Richard Black, "Why Did Copenhagen Fail to Deliver a Climate Deal?", in *The Hindu*, December 24, 2009, p. 11; M.S. Swaminathan, "Copenhagen, Tsunami and Hunger", in *The Hindu*, December 26, 2009, p.12.

Chapter 10

# Prophetic Anger and
# Sapiential Compassion
*Grappling with Evil Today*

---

*"A fundamental sanity of Indian civilization has been due to an absence of
Satan"*            - Romila Thapar[1]

*But he said, 'No, lest in gathering the weeds you root up the wheat along with
them. Let both grow together until the harvest; and at harvest time, I will tell
the reapers, "Gather the weeds first and bind them in bundles to be burned, but
gather the wheat into my barn (Mt 13: 29-30)."*

If there is a single most anguishing issue that calls for the
concerted effort of all religious traditions, it is the problem of evil. In
spite of their best efforts, no one religion has succeeded in explaining
satisfactorily the genesis of evil, nor has any one of them come out with
appropriate strategies and praxis to respond to evil, especially when it
confronts us as the suffering of the innocent. Whether the story of the
original fall, or the theory of *karma* or the belief in predestination, or the
ingenious philosophical argumentation around the traditional question
of theodicy – they all leave us high and dry in coming to terms with the
concrete experience of evil. At best, they are scattered flickers while
humanity is struggling - in the proverbial sense - to look for a black cow
in the pitch darkness of the night; and at worst they are like the plight of
Sisyphus, sadly witnessing all the painstakingly worked out theoretical

---

[1] Romila Thapar, *Early India. From the Origins to AD 1300*, Penguin Books,
Delhi, 2002, xviii.

constructions roll down the hill, to begin the struggle once again. May be when these flickers come together more light is thrown on this vexing issue; may be when the hands of religious traditions all join together in the ascent, there is more hope at the end.

Obviously, it is not my intention here to go into any study and analysis of the question of *unde malum* - where does the evil come from - or describe the ways in which it has been responded to by the various religious traditions, or the extent and nature of human freedom and responsibility. The scope of this chapter is a limited one. It falls in the larger area of how we respond to evil, given the inexorable fact that it is there. In seeking an answer it proposes that evil, like in the case of all reality, requires a *ying-yang* response. This is what I mean when I say *"prophetic anger"* and *"sapiential compassion"*.

## Convergence of Anger and Compassion in the Divine

In the Biblical tradition Yahweh is an angry God, but at the same time she is a God of compassion with maternal qualities. What is humanely thought as irreconcilable is united on the divine manifesting two important dimensions of the divine mystery.

Conjoining the opposites – *coincidentia oppositorum* – is a typical pattern of the Hindu conception of the divine. As conqueror of evil, goddess Kali is fearsome and terrifying, and at the same time her anger is the expression of her motherly protection from evil, and she is most compassionate. Shiva, the supreme deity in the Saivite tradition, is known to be fierce and is depicted with a third eye, which when opened, destroys and reduces to ashes the evil. The same Shiva is also known to be a beneficent god who confers happiness.[2]

To deploy Jungian categories of *animus* and *anima*, we may say that the prophetic anger is the *animus*, whereas the sapiential compassion is the *anima* – the healing touch. It cares for the victims and is concerned about the subject as he or she is, and aims at transformation. If Jesus' attitude towards the evil of the society of his times was the expression of his prophetic anger (Jn 2:14-16), we find in his Sermon on the Mount the *anima*, the sapiential compassion. His stance depicts God's approach to the human reality dotted by evil. In Buddhism compassion (*karuna*) is

---

[2] *Rudra* and *Shankara* are the two different names with which Shiva is referred. They mean respectively "the fearsome" and "the beneficent".

closely related to the quality of wisdom (*prajna*), which is feminine. In fact, the compassion results from wisdom which perceives each event, and each aspect of reality as part of an organic whole. It is this perspective of wisdom that flows as the river of compassion to enliven all human beings and the entire universe. It is not a sign of weakness but of strength, no less than that of the prophetic anger.

## A World Not-Angry Enough

More than the way we try to find ingenious solutions to the reality of evil, which anyway eludes our intellectual prowess, what defines us more as individuals and groups is the way we react to evil and respond to it. This is a crucial question. For, as Hannah Arendt has drawn our attention, there is something like *banality of evil*.[3] Its everyday genesis and manifestations do not involve any sensation as it is mostly committed by ordinary men and women who go about their daily lives, and are, by no means, moral monsters.

> For what Arendt meant in saying that evil may be banal was simply that
> it need not be demonic. After Auschwitz, at the latest, we learned that
> the greatest crimes can be committed by people less likely to arouse terror
> and awe than contempt and disgust. Thoughtlessness can be more
> dangerous than malice; we are more often threatened by self-serving
> refusal to see the consequences of conventional action than by defiant
> desires for destruction.[4]

The first sentiment in responding to evil should be a sense of horror, trembling and indignation at the injustice and suffering inflicted on the victims, and that is very important. We note that the environment we live in is so politicized that human beings are less and less shocked by the horror of evil. Evil has become a matter of statistics, codification, media-commercialization and photography.[5] There is more a techno-managerial

---

[3] Hannah Arendt, *Eichmann in Jerusalem*, Viking Press, New York, 1977.

[4] Susan Neiman, *Evil in Modern Thought*, Princeton University Press, Princeton – Oxford, 2002, p. xii.

[5] I want to refer here to the photograph by Kevin Carter, which brought Pulitzer Prize *New York Times* published it in 1994. The photographer captured this symbol of the suffering of the innocent. A little girl in Sudan, reduced to skeleton by starvation, pulls up her remaining strength to crawl to a neighbouring feeding centre, but collapses, and a vulture is perching near the little girl. For the photographer it was a moment of glory to have caught this moment into a picture. But later on, Carter was tormented by the question: What did I do at that moment to save the little starving child? This anguishing

response than a *human* response. What point is there, for example, to lament that the arms may fall into the hands of "terrorists" when there is no effective will to abolish arms and the arms-race? We need to be angry about a whole system that allows the proliferation of deadly arms. Terrorism is nothing but the byproduct of a world which is not angry enough with the production, marketing and accumulation of deadly arms and lethal weapons.

What strikes us is the fact that anger characterized men and women of great leadership, because they were upset with the existing situation and they imagined a different order of things. Moses was such a man in the Biblical tradition. In modern times, such was the case for example with Ambedkar, the foremost leader of the Dalits ("Untouchables") of India, and Dr. Martin Luther King of the civil rights movement in the USA,[6] both of whom were great angry leaders. We could characterize this as "holy anger". It aims not at destroying the enemies or punishing them but at redeeming a society of the consequences of evil. In this context we may recall Rabbi Heschel who not only wrote a classic work on prophets, but like them was angry and was involved in civil rights movement and walked with Dr Martin Luther King in the second Selma march in Alabama, in solidarity with the victims. When asked about that experience, Heschel is supposed to have replied that he "felt as if his feet were praying." It is the same Rabbi Heschel who characterized the prophets as those who spoke "one octave too high".[7]

## A World of Acquiescence and Political Correctness
Conformity to the system, to the given, seems to be the dominant philosophy. It advocates political correctness and prescribes standards of social acceptance. There is a large dose of pragmatism in it, but also the lack of courage for confrontation, challenge and the building of a counter-culture. The symbols of the counter-culture of once are trivialized today. There are few who are ready to tell the plain truth that the emperor is naked. There is something like the politicization of evil.

---

question led him to commit suicide in the month of July of the same year 1994. See Arthur Kleinman – Veena Das – Margaret Lock (eds.), *Social Suffering*, Oxford University Press, Culcutta-Chennai-Mumbai,1998, pp. 3 ff.

[6] Cf. Martin Luther King Jr., *Where Do We Go from Here: Chaos or Community?*, Harper & Row, New York, 1997; Thomas F. Jackson, *From Civil Rights to Human Rights. Martin Luther King Jr., and the Struggle for Economic Justice*, University of Pennsylvenia Press, Philadelphia-Pennsylvenia, 2007.

[7] Cf. Abraham J. Heschel, *The Prophets*, Harper Collins, London, 2001.

Covering up evil and acquiescence brings rewards. Hence there is the temptation to leave evil wide-open to ambiguity. There is certainly the need to be restrained at times lest no greater evil occurs. But this principle could become a justification for acquiescence with the existing order of things. The contentment with the status quo can be characterized as the *"royal consciousness"* which is challenged by the prophets who evoke a different consciousness and perception about the culture and evil around, and through their "prophetic imagination" project alternatives and thus nurture hope.[8]

It is a fact that people are moved when they see suffering which is reminiscent of their own struggles and are less sensitive when it is the suffering of others who are ethnically, geographically and culturally different and distant.[9] If it is true that some good could come out of evil, it is this: The evil and sufferings the victims undergo is a challenge to the dominant interpretation of history; it is a challenge to the model of development and the projection about the future of humanity. On all these fronts, the victims challenge us.

In our world we experience an abundance of communication. But the growth in communication is not matched by a growth in resistance. We would expect communication to bring greater knowledge and truth about reality resulting in revolt and resistance. But, alas, this does not happen. For parallel to the process of communication which reveals, there is also a process of cover-ups deftly manipulated, creating a world of make-belief. The unmasking of evil is a serious problem in the global empire controlled by innumerable anonymous power-centres and operators, who benumb and "mystify" the consciousness of the masses.

As a result, today, the question is no more why people rebel; rather the question is why people do *not* rebel and rise up in protest, in spite of the fact that evil has not abated. The question becomes all the more complex in our global world where it is difficult to identify the enemy against whom we should rebel and resist.

The intricate and ingenious ways in which the distortion in representing evil and suffering in our world - especially the suffering of the other in the ethnic, religious, and cultural sense - takes place, should

---

[8] Cf. Walter Brueggemann, *The Prophetic Imagination*, Fortress Press, Minneapolis, 2000.

[9] Arthur Kleinman et al. (eds.), *op.cit.* p. 272.

provoke prophetic anger. Such an anger is necessary lest our sense of hope and confidence is not vanquished, and we settle down with compromise by opting for what is comfortable and unsettling.

## A Question of Method

Since evil is a universal phenomenon affecting the entire humanity, cutting across all religious traditions, in responding to it, we may not simply rely on any one single theology.[10] There needs to be conversation among the various theologies of religious traditions in order to respond to this all embracing reality of evil.

The methodology we adopt to approach the question of evil needs to be holistic. Mere rational tools show their utter inadequacy when confronted with the issue. That is why the whole person needs to be involved in responding to evil, including one's emotional resources and energies. This goes against any compromise or acquiescence to evil. Just as a cosmic acquiescence to evil as something inevitably part of creation – an evolutionary perspective espoused also by Teilhard de Chardin - needs to be overcome by the perspective of the agency of human intervention, so too the historic acquiescence and compromise to evil needs to be challenged by prophetic anger. And since the good and evil are mixed as we find in the parable of grain and weeds (Mt 13:24-30), and since, as Augustine says, "the rise, the development and the destined ends of the two cities…[are] … interwoven and mingled with one another,"[11] there is need for true wisdom to discern – something that goes beyond the power of reason. This wisdom is the spring of compassion.

## Multiple Perspectives

Evil, which is a mystery and which clouds our understanding, cannot be responded to with any one single perspective or view. It is not a question like in other areas, where maintaining one perspective consistently and deducing conclusions logically is a matter of strength. But it is sheer weakness in the case of evil. Therefore, we need to hold many perspectives together and allow a little more light to fall on the darkness that evil represents. This is precisely the strength of India's thought on evil that it

---

[10] Max Weber identified three explanations for evil: *dualism* which makes evil and good two polar forces, *predestination* and the theory of *karma*. Of all the three he found most satisfying the approach taken by the theory of karma for a problem which ultimately defies all solutions.

[11] St. Augustine, *The City of God*, Book XI.

holds together at least two different perspectives. At one level is the monistic view that holds that good and evil are *indivisible* and forms part and parcel of human life.

> The individual creates his life not out of the full range of materials but, as it were, out of *objects trouvé*, and each individual is expected to create a different part of the mosaic, some of these parts necessarily involving suffering, heresy or other evils, provided by the gods, who are caught up in *karma* as we are.[12]

Evil is seen, in the Indic tradition, for example, as the constant threat to purity, and this is how it is explained as something inevitable; there is no way in which impurity could be totally avoided.[13] The second perspective is the one in which good and evil are viewed *antagonistically*,[14] (which is not the same thing as dualistically), and this is represented by Buddhism which challenged the monistic perspective, and later on by the *bhakti* tradition in Hinduism itself. The Buddhist tradition saw in the human intervention the means not so much to conquer and triumph over evil as to bring the evil-doer with compassion to the path of righteousness.[15] These traditions also challenged the conception of evil as something cosmic beyond the control of the human and as something to be accepted as inevitable.

### Theological Character in Response to Evil

There is a theological character in the response to evil. It is by listening to God's call and to the voice of the Spirit who direct our steps that we respond at one moment with anger and another moment with compassion. In this way, there is no need for unifying these apparently contradictory attitudes and sentiments. They both get united in God's call as a common point of reference. What is required of human beings is that there be sensitivity to the call of God and that the call is discerned every moment afresh. This way of acting and responding reflects precisely the manner of Jesus. He could be compassionate at one moment and at another moment

---

[12] Wendy Doniger O'Flaherty, *The Origin of Evil in Hindu Mythology*, University of California Press, Berkeley, 1976.

[13] This is closer to the perspective which sees evil as an inevitable byproduct of a world in evolution.

[14] Cf. O'Flaherty, *op.cit.* p. 378.

[15] Cf. H. Schwartz, *Evil. A Historical and Theological Perspective*, Fortress Press, Minneapolis, 1995, p. 195.

he could chase the vendors from the temple, and call Herod the king, a fox (Lk 13:31).

The theological character is also to be discerned in the fact that the response to evil is an object of revelation, even as evil itself remains a mystery. Light on this dark reality does not come through the powers of mind and reason, but is something that is hidden to the wise and revealed to the babes (Lk 10:21). The traditional question of theodicy grappling with the problem of how to reconcile the image of a benevolent and powerful God with the reality of human suffering has been given a new turn by liberation theology, in which the traditional question is turned into a question of how to speak about God amidst the suffering of the innocent.[16]

### Mythical, Mystical and Prophetic Language in Responding to Evil

In his contribution to *Encyclopedia of Religion,* Paul Ricoeur begins his article on "Evil" with a pregnant statement: "If there is one human experience ruled by myth, it is certainly that of evil".[17] Evil is one reality where we reach the limits of reason, and myth seems to take over. Myth has the advantage of bearing contradictions in itself. One does not rationalize and systematize the contents of a myth. Myth as a narrative is open-ended. One could add, subtract, etc. It is a companion on our journey. By placing our demands and expectations on it, we shape the myths as we move along. Myths and symbols also play an important role by offering hope for the future. This hope is not for a magical change of things; it comes in the form of courage and strength against any sense of defeatism or despondency before evil.

The other language that is able to approximate some understanding of evil is the mystical language. At that level, one understands evil in the light of the overwhelming greatness of God's love. "The language of contemplation acknowledges that everything comes from the Fathers' unmerited love and opens up 'new horizons of hope'".[18] The mystical language is not something that simply fosters resignation but has prophetic overtones. Powerless though, the victims bring out their anger against

---

[16] Cf. Gustavo Gutierrez, *On Job. God-Talk and the Suffering of the Innocent,* Orbis Books, New York, 1987.

[17] Paul Ricoeur, "Evil" in *Encyclopedia of Religion,* vol 5, Collier Macmillan, New York, 1987, p. 199.

[18] Cf. Gustavo Gutierrez, *op.cit.* p. 97.

inflicted suffering in prophetic language, as in the case of the "Untouchables" against those who practice discrimination on the basis of purity and pollution. This language shocks their oppressors, which leads either to their (oppressors') changing of ways, or serve as provocation for further suppression. The victim's language of anger is often tinted with lamentation, and lamentation does not imply loss of hope, but it is a manner of coping with the evil they suffer, and it has cathartic effect.[19]

### Prophetic Anger – Some Salient Features

When we speak of prophetic anger, the question that could be raised is: Whose anger? It is first and foremost the anger of the victims. For it is they who know the pain that evil inflicts in the form of grinding poverty, violence, etc. Along with the victims, we have those in solidarity with them who express rage at the situations of gross injustice. Anger is of different kinds. Anger can and does often accompany the spirit of vindication and revenge.[20] This anger is aimed at others as enemies, as threats, etc. But prophetic anger has a direct reference to justice. The anger of the victims has something visceral about it. The whole being of the victim reacts to the injustice and oppression suffered – be it women, the discriminated ethnic, religious or linguistic minorities or any victim of human rights violation. There is then ample room to speak about "black rage" and similarly gender-rage etc., which express the anguish of the victims pushed to the wall through long-standing oppression, and yet having the strength to imagine something different. Prophetic anger is a healing anger. It opens the wounds of the society, and has ultimately the goal of healing them.

Moreover, prophetic anger is the result of being gripped by an encounter and experience of something wonderful and exceedingly beautiful beyond the present disfiguration of reality. This is something different from a mere human passion. Like symbols which help us convey what words and speech are incapable of, so anger is a medium to bridge the gulf that divides the lofty realities and the misery of the prevailing

---

[19] We could note all these characteristics in the literature of the oppressed Dalit ("The Untouchables"), especially in their poems and their *testimonies* or autobiographies.

[20] The Letter to the Ephesians tells us as to the nature of just anger. It should not be nurtured by hatred or revengeful intent. "In your anger do not sin; do not let the sun go down while you are still angry and do not give the devil a foothold" (Eph 4: 26-27).

situation. The encounter and experience which is in the prophets also finds expression in the prophetic anger as it is directed at the cause behind the suffering of the innocent.

The force of the prophetic anger is derived from the fact that it addresses evil very concretely and with reference to a specific context. Only when placed against the context, the nature of evil stands out in all its horror. The challenge then becomes so powerful that evil cannot take shelter under convenient pretexts.

Prophetic anger is directed at awakening people from their slumber, their numbness. People do not want to face the suffering of others in everyday life. There is an attempt to put up a brave front and convince oneself that everything is fine. The reality all around us benumbs people. Prophetic anger provokes people out of their complacency, their situation of being anesthetized by the manipulative techniques of the empire, of the dominant powers. There is anger because there is a violation of human dignity and rights, and a distortion of the vision of something beautiful. Loss of vision is the cause for the perpetuation of the present as the optimal situation. It works to the advantage of the powerful and causes suffering to the victims.

### Some Components of Sapiential Compassion

Whereas prophetic anger points to the human responsibility in perpetrating evil, compassion proceeds from another perspective that goes beyond human culpability. It derives from the conviction that evil is the product of ignorance;[21] or that it is the result of a particular existential situation into which human beings are thrown by circumstances of history.

Compassion is a response as well to evil understood as suffering, and indeed as the suffering of the innocent. What moves one to compassion is the wisdom that the entire reality is bonded together. Human beings, sentient beings and nature – all are part of the cosmic family and their destiny is also bound together. To view every aspect of reality as the part of a whole is indeed a practice in wisdom. In this holistic perspective of reality, suffering of any being becomes one's own suffering since every part goes to make up the whole. The *karuna* or compassion of which

---

[21] In the West, this tradition is represented by Socrates and Plato, and in the Indian tradition we have the advaitic (non-duality) school represented by the medieval philosopher Sankara.

Buddhism and Hinduism speak so very insistently is precisely inspired by this holistic and sapiential vision. It is not sign of any weakness; it has the power to break the mountains, and make the stones cry in repentance.

Sapiential compassion signals also to the consequences of evil-doing. One has to steer through a dilemma: On the one hand is the existential condition of the evil-doer with his or her personal history provoking compassion. On the other hand, there is the legitimate demand for retribution to uphold justice and moral standards. Mercy and compassion could become a matter of leniency and arbitrariness. St. Anselm's difficulty was how could God punish some who are unworthy, while showing mercy to equally unworthy people. Kant, on his part, feared that the role of compassion in criminal law could lead the sovereign to the dereliction of his duty of justice.[22] What saves compassion from such dangers is that its genuine practice has reference, like in the case of prophetic anger, to something beyond, to a motive that surpasses the conventional ways and manners. Theological motive consists in that, human beings by practising reflect the divine. For it is the God who allows rain over the just and the unjust, and it is to this we are exhorted when Jesus says, "be merciful as your Father is merciful" (Lk 6:36). One who experiences this gratuitousness, and abundance of God's love and mercy, approaches evil with great wisdom and compassion.

In compassion we understand more deeply not only the divine, but the human mystery as well. It is the mystery of the "bruised reed". It is this divine-human justice and compassion that prophet Isaiah seems to depict when he speaks of the Lord's servant, as someone who "will bring forth justice to the nations. He will not cry or lift up his voice, or make it heard in the street; a bruised reed he will not break, and a dimly burning wick he will not quench; he will faithfully bring forth justice" (Is 42: 2-4). Where there is compassion and mercy, people do not lose their dignity; they are not humiliated. There is a hope of being accepted. For compassion is able to draw good from the evil existing in the world and in human

---

[22] The response to these questions lies in a distinction between criminal law model and private law model. In the former case a judge has the obligation and responsibility to safeguard justice by imposing sanctions proportionate to the crime, and may not act on the basis of personal compassion. In the private law model when a person has certain rights as in the case of a contract of loan, he or she can forego or waive this right by being compassionate. Here there is no offence against justice. Cf. Edward Craig (ed.), *Routledge Encyclopedia of Philosophy*, vol. 3, Routledge, New York, 1998, p. 700.

beings. It knows that it is the veil of ignorance that creates enemies. What that compassion bathed in wisdom is we recognize in a poem of the Vietnamese Buddhist monk Thich Nhat Hanh known as "Call me by my true names:"

The rhythm of my heart is the birth and
death of all that are alive

I am the mayfly metamorphosing on the surface of the river,
and I am the bird which, when spring comes, arrives in time
to eat the mayfly.

I am the frog swimming happily in the clear pond,
and I am also the grass-snake who, approaching in silence
feeds itself on the frog.

I am the child in Uganda, all skin and bones,
My legs as thin as bamboo sticks,
And I am the arms merchant, selling deadly weapons to Uganda.

I am the twelve-year-old girl, refugee on a small boat.
Who throws herself into the ocean after being raped by a sea pirate,
and I am the pirate, my heart not yet capable of seeing and loving.

I am a member of the politburo, with plenty of power in my hands,
and I am the man who has to pay his"debt of blood" to my people,
Dying slowly in a forced labor camp.

My job is like spring, so warm it makes flowers bloom in all walks of life.
My pain if like a river of tears, so full it fills the four oceans.

Please call me by my true names,
so I can hear all my cries and laughs at once,
so I can see that my joy and pain are one.

Please call me by my true names,
so I can wake up,
and so the door of my heart can be left open,
the door of compassion.[23]

Sapiential compassion involves also a self-critique and reflexivity. It is a confession of human limitations and judgment. It is a realization that the task of discerning good and evil is fraught with risks, and deciding one way or the other has serious consequences. Sapiential compassion,

[23] Thich Nhat Hanh, *Call Me by My True Names:* Collected Poems and Their Nhat Hanh, Parallax Press, Berkeley, CA, 1999.

however, needs to be understood in an active and dynamic sense. It would simply be a cover-up of evil if it does not lead to a sense of repentance, readiness for expiation and transformation of the self of the evil-doer, or the group that was instrumental in bringing forth a particular evil. Here is the real struggle to be human in responding to evil.

## Conclusion

The human response to evil can be modeled after two symbols which are pertinent to our discussion. One is *the symbol of the cross* which is the result of having been angry with all the wrongs and injustices of society and refusing to be politically correct, and at the same time filled with compassion for a humanity that is under suffering, by taking upon oneself voluntarily the suffering. I need not elaborate this image well known to us.

I would rather highlight another model image – the image of the angry and compassionate god Shiva. Seeing the creatures dying for want of *amrita* – the immortal food, the compassionate gods were engaged in churning the ocean of milk to produce *amrita*. For that purpose they used a mountain called *Meru* as the stick and the cosmic serpent *Vasuki* as the rope. When after prolonged efforts in churning, the *amrita* was emerging, the snake Vasuki, heated up, spewed venom. It threatened to poison the very food that was produced with so much of labour for the life of the universe. At this point, provoked by compassion for all beings, Shiva instantaneously took the poison and swallowed it. It landed on his neck which turned blue.

The iconography of Shiva shows him as blue-necked and with the serpent coiled around his neck. The blue neck is the symbol of Shiva's compassion for all creatures, and the tamed snake purged of its poison is the transformation effected on the evil that was a threat and danger. The concentration of the myth is not so much on the power of god to control evil; rather on the gratuitous compassion of God, on God's *dharma*, or sense of righteousness which want all creatures to sprout, flourish and blossom in full.

If responding to evil is a struggle, even greater struggle is to be *human* in our response to evil. When we touch the core of what it means to be human, we comprehend the blurred 'greyness' in the motives and attitudes of people beyond the black and white demarcations. Then the human response to evil as prophetic anger and sapiential compassion can model on the divine response to the *mysterium iniquitatis* – the mystery of iniquity which is beyond clear cut definitions and boundaries.

# Part III

# Theological Crossroads

Chapter 11

# Christianity between Decline and Resurgence

*"Christianity is flourishing wonderfully among the poor and persecuted. While it atrophies among the rich and secure....If it is not exactly a faith based on the experience of poverty and persecution, then at least it regards these things as normal and expected elements of life...Christianity can certainly succeed in other settings, even amid peace and prosperity, but perhaps, it does become harder, as hard as passing through the eye of a needle."* – Philip Jenkins[1]

The global status of Christianity is important for Asian Christianity to come to terms with the public issues and questions of the continent. Nobody can seriously dispute the fact that some years ago in the American presidential re-election of George Bush, Christian religious sentiments and convictions played an important role; Evangelical and neo-orthodox forms of Christianity exerted great influence. Critically thinking and secular-minded Europeans were ill at ease with this mix of religion in politics which they were used to associate with the Muslims. Let us look at another fact. The European Union drew up the draft of a Constitution in which there was no mention of Christianity, in spite of the fact that the European culture and history have been impregnated by this religious tradition.[2] When we place these two facts side by side, the

---

[1] Philip Jenkins, *The Next Christendom. The Coming of Global Christianity,* Oxford University Press, New York, 2002, p. 220.

[2] Pope John Paul II made repeated appeals to include the Christian roots in the Constitution; so did the Bishops' Conference of European Community, but these went unheeded. Space does not permit elaborate documentation and references.

question whether Christianity is in crisis turns out to be a very difficult and complex question to respond to.

If we add to this the fact of the resurgence of Christianity in Africa through indigenous forms and expressions, and the emergence of a different form of Christianity in Asia, shaped by religious experiences of other traditions, the question becomes compounded, and all the more difficult to answer. Speaking of African Christianity, Lamin Sanneh notes that, 'African Christianity, then, is the irony of mass religious enthusiasm pitted against mass disenchantment with political structures'.[3] Whether Christianity is in decline yielding to post-Christian situation, or in resurgence will depend upon how the present state of Christianity is being viewed and assessed in differing world-contexts.

Is Christianity in crisis? Any attempt to answer this question would call for a certain conceptual clarification regarding what is meant by *crisis*, what are its processes, and in what ways crises are sought to be resolved. After some elucidation on the fundamental concept of crisis and its dynamics, we will take up the question whether Christianity is in crisis through three interpretative keys before we look at the resurgence of Christianity in the South in its varied forms, and conclude with some brief thought on what Christianity could mean for a world in crisis.

## Two Approaches in Crisis
Various sociological theories try to analyze and explain the origin, dynamics, climax and the prospects of ending a social or political crisis. For example, Marxist crisis theory relates the analysis of crisis to developments within the economic processes with social and political consequences. The approach to crisis will differ according to the basic paradigm in the understanding of society. In a *functionalist paradigm* crisis will be a matter of dysfunction, disturbance or sudden disruption in the system, which calls for the stabilization or equilibrium of the system through the application of appropriate means. It could be also a perception of threat to the system and its structures. In this functional perspective the means (tools, expertise, resources, etc) are thought to be available *within the system*, and in this context one speaks today of *crisis management*.

But in more *critical approach* to crisis analysis, the capacity for coming to terms with crisis would go beyond, calling for decisive *critical*

---

[3] Lamin Sanneh, *Whose Religion Is Christianity? The Gospel Beyond the West*, William B. Eerdmans Publishing Company, Grand Rapids, 2003, p. 28.

*interventions*. This latter approach can invoke support from the *medical use* of the terminology of crisis – which seems to be very basic for the concept – in as much as the situation of a patient could undergo a sudden change either towards deterioration or towards improvement, causing both anxiety and hope. In this understanding, crisis would denote a crucial situation for the resolution of which the available means within the system are inadequate, and would call for external measures. The structural paradigm to society and its processes would view crisis as a crucial point which could cause a total collapse or disaster, or turn out to be a qualitatively different and abrupt turn.

There is yet another aspect to the understanding of crisis which goes back in some of the European languages to seventeenth and eighteenth centuries in the context of martial expedition. Crisis is a battle situation in which crucial *decisions* have to be taken, and decisive strategic measures are to be adopted, and this reflects the original Greek etymological sense of *krínein*, meaning decision, decisive change, etc. Subsequently, the word "crisis" was used also to characterize certain political and social situations of deep contradictions calling forth the outbreak of revolution as a way out of the situation, or abrupt changeover from one particular social formation to another.[4] In today's world, the use of the term "crisis" has undergone inflation; it is employed to refer to any personal or institutional situation of stress, and is applied to every possible field. Besides society, politics, economy, culture and religion, crisis is referred in this inflated sense to any unpleasant and undesirable situation in everyday life. That would be a very diluted sense in which we do not employ crisis in relation to Christianity.

As regards the significance, crisis could be viewed as a normal growth process in any individual or institution, in which case the facet of *opportunities* it offers gets highlighted. One begins to think of the new prospects opened up by crisis. On the other end of the spectrum of significance, crisis is viewed as nothing but deviance, the norm being the functioning of a system or institution as it has been, and the goal being the restoration and reestablishment of the old. In this latter context, the *discourse on crisis* could serve also as *a pretext* and *legitimation* to impose one's views and positions.

---

[4] In terms of time, crisis indicates a situation of short duration, but could also be a prolonged situation as in the case of some economic crisis characterized by poverty, unemployment, lacking in trade and investment period of sustained economic recession and crisis is called "depression".

## Christianity in Crisis – Three Diagnostic Keys

For *neo-orthodoxy*[5] fighting on many fronts, the diagnosis of crisis, its definition and its solution are characterized by what it is claiming to do in all these – *defensio fidei* – the defence of faith and its integrity. The farthest extent neo-orthodoxy could go is reformism, even that, on its own terms. It is not strange then that in the Roman Catholic Church, for example, neo-orthodoxy could invent queer and perplexing interpretations of Vatican Council II in a bid to re-establish old certainties, and thus to refurbish its eroding self-confidence. Neo-orthodoxy, ironically, presents today a challenge to the secular, making this latter shudder at the onslaught of religion, thus completely reversing the roles that characterized secularity and religion not long ago. The same neo-orthodoxy with its multiple limbs, as in the mythical image of Ravana in the Hindu epic, would not hesitate to pull down emerging theologies of religion. Militant as it is, it could crush with its institutional power anyone challenging its war against secularity and other religions.

What we could observe in neo-orthodoxy is that it has progressively changed its accent on crisis *from secularisation to pluralism*, and more specifically to the plurality of religious experiences, since these seem to put into crisis the certainties of the past in a way and to an extent, secularisation did not do. Even as neo-orthodoxy struggles hard to subordinate culture, society and religions under its interpretation of faith, the sense of crisis is reaching a high-point with the crisis of authority in the Church – a crucial preoccupation which colours all neo-orthodox attitudes and interpretations. The progressive marginalisation of Christianity from the consciousness of Europe and its public sphere seems to loom large in the horizon of neo-orthodoxy, accentuating further the sense of crisis.

*Neo-liberal theology*, true to its tradition, has laid emphasis on experience, freedom and the agency of the subject. And these, according to it, would be in tune with modernity, and hence the solution to the crisis situation of Christianity is to thoroughly secularise it by abandoning some of its dated world views, mythical conceptions, practices, orientation to

---

[5] I am using *'neo-orthodoxy'* here not in its restricted technical sense of a development within Protestantism. Rather the term is used here to refer to a trend across denominational borders, and especially as manifest today in Roman Catholicism. It is a trend which, among other things, includes certain political leanings, attitudes, and wants to save Christianity from heterodoxy and marginalisation.

ethics, etc. In other words, the shape of traditional Christianity was contested for its inability to respond to the challenges of modernity, and the solution was found in an accommodating secularisation. There is no need to go in detail into these aspects of liberal theology.

What is most preoccupying, however, is *the new avatar of liberal theology* in the form of a theology of wealth and prosperity. It is a theology which reminds me of the critical words of Richard Niebuhr who spoke of, "a God without wrath [who] brought men without sin into a kingdom without judgment through the ministrations of a Christ without a cross."[6] In the liberal reading, the survival of Christianity is bound together with the success of liberal capitalism and political liberalism. Capitalism is for Michael Novak a "moral case"[7] for Christianity, and wealth, a sign of God's blessings. For him, democratic polity, market-economy and liberal culture would translate Christianity into practice. The implication is that in the absence of capitalism and wealth Christianity would be steeped in crisis and turn ultimately into a failure. This version of neo-liberal reading of crisis of Christianity would converge ironically with neo-orthodox positions such as the ones held by John Milbank, John Neuhaus and others. It is the case of extremes meeting together. For Neuhaus, for example, the trouble with the Catholic Church in Latin America is that it has thrown itself into a crisis by failing to instil values and attitudes that would promote capitalism![8]

For a *postmodernist reading*, the crisis of Christianity is part of the general crisis of all "grand narratives". More specifically, Christianity's fate is sealed with the advent of a post-metaphysical world and culture, characterized as "weak thought". *Postmodernism*, however, is not necessarily anti-religious and anti-Christian. In fact, in some of its versions it has created space for the reappearance of religion which had vanished on the horizon of modernity and secularity. A case in point is that of the Italian Gianni Vattimo who claims to have found back his Christianity through postmodernism.[9]

---

[6] H. Richard Niebuhr, *The Kingdom of God in America*, Harper and Row, New York, 1959, p. 193.

[7] This well-known position of his, he reiterated in a speech delivered before the Mont Pelerin Society in Sri Lanka on January 11, 2004. The positions of George Weigel, John Neuhaus and Robert Sirico are all along the same lines.

[8] John Neuhaus, *Appointment in Rome: The Church in America Awakening*, Crossroad, New York, 1999.

[9] Gianni Vattimo, *After Christianity*, Columbia University Press, New York, 2002.

Postmodernism and Catholicism are not strange bedfellows. The *distancing* of postmodernity from modernity (to avoid speaking in terms of *opposition* between the two which may not be accurate) and the anti-modernity of Catholicism converge at certain points. It should be no surprise then that postmodernism has allowed space for religion in general and Christianity in particular. With the crisis of modernity blown past, the postmodernism of Vattimo could find a place for his Catholicism.

For me what transpires out of this is that, at bottom, Christianity could be identified with Europe only as much as metaphysics could be considered as inalienable presupposition for Christian message. There is however in practice an overlap between the former identification and the latter presupposition which could be seen in the fact of the decline of Christianity in the West with the dissolution of metaphysics in the western culture. What has been said has far reaching implications for Christianity in Asia and in the South in general.

I must immediately add that the resurgence of Christianity in the South goes to show that neither the crisis of Christianity in the West, nor of its metaphysics constitute any threat to the message of the Good News to the poor or to the reality of love - both of which represent the core of the Gospel. What is happening in the South is the expression of a Christianity not tied to any metaphysics, and hence open to a plurality of ways and expressions in experiencing and living out the Gospel. A message that came to us through Jesus Christ is credible not because of its presumed metaphysical basis, but through its radical appeal to our deeper humanity and the contingencies of our lives (individual and collective), and indeed through Jesus' unconditional love and grace, and through his becoming one in solidarity with the poor and embodying in himself the pact of God in defence of the poor. Such a message of love and defence of the poor could hardly be in crisis, all the more so when the axis of Christianity is shifting to the South with more and more Christians from among the poorest of the poor. To put it differently, those with below $ 500 dollars as annual income are the ones who will be, if not already, the most numerous Christian disciples in our world. The shift is not only from the West to the South, but a shift of Christianity from the rich and the middle-class to the poor. A Christianity which is becoming a faith of the poor of today's world, reminding of its origins, can hardly be considered to be in crisis in any negative sense.

None of the above three diagnostic keys seem capable of responding to the new shape of Christianity in the South. They are basically euro-centric optics which view the crisis of Christianity from a particular perspective and against the background of definite historical experiences. Once again, all the three are equally bad instruments to diagnose the crisis of Christianity in the South. The opportunities for Christianity seems to be immense, not in the sense of mission conceived in the West and imposed on the South, but as a result of creative engagement by the peoples of the South themselves in their encounter with the social, political and cultural realities of their context. Obviously, there are many aspects to this engagement, all of which cannot be treated here. Let me highlight one or two aspects which would enlighten us how the crisis in Christianity means new opportunities in the South.

### Future Christianity – A Learner in the School of Tolerance

The future of Christianity will depend upon the extent there takes place a metamorphosis of it as a religion of great tolerance and as a promoter of understanding, capable of creating community in our fragmented world. This could happen, among other things, through a powerful theological engagement with other religious traditions. Implied therein is not that other religious traditions are all but examples of perfect tolerance, but rather the very open engagement of Christianity with other religious traditions is itself a process capable of bringing its deepest truths about tolerance, justice and peace into the open. The overcoming of crisis and the resurgence of Christianity could come about especially in Asia precisely through the above process, and it will contribute to a reinvigorated Christianity. Crisis will apply to Christianity in the South, especially Asian Christianity, in its positive sense of opportunities.[10]

Christianity, in spite of the new opportunities it has in the South, has to wrestle with many aspects of its past, especially the neo-orthodox phobia of religious pluralism. Even a Wolfhart Pannenberg, not known especially for his liberal views, does not hesitate to name where *"the disastrous sin"* lies in Christianity, which is important at this juncture to redeem the future of global Christianity.

> Intolerant dogmatism was probably the most disastrous sin of traditional Christianity from the early centuries up to the beginnings of modern times. Intolerance contributed more to the ambiguity of the Christian past than any other factor, and it is therefore necessary to understand

---

[10] Felix Wilfred, *Asian Dreams and Christian Hope*, ISPCK, Delhi, 2004 (2nd edition); Id., *The Sling of Utopia. Struggles for a Different Society*, ISPCK, Delhi, 2005.

the roots of the phenomenon. We must ask ourselves whether dogmatic intolerance, with all its ugly consequences, belongs to the essence of religious passion for truth, at least in its Christian form. If the answer is yes, the exclusion of religion from the arena of public culture - an exclusion introduced in early modernity after the confessional wars of the post-Reformation period - was justified then and is justified now. But the religious dogmatism that emerged as early as the Constantinian period can also be viewed as a distortion, even a disease, of the religious mind. If it is that, it can in principle be overcome without extinguishing the religious commitment to truth.[11]

Such has been the impression about Christianity in the minds of many Asians too that Arvind Sharma has been driven to ask to what extent we in Asia should be "tolerant of intolerance", and whether we should not develop "intolerance of intolerance".[12] If commitment to truth can be practiced without recourse to the kind of dogmatism and intolerance that is sure to make Christianity ineffective in the public sphere of the developing world, then the wise course of procedure is to open up new approaches to truth in which Christianity will be a prime contributor to tolerance and understanding. This is very important to overcome the crisis of Christianity and make it respond to the resurgence of Christianity in the Asian continent.

But the consoling and hopeful thing is that Asia, for example, is not awaiting anybody's permission to turn Christianity into a religion of tolerance – not the least from the Western Christianity and its centres of authority. The dialogue with peoples of other faiths, the challenge of creating communities of love and reconciliation, and the agency of the people appropriating the Christian message and spirit - these are reinventing Christianity as a religion of tolerance. That leads me to the next consideration.

### Christianities – The Plurality of the Future
What is again hopeful about Christianity in the South is the developing plurality of its forms and expressions. There is less and less reference in the South to the diversity of Churches deriving from the turbulent

---

[11] Pannenberg's 1994 Erasmus Lecture, sponsored by the Institute on Religion and Public Life. The text of the lecture is published in *First Things* 48 (December 1994), pp. 18-23.

[12] Arvind Sharma, *Hinduism for our Times*, Oxford University Press, Delhi, 1997, p. 69.

European history of division, which was sought to be overcome through the ecumenical movement. The attention is focused rather on the *various types of Christianity* – some inspired by the importance of human body and its healing in the practice and understanding of religion, as is the case, for example, in Africa. This is quite subversive of the head-approach Christianity has been made to assume. *"I think therefore I am"* of Descartes finds a counterpoint in the African thinker Eboussi Boulaga, when he says, *"I dance, therefore I live"*[13] – an insight from African experience which we could see shaping also certain forms of African Christianity with emphasis on human body and care of it through healing and exorcism.

The Christian message intersects at certain points of the history of a people and their experience and finds a new avatar and expression. This is what has enabled resurgence of Christianity in the Southern hemisphere. There is the shaping of new Christianities in Africa, Asia and Latin America, where euro-centric Christianity and many of its present apparatuses of operation are becoming matters of historic memory. I am more and more convinced that the question of religious pluralism as we know it in our parts of Asia is part and parcel of the even broader issue of plurality of Christianities. This latter issue will supersede the former.

The future of Christianities in the South will not be a matter of numbers but of *quality* and *diversity*. The diversity will not be like the confessional diversity witnessed in the Western history of Christianity. It will be one of different appropriation through culture and experiences of the peoples of the South. It will be a diversity deriving also from the different ways the Christian message exerts influence on the various realms of individual and collective lives. The expectation of an expansion in numbers of Christians in the South, especially in Asia, would be but nostalgia to find back elsewhere what has been lost in Europe – the Christendom. A crass ignorance of the ground-realities could prompt even well-meaning people in the West to misjudge the resurgence of the Southern Christianity from the perspective of the Western crisis of Christianity.

When I study what the Western postmodernists have to say, I begin to think that if this is postmodernism, we have been in the postmodern era in India since four thousand years! This is true also of many parts of Asia. The point I want to underline here is that an Asian appropriation of Christianity cannot be expected to be a presumed comprehensive

---

[13] F. Eboussi Boulaga, *La crise du muntu*, Presence Africaine, Paris, 1977, p. 56.

totality. The Asian discovery of Christian message and spirit will bear upon certain issues and questions and not others, depending upon the *journey* the people make. The same could be said also about Africa and other parts of the Southern hemisphere. We need to place accent on the *discovery* of Christianity by Asians and Africans and Latin Americans which will happen in relation to their needs and experiences as they move ahead. In this process, the subjecthood and agency of the people will be very important, and not structures and institutions, nor a presumed comprehensive package of Christianity. These in fact could turn out to be deadwood and impede a creative encounter and discovery of Christianity by the people living in a world bursting with crisis.

The crisis which leaders of neo-orthodoxy proclaim as taking place in Asia for example is only a construct from an euro-centric and narcissistic form of Christianity which is immobilized within its own past traditions. In fact something else is happening with Christianity in the southern hemisphere. The temptation is strong to think that a religion that has become a spent-force in Europe (post-Christianity) is "dumped" as unwanted medicine into the Third World where it is finding a flourishing market. This would be too simplistic an approach. What is happening is not a replication of a worn-out Christianity but a discovery of Christianity by the people from the South in their own ways.[14] This is the most hopeful and refreshing aspect about Christianity and its survival in the future.

## Conclusion: Christianity for a World in Crisis

We live in a world enveloped in deep crisis, and indeed to an extent as never before in history. Imperialism and escalating conflicts, violence and wars, ecological destruction, poverty and exploitation – to name a few – are turning the world into the most dangerous planet to live in. What does really Christianity stand for in a world that is enveloped in a deep crisis? Whose interests does it serve?

---

[14] In the milieu of ideological vacuum, for many in China, Christianity has become important as for as an entry-point for the encounter with modernity and its benefits. So, we have the so-called *"cultural Christians"* in China, Japan and in other parts of Asia without being *confessional Christians*. For others in the same continent like the "untouchables " of India the Gospel has profound attraction as a message in their struggle for justice and human dignity. Cf. Felix Wilfred, "Asian Christianity and Asian Modernity: Forty Years After *Gaudium et Spes*", in *East Asian Pastoral Review,* vol. 42, no. 1/2 (2005), pp. 191-206.

In the past few decades it was assumed that the future of Christianity in the developing world would be ensured by adopting Christianity to local culture, tradition, etc. There is certainly a point in this endeavour. But as Marc Ela has pointed out with reference to the African continent, the most important question is not inculturation or African authenticity.[15] The key question is how Christianity is going to come to terms with crucial problems and issues affecting the people. The future of Christianity in the developing world of the South as well as in the developed world will depend upon the extent it will be able to contribute to overcome the *crisis of the world* in its micro and macro manifestations.

This crisis is characterized by the inability of humanity to create by itself an order of society that is respectful of everyone and equitable in spirit and practice; its inability to cultivate wisely and reverently this delicate garden of the earth committed to it by God for the well being of all. The heightened capacity of humanity to control nature, its laws and working, is not matched by its readiness to regulate just relationships among human beings; rather science and technology have become part of the problem contributing to inequality, violence and war, and unequal distribution of resources.

The situation is like that of a house on fire. It is the moment of challenge for Christianity everywhere to save the world by getting back to the basics of the Gospel message. Here lies also the ultimate diagnosis whether Christianity is really in crisis and to what extent. This time it has to do the fire fighting not all alone, but with other actors on the scene. The West will find back its Christianity not as a nostalgic Christendom or as an identity-marker of its history and civilization, but by responding to the crisis of the world, and drawing from the living waters of the Gospel. In the process, it will also learn how much to remember of its past, and how much it should leave behind to be able to follow unencumbered the call of the Spirit.

---

[15] Jean-Marc Ela, "Christianity and Liberation in Africa," in R. Gibellini (ed.), *Paths of African Theology*, Orbis Books, New York, 1994, pp. 136-150.

# Chapter 12

# Asia and Christian Social Message

*"I will give you a talisman. Whenever you are in doubt, or when the self becomes too much with you, apply the following test. Recall the face of the poorest and the weakest man whom you may have seen, and ask yourself, if the step you contemplate is going to be of any use to him. Will he gain anything by it? Will it restore him to a control over his own life and destiny? In other words, will it lead to swaraj for the hungry and spiritually starving millions?[1] Then you will find your doubts and your self melt away."* — M.K.Gandhi

It is said that Christianity right from its inception carried a strong social message which made it attractive to the underdogs of history at all at times. Even in the most arid seasons of its history, there have been oasis of love, compassion and concern to the least and the last. Various social movements within Christianity and some of the saints and sages have borne the good news to the poor. That is why Asian Churches could with a lot of hope look to the Christian tradition and learn many lessons to respond to the public issues affecting the continent. By way of example, in this chapter, we focus on one of these traditions – the social teachings of the Catholic Church, aware of the fact that similar studies can be done also regarding other Churches. The social message of the Gospel remains a common challenge to all of them.

There is, perhaps, no other religious tradition in which *faith is related so very closely to social realities* and developed into a body of social teaching as in Catholic Christianity. Though there have been many efforts in the past to trace the development of Catholic social thought and highlight its salient features, this was confined by and large to a relatively small group of theologians and other experts in the field. There has been a lacuna to

---

[1] Pyare Lal, *Mahatma Gandhi* [Last Phase, Vol. II (1958)], p. 65.

bring this rich Catholic heritage to the larger body of believers and relate them to the concrete realities of society, economy, politics, culture, etc. The publication of the *Compendium of the Social Doctrine of the Church*[2] fills this lacuna by bringing out the quintessence of this corpus of teaching in a manner accessible to all Christian faithful. The Pontifical Council for Justice and Peace deserves our appreciation and thanks for the important and timely service it has done from which Asian Churches can benefit immensely.

On the other hand, it is regrettable that *enough attention has not been paid to the Social Teachings* in Asian Churches as it should be, in spite of the fact that the Federation of Asian Bishops' Conferences (FABC) has been very active in understanding and interpreting the social teachings.[3] The efforts of FABC are far from being matched by the various Bishops' Conferences or individual bishops - barring some laudable exceptions. Unfortunately, the social teachings still remain in Asia "the best kept secret". For example, the Bishops in different countries of Asia, dealing with pastoral issues give disproportionately greater attention to liturgical questions and sexual morality than burning issues of society. In this sense, the Social Teachings remain a pastoral challenge to the Asian bishops, priests, religious and laity.

Admirable, indeed, is the earnestness with which the *Church tries to update itself* by interpreting in the light of its religious sources the reality of the society, the economy, culture, politics, etc. The Church's reading of the "signs of the times" helps the Christians to more easily relate their faith with the societal realities they experience. One of the difficulties encountered in interreligious dialogue is the fact that religions are mostly centred on tradition and belief-system, and rarely address the significance of belief to life in contemporary times. In spite of the rich resources of

---

[2] *Compendium of the Social Doctrine of the Church*, Libreria Editrice Vaticana, Vatican, 2004.

[3] At this point we need to acknowledge the crucial role played by the Office of Human Development (OHD) from its very inception to relate faith with the Asian social realities. In particular I would like to highlight the Conference OHD organized on the occasion of the centenary celebration of *Rerum Novarum* in 1991. The other offices of FABC, especially the Office for Theological Concerns (OTC), have brought out a rich body of materials on Church in relation to Asian social, economic and political situations. Cf. Vimal Tirimanna (ed.), *Sprouts of Theology from Asian Soil. Collection of TAC and OTC Documents (1987-2007)*, Claretian Publications, Bangalore, 2007.

wisdom each religion enshrines, the failure to relate and interpret them in the light of contemporary experiences turn even well-intentioned people sceptic about the role religion could play in transforming our world and society. Catholic Christianity by addressing the social issues of contemporary times has set a good example.

We can observe certain *dynamism* within the Church at work in formulating the social teachings. Before getting crystallized into teaching, many of the social questions and issues first get discussed and debated in the Church. Pastoral efforts are taken to grapple with many concrete situations. All this contributes to greater clarification of issues and questions. One may, for example, point out the tardiness in the response of the Church to the issue of workers at the height of their exploitation in mid-nineteenth century. However, what is to be taken note of is that there were many initiatives taken by Catholic individuals and groups to respond to the situation even before any official teaching on the question was made. The official teaching could benefit from these experiences and debates at the grassroots that preceded the formulation of workers' issues by Leo XIII.

The significance of social teachings derives also from the fact that they represent the overcoming of all too common a tendency among religions to dichotomize between the spiritual and the material, *the sacred and the profane*. Religions generally tend to confine themselves to the realm of the sacred and refuse to be affected in their beliefs and practices by socio-political realities. Social teachings are bound to generate widespread interest not only among Christians but among all sections of people as these teachings touch upon issues which cut across borders and boundaries and address public issues and questions.

## THE SIGNIFICANCE OF SOCIAL TEACHING OF THE CHURCH IN THE CONTEXT OF CHRISTIAN CONTRIBUTION TO ASIA

To be able to appreciate the social teachings, we need to place these against the background of a much larger question: What could possibly be the contribution of Christianity in the Asia of today? I mean to say that the social teachings of the Church need to be placed against the context of Asia where Christianity seeks to make its presence felt through its witnessing and involvement. We could identify at least five major areas in which Christianity could make sense to Asians.

1. Opening up Asian Nations to Inter-cultural and Inter-religious Understanding and Praxis

The unity of human family is truly a humanistic task that cannot be really achieved by the process of globalization driven by the spirit of competition, market and profit. The trouble with globalization is that it is a new technology with an old philosophy. Utilitarianism is not capable of bringing about unity and solidarity.[4] Spiritual forces are required to bring peoples and nations to a deeper encounter with each other. In the past, Buddhism was a great force that brought together different peoples and cultures of Asia. For example, India and China considered each one to be the centre of the world, and viewed other peoples as "untouchables" (*Melecchas*) and as "barbarians". Buddhism broke the self-centredness of these two ancient civilizations, and led them to learn from each other. For example, during the Tang Dynasty in the seventh century, Hsüan-tsang, a renowned Buddhist monk of China journeyed to India and after studying a decade the Buddhist scriptures, he took with him to China thirteen hundred and thirty-five scrolls.[5] On this basis, during the Ming Dynasty Wu Chengen created a popular story of great imagination under the name "The Pilgrimage to the West". *Buddhism was a means which facilitated more secular pursuits like the exchange in science, technology, art, literature, etc. between India and China, and in our parts of Asia as a whole.* Particularly striking has been the role it played in the education or enlightenment of people.

> It is, for example, remarkable that nearly every country in the world with a powerful presence of Buddhist tradition has tended to embrace widespread schooling and literacy with some eagerness. This applies not only to Japan and Korea, but also to China, Thailand, Sri Lanka and even to the otherwise retrograde Burma (Myanmar). The focus on enlightenment in Buddhism (the word "Buddha" itself means "enlightened") and the priority given to reading texts, rather than leaving it to the priests, can help to encourage educational expansion.[6]

---

[4] Cf. Gnana Patrick, "Auditing Utilitarianism. From a Subaltern Perspective", in Felix Wilfred (ed.), "Subaltern Perspectives and Ethical Auditing" Jeevadhara, 37 (January 2007), pp. 69-87.

[5] Cf. D. Devahuti (ed.), *The Unknown Hsüan-tsang,* Oxford University Press, Delhi, 2001. It is significant that the memory of this Buddhist monk remains a powerful historical link between India and China. In fact, a statue of this Chinese monk has been erected at the site of the ancient university of Nalanda where he was a student, and this monument was opened by a visiting Chinese minister. See *The Hindu*, 13 February, 2007.

[6] Amartya Sen, *Identity and Violence. The Illusion of Destiny,* Penguin Books, London, 2006, p. 109.

Christianity could follow the great example set by Buddhism in Asia in bringing peoples and cultures together. These are the times when Asia is torn by ethnic, linguistic, religious and cultural divisions. The divisions and conflicts are particularly visible in South Asia and South East Asia. To name a few, there are serious ethnic and religious conflicts in Sri Lanka, India, Myanmar, Malaysia, Indonesia, etc. Then, there are deep-seated resentments in the relationship of nations, deriving from past history and experiences, as is the case for example between China and Japan, China and Taiwan, Korea and Japan, India and Pakistan. The role of Japan during the Second World War has left deep scars in East Asia and South East Asia. The process of globalization and the economic and political competition attendant on it, have aggravated and sharpened these conflicts rather than helping to overcome them.

In the new circumstances of today, Christianity could provide the spiritual foundations to bring people and nations together in mutual understanding and in the spirit of true catholicity. It can function as a force to create the whole of humanity into one single family.[7] The Christian vision as we find in the Scriptures is precisely one of unity of the whole of human race as children of God, a vision that overcomes all kinds of ethnic divisions. "There is no longer Greek or Jew, there is no longer slave or free, there is no longer male or female; for all of you are one in Christ Jesus"(Gal 3:28). The fact that the Christian Scriptures were translated into the language of different peoples (Bible translation) is itself an act of catholicity or universality.[8] *This Christian faith in catholicity and unity of the human family runs through the whole of social teaching, and in the Compendium.* It is the fundamental premise underlying the entire corpus of social teaching. This faith in unity and catholicity will be marred if it is not accompanied by an appropriate theology of religions that is capable of cementing the relationship among the peoples of Asia.

---

[7] In the nineteenth century, the Church defended the unity of human family against the ideology of racism based on a misinterpreted theory of evolution. Today the Church is called upon to defend the unity of the whole of human race against theories which proclaim "clash of civilizations" as the future. Samuel Huntington writes unabashedly that "it is human to hate. For self-definition and motivation people need enemies." Samuel Huntington, *The Clash of Civilizations and the Remaking of World Order*, Simon and Shuster, New York, 1997, p. 130. We are reminded of Thomas Hobbes (*Homo homini lupus*) and of Machiavelli of *The Prince* fame.

[8] Cf. Lamin Sanneh, *Translating the Message. The Missionary Impact on Cultures*, Orbis Books, New York, 1996.

## 2.   Christianity and Modernity

I do not want to enter at this point into the Western discussion whether there is a continuity between Christianity and modernity, or whether modernity results from the disintegration of Christianity, or whether modernity is the extrapolation of Christianity and its spirit in the secular realm.[9] It is strange that, whereas in the West, Christianity has been viewed as a force against modernity and science, in most parts of Asia, Christianity is viewed as an ally of modernity. The perception of Asian Christians both in the past and in present times is one in terms of *continuity rather than a caesura between Christianity and modernity.* This is especially true of China and Japan. Ricci's huge maps adorned the palace of the Chinese emperor Wanli. His mastery in mathematics of the time (having been a student of the great mathematician Clavius in the Roman College) and astronomy brought him widespread admiration. Some of the first converts of Ricci, in fact, were those who were attracted by what they believed to be his power of science. The great scholar Xu Guangqui was attracted to Ricci for transmitting the Euclidian geometry, and Qu Rukuei was attracted by what he believed were the alchemical powers of Ricci, and Li Zhizao turned to Christianity by having been taken up by the cartography of Ricci.[10]

Given this tradition, it is no wonder that even today, in China and Japan Christianity has been welcomed as a gateway to science and modernity, which also explains the increasing interest and study of Christianity in those parts of Asia.

Christian social teaching is significant today for Asia because it deals with many questions and issues thrown up in our present world through new developments in science, technology, economics, politics, etc. Modernity in Asia requires deeper study and reflection. In the social teachings of the Church, Asia could find a point of reference in which questions of modernity are approached from a humanistic perspective. These teachings could support and facilitate a deeper encounter of Asia with modernity.

---

[9] These questions drew much attention in recent times in connection with the discussion on drafting the Constitution of European Union. At issue is the question to what extent Christianity is part of European legacy and foundation for its unity. Opinions were sharply divided.

[10] Cf. Jonathan D. Spence, *The Memory Palace of Matteo Ricci,* Penguin Books, 1985, p. 152.

The significance of these teachings derives also from the fact that the encounter with modernity in many parts of Asia has been only partial. I mean to say that adoption of modern economic policies or deployment of the means of science and technology is not to be equated with modernity. There is more to modernity than these factors. Modernity has to be seen also in the way society is organized, nations are governed and human rights are practiced. In this respect, in several parts of Asia, democratic governance as an integral part of modernity is absent, and this in spite of fast economic development, as for example is the case in China. Participation of people in what affects them and *democracy* are integral part of modernity without which modernity will remain only partial and selective.

## 3.   Christianity and Social Justice in Asia

There is no gainsaying the crucial importance of social justice in Asian societies. The present mode of economic development, and past traditions have created a situation of much oppression and violence. At the root of it all is the absence of solidarity and the failure to provide equitable access to resources.

Christianity in Asia could make a difference by its involvement for the creation of a just and equitable society. This is the context in which the social teachings of the Church could be most helpful. They could make the Christian presence meaningful and effective. The teachings of the Church on social justice rest on solid Biblical foundation and are inspired by the example of Early Fathers of the Church. The introduction of the concept of *social justice* was an important turning point in the modern social teaching of the Church. It helped the Church to go beyond charity, almsgiving and developmental ideology. What is especially remarkable is the fact that involvement of justice was intimately linked to the evangelizing mission of the Church.[11] That is why the teachings on social justice can motivate the Asian Christians to engage themselves in the Asian situation of today on the basis of their faith. As a shared concern, the issue of social justice provides also a common platform for involvement with peoples of other faiths in Asia.

## 4.   Contribution to Peace and Harmony

Peace is a language addressed to all. It has a universal character and appeal; because it has formed the object of yearning of peoples at all times and

---

[11] Cf. Roman Synod, *Justice in the World*, 1971.

ages. Peace, however, is not a matter of chance or fate. Peace as much as conflicts are of human making. Promotion of peace and resolution of conflicts, therefore, call for human engagement on the basis of values. The values that need to be fostered for the construction of peace are truth, justice, love and freedom.[12]

If we leave out the geopolitical considerations (into which I do not enter here) in the relationship among Asian nations, we can identify two important sources which threaten peace in Asian societies. They can be summarized in two key-words - *disparity* and *identity*. The disparity is being caused through the model of development being followed under the aegis of globalization. The fast economic development in Asia is taking place at great social costs. The second danger that constantly threatens peace is the conflict that erupts on the basis of ethnicity, language, and particularly religion. There is a connection between these two - disparity and identity. The growing inequality will increasingly trigger conflicts in the name of religion, language and ethnicity. In the relationship among the various ethnic and religious groups, a perceived sense of injustice sets off conflicts and confrontations. Speaking of development as the new name for peace, Pope Paul VI reminds us "Excessive economic, social, and cultural inequalities ...are a danger to peace".[13]

It may be recalled here, for example, how the East Asian economic crisis of 1997 provoked in Indonesia ethnic conflicts between the local people and the affluent ethnic Chinese communities in that country. The Hindu-Muslim conflicts in the state of Gujarat, India, were caused by the ruthless commercial competition between the two communities in the wake of globalization. Besides the growing religious fundamentalism of the established religions, threat to peace also derives from increasing poverty. In this regard, the United Nations Development Report notes,

> The interaction between poverty and violent conflict in many developing countries is destroying lives on an enormous scale - and hampering progress...The human development costs of violent conflict are not

---

[12] One of the accusations against Christians in the Roman Empire was that they advocated peace and concord, whereas the Empire relied on wars for its growth and expansion. Christian pacifism created many martyrs. Nevertheless, the Christians contributed to public life. See Bruce W. Winter, *Seek the Welfare of the City. Christians as Benefactors and Citizens,* William B. Eerdmans Publishing Company, Grand Rapids, 1994.

[13] *Populorum Progressio,* no. 76.

sufficiently appreciated...Conflict undermines nutrition and public health, destroys education system devastates livelihoods and retards prospect for economic growth...The immensity of these costs make its own case for conflict prevention, conflict resolution and post-conflict reconstruction as three fundamental requirements for building human security and accelerating progress...[14]

There are innumerable micro initiatives taking place everyday all over the world in which religious communities positively contribute to the cause of peace and resolution of conflicts.[15] In more recent times, Christianity did play an important role for peace, harmony and reconciliation in South Africa, East Timor, Northern Ireland, etc. How could Christianity become truly a promoter of peace in Asia today? It can play a significant role by involving itself in the dynamics of peace. First of all, no social harmony is possible without *recognition of the dignity and rights* of people. By defending human rights Christianity will effectively champion the cause of peace in Asian societies. Secondly, Christianity could become an active force in *developing the values and attitudes required for the creation of peace.* Thirdly, the contribution Christianity could make is to instill the spirit of *dialogue* as an indispensable and effective method for the promotion of peace. The contribution at these levels will bring Christianity into dialogue and cooperation with other religious traditions of Asia.

On the other hand, harmony is an important value cherished in Asian traditions and cultures. But this could be, as is often the case, misinterpreted. Situations of blatant injustice could be covered up in the name of harmony and loyalty. Fear of disturbing the established order can prompt compromise with injustice. But this kind of harmony which covers up injustice is very costly for the poor and the marginalized.[16] Their

---

[14] *Human Development Report 2005*, United Nations Development Programme (UNDP), Oxford University Press, Delhi, 2005, pp. 12-13.

[15] This needs to be said because of the fears that involvement of religion could cause social divisions and violence. See Mark Juergensmeyer, *Terror in the Mind of God. The Global Rise of Religious Violence*, Oxford University Press, Delhi, 2000. From a theoretical perspective, well-known is the thesis of Girard who tried to show an intrinsic connection between religion and violence. See René Girard, *Violence and the Sacred*, Continuum, London, 2005.

[16] When I was the secretary to the Office of Theological Concerns of FABC, the Office undertook a study on harmony in Asia, and the final document is entitled: "Asian Christian Perspectives on Harmony". The text can be found in Vimal Tirimanna (ed.), *op.cit.* pp. 111-166.

well-being will depend upon peace and harmony nourished by justice - *pax opus iustitiae* (peace is the work of justice).

## THREE MAJOR ISSUES OF SIGNIFICANCE FOR ASIA

After having surveyed the context in which we have to make sense of the social teachings of the Church, in this second part, let us take a closer look at the social teachings. We will do this, by highlighting some issues of great significance for Asia; by examining some of the factors that inhibit the effectiveness of these teachings; by probing into some questions that deserve attention; and finally by pointing out some possible directions for the future.

### 1. The Dignity of Human Person

The dignity of human person rests on the Christian understanding of God's creation. Reason and freedom are keys to human flourishing, and are important markers of human dignity. Much of the social teaching, then, has to do with the expansion of human freedom, supported by human rights. Part of this recognition of human dignity is the religious freedom (*Dignitatis Humanae*). The developments that have taken place in the teaching of the Church have overcome some of the theological difficulties of the past and have created, at least in principle, an open space for the recognition of the freedom of faith of our neighbours of other religious traditions. This was not something easy for the Church. It was a breakthrough. This was possible, because, from a generic recognition of human dignity based on creation, the social teaching has gone to acknowledge the subjective dimension of the human person. This is an important milestone. There is no subjectivism here. Without undermining the objective, the shift has taken place to the subjective in the human person and her conscience. We could see it in the Vatican Council II documents of *Dignitatis Humanae* as well as in the orientation of *Gaudium et Spes*. This is far from the objective approach epitomized in the axiom "error has no right to exist". This shift has created the condition for greater interreligious understanding and cooperation on social issues of Asia.

Two points however need to be stressed here: The dignity of human person is incomplete unless *the full humanity of woman* is affirmed. This implies recognizing women's subjecthood and intellectual agency. And this calls for a new anthropology. I mean to say, without affirmation of full dignity of woman from a proper anthropological orientation, the statement about the dignity of human person by the social teachings remains only partial. Neither an *anthropology of complementarity* in man-woman relationship, nor the view that men and women are different (implying that they have different roles) could do justice to the dignity of woman. For the full dignity of woman we need *an anthropology of partnership*: Women and men are equal, but different *and engaging in a relationship of mutuality*. Mutuality implies recognizing the contribution of women in every aspect of human functioning. Such an anthropology on a *partnership model* is the condition for the acknowledgement of full dignity of woman. This integral anthropology seems to be missing in the social teachings of the Church, whereas it is important in the Asian societies in which the dignity of women is trampled upon both by modern and traditional forces, supported by strong patriarchal ideologies.

A second observation concerns the human rights which flow from the dignity of human person. Here too there is an incompleteness. From an Asian perspective, there are not only rights - after all Tatas, Birlas, Ambanis and Bill Gates are all fighting for their rights! Deriving only rights from human dignity leaves out an important dimension of this reality. There is the need to inculcate the *duties* which binds a person to society. Doing the duties towards the other and being in solidarity with the other too flow from the dignity of the human person. This is what in the Asian tradition has been known as *Dharma* or *Dhamma*. It is very often easier to begin dialogue with peoples of other faiths regarding the dignity of human person starting from duties rather than rights. Dharma shows the embeddedness of human beings and their dignity in a web of relationships with mutual obligations and rights.

## 2.   Partakers of the Same Inheritance

In recent times, particularly since Vatican Council II, the social teachings of the Church clearly affirm, consistent with the teaching and the spirit of the Fathers and the unambiguous position of Thomas Aquinas, that the goods and resources of the earth belong to the entire humanity from which everybody could attain what is necessary to fulfil her or his needs. In the face of this primary and universal destination of the goods of nature, titles of ownership and right to ownership acquire a limited and secondary validity. This has been such a strong conviction that it was held that in dire necessity everything becomes common, and those in extreme necessity for their livelihood could take it from others, disregarding any claim or title to ownership. Such an act may not be considered as theft. This shows how private property, possession and ownership are relative and are subject to the needs of others. In his *Sollicitudo Rei Socialis*, Pope John Paul II notes,

> It is necessary to state once more the characteristic principle of Christian social doctrine. The goods of this world are originally meant for all. The right to private property is valid and necessary, but it does not nullify the value of this principle. Private property, in fact, is under a "social mortgage" which means that it has an intrinsically social function, based upon and justified precisely by the principle of the universal destiny of goods.[17]

Now, this position so strongly affirmed and emphatically repeated in social teachings of our times has enormous consequence for the Asian peoples. In many countries, land-ownership is the cause for the scandalous wealth on the one side and dire poverty on the other. Land reform and equitable distribution of resources remains one of the great challenges in Asian societies. Wherever such basic reforms did not take place, the poor have been most hit by economic globalization and market.

## 3. The Issue of Labour

This is one of the pillars of Catholic Social Teachings. The development of the Catholic social thought hinges on this central question of labour and has found its stimulus in the workers' movements. The Church with all its teaching of over one hundred years on the issue of workers and their rights could be a catalyst in Asia for protecting their interests and well-being. This is particularly necessary in our times when all that has been achieved through the struggles of workers and workers' movements since the industrial revolution seems to be thrown to the winds overnight by new economic policies and by the process of globalization. The plight of workers is under worst conditions in Asia. Women workers, working children and migrant labourers bring out the pathetic labour-conditions in Asian societies in a rat race to catch up with developed countries.

It is here that some of the basic orientations set by the social teachings assume great importance. For example, in the present-day conditions we need to underline as the social teachings do, *the priority of labour over capital*.[18] Basing itself on the Biblical account of Genesis, the social teachings, especially those in more recent times, have underlined the agency and subjectivity of the human person involved in labour which stands above

---

[17] *Sollicitudo Rei Socialis*, no. 42.

[18] In fact, this is one of the central points in *Laborem Exercens* of Pope John Paul II.

the instrumental role of the capital. Consequently, any efforts to centre economic activities on the accumulation of capital by individuals, corporates and institutions would mean a lopsided development in Asia. Unfortunately, this is precisely what is happening in our societies. Labour as flowing from the subjectivity and agency of the human person (the meaning of dominion in the sense of Genesis) is endowed with an ethical character. It cannot be treated as an object. Therefore, competition to accumulate wealth needs to be checked and controlled by the more important ethical question labour involves, since it deals with human subjects. The priority of labour over capital and the subjectivity of the workers create space for the claim of just wages, participation of the workers in the process of production as well as the sense of equality and solidarity among the workers.[19]

## INHIBITING FACTORS OF THE SOCIAL TEACHING

### 1.    The Gap between Teaching and Praxis

This gap could be looked at from three different angles. First, like in other fields, also in social questions, the effectiveness of teaching suffers because the praxis in the Church does not correspond to many noble ideals presented. Critical questions could be raised in this regard, for example, concerning the way women are treated in the Church, the extent of freedom of expression in the Church, the extent of participation of the people in the internal matters of the Church, etc. Secondly, the gap is there because the social teachings are often couched in an abstract philosophical language that makes it difficult for many people to relate the concrete realities of daily life with what these teachings say. Thirdly the cleavage between theory and praxis derives from the fact that the social teachings of the Church do not relate themselves to the strong social ferment at work in the larger world, nor reflect the aspirations and efforts for social justice and societal transformation in which so many people all over the world are involved.

In different parts of our continent, there are significant new social movements with concrete agenda to attain the very goals the Church teachings state in theory. The social teachings seem to run parallel to these developments in the world. The gap between theory and praxis could be reduced if there are elements which facilitate a mediation between praxis and theory. I mean to say that, if social teachings are developed closely

---

[19] Cf. *Laborem Exercens*, no. 8.

with these experiences and experiments, the gap between theory and praxis could be significantly reduced, and the social teachings will gain greater credibility.

## 2. Condemnation and Non-Condemnation

The effectiveness of the social teachings of the Church cannot be dissociated from the Christian legacy of the past and the Christian image in the minds of Asians. The attitude towards Christianity conditions also the extent the social teachings of the Church can have influence on the Asian societies. Instead of going into a detailed analysis of this statement, let me point out two historical facts. There is one condemnation that has profoundly affected the Asian attitude towards Christianity: The controversy that started at the time of Matteo Ricci on the rites of Chinese ancestral veneration, ended with the condemnation of them by Rome, not once, but three times. It alienated the whole of Asia under the Confucian civilizational influence.

As for South Asia, we have a case of non-condemnation. Caste was one of the most difficult issues the missionaries had to face. The hierarchical ordering of the society on the basis of the principle of purity and pollution made some people by birth pure, superior and privileged. Christian missions could have challenged the caste-system to bring about the Gospel message of the equality of all children of God. Instead, the Church failed to condemn this social evil and allowed the discrimination against the lower castes and the untouchables to continue. What is even more unfortunate is that policies were adopted in the Church which even legitimised the existing caste-division. This was done because, the Church feared that if it challenged the caste-system it would upset the existing social order which in turn will affect its mission of winning souls.

The social teachings will find welcome in Asia if the Church openly expressed its regret for this condemnation and non-condemnation. The absence of any expression of regret on the part of the Church regarding Christian past in Asia, will only make Asians look with scepticism at its lofty social teachings. What is surprising is that on issues such as anti-Semitism, opposition to science, etc., the Church was quick to confess its past failings. But little of that openness is seen as for the societies in our parts of Asia are concerned. Even now it is not too late.

## 3. Absence of Self-Critique

It is an undeniable fact that religious freedom was denied for many centuries and was supported by theological arguments. It is only since

Vatican II, we find any clear admission of religious freedom by the Church. We need to recall here that Pope Pius IX and Pope Leo XIII condemned religious freedom. Where religious freedom was inevitable it was grudgingly tolerated as lesser evil. Similarly, we know also about the serious difficulties the Church had in accepting democracy as a legitimate form of governance. It is again only in relatively recent times democracy has been accepted as a mode of governance to be fostered. We hear of a positive note on democracy for the first time in a radio message of Pope Pius XII during the Second World War: "A democratic form of government appears to many people as the natural postulate imposed by reason itself".[20]

A sign of the lack of self-criticism is the claim that the social teachings of the Church have a consistent and progressive development, something that cannot be reasonably maintained. There are continuities and discontinuities in the social teachings. To claim that there has been a steady and organic growth of social doctrines contradicts actual facts. Some of the things claimed to have been professed from the beginning consistently does not seem to be so. For example, there is a marked difference between what Leo XIII said about the absolute character of private property and what Pius XI said abut the social dimension of private property. One could hardly speak about a continuity in this matter, which would only foster scepticism about the social teaching of the Church. Moreover, there is hardly any recognition of the fact that some of the social teachings of the Church owe a lot to developments in the larger society and in the secular field as was clearly the case regarding religious liberty. A realistic admission of the struggle the Church itself had to undergo in getting greater clarity on various social issues will enhance the credibility of its social teachings. It will make the Church a partner in the common journey of the entire humanity as it gropes from less justice and peace to more of justice and peace, from refusal of democracy to acceptance of it and its consolidation.

## 4.  Limping Social Teachings of the Church

There is an asymmetry between the social teachings and theology of religions. Both these are inextricably bound up in Asia. It is anomalous to have a very advanced teaching on social issues, while holding on to views about religions that are far from acceptable for Asian peoples, and which cannot form a basis for serious interreligious understanding and harmony. While one foot is strong, namely, the social teachings of the Church, the

---

[20] *Christmas Message, 1944.*

other foot, namely the official theology of religions, is handicapped. This situation undermines the body of social teachings and it can move at the moment ahead only by limping.[21] *There is a need for a thorough revision of the official theology of religions, for the social teachings of the Church to have effect on the larger masses of Asian peoples.*

Certainly, looking against the background of the past history, the affirmation of religious liberty in the teachings of Vatican Council II through *Dignitatis Humanae* was, as I noted earlier, a breakthrough. It makes sense against the longstanding tradition of refusal to accept this freedom in Christian history and theology. However, as far as Asia is concerned, this affirmation of liberty needs to be accompanied by a theology of religions that goes beyond the present position. It is where the social teachings get stuck especially when it is a question of engaging neighbours of other faiths in common public issues.

## QUESTIONS REQUIRING ATTENTION

### 1.  Selective Specificity

There are many issues and questions relevant to Asia, that are dealt with in the social teachings. But there are also many more issues of very vital and central importance for Asia which are absent in the social teachings. One may respond to this remark saying, that the Universal Church can speak only in general terms and cannot go into specificity of the contextual issues. The universal teaching requires only to be applied to particular contexts. However, the point to note is that the social teachings do in fact deal with specific issues when they belong to *European experience and history*. For example, the question of workers has its experiential roots in European industrial revolution; religious freedom in the European experience of the conflictual relationship of altar and throne; the issue of ideology is centred on Marxism, an ideology of European origin. In fact these issues so very close to European history and experience occupy the major portion of the social teachings.

### 2.  Eclipse of Asian Specificity

There is a need to give attention to issues and questions of other contexts, and these to be treated with the same earnestness as issues affecting

---

[21] In employing the expression "limping" to the social teachings, I am inspired by St Augustine who speaks of a limping Church. "*Modo clauda est ecclesia, unum pedem fortiter point, alterum invalidum habet*" St Augustine, *Sermo* 5, 8 (P.L. 38, col. 59).

Europe. How could one understand the Asian realities of today without referring to the colonial experience of many Asian nations and their struggles for national independence? These are questions which impinged upon Asian peoples and in which the European colonizers were involved. Even at the height of colonial exploitation, we never hear a word of condemnation of colonialism by the Church, nor any support to the struggles of Asian peoples for their sovereignty. If such is the past, how could anyone, then, expect that Asia will today suddenly warm up to the social teachings? As for the contents of social teachings, Asians hear very little about tribal culture, caste, question of identities and minorities, etc. - issues which affect almost all the nations of Asia. If the absence of such issues in the social teachings are justified by invoking the universal nature of the social teachings, many of the actual issues found in the social teachings could also be shown as being specific and peculiar to European experience. How are we to justify the absence of those and presence of these, except to say that there is a selective specificity in the social teachings?

## 3.  Assumption and Methodology

The body of social teachings assumes that the society can be changed if only we impart the truth and employ human reason. The very expressions "social doctrine" and "social teaching" seem to indicate such an assumption. The social teachings make appeal in the name of truth, knowledge and reason, and these are expected to bring about change in society - a too neat and optimistic assumption. The teachings do not take into account sufficiently the sinful human nature. Those in power often act unjustly even after knowing the truth; hold on to power and maintain oppressive structures because of the advantage they derive over others, even when they know that it is an unjust situation. In other words, the conflict of interests in society, and asymmetry of power are not addressed sufficiently and in depth in the social teachings. These are quite central in addressing the social and political issues of today's Asia. But these aspects have been in general watered down under the assumption that imparting knowledge and truth and appealing to reason will bring about change. This assumption is reflected in the basic methodology we find in the social teachings. It is a methodology from theory to praxis. However, if the methodology is one that starts from praxis, the actual conflictual realities in the realm of politics, economy, etc., will be taken more seriously for reflection.

## 4. Anthropocentrism Overshadowing the Cosmic

Anyone reading the corpus of the social teachings from an Asian perspective will be struck by the fact that these teachings reflect an excessive anthropocentric world view. There is a general lack of emphasis on the bonds that unite human beings with the nature and the whole universe. These bonds are so intrinsic and vital that the human cannot be defined without reference to them. This is something that does not turn out clearly in the anthropology behind the social teachings. Here again we note how these teachings are still attached to the anthropocentrism of the classical Western thought. I say "classical", because today in the West itself new developments are taking place in the world view, more sensitive to the earth and nature, as revealed in many vibrant ecological movements. In Asia, the understanding of the human in relation to nature has been something that is inscribed in its cultures and civilizations. This has contributed to the development of a holistic vision of reality and of human beings. In fairness, we must admit that the social teachings do speak about environmental issues. However, they lack force, and do not seem to come out of a nature-sensitive cosmic world-view.

## SOME POINTERS TO THE FUTURE

Let me now point out a few areas in reference to which the social teachings of the future could become a language closer to the understanding of peoples in our parts of Asia.

1.  The fact that the *axis of Christianity has already shifted from the West to Asia and other continents, the future of social teachings necessarily will have to reflect this new situation* and draw from Asian experiences many fibres for weaving the future social teachings. There is the need, for example, to pay greater attention to what is happening at the *grassroots in Asia.* These are extremely rich and important resources for the future social teachings of the Church. It is undeniable that there is also a strong social and political ferment in Asia, especially at the level of everyday life. All these experiences from the bottom could flow into the future social teachings of the Church.

2.  The Asian Bishops on their part should make *forceful representation of Asian questions* at the level of the universal Church, so that the entire Church could benefit from the rich Asian experiences. The Federation of Asian Bishops' Conferences has contributed to deepen many social issues of vital importance. There is little evidence that the insights

coming from the intense social engagement of the Asian Churches have found its place in the social teachings.

3.  The social teaching should not be merely "teaching" and "doctrine", but should have bearing on concrete praxis. Hence, we need to think of ways and means in which they could impact upon the larger society. Moreover, these teachings should go beyond motivating Christians for social engagement. Most effective are the *formulation of public policies in a state or country*. We need to think how the spirit and insights of social teachings could influence the public policies. This is again an important reason why we need to be attentive to the Asian resources on social and political questions. This will make the influence more natural and acceptable.

4.  There is need *to draw resources from Asian history and tradition*. For example, there are global roots for democracy, which cannot be reduced to Western sources. Similarly we have rich resources on human dignity, rights and duties in the various cultures of Asia.[22] These need to be brought into dialogue with the social teachings of the Church.

## CONCLUSION

To conclude, Asian Churches today stand before two imperatives: to be rooted in the soil and at the same time to be prophetic. If, on the one hand, being rooted in the soil and being accommodative to the political and social order could end up in Churches devoid of prophecy and critique, on the other hand, trying to be prophetic without roots among the people can make the voice of the Churches alien and ineffective. Asian Churches have to live with this tension, and it cannot be easily resolved. In fact, it is a healthy and productive tension. False rootedness as much as misleading prophetism with its martyrdom complex is to be avoided. The social teachings could help the Asian Churches in the struggles they are going through in their double-task of being rooted and at the same time prophetic. Christian witness and prophetism will be convincing when they become expressions of deep *immersion* into Asian life and history. But as it is, the social teachings have more of prophetic character and do not reflect the concerns and questions of Asian societies. This imbalance could

---

[22] See for example, Stephen C. Angle, *Human Rights and Chinese Thought. A Cross-Cultural Inquiry,* Cambridge University Press, Cambridge, 2002.

be made good with ever-greater attention to the Asian experiences and concerns in these social teachings.

I see another basic role for the social teachings in Asia. They can assist the Asian Churches to free themselves from narcissism and self-centredness and give impetus to reach out to the larger society. Trying to face the questions and issues of the larger society can spare the Churches from the excessive preoccupation with internal matters. In fact the entire body of social teachings is an invitation to address questions which affect humanity and the different facets of society.

Finally, any future social teaching has to take into account the fact that Asian Christians live in the midst of peoples of other faiths. Co-operation with our neighbours of other religious persuasions is extremely important for common involvement towards the transformation of society, for the defence of human dignity and rights and for the promotion of justice. Let me make a suggestion in this regard: *The future social teachings of the Church draw also from the rich religious resources of our neighbours -* Buddhists, Hindus, Confucianists, Daoists and so on. These traditions have such important insights on the various aspects and issues affecting humanity and Asian societies. Drawing from these treasures will give a truly *interreligious dimension to the social teachings of the Church,* and Asians will find their culture and traditions reflected in these teachings.

# Chapter 13

# Asian Ethics –
# New Shifts and Paradigms

*"As increasing globalization and advances in science and technology bring about changes in peoples' perspectives, ways of life and relationships, it becomes more and more imperative to reflect on our Asian heritage and affirm the fundamental value of life and human dignity rooted in our varied cultural and religious traditions of Asia."* – FABC – Office of Theological Concerns[1]

We are experiencing today a revival of ethics all over the world, and Asia is no exception. Ethics is developing into a common language that can overcome the hurdles religions may pose in relating peoples and communities.[2] There is even an effort to dissociate ethics from religions and religious beliefs. The growing complexity of life and of societies has necessitated the search for a new ethical direction.[3] Science and technology may be imposing, but when it comes to responding to intricate human and societal issues, they are clueless.

---

[1] Vimal Tirimanna (ed.), *Sprouts of Theology from the Asain Soil. Collection of TAC and OTC Documents 91987-2007)*, Claretian Publication, Bangalore, 2007, p. 384.

[2] Cf. Louis P. Pojman, *Ethical Theory- Classical and Contemporary Readings*, Wadsworth Publishing Company/ Belmont, California, 1988; W.I. Jones et al., (eds.), *Approaches to Ethics*, McGraw-Hill Inc. New York, 1977; Peter Singer (ed.), *Ethics*, Oxford University Press, 1994.

[3] Cf. Zygmunt Bauman, *Life in Fragments. Essays in Postmodern Morality*, Blackwell, Oxford, 1995; Id., *Does Ethics Have a Chance in a World of Consumers?*, Harvard University Press, Cambridge, 2008; cf. also Robert Wuthnow, *Meaning and Moral Order. Explorations in Cultural Analysis*, University of California Press, Berkeley, 1987.

Asia has nurtured ethics throughout its millennial history as can be seen in its abundant ethical literature, like the *Thirukkural* in Tamil, or the works of Chinese Confucian philosophy. The rapid changes taking place in this continent are posing challenges to traditional values, social mores and practices. What kind of support could Christianity give to the development of an ethics which would respond to the new questions and dilemmas faced by the continent? We begin our reflections by reading the global situation. For, many ethical questions Asia faces today has global roots.

### Global Developments Impacting on Asia

Reading the signs of the times is something very invigorating. It makes the journey of life exhilarating, because new possibilities and challenges appear on the horizon. But it is a difficult task too. For, the reading happens in a world of ambiguities with too many confusing signs. Globalization with its opportunities and dangers; hegemony of market forces and consequent culture of consumerism; endemic poverty and oppression; mass-migration with the inherent possibility of cross-cultural and economic enrichment, which, at the same time, gives rise to xenophobia; the escalating terrorism in every part of the globe expressing a deep sense of discontentment with the established systems and international order; ambiguous nuclearization of nations – these signs coexist with a deep and persistent search for peace with justice; democratisation that facilitates participation of people in all areas of life; longing for new forms of community; emergence of the periphery to the fore; and the visibility and force of new social movements to bring about transformation.

The quest for *identity* is one of the major signs of the times of the contemporary world.[4] It is also an issue around which some of the more serious ethical problems confronting humanity today get crystallized. The issue of identity has turned out to be a crucial question in different regions of Asia. What is most preoccupying is the fact that the ambiguity surrounding identity and its construction has become a source of conflict and violence worldwide. Identity can kill as much as it can enliven life and infuse confidence. Fundamentalism of every colour and hue, and ethnicity can be traced to unresolved identity-questions. Peace, harmony and justice are, therefore, inextricably related to the approach humanity adopts to resolve the issue of identities.

---

[4] Cf. Amartya Sen, *Identity and Violence. The Illusion of Destiny*, Penguin Books, New York, 2006.

The issue has many facets: At one level, the question could be described as an ambiguous conflict between affirmation and negation of identities. Affirmation could mean either a move towards consolidation of power, as for example when Samuel Huntington in his book *"Who Are We? The Challenges to America's National Identity"*,[5] calls for a recovery and assertion of Protestant identity of his country. On the other hand, identity-assertion is often a means to gain the dignity and rights a people have been denied, as for example when the Dalits, the *Los Indios* of Latin America and the Aboriginals of Australia assert their identity. This latter type of assertion calls for a shift from the centre to the margins. It challenges the imposition of identities on the basis of tradition and conventional basis of power. Earlier, the centres claimed to possess true identity and arrogated to define the identity of the other. Today there is a strong movement to challenge such claims.

There are some positive signs emerging as to how we need to go about this major issue. One clear line of conviction which promises a lot of hope is that we need to cross borders of every kind – cultural, national, ideological disciplinary or religious – and overcome the syndrome of single identity, and recognize that in reality there are multiple layers of identity.[6] There is the urgent need to build up the ethical values and attitudes necessary to enable negotiation of borders which will help redefine one's identity in relationship to the other – a great enrichment – or to discover the self through a journey across borders and boundaries – an exciting experience full of surprises. Yet another sign of hope is the convergence towards the creation of a world community as an ethical and spiritual project calling forth a different set of values and attitudes than the ones identified with globalization

The agenda of identities has mighty challenges for Christian ethics both in terms of redefining its own identity by forging new relationships across socio-cultural borders, and in terms of contributing to resolve the dilemmas humanity is facing with the question of identity that has its own specific configuration and contours in different contexts. All this certainly is an invitation for a rethinking and redefining the nature and role of Christian ethics today.

---

[5] Samuel Huntington, *Who Are We? The Challenges to America's National Identity,* Simon & Schuster, New York, 2004.

[6] Cf. Patrick Gnanapragasam – Elisabeth Schüssler Fiorenza (eds.), *Negotiating Borders. Theological Explorations in Global Era. Essays in Honour of Felix Wilfred,* ISPCK, Delhi, 2008.

In one sense, the issue of gender exemplifies in its most basic and radical form the question of identity. It is an important ethical issue of our times. Down through the ages, the fullness of being human has been appropriated and defined by the male. This illegitimate monopolizing of the human – belonging equally to man and woman - by the male alone is the reason why women are relegated to the margins and their identity defined as mere bodies incapable of thinking, acting and being themselves. Thanks to the feminist movement and women's negotiation of borders between the domestic and the public space, humanity is challenged to redefine itself and grow towards greater wholeness. A new space of ethics is thereby opened up.[7]

The rapid developments in every segment of life have also thrown up new and unprecedented ethical dilemmas. The novelty and speed of the new developments in science and technology have had their social and cultural repercussions, the most obvious of which is the glaring imbalance in sharing of the resources of the world, its goods and services, and the disparity in availability of opportunities. A striking fact is that a fitting ethical response has neither kept pace with these developments, nor has it been able to convincingly address the most intriguing moral questions and dilemmas of our times.

There is also the imbalance caused by the use of calculative reason in studying and controlling nature and the laws of its working and application of these in the field of very complex technologies. These developments with the help of calculative reason have not been synchronized with the development of *moral reason* that would ensure justice in inter-human relationships, and with ecological reason – if I may say so – which will integrate the human development within sustainable limit and not disrupt the rhythm of nature. Moreover, explorations in genetic and biological fields have opened up new questions which are so radical that they call for a revision of conventional understanding of the human and of nature.[8]

As for religions, their traditional role as moral teachers have undergone an erosion of credibility, not only due to the gap between the ideals they project and the actual situation but also, often, because of their failure in

---

[7] Barbara Andolsen - Christine Hilkert et al. (eds.), *Women's Consciousness, Women's Conscience. A Reader in Feminist Ethic*, Winston Press, Minneapolis, 1985.

[8] Cf. Richard Scherlock – John D. Morrey (eds.), *Ethical Issues in Biotechnology*, Rowman & Littlefield Publishers, Lanham-Boulder-New York-Oxford, 2002.

intervening effectively in defence of the poor and the weaker ones. There are other moral agencies such as new social movements (ecological movements, human rights movements, etc.) which are bringing a new moral consciousness to humanity. In the Roman Catholic Church, one of the great realizations of Vatican Council II was that the Church does not have solutions to all the problems and questions assailing our world.[9] The openness it entails and the dialogue it calls for with the world remain permanent features of the praxis of faith today with all its ethical implications. It places Church, faith and theology in a common journey. This journey involves crossing of many identities, borders and boundaries.

## Christian Ethics and Its Humanistic Basis

Christian ethics is not a particular religious category of ethics as Christian ethics ultimately overlaps with truly humanistic ethics. This requires some elaboration.

There are some important ways in which Christian faith and Gospel can influence moral and ethical life. Faith can be understood as providing a theological justification for moral life and our ethical practices. The love of God and the promise of the Kingdom of God invite a response in the form of a way of life that is in conformity with these great realities. Following the path of Jesus and the manner of his living is itself an ethical experience. It goes beyond the horizon of laws and commandments. That is why one may not reduce the Gospels into a source from which to draw practical application for our daily lives. That would be to convert the Gospels into what they are not intended to be. Moreover, the circumstances of our world and society are so different that any concrete injunction or practice culled out from the Gospels could be anomalous.

Following the teaching of Jesus and the ideal of the Kingdom of God, do not bring about Christian character to ethics. Rather, this way of life and this quest makes ethics into truly a humanistic enterprise, enlarging its scope far and wide. To put it differently, one does not follow Christian ethics because one practices the Sermon on the Mount. Rather the practice of Sermon on the Mount makes one truly a human being. The Sermon on the Mount, the teachings of Jesus, his life and the mystery of his death and resurrection – all these lead to a fuller life. They do not create a separate code of conduct. They help us live in a deeper way the calling to be human.

---

[9] See especially its document on "Church in the Modern World" (*Gaudium et Spes*).

It is a fulfillment of the vocation of every human person given through creation. I am convinced that if we live deeply the human life we will reach the Sermon on the Mount as the life-sustaining waters. It is not something of more to human life; it is essential and fundamental to human life – the ethics that is enshrined in the Sermon on the Mount. It has then a universal applicability. No wonder then that it has found greatest echo in our country among our Hindu neighbours who have not ceased to comment upon it.

## A Missed Opportunity

When Ram Mohan Roy, the father of Indian Renaissance, wrote a little book on *"The Precepts of Jesus"* he was attempting to read universal ethics in the life and teachings of Jesus. Ethics in the Gospels was the beginning of a Hindu appraisal of Christianity in modern times. Roy noted:

> I feel persuaded that by separating from the other matters contained in the New Testament, the moral principles found in this book, these will be more likely to produce the desirable effect by improving the hearts and minds of men in different persuasions and degrees of understanding.[10]

At a time when India required the moral resources for its regeneration, Roy found one important source in the ethical teachings of Jesus. But then sadly, instead of welcoming his attempt to relate Jesus the moral teacher with the Indian situation, his approach was resisted by missionaries, because it did not tally with what they thought was the Christian belief-system.[11]

Today, in the face of critical situation in the country and the world at large, we need to revisit Christian ethics unencumbered by doctrinaire concerns. A meaningful presence of Christianity in Asia seems to lie in what it could offer in terms of ethics than in terms of beliefs. In the light of the human predicament at the global level and in Asia, such an approach from a humanistic basis seems very important. Christian ethics, in other words, is not something that addresses the Christians who explicitly

---

[10] Ram Mohan Roy, *The Precepts of Jesus*, Baptist Mission Press, Calcutta, 1820 (Reprinted in London in 1823), p. xxvii. See also J.N. Farquahar, *Modern Religious Movements of India*, (1915). Cf. also David Kopf, *The Brahmo Samaj and the Shaping of the Modern Indian Mind*, Princeton University Press, Princeton, New Jersey, 1979.

[11] Robert Ellsberg, (ed.), *Gandhi on Christianity*, Orbis Books, New York, 1991.

profess faith in Jesus Christ and form a community of believers. Rather Christian ethics has universal import, and has a message for the entire humanity – something that could be followed even if one does not belong to the Christian community.

## Challenges to Christian Ethics

*1.   Shift from Individual Morality to Social Ethics and Ecological Ethics*
Christian morality came to be narrowed down to such an extent that its scope was limited to telling the believers what constituted sin and the degree of its gravity. The Roman Catholic tradition was so obsessed with it that every faithful was required to confess his or her sin according to the number of times it was committed and according to its species. Moral theology became a matter of preparing the clergy regarding the varieties of sin and the penance to be imposed to the faithful at the confessional.[12] Similarly, in the Protestant tradition, sin and salvation got highly privatized within the realm of an individual's life. It meant the cultivation of thrift, discipline, hard work, etc. – something that lent substance to the sociologist Max Weber to make a connection between Protestant ethics and capitalism.[13] Besides, the virtue ethics of the Greeks, especially of Aristotle, had a profound influence on the Christian tradition.[14] This ethical orientation is focused on character-formation and education of the individual to opt for the noble ideals and reject the contemptible. This ethical orientation though has the advantage of transforming the individual through moral skills and habits, turned out to foster also moral individualism.

A great challenge before Christian ethics is to transform itself in such a way as to reflect the concerns of the larger realities of human predicament and the survival of nature. Such a perspective would make ethics inherently social and ecologically sensitive. It will be an ethics based on a wholistic vision, weaving together the individual, the communitarian

---

[12] Cf. Charles E. Curran, *Catholic Moral Theology in the United States- A History*, Georgetown University Press, Washington D.C., 2008.

[13] Cf. Max Weber, *The Protestant Ethic and "The Spirit of Capitalism"* (1905). Translated by Stephen Kalberg, Roxbury Publishing Company, Los Angeles, 2002.

[14] Aristotle in his Nichomachean Ethics states that a good human life (*eudaimonia*) would consist in the exercise of virtues. See also MacIntyre, Alasdair C., After Virtue. A Study in Moral Theory, 2nd edition, University of Notre Dame Press, Notre Dame, 1984.

and ecological concerns. The reality of sin, grace and salvation are to be understood in close relationship to the realities of society and of nature. This shift may prove difficult for many Christians, accustomed as they are to separate the theological from the human and the societal.[15] In this connection it needs to be emphasized that the path of nature and human reason are not opposed to revelation.

In the Roman Catholic Church there has been so much insistence on nature and natural law as foundations for ethics, and outright rejection of these in general in the Protestant tradition. While one may not subscribe to a fixed and pre-conceived notion of nature and natural law, nevertheless today we are challenged to rethink traditional positions to make a reappraisal of conceptions of nature in more dynamic terms. In the last few decades, there has been heated debate on the conception of nature and natural law in the Roman Catholic Church. And in recent times in certain Protestant circles, one has begun to realize the importance of acknowledging a mediatory role for nature. This is also occasioned by the thought that the social teachings within the Catholic Church which succeeded in exerting some influence on the society is due to its discourse of society not basing simply on revelation but on the basis of an ethics evolving from nature and human reason.

## 2.  *From Utilitarianism to an Ethics Based on Aesthetics*
Christian ethics faces another challenge in the form of utilitarianism and pragmatism characterizing the dominant culture today. Utilitarian ethics promotes a way of life and values driven by instrumental reason. We need an ethics informed by aesthetics. When I say ethics based on aesthetic experience, it should not be interpreted as any romanticization. Rather I am referring to two fundamentally different experiences in human life. There are many realms in which we operate with tools and instruments, and therefore we tend to ask about the use or utility of the various things in daily life. Our decisions are most often conditioned by the utility or instrumentality of a particular thing. But then there is another whole realm of human experience that defies any characterization in terms of utility or instrumentality. Even more, to think of sublime realities in these terms is to profane and desacralize them. For instance, it would be odd to ask what is the use of friendship, of love, of an artistic work, etc. The experience we have of them can in no way be classified in terms of a particular end to

---

[15] Cf. David Hollenbach, *The Common Good and Christian Ethics*, Cambridge University Press, Cambridge, 2002.

which they are a means; rather they are the end in themselves. The experience with these realities I call aesthetic experience. These two kinds of experiences produce two different orientations to ethics.

Simplifying the matter, we could present two figures who typify these two ethical experiences. Jeremy Bentham who is known as the father of utilitarianism proposes the principle of utility for ethical decision and action in any circumstance. Good and evil are viewed as that which brings pleasure and that causes pain respectively. According to him,

> By the principle of utility is meant that principle which approves or disapproves of every action whatsoever, according to the tendency which it appears to have to augment or diminish the happiness of the party whose interest is in question. By utility is meant that property in any object, whereby it tends to produce benefit, advantage, pleasure, good, or happiness ...or ...to prevent the happening of mischief, pain, evil or unhappiness to the party whose interest is considered.[16]

In a world of technology and science which have created a culture of calculus and instrumentality, utilitarianism squares perfectly. In fact, much of the ethical practices today are conditioned by the utilitarian philosophy. But the other pole of human experience is represented by Augustine, who while acknowledging a realm of use in human life, tells us about another human experience, namely that of *enjoyment*. Enjoyment characterizes the experience of friendship, love, art, truth, goodness and beauty. Here, things and above all people are valued not in view of the purpose they serve, but what they are in themselves. An ethical practice informed by such an aesthetic experience has a profound transformative value.

Now in our contemporary world gripped by instrumental reason and utilitarian consideration, there is scarcity of an ethics of aesthetics or enjoyment. Ethics should, of course regulate the way things are used, and in this sense ethics serves as a restraint to power. But there is more to ethics. It becomes truly transformative when it is based on aesthetic experience. Christian ethics may not get bogged down to regulating the use of things but to help people and societies to pass on to the realm of an aesthetic ethics. This is the type of ethics that requires to be imparted also in the educational field.

---

[16] Jeremy Bentham, *An Introduction to the Principles of Morals and Legislation* (London, 1789), as cited in *Approaches to Ethics. Representative Selection from* edt. By W.T.Jones et al., McGraw-Hill Book Company, New York, 1977, p. 252.

An ethics focused on aesthetics will turn out to be truly an ethics of care. It pays attention to the reality in itself – its truth and beauty – and not for what it would serve. We are very much in need of such an ethics in our relationship to nature. Nature is respected for what it is and does not become a "thing" to be exploited. Human conduct should manifest responsibility towards nature and all of creation.[17] A responsible ethics towards nature will create a habit of mind that in turn will appreciate and value all human beings beyond considerations of their productivity. Therefore, it will be an ethics that will care for the sick, the wounded, the physically and mentally challenged and others. We may recall here how the Nazis got rid of all those who were not capable of producing, in gas-chambers and camps of death. The ideology that values productive capacity as the sole criterion will exploit nature and at the same time also ignore and sideline humans who are not productive in the capitalistic sense. In the situation of growing modernity where exploitation of all kinds is growing, Christian ethics will stand for an ethics of care.

## 3.    Shift from an Ethics of Conformity to an Ethics of Refusal and Dissent

By and large, traditional morality was centred on making people fall in line with what is given – the law, the established order, the authorities, etc. Often these given were held as absolute values, crippling human growth in freedom. The degree of morality was measured by the extent of one's compliance to what is prescribed. This attitude was characterized as the virtue of "obedience" which became a supreme value. Where law is the norm for morality, one is not expected to go behind what is commanded or legalized and critically examine their validity. Such a moral orientation could be found among all peoples in different degrees. But such a moral orientation, as could be inferred, has also disastrous consequences. The case of Adolf Eichmann exemplifies the extreme form this could take. Eichmann was a Nazi war-criminal who had killed thousands of innocent people. During his trial in Jerusalem – about which Hannah Arendt has written an entire book – he pleaded innocence, stating that he was morally and legally correct as he only obeyed orders from above, and he remained unrepentant till the end.

---

[17] Cf. Nicholas Low (ed.), *Global Ethics and Environment*, Routledge, London, 1999; D.C. Srivastava, (ed.), *Readings in Environmental Ethics. Multidisciplinary Perspectives*, Rawat Publications, New Delhi, 2005; Mark Sagoff, *The Economy of the Earth. Philosophy, Law, and the Environment*, Cambridge University Press, Cambridge, 1988.

Christian ethics during the course of history has often supported a practice of conformity, obedience, compliance, etc. It is interesting to note that many missionaries judged the actions of nationalists during the Indian Independence as unethical because actions like *satyagraha* and protests were viewed as challenge to the established authorities and therefore unethical. In the face of growing political and social oppression and cultural hegemony we require another set of values and a different mode of ethical conduct. What is often required today – and rare to find – is an ethics of refusal. Ethics of refusal challenges the injustice of the established order and legitimation of institutionalized modes of conduct. Interestingly, in the Chinese tradition, the refusal to conform is a character of a gentleman. In fact, Confucius, a great Chinese sage said: "The gentlemen are harmonious without conformity, and the small men conform without harmony"[18]

Christian ethics needs to move from an ethics of conformity to which it is prone, to an ethics of refusal. Resistance to what is unjust and what is falsity becomes an ethical imperative. Here there is no "cheap grace"; rather here we realize the "cost of discipleship" – to use the expression of Dietrich Bonhoeffer.[19] Jesus' mode of action in the face of the society of his times and the ruling powers was an ethics of refusal as he challenged the conventional modes of action. It is an ethics of refusal when we challenge an economy that leaves millions below poverty line to a life just with one dollar per day. 50% of the people in our country are below 25 years of age. It is a country full of human resources. But let us look at the stunting of opportunities for the vibrant millions of youngsters, and the lot of starvation of innocent children. We cannot tolerate but can only be angry when the buds do not blossom; and saplings whither away, for want of nurturing. What would be Christian ethics if it does not respond to such situations? The need of the hour is truly a liberation ethics which will go into the present state of oppression and move towards a praxis of liberation.[20]

---

[18] *Analects* 13:23.

[19] Dietrich Bonhoeffer, *The Cost of Discipleship*, SCM Press, London, 1959.

[20] Cf. Enrique Dussel, *Ética de la Liberación en la edad de la globalización y de la exclusión*, Editorial Trotta, Mexico, 1998. There has been a lot of debate and discussion between liberation ethics and discourse ethics represented by Jürgen Habermas. I have been participant in some of the conferences organized for a dialogue between these two forms of ethics. The proceedings of the conferences have been collected into many volumes. The following works could be usefully

## 4.  Developing an Ethics of Identity

I already observed how in Asia we have endemic conflicts and violence in relation to identity question. Some of these problems stem because of misconception about the other - religiously, ethnically, linguistically, etc. To be able to come to terms with this question, there is a need to develop an ethics of identity. Conflicts result because the other is viewed as a threat to one's own identity. The creation of communities in a highly pluralistic situation like in Asia calls for an ethics that would include and not exclude the other. Asia has such a rich history of dealing with difference and plurality and rich resources that could be tapped to develop an ethics of identity. This may be contrasted with the Western situation today where one is at a loss to deal with the other and to accept difference exemplified in the struggles of Europe to negotiate with its Muslim citizens and with Islam.

## 5.  Challenge from Science and Technology

Science provides us with knowledge for the understanding of nature and its working, and technology provides the tools to control nature and its processes. As they open up new possibilities for humanity and its future, they also represent a serious threat for human beings and for nature. Traditional ethics is far from being able to respond to the new questions that are thrown up by science and technology and the ambiguities surrounding them. The new situation calls for an ethics that is based on a closer understanding of developments in the fields of science and technology. In particular, we are confronted with vexing questions in the fields of human and agricultural reproductive technologies, organ transplantations, stem cells, gene therapy and so on. All these involve serious experimentations. We may not find any direct answers to these questions in the Christian Scriptures or in tradition. At the same time the present situation signals the need for a certain orientation and direction. Unfortunately, Christian ethics in Asia has not directed sufficiently its attention to these crucial questions of our times. The challenge from the fields of science and technology can be met adequately only by a re-orientation and a radical renewal in dialogue with many other forces in the society. More about it when we speak about the method.

---

consulted: Raúl Fornet-Betancourt (ed.), *Die Diskursethik und ihre lateinamerikanische Kritik*, Verlag der Augustinus Buchhandlung, Aachen, 1993; Id., *Konvergenz oder Divergenz?* Verlag der Augustinus Buchhandlung, Aachen, 1994.

### 6. From Bourgeois Ethics to Subaltern Ethics

Ethics is not and cannot be neutral; it has a perspective. The dominant ethical discourses have a bourgeois character. Good and evil, right and wrong are viewed from the bourgeois perspective; so too the idea of a good life about which so much is talked about today. Bourgeois ethics is concerned about determining the right course of action in the face of moral dilemmas. It speaks about duties with reference to a predetermined order of things, and is not concerned about the social position from which right and wrong are viewed and judged. Bourgeois ethics in its economic application sees justice as fairness – something that happens automatically when self-interest is cultivated and set in motion. There is but a small step from bourgeois ethics to market and its dynamics.

The kind of ethics we require today is subaltern. Every aspect of human, social and ecological conduct needs to be viewed from the perspective of the weaker sections, and moral theorizing will revolve around their concerns as the focal point. This will put the society on the path of a common future for all. The challenge to Christian ethics is to transform itself into a subaltern ethics. The more it becomes subaltern, the more it becomes Christian. When we know that at the top level decision-making is dominated by upper castes and classes with almost no representation of Dalits or tribals, for example, it is difficult to expect ethically just and fair dealings for the marginalized. Similarly if we analyse the economic and political fields from the perspective of the subalterns, we will realize the bourgeois character of the dominant ethics coloured by caste and class interests. This is all the more reason why Christian ethics to be true to the Gospel needs to become an ethics in favour of the subalterns.

### Methods and Sources for Pursuing Christian Ethics Today

### 1. Critical Analysis

Bourgeois ethics is a-historical. It does not pay attention to the particular context or situation in which the ethical principles are to be practiced. Christian ethics will be an antidote to a bourgeois ethics in as much as it will be a contextual ethics, and historically rooted. For this to come about it is crucial that there take place an analysis of the social, political, economic and cultural conditions of a particular society. In this way, Christian ethics will be empirically based, and it will address the problems and questions of a particular time in a specific context. This will provide a cutting edge to Christian ethics. The analysis and interpretation of the context will also save Christian ethics from turning into a mere series of prescriptions.

## 2.  A Dialogical Method

There were times when religions functioned as the chief repositories and ultimate points of reference for ethics. Today, the failure of religious traditions to keep pace with the changing times has led to a distrust regarding them when it comes to ethics. This has been further accentuated by the scandalous divide in the religions between the ethical ideals they project and their actual practice. Moreover, human and societal life have become so complex that no one single religion, however rich in its ethical heritage, is able to meet the challenges of present times. All this forces Christian ethics to follow a dialogical method. It needs to relate itself not only to other religious traditions but also to many new social movements. For, some of the major ethical concerns of present times are taken up more concretely and insistently by social movements than by religions. For example, gender-ethics is more convincingly embodied in feminist movements and in their theorizing. So too, the issues of social ethics are practiced and reflected upon more sharply by anti-caste movements. That is why it is crucial for Christian ethics to continue to dialogue with the various new social movements.

## 3.  Religious Scriptures

The Dharmapada, Bhagavadgita, Bible, Qur'an, etc., contain a rich fund of moral and ethical teachings and in fact these sources have been guiding the conduct of the believers of each of these religious traditions for centuries.[21] They also explain the different ethical orientation and emphasis among the followers of various religions. To this we need to add such works as that of Confucius, Mencius and others who distinguished themselves as ethical guides for all the peoples influenced by Chinese thought and world-view. This religious and philosophical heritage of Asia will help Christian ethics to strike roots in the Asian soil and understand its ethical values, traditions and practices.[22] Since ethics, as we noted, is inherently something social, and the people we interact with belong to other religious traditions, it is important that Christian ethics relates itself with these many Asian sources.

---

[21] Cf. Ninian Smart – Richard D. Hecht (eds.), *Sacred Texts of the World. A Universal Anthology*, Quercus, London, 2007.

[22] Cf. Roderick Hindery, *Comparative Ethics- in Hindu and Buddhist Traditions*, Motilal Banarsidass Publishers, Delhi, 1978.

## 4.  *Literature and Narrative Ethics*

Stories and literature make us aware of the role of emotions and imagination in human life. They are so very essential in interpreting human intentions and actions. That also tells us about the limitation of a mere discursive and rational approach to ethics.[23] In fact the peoples of Asia in their daily lives have used stories and epics as guidance for a righteous and virtuous life. The immense lore of stories in India and in other parts of Asia have great potential of inspiration than other forms of ethics.[24] Since narratives bring out the many facets of human and societal life in all its complexity and portray varied emotions, we need to look at literature as an important source for ethics. Literary narratives of hope, anxiety and despair, joy, pain and suffering give us profound insights into human condition. Such being the case, Christian ethics need to be continuously in conversation with local literature. This would help Christian ethics also to get rooted in the soil and respond to issues of the context.

## Conclusion

We may not reach far with our truths of faith and with the Bible. But with ethics inspired by faith and Bible we have greater access to the life of the people across borders and boundaries. In that sense, Christian ethics is an entry point to the life of society, the world and nature. In a world situation and Asian situation characterized by many challenges and ambiguities, Christian approach to ethics needs to acquire more and more a humanistic character and develop into a strong social ethics; even more, it needs to become a subaltern ethics. The Christian Gospels speak of the poor and those rejected and oppressed as blessed. The many parables of Jesus present the poor as those who are especially cared for by God. The Scriptures present to us a "God of Life".[25]

In the context of the glaring divide between the rich and the poor, the Christian message of God's privileging of the poor needs to find also an ethical expression. That is why there is a need to develop an ethics of refusal in order to challenge the powers that be. In this way, Christian ethics will be in service of life and its promotion and it needs to intervene

---

[23] Cf. Farrell, Frank B., *Why Does Literature Matter?* Cornell University Press, Ithaca, 2004.

[24] Cf. A. K. Ramanujan, *Folk-tales from India*, Viking, Delhi, 1993; ID., *A Flowering Tree and Other Oral Tales from India*, Penguin Books, Delhi, 1997.

[25] Cf. Gustavo Gutierrez, *God of Life*, Orbis Books, New York, 1991.

decisively whenever and wherever life is threatened, corroded, maimed or suppressed. This includes also the condition of the nature which has been jeopardized by the dominant model of development. This basic agenda of Christian ethics today will lead it to a closer collaboration with new social movements and dialogue with the many rich resources in various religious traditions and in the stories and literature of Asian peoples.

## Chapter 14

# Asia's Struggle for Religious Tolerance

## The Swing and Sway of the Bamboo

*"The golden rule of conduct...is mutual toleration, seeing that we will never all think alike and we shall always see Truth in fragment and from different angles of vision. Conscience is not the same thing for all...Even amongst the most conscientious persons, there will be room enough for honest differences of opinion. The only possible rule of conduct in any civilized society, is therefore, mutual toleration."*

– M. K. Gandhi[1]

One of the most critical issues humanity faces today is the negation of diversity and plurality. Be it the question of immigrants in Europe or the innumerable ethnic groups in Asian countries or the tribes in Africa, or the indigenous peoples in Americas – the question of coexistence in peace in the context of plurality has become a challenging one. That explains the importance of tolerance as an attitude and toleration as a practice vis-à-vis modes of thought, beliefs and ways of life by the others living in the same society.

The responses to diversity rest on different ideological orientations, and these could span from extreme view of steamrolling all differences in the hope of creating unity, or could be a posture of cultural relativism that may not dare to challenge in the cultures what is counterproductive to common good. The question of different identities also touches upon

---

[1] *Raghavan Iyer (ed.), Essential Writings of Gandhi,* Oxford University Press, Delhi, 1998, p. 246.

institutions like the state which has the duty towards its citizens, all of whom may not have the same culture, nor may share the same worldviews and values.[2] In what ways the state comes to terms with diversity becomes a political question, calling for policies that would be fair and would not prejudice the interest of any group in the same polity. Here again tolerance becomes politically very significant.

In the heart of Asia there are, unfortunately, some intolerant states. It is really a contradiction that a tolerant people like the Buddhists in Myanmar should be ruled by an intolerant military junta. The mode of governance in that country, in Vietnam, North Korea and China present a picture of intolerance affecting the daily lives of the people. China's intolerance towards Tibet and the Muslim-dominated Xinjiang province and the way the culture and tradition of the peoples of these regions are suppressed are well-known. The socialist regimes in Asia are intolerant of any legitimate expression of the aspirations of the people, and there is continuous protests and resistance from the people and various groups which are suppressed violently.

The question of tolerance could be approached from these various angles. However this chapter limits itself to consider the question of religious tolerance in Asia, its practices, difficulties and the ways to overcome intolerance and religious fundamentalism. Though religious tolerance is but one aspect of a larger question, it nevertheless is a mirror on which the situation of the Asian societies gets reflected.

### New Facets of Religious Intolerance
In spite of the fact that Asian worldview and ethos are oriented towards tolerance and peace, there have been, unfortunately, many incidents of intolerance in recent decades. For many it may come as a surprise that in India, a country which is known for its tolerance, such incidents as the attack on Muslim community in the state of Gujarat and more recently the attack of Christians in the state of Orissa could take place. Attacked by the violent Hindu fundamentalist groups, tribal Christians of Orissa were forced to flee to the forests to save their lives.[3] There is growing

---

[2] Cf. Urmila Phadnis – Rajat Ganguly (ed.), *Ethnicity and Nation-building in South Asia*, Revised Edition, Sage Publications, New Delhi-Thousand Oaks-London, 2001; Mark Juergensmeyer, *Religious Nationalism Confronts the Secular State*, Oxford University Press, Delhi, 1996.

[3] Cf. Anto Akkara, *Kandhamal a Blot to Indian Secularism*, Media House, Delhi, 2009.

intolerance towards the Christian community in Pakistan, against whom the blasphemy law is applied. There was a serious debate and controversy in Malaysia regarding the use of "Allah" by Catholics in their newsletter *Herald*. And after prolonged dispute when the court ruled that Christians could use the word "Allah" to refer to God, there were firebomb assaults on churches. Philippines, though is an exceptional case in Asia of a country with overwhelming majority of Christians, there has been endemic conflict between Christians and Muslims in Mindanao with a strong Muslim population. There is still armed struggle, violence and kidnapping in that part. Further in the southern part of Thailand there is religious conflict between Buddhists and Muslims.

More and more studies and analyses have shown that in Asia, while people still mutually respect each other in their religious expressions, the cause for intolerance is to be traced to political and economic factors. In the above referred case of Malaysia, for the large majority of the people, the use of "Allah" was not an issue, while it was objected by the state on the ground that it might flare up into a communal trouble, which became a self-fulfilling prophecy. The struggle for political power and economic dominance produces intolerance, and religions are used, given their strong symbolic and emotive potential, as instruments in political conflicts and economic competition.[4]

In South and South East Asia, the colonial legacy is very strong. The growth of intolerance is due to the reaction to colonialism and its policies which, in the perception of many Asians, favoured the religion of the colonizers – Christianity.[5] Moreover, a common factor that has led to intolerance towards other religious traditions, especially Christianity, is what is perceived as its strong proselytizing tendencies. From Pakistan to Japan in almost every Asian society, there has been resistance and expressions of intolerance towards Christian proselytization. Coupled with this practice is the belief that Christianity is not tolerant of other religious traditions.

---

[4] Cf. Ninian Smart, *Religion and Nationalism. The Urgency of Transnational Spirituality and Toleration*, Centre for Indian and Inter-religious Studies, Rome, 1994; Anthony Giddens, *The Nation-State and Violence*, University of California Press, Berkeley and Los Angeles, 1987.

[5] In fact, the uprise of Indian soldiers (so called 'mutiny' of 1857) had as its target the colonizers, colonial institutions and the Christian minority. Subsequently the British took much care to be neutral in their religious policies.

## Asian Practices of Tolerance

The Asian ethos of tolerance and the means it developed to uphold and cherish difference distinguish it from other forms of tolerance. The *millet system* developed in the Ottoman Empire allowed each religious community to have its own self-governing organization without impinging upon Islam. Thus Jews, Greek Orthodox and Armenian orthodox could follow their own customs and traditions irrespective of the numerical strength of the community. This model while is tolerant towards each other, has the lacuna of sealing off communities from each other as well-defined entities.

Asian tradition followed a different path. There was an encounter among the religious traditions allowing each one to receive and learn from each other, and to mix and mingle to the extent of even participating in the worship of others. In this way, each religion was shaped by the other. The difference of Indonesian Islam from other Islamic communities is due to the influence of Hinduism and Buddhism on it. We could also cite the case of Buddhism which through encounter with Confuciansim and Daoism developed indigenous versions of it in China, Korea and Japan.

*Multiculturalism* is another proposal for tolerance and it is today discussed by many neo-liberals as a means for peace.[6] The philosophy and political theory of multiculturalism is certainly an antidote to homogenization and standardization or assimilation policies.[7] Here the

---

[6] Cf. Will Kymlicka, *Multicultural Citizenship. A Liberal Theory of Minority Rights*, Oxford University Press, Oxford, 2000 (Reprint); Will Kymlicka (ed.), *The Rights of Minority Cultures*, Oxford University Press, Oxford, 2000 (Reprint); Will Kymlicka and Wayne Norman (eds.), *Citizenship in Diverse Societies*, Oxford University Press, Oxford, 2000; Charles Taylor and Amy Gutman (eds.), *Multiculturalism. Examining the Politics of Recognition*, Princeton University Press, Princeton, New Jersey, 1994.

[7] Unfortunately France is following a standardized approach in the name of *laicité* – secularity. There appears to be in its approach a limited understanding of nationalism and it is conditioned by its own history of the secular. This became evident the way it dealt with the case of the scarf of Muslim children. It may be pointed out that in a similar situation, in India, the scarf was allowed precisely for the reason of the secular! What we have in the former case is an "Enlightenment Fundamentalism" calling for a universal mode of rationality, whereas in the latter case it is a question of reconciling the Enlightenment heritage with due acknowledgement of cultural pluralism and its consequences for day-to-day life.

mere fact of recognizing diversity does not help. What we require is a clear affirmation of human diversity as an important *value*.[8] Moreover, tolerance cannot limit itself to let each culture and people have their own way, but needs to go beyond to promote interaction and exchange among the different ethnic, linguistic and cultural groups on an equal footing. It is possible that a society may allow multicultural co-existence, but then one or other culture may dominate. Here tolerance lets the other live, and it does not matter whether the other is considered inferior. "If tolerance is the product of compassion", as R. Balasubramanian notes, "it amounts to a concession and not a recognition".[9] In other words, it is important for tolerance that every culture, every ethnic group is equally valued and recognized as significant to the integrity of the whole.

The assumption that we could create equality by making everyone the same – even assuming this to be the best interpretation for assimilation and integration - has not worked for the simple reason that the culture or group to which one is supposed to assimilate becomes the standard one. When a religious fundamentalist, ethnic or national chauvinist considers his/her own religion or group identity above those of others, in this case what is required of him or her would be not tolerance towards the other, but rather adopting other means and measures so that the religious or ethnic prejudice is overcome. To put it more concretely, what is expected of a white man or woman is not simply to tolerate a black person. Here tolerance does not make sense. What is expected is rather that the white man or woman overcome his or her racial prejudice. This is fundamental. The same thing could be said of a Brahmin or upper caste person. He or she doe not become just, by tolerating the Dalits. Rather the Brahmins and upper castes need to rid of their caste-prejudices. This makes us see why tolerance as an attitude and toleration as a practice presuppose acceptance of *equality* of all members with their diverse worldviews and their different conceptions of good life – as long as these are not prejudicial to the common good.[10]

---

[8] In Britain after a period of insistence that the immigrants assimilate to British culture and way of life, there took place from 1970's a shift in policy towards multiculturalism, something that has not happened in countries like France whose public policies still insist on assimilation and integration.

[9] Cf. R. Balasubramanian (ed.), *Tolerance in Indian Culture,* Indian Council of Philosophical Research, New Delhi, 1992, p. 3.

[10] Cf. Imtiaz Ahmad – Partha S. Ghosh – Helmut Reifeld (eds.), *Pluralism and Equality. Values in Indian Society and Politics,* Sage Publications, New Delhi-Thousand Oaks-London, 2000.

How one could be tolerant and yet mete out unequal treatment to others is exemplified by the caste-system. This system is one in which everyone is integrated in such a way that one needs the other. The mutual interdependence creates an atmosphere of tolerance in daily life. But what is lacking here is the absence of equality. The Brahmin needs the "untouchable" to deal with the impurities, but could never consider the "untouchable" as equal to him. Here is a case of tolerance in a hierarchical system.[11]

Tolerance is something not only an inter-religious matter, but also an *intra-religious* question. The Semitic religious traditions have been in general very rigid and uncompromising with internal differences, and history amply bears witness to the regime of intolerance towards heretics and the unorthodox. The fluidity of Hinduism and Buddhism, on the other hand, had allowed multiplicity of views in doctrines and practices to co-exist in a spirit of tolerance. In fact, as many studies have shown, Hinduism itself is a confluence of many religious experiences and it keeps including new ones, so that nothing is lost or gets excluded.[12] Even *tantrism* – shocking as it may be for many religious puritans – found a niche within Hinduism. Moreover, for Hindus, truth is not something once for all given and to be transmitted, but something to be discovered in every experience of fragments which sets in motion a quest for fuller truth.[13] There is no pretension of having ever attained the fullness of truth.

---

[11] Cf. Wilhelm Halbfass, *Tradition and Reflection. Exploration in Indian Thought,* State University of New York Press, Albany, 1991, pp. 347-405.

[12] Cf. Vasudha Dalmia – Heinrich von Stietencron (eds.), *Representing Hinduism. The Construction of Religious Traditions and National Identity,* Sage Publications, New Delhi-Thousand Oaks-London, 1995; Günther D. Sontheimer – Herman Kulke (eds.), *Hinduism Reconsidered,* Manohar, New Delhi, 1991.

[13] Entering into this question here may take us far afield. Nevertheless it is important to note the contrast between the flexibility of vision and the rigidity of the social system of caste. Jamal Khwaja notes in this regard: "While Indian culture admirably tolerated doctrinal differences, it failed to develop the idea of toleration into the concept of humanistic respect of man [sic] as such. The humanistic protest of Jainism and Buddhism against caste could not be assimilated by Hindu orthodoxy, despite the spiritual renewal produced by these movements and the legacy left by Ashoka... If tolerance remains incomplete without equality of status, the Hindu concept of tolerance has only one leg to stand upon." R. Balasubramanian, *Tolerance in Indian Culture,* p. 100.

One of the important expressions of tolerance is the practice of pilgrimages across religious borders. People of one religious group visiting and praying in the religious places of others are quite common throughout Asia. This has been practiced even today. There are many *darghas* – tombs of Muslim holy persons – visited by Hindus. In fact the Khwaja Banda Nawaz Dargha and the shrine of Sufi saint Khwaja Moinuddin Chichti at Ajmer, receive perhaps more Hindu visitors than Muslims. The same thing is true also of the Marian shrine of Vailankanni, where Hindu pilgrims are said to outnumber Christians. There are also a few instances of Indian Christians going on pilgrimage to Hindu shrines like Sabarimala in Kerala. In the Philippines, where there is a long history of violent conflicts between Christians and Muslims in Mindanao, examples of initiatives for tolerance between the two communities abound. We may cite here the case of *Silsilah*[14] movement in Zamboanga City and around. The movement promotes day-to-day forms of dialogue among the two communities – Christians and Muslims.

Yet another force for tolerance has been the personalities of saints and sages who through their universal spirit have taught us what it means to cross borders and boundaries and reach out to the other, to the different. In the Indian tradition we have the example of Kabir – the mystical saint who was a bridge between the spiritual heritage of Hinduism and Islam. Both these religious traditions consider him as their own. We could cite many models of tolerance who even today could serve as guiding lights.[15] Besides Ashoka in the ancient period, we have in the Medieval India the example of the great Mughal emperor Akbar (1542 – 1605). The need for tolerance and mutual trust among the religious communities, especially

---

[14] The movement was started by Fr Sebastian D'Ambra PIME on May 9, 1984, moved by the eruption of violence and endemic conflicts between Christians and Muslims, political in origin, took practical steps to create tolerance and understanding among the two groups. Even today it remains a symbol of hope for peaceful co-existence in the region. Today the movement has tried to include in its common journey not only Muslims and Christians but also peoples of other faiths. Part of the movement is the creation of harmony villages where people of different religious traditions live and work together as one community. Sisilah offers also training programmes for tolerance and harmony.

[15] Well-known is the tolerance Ashoka (304 BC – 232 BC) advocated among the various religious "sects" noting perceptively that dishonour done to another religion is done to one's own. Cf. N.A. Nikam – Richard McKeon (eds.), *Edicts of Asoka*, The University of Chicago Press, Chicago, 1978.

between Muslims and Hindus, led him even to found a religious path which all could share and he called it *"Din-i-Ilahi"*. He promoted dialogue among Christians, Jews, Parsis, Jains and even atheists. Such was the trust Akbar reposed in his Hindu collaborators that he did not hesitate to appoint them as generals in his army. This confidence and trust showed the openness of this Muslim ruler. Akbar also revoked the jizy tax collected from the Zimmis or non-Muslims in 1563, and in the following year he did away with the obnoxious pilgrimage tax imposed on the Hindus. His great grandson Dara was the one who translated from Sanskrit into Persian the *Upanishads* – the Hindu Scriptures.

## Asian Foundations for Tolerance

Asian approach to tolerance derives from a sense of fluidity of borders. The cultural ethos of peoples in the continent is nurtured through Hinduism, Buddhism and Daoism, etc., which do not erect walls of separation between religions on the basis of doctrines, orthodoxy, etc. As for human fulfilment, a religion like Hinduism believes that it cannot be framed or prescribed. As a result, each person is to follow the path that is most suited to him or her. It could be the path of knowledge (*gnana*), or of devotion (*bhakti*) or of action (*karma*). Closely related to it is the conception of *adhikara* which acknowledges different competence of people and levels of understanding, and it advocates tolerance. Tolerance is also manifest in the freedom each one has to choose one's deity of predilection (*istadevata*). As for Jainism, the concept of *anekanta-vada* or pluralism in the approach to truth has served as inspiration for tolerance.

Moreover, there is a sense of respect for the belief of others which derives from the conviction that the sacred is present and operative in the beliefs and practices of others. To put it differently, there is an embedded sense of mystery in the Asian ethos that recognizes the sacred in the religious tradition and rituals of others, even though these are quite different from one's own. Implicit herein is also the conviction that the sacral mystery may not be encapsulated in any one single frame or limited to one path. It is not by trying to create unity of creed that harmony and concord result, but by moving together in a common quest.

Metaphorically the ideal of co-existence could be captured by the image of *bamboo*. The winds are not able to break it, because it knows to swing and sway while firmly rooted in the ground. This is different from the image of *wall* that separates one religion and its doctrines from others. In South Asia, there has been rarely conflicts and violence on the basis of doctrinal issues. The plundering of Hindu temples like Jagnath in medieval times was not due to any disrespect to the Hindu gods or Hindu doctrines, but motivated by the wealth – gold, jewels etc. – these places of worship contained. This is different from the doctrinal intolerance expressed through inquisition and witch-hunting, for example.

The advent of Islam brought a new dimension to the traditional Indian culture, and there was exchange in various areas giving birth to new genre of arts, music, architecture, etc. There are numerous instances of Muslim rulers like Tippu Sultan making endowments to Hindu temples, and this was meant to create good understanding and tolerance among the citizens. Another important means that was common was the practice of marriage that straightened strained relationships and created good will. In India the mutual influence of Hindus and Muslims led to the emergence of Urdu language which harmoniously blends Hindi, Persian, Arabic and Turkish languages.

### Tolerance – the Secular and the "Rational"

It is well-known that amidst religious wars between Protestants and Catholics, the ideal of the secular presented a *tertium quid* in the European history, and it was fostered further through the Enlightenment tradition. In contemporary times, unwittingly, one thinks of this as the solution for the intolerance in the world. Unfortunately, the secular of the European vintage may not respond to the challenges of Asian societies, and perhaps also of other parts of the world.[16] One of the assumptions behind this secular approach is that religion and public life are separate. But then, as J. Habermas has pointed out quite perceptively, this position that religion is private and has nothing to do with public life is an exception than the norm,[17] since other parts of the world show intimate connection of religion and public life, and that is true as well of the United States, not to speak of Asia, Africa, Latin America, etc. Therefore, for Asians, the question of tolerance is not answered by taking recourse to the ideal of the secular defined in the Western manner, but by fostering closer bonds and relationships among peoples of various religious traditions. Dialogue,

---

[16] Cf. Rajeev Bhargava (ed.), *Secularism and Its Critics*, Oxford University Press, New Delhi, 1999.

[17] This was expressed in a lecture he delivered at Tilburg University on 1 March, 2009. Cf. also, Ninian Smart, *Religion and the Western Mind*, State University of New York Press, Albany, 1987.

friendship and harmony are important for realizing the ideal of harmony. These are embedded in the Asian cultures and religious traditions.[18]

What we have said also makes us aware of those approaches that overemphasize the procedures, ideal conditions of dialogue or communicative rationality. But the point is, the way Asia understands rationality goes beyond such procedural modes abstracted from concrete situations. Rational argumentation could bring about tolerance is an utopian proposal when it does not attend to concrete social and cultural conditions of different contexts, and when it does not take into account that in intricate issues like inter-religious relationships a host of other factors like emotions, symbols, history, etc., are involved. Further, any assumption that rationality will bring about also the attitude of tolerance and the practice of toleration could be disputed. Legal and constitutional means are certainly a great aid to the practice of tolerance. But they cannot substitute the change of attitude and consciousness required for tolerance, nor dispense with other important ways and means to overcome intolerance.

More than Asia becoming secular in the European way, it is Europe which is becoming more like Asia with its growing multi-religious societies. In these "post-secular" times, probably the secular solutions may not lead the European community towards tolerance and peace in the growing multi-religious and multi-cultural societies of that continent. Probably Europe needs to go back to its Christian roots to find the sources for the understanding of the religiously other in love, compassion, acceptance, and friendship. Let me venture to suggest, from a long range perspective, many of Europe's philosophies and speculations may be treated as footnotes to its deeply embedded Christian tradition which Europeans need to reinterpret in response to the challenges of the present times, especially in relation to people of other faiths, who are becoming increasingly their neighbours.

### Limits of a Theology of Inclusivism

What we have said leads us also to understand that the theological position of inclusivism for example vis-à-vis other religious traditions may not be characterized as tolerance. For the other religions are not taken as having

---

[18] Cf. Francis Loh Kok Wah (ed.), *Building Bridges. Crossing Boundaries. Everyday Forms of Inter-Ethnic Peace Building in Malaysia*, The Ford Foundation-Persatuan Sains Sosial Malaysia, Jakarta-Selangor, 2010.

equal standing and right as one's own. Here the value of religious traditions in themselves is negated, and they are viewed in what they could signify in relation to one's own religious truth to which the others are subordinated. Inclusivism is then a kind of intolerance as it does not value other religious traditions in themselves. Theology of inclusivism rests on the ideology that what is lower is contained in the higher and is assumed into it (one may think of Hegel's concept of "*Aufhebung*"). Inclusivism does not make tolerance. That is precisely the point of Paul Hacker for whom one should speak more of inclusivism in Hinduism rather than tolerance.[19] That may be true of doctrinal level. But the every day practice shows another facet of Hinduism that could accommodate other religious experiences.

But there is a basic point to be considered here. Since Europe made a separation of the private and the public and confined religion to the private realm, it was forced to seek the resources for religious tolerance within the doctrinal realm. But the doctrinal realm does not give us the tolerance required for day-to-day life. The separation of the public and private of the European Enlightenment tradition stands in contrast to the belief system of Islamic migrants for whom religion is a total way of life and it cannot be confined to the private realm. Such being the case, it is doubtful whether mere theological approaches will bring about tolerance and peace. It requires many practical approaches that touch upon other realms. A more comprehensive approach to tolerance is needed within which the religious tolerance could be addressed.

### The Future of Tolerance in Asia
Could we really hope for tolerance in Asia? What are some of the ways that could eventually lead us to greater tolerance? How do we overcome the growing religious fundamentalism in the continent?

It is too evident that there is no panacea for intolerance and religious fundamentalism. We need a multi-pronged approach that will pull together all the resources available. I would like to highlight six important areas on which we need to concentrate for a harmonious and tolerant societies in Asia. What is said here may be applicable also elsewhere.

---

[19] Cf. Wilhelm Halbfass, " 'Inclusivism' and 'Tolerance' in the Encounter Between India and the West", in his *India and Europe: An Essay in Philosophical Understanding*, Motilal Banarsidass, Delhi, 1990, pp. 403-418.

## 1. *Affirmation of Multiple Layers of Identity*

For the nurturing of tolerance in a society, certain materials conditions (in the Marxian sense) need to be created. The point could be illustrated with an example. Indonesian society, as we noted, has a form of Islam quite different from the rest of the world. The Javanese culture has contributed to the creation of an Islam open to other religious traditions and experiences. However, the absence of democracy and social justice has lent substance to radicalization of Islam and the birth of religious fundamentalism.[20] The cultural resources may not sustain Indonesia in tolerance, unless conditions are created for the removal of poverty, for a democratic life and for a modicum of justice. Much of the wind from the fundamentalists' sails could be taken by a process of democratization and pursuit of justice. In the absence of this process, the rich multi-cultural society of Indonesia could turn towards radical Islamization fixating on one single identity of the religion of the majority community.

Very often religious hostility and prejudices arise because people are branded with one single identity. The truth is that people have multiple identities.[21] Exchange and interaction take place at different levels. Religion is not an all-engulfing identity. All this tells us that inter-religious relationships are to be placed within the broader social and cultural context in which individuals and communities are situated. It also makes us aware that tolerance does not follow by simply responding to the demands of religious identity. A historical example is that of Pakistan, which at the time of partition in 1947 had a Western part and Eastern part separated by thousands of kilometres and supposed to be united because of the Islamic religious identity. But then as history tells us, the cultural and linguistic factors were so overriding that religious identity could not hold together a nation and the creation of a different nation as Bangladesh became inevitable.[22] Like the equality of status which is an essential

---

[20] Cf. Thomas Michael, "Emerging Trends in Religious Fundamentalism", in Anthony Rogers (ed.), *Asian Consultation on Harmony through Reconciliation*, FABC - Office of Human Development, Manila, 2007, pp. 153-165.

[21] Cf. Amartya Sen, *Identity and Violence. The Illusion of Destiny*, Allen Lane, London, 2006.

[22] Historically, this is illustrated by the fact that tolerance was created through regimes of empires and kingdoms, where people of different religious traditions could co-exist and interact. See Michael Walzer, *On Toleration*, Frank Bros. & Co., Noida, 2004.

requisite for a more complete tolerance, it is important that multiple identities of individuals are recognized. The tolerance within the religions is in itself a vast area which is becoming more and more important today, but dealing with this issue goes beyond the scope of this chapter.

## 2.   Promoting Intra-religious Understanding

One may not take for granted that religious tolerance has to do between religions, as if every religious tradition is a homogenous entity. Many Hindus and Muslims do not clearly share what some of their radical co-religionists think and act. The diversity we find in each religious tradition makes religious tolerance a much more complex issue than what may appear to be. It could easily happen that people of a particular religious group may be closer in terms of their vision and values to another group of a different religion. The Sufi saints with their spirit of universalism, tolerance and innovative interpretation of *Quran* may be closer to Christian saints and mystics than Islamic jihadists and theocratic rulers.[23] Similarly, there may be greater understanding and tolerance among Muslim Sufis and Hindu saints than towards their co-religionists. This mutuality across conventional religious boundaries needs to be cultivated. But that poses the question of the extent of freedom individuals may enjoy within their religious community to uphold views and convictions that empathize with other religious communities. Therefore, for the future of tolerance, it is crucial that religious communities become self-critical and are open to other voices within their group. These voices may not be suppressed in the name of orthodoxy or by unenlightened group-loyalty.

## 3.   Challenging the Use of Religion as a Political Weapon

It is precisely the strategy of religious fundamentalists to make people forget all other identities and invest their entire energy and emotions into one single identity – that of their religious belonging. In this way, religion is converted into a political weapon meant to defend the group.[24] The analysis Christophe Jaffrelot has made regarding Hindu fundamen-

---

[23] Cf. Omid Safi (ed.), *Progressive Muslims. On Justice, Gender and Pluralism*, Oneworld Publications, Oxford, 2006; Bernard Lewis, *The Crisis of Islam. Holy War and Unholy Terror*, Phoenix, London, 2004.

[24] Cf. Mark Lewis Taylor, *Religion, Politics and the Christian Right. Post – 9/11 Powers and American Empire*, Fortress Press, Minneapolis, 2005; Mark Juergensmeyer, *Terror in the Mind of God. The Global Rise of Religious Violence*, University of California Press, Berkeley-Los Angeles-London, 2001.

talist strategies are applicable also to other forms of religious fundamentalism.[25]Fundamentalism and intolerance thrive by *stigmatization* of the "threatening other". Paradoxically, the threatening other also becomes in the politicization of religion, the ideal to be emulated. Hindu fundamentalists, for example, wants to emulate Christian and Islamic model of what it views as their aggressive proselytization.[26] This phenomenon has been referred to as "semitisation of Hinduism".[27] The third strategy in politicization of religion is that of *mobilization*. The fomenting and popularization of prejudices and emulation of the other ends in riots, conflagration and violent acts of terrorism. Many of these are not spontaneous outburst of violence but are well-planned and engineered religious riots.

Now for the future of tolerance we need to respond at all three levels. Stigmatization needs to be responded to by educational praxis – both formal and informal – through which knowledge of other religious traditions as its believers would like to be understood - is imparted and made available to the people. The formal educational system needs to include education for religious harmony as an integral component of curriculum. The educational process could rely on the rich and longstanding Asian tradition of harmony and concord. The whole problem today is that the rich religious heritage of tolerance is set aside, and they are viewed from a political angle or exploited as identity-markers of groups and communities. Asia cannot live on borrowed conceptions of tolerance but has to find within its own tradition the resources for religious harmony and understanding.

The question of emulation needs to be responded to by highlighting the unique character of each religious tradition. There is an incommensurability of religions. Emulation of one religion by another does not respect the different historical trajectories each religion has followed. Efforts need to be made to highlight the vision, values, and

---

[25] Cf. Christophe Jaffrelot, *The Hindu Nationalist Movement and Indian Politics 1925 to the 1990s*, Viking, New Delhi, 1996.

[26] Cf. David Ludden (ed.), *Making India Hindu. Religion, Community, and the Politics of Democracy in India*, Oxford University Press, Delhi, 1996; Walter K. Andersen – Shridhar D. Damle (eds.), *The Brotherhood in Saffron. The Rashtriya Swayamsevak Sangh and Hindu Revivalism*, Vistaar Publications, New Delhi, 1987; Tapan Basu et al., *Khaki Shorts and Saffron Flags. A Critique of the Hindu Right*, Orient Longman, New Delhi, 1993.

[27] Rajni Kothari, "From Religion to Religiosity", in *Jeevadhara*, 20 (1990), p. 74.

ethical ideals that are unique to each religious universe. Finally, the mobilization for intolerance and assault on peoples of other religious traditions and minorities need to be responded to by creating at the grassroots movements that would counter the manipulations of the elite and the powerful who make use of the poor and the marginalized to create violence in the name of religion.

## 4.   Re-interpretation of Religious Sources

Religious scriptures, traditions, laws, regulations, rituals, etc., are the religious sources with which believers are fed. But when they are not interpreted properly, or taken in their literal sense, this has serious social consequences, especially so when fundamentalists see the degeneration of their religion and would want to restore it to its purity. Such a trend is observable in Islam, Christianity, Hinduism, etc. That explains the need for a proper hermeneutical approach to religious sources interpreting the message of a religious community in relation to the broader society. Further, it requires that adequate means are taken to remove the sense of insecurity among the believers. In fact, it is the insecurity that causes the fundamentalists to withdraw themselves into their world in which they believe purity is safeguarded by banning any interpretation other than the one of tradition or of authority. The narrow interpretations fomenting intolerance will be best addressed by people of the same religious community proffering more open interpretations. Religious authorities and theologians have a great responsibility in challenging fundamentalist interpretations, and thus promoting peace and harmony.

## 5.   Promoting Critical History

It is a fact that the way history is perceived and interpreted by contending groups in a nation or society is one of the ideological sources of intolerance. In this sense writing of history is also a play of power. Sometimes no distinction is made between history and myth. Histories about the glories a group enjoyed in the past and now deprived of, or the humiliations suffered ignite sentiments of enmity and revenge.[28] Distorted historical

---

[28] For example, V.D. Savarkar, one of the ideologues of the Hindu right, wrote a book entitled *Six Glorious Epochs of Indian History*. He tries to portray Indian history as a struggle by the Hindus against outsiders like the Muslims and Christians, who are then the enemies. In Sri Lanka, the Tamils are viewed by the majority Sinhalese as foreigners and the history of Sri Lanka is identified with the history of the majority Sinhalese Buddhist community.

narration, especially when popularized, serve as ammunition for intolerance and violence. Examples can be drawn from almost every country in Asia. Given this situation, the future path of tolerance calls for clearing the misrepresentations of the past.[29] This needs to be done through revising the content of how the history of a nation or a society is portrayed in educational text-books, for example. History needs to become also a point of dialogue and discussion in the civil society with the possibility of all concerned to participate in this exercise. Here the historians and honest intellectuals have the task of producing evidence and critically study the claims about the past. The critical approach could have a restraining effect on intolerance.

### 6. *Availing Constitutional and Legal Means*
The various ways and strategies we have viewed need to be supported by constitutional means and by a judiciary that would be free and fair. In every Constitution – especially those espousing secular and democratic spirit – there is room for challenging religious intolerance. This is for example the case with Indian Constitution. Since national constitution is a common point of reference, citizens need to be trained and educated to avail the provisions of it. In the case of the use of "Allah" to which I referred earlier, the judiciary came out with a verdict that challenged the intolerance of extremist groups. That this could happen in a country as Malaysia with its strong Islamic spirit is significant and evokes a lot of hope for the future.

### Conclusion
What we have said about Asia may have some insights for the global issue of tolerance today. One thing that is becoming evident is that there is no one single formula to create a tolerant people and society. Lest tolerance become condescension, it is important that it is not dissociated from the concern of equality. The overcoming of intolerance and paving the way for a harmonious society in justice and peace will depend upon each society with its unique, history, tradition, practices, etc.

Manifestations of religious fundamentalism too differ according to societies and its origin may have different causes. The response also has to be different. Constitutional and legal means are certainly important. But they may prove to be quite inadequate. They need to be supported by

---

[29] Cf. Felix Wilfred – Jose Maliekal (eds.), *The Struggle for the Past. Historiography Today,* Department of Christian Studies, University of Madras, Madras, 2002.

everyday practices of mutuality through informal ways, such as fostering of friendship,[30] mutual visits of places of worship and pilgrimage centres, inter-religious marriages, etc. For, as in the case of justice, the best theories of it do not bring about effective justice, which presupposes that there be change of behaviour patterns. Tolerance is a value that needs nurturing and a broader environment of acceptance. The bamboo-like flexibility is required not only for Asian societies; flexibility is increasingly becoming important for people all over the world to resolve conflicts and overcome intolerance.

Finally, tolerance is a much larger matter than religions. However, today with growing realization of the role of religion in public life – whether positively or negatively – the measure of tolerance in the religious field becomes also the index for general tolerance in society. In this respect, many of the Asian states, despite the long-standing civilizational ethos of tolerance, curb religious freedom. There is little room for religious traditions to interact among themselves since all relationships of religions are directed to the state which controls them. In such situations channels of communication need to be opened, so that religious groups could interact among themselves. Dalai Lama of Tibet and Aung San Suu Kyi of Mynmar – both of them Nobel Prize winners for peace – stand as 'voice of hope'[31] and sanity for a more tolerant and harmonious Asia.

---

[30] The practice of friendship can overcome many difficulties and differences and foster a genuine process of growth of all the communities involved. Here it may be pointed out how the spirit of friendship and concern for the Muslim community led Pope John Paul II not to feel confronted by the construction of a big mosque in Rome. On that occasion, he sent out a message of friendship to the Muslim community which eased highly charged political tensions.

[31] Aung San Suu Kyi, *The Voice of Hope. Conversation with Alan Clements*, Raider, London, 2008.

Chapter 15

# Theological Education
# for Public Life

*"We are deeply concerned with the fact that theological education in India does not evolve itself out of the very life struggle that characterizes the Indian situation. This situation would include the socio-economic-political reality, the varied religious heritage and practices, the phenomenon of India being both urban and rural and the scientific secular world-view of modern India. All these form part of the ongoing self-revelation of God to us that should be an essential part of our biblical hermeneutics and theological reflection."*

- ITA Statement[1]

Recently during a brief stay in Dar Es Salaam, Tanzania, I was interested to trace the trail of East African slave-trade. So, I took a boat and reached Zanzibar after two and a half hours of voyage. Zanzibar was a hub for the meeting of peoples, nations, cultures, religious traditions, etc. It was also a notorious centre for slave-trade. From Bagamayo and other places in the mainland, slaves were transported to Zanzibar for sale.[2] They were well-fed and their bodies were smeared with oil, so that they prove attractive and profitable for the prospective buyers. Today in the place of the slave market stands St Monica's Church, and the very spot where slaves were flagellated is erected the main altar, powerfully invoking the memory of the "crucified people".

---

[1] Statement of the Indian Theological Association (ITA), 1984., No. 16. For the text of the statement see Jacob Parappally (ed.), *Theoogizing in Context. Statements of the Indian Theological Association*, Dharmaram Publications, Bangalore, 2002, p.95.

[2] Cf. Amir A. Mohammed, *A Guide to a History of Zanzibar*, Good Luck Publishers, Zanzibar, 2006.

What touched me deeply was the visit to the house of an erstwhile slave-owner, adjacent to the Church. There beneath the ground floor, I found two dark rooms, each one measuring no more than ten by ten feet. In those dungeons were crammed fifty men chained together; so too fifty women. There was a small opening in those rooms to let in a little light and air, and a small pit that served as toilet for the slaves. Even animals deserved better treatment than this! Here is the saga of deep human suffering, that is not sufficiently brought to the consciousness of humanity. The victims of slave-trade deserve all honour, but it is also a warning to the living.

What came to my mind while visiting the sights of horrendous crimes against humanity was the thought about Christian mission and theology. Even while slave-trade was flourishing, theology was pursued; missionaries were in full action; pastors and priests were trained in theological institutions; and they were ordained; bishops were consecrated and they did their pastoral work. And yet, they were totally blind to the realities all around them. Theology, mission and pastoral work were completely insensitive to what was happening to human beings, engrossed as they were in certain ideals and values that centred around the soul and its redemption. The issues that were most crucial did not invite any response from theology or theological institutions of the times. In the case of East Africa, it was a layman, David Livingstone, who was ignorant of the theology of the times, but deeply human, who became the pioneer in liberating the salves and bringing an end to this practice.

We could trace further examples from modern times when theologians like Karl Rahner could elucidate the deep meanings of Christian faith and doctrines, without needing to refer to World War II and Auschwitz. Before him, in medieval times, Thomas Aquinas could construct such an impressive theological edifice in which the condition of the feudal society of his times and its oppression found no place.[3] I think these instances provide us openings to begin our reflection on theological education in relation to public life of Asia.

---

[3] Cf. Samuel Rayan, "Theological Education in the Social Context of India Today", in Felix Wilfred (ed.), *Theological Education in India Today, The Statement, Papers and the Proceedings of the Eighth Annual Meeting of the Indian Theological Association, Pariyaram, Kerala*, Asian Trading Corporation, Bangalore, 1985, p. 13.

## The Asian Scene

The innovation in theological education was a sequel to the autonomy and independence which the various Asian Churches sought from the West.[4] The independence meant deploying indigenous categories to express beliefs, or conduct worship adopting local symbols and rituals. Moreover, there was a lot of new initiatives in the way of pasturing the Christian congregations, and theological education adopted a lot of practical means and measures. By and large, then, theological education confined itself to doctrines, worship and its space was limited to the Christian community.

The main question today is to re-conceptualize theological education in order to respond to the public issues and questions in Asia . I think this will happen if we widen the scope of theological education and not limit it to the formation of  pastors, priests and ministers in the Church. Theological education concerns the entire Christian community and its relationship to the larger society. In the following pages we shall reflect on these concerns.

## A Fundamental Issue of Orientation

One of the major concerns of theology since European Enlightenment has been to secure for it a legitimate place in the comity of other sciences. A deeper analysis of various theological enterprises and movements since the Enlightenment will amply testify to this.[5] This concern had on its positive side the attempt to respond to the questions modernity posed to theology and theological education. The response, however, was by and large in terms of explicating the meaning of Christian belief for modern times and demonstrating its intelligibility. A radical re-orientation in

---

[4] See for example the proceedings of a consultation held in 1978: K. Rajaratnam – A.A. Sitompul (eds.), *Theological Education in Today's Asia*, CLS, Madras, 1978. The question of liberation from the Western patterns and of self-reliance in theological education is still with us. However, the accent has shifted, with new experiments in theological education, to new questions and areas. In the post-secular world of the West, new issues and questions have emerged, including the relationship between theology and religious studies. Cf. David F. Ford, *Theology. A Very Short Introduction*, Oxford University Press, Oxford, 1999; Sheila Greeve Davaney, "Theology and Religious Studies in an Age of Fragmentation", in Erik Borgman – Felix Wilfred (eds.), "Theology in a World of Specialization", *Concilium* 2006/2, pp.35-44.

[5] Cf. Jürgen Moltmann, *Was ist heute Theologie?* Herder, Freiburg, 1988.

theology came with the advent of a new methodology. Starting from the challenges of praxis, it tried to reconstruct Christian Scriptures, tradition, history and faith in order to transform the prevailing order of things. We could think of the emergence of liberation theologies, various forms of contextual theologies, feminist theologies, Dalit and tribal theologies. As a consequence, inspired by this new turn, there has taken place a fresh understanding of Christian praxis faith and theology.

This orientation of theology and a corresponding mode of theological education are challenged by another paradigm represented by the so called "radical orthodoxy" and "post-liberal theology", which have surfaced today by invoking the Barthian heritage which for the last few decades had fallen in disfavour. According to this paradigm represented by George Lindbeck, Hans Frei, John Howard Yoder, Stanley Hauerwas, and others, theology has its own autonomy in the Barthian sense, and therefore it seeks to present the story of God's salvation to the world, and in this way, makes its unique contribution.[6] Once again it is not a movement of reaching out to the world, but of bringing the world into the orbit of God's Word and God's salvation. For Lindbeck the question of responding to the culture and the issues of the world do not arise. Much less is he interested in viewing cultures, traditions, histories and religious experiences as mediating God's Word.[7] According to him, there is no need to look for other categories drawn from cultural and religious resources of others for the transmission of the message of the Scriptures. In a world of plurality, Christian faith and theology need to affirm themselves; it is by strengthening themselves that they can contribute their part to the world.[8] There is no room for any mediation of the message through the culture and traditions and histories of people.[9] In this context, Lindbeck makes use of the linguistic model of Wittgenstein to explain his point.

---

[6] Cf. David Hollenbach, "The Foundation of Theological Knowledge", in Rodney Petersen (ed.), *Christianity and Civil Society*, Orbis Books, New York, 1995, pp. 89–98.

[7] This contrasts with the contextual theologies we are promoting in India and in Asia at large. For these theologies, cultural and historical mediation is of crucial importance, since these go to mark the specific characteristic of any contextual theology. Similarly, in contrast to the position represented by Lindbeck and others, the theologians of correlation such as David Tracy, Langdon Gilkey, Shubert Ogden, Paul Ricoeur and others.

[8] Cf. G. Lindbeck, *The Nature of Doctrine: Religion and Theology in a Postliberal Age*, Westminster Press, Philadelphia, 1984.

[9] In this connection, it may be interesting to recall here the position of Lamin Sanneh , for whom, the distinguishing mark of Christianity is that it allowed

I see the basic problem of theological education today in the oscillation between these two paradigms and a lack of consistency. I mean to say that there is a frequent jump from one plane to the other, in such a way that the same theologian may be employing one paradigm for addressing a particular issue, and then quickly turn over to another paradigm while addressing a different theological issue. This happens also in the Christian communities in their understanding of mission and witness. Therefore, for an effective theological education, there should be a clear choice of the theological paradigm we want to follow. When in the same theological institution different faculty members follow different paradigms, there results confusion in the minds of the students. That is why there should be constant dialogue and interaction in theological institutions and Christian communities so as to have a clear direction for its mission and witnessing.

## A Single History

Looking at the matter from another angle, we may say that a dominant paradigm in theology is one that is centred on the idea of two histories – the one is salvation history and the other history of the world, parallel to the former.[10] This dominant paradigm views the world as the large theatre on which the one story of salvation needs to be narrated and represented in different ways.

Theology and theological education modeled after this division of two parallel histories need to be overcome by narrating the stories of all God's peoples, and these stories continue. Such a framework will help incorporate within theology the present concerns of society and humanity at large as integral part of a single story of God's dealing with humanity, and therefore deserving our utmost attention. The dominant conception of Christian identity is viewed as a matter of retelling this story. Theological education needs to overcome such a limited conception of Christian

---

God's Word to be mediated and translated which itself was an act of valorizing the cultures of peoples. In fact, from the beginning, Christianity allowed its Scriptures to be translated in different languages. This is different from Islam which holds that, since God's revelation was in Arabic, it remains the authentic voice of God. Lamin Sanneh, *Translating the Message. The Missionary Impact on Culture*, Orbis Books, New York, 1989; Id., *West African Christianity: The Religious Impact*, Orbis Books, New York, 1983.

[10] Cf. Felix Wilfred, "A Matter of Theological Education – Some Critical Reflections on the Suitability of 'Salvation History' as a Theological Model for India", in *Vidyajyoti Journal of Theological Reflection,* 48 (1984), 538–556.

identity, and view it in relation to the still unfolding history of evil in the world and the struggles to overcome it in ever new circumstances through the power of God's Word that is being spoken today. Theology and theological education are to be seen in service of this larger project that embraces our present history and the history of the entire humanity.

The question about history requires also a choice in the theological education. Like the earlier issue of orientation, here too the conflict between these two paradigms could leave theological institutions and Christian communities in a state of confusion. Therefore, for a focused theological education one needs to be clear about the choice of orientation regarding history.

### The Conflict of Theory and Praxis

Let me begin by sketching the larger background of this question in the field of theological education. When a research university was started in Berlin in early nineteenth century, Schleiermacher, who was one of the architects of this project, wanted to create room for theology amidst other sciences.[11] How could theology which has presuppositions of faith that are not subjected to scientific study and analysis form part of university education along with other sciences? Schleiermacher took a more practical approach to the question and justified its existence. His basic argument was that theology dealt with an important dimension of life, namely religion which has great impact on people and society, similar to the study of law and medicine. If such is the case, then, for the good of society (to which religion contributes) leaders should be professionally trained. This professional training (which has a practical dimension) should be accompanied by a spirit of inquiry and research. The theoretical aspect envisaged here (*Wissenschaft*) is not the imparting of a set of doctrines, teaching of history, etc. but the enabling of a critical research orientation as an aid for the professional training of leaders.

In the course of time, the professional training got narrowed down to mean the imparting or acquiring of tools and skills to be able to function effectively as a pastor or as a priest. One of the serious limitations of theological education is precisely its clericalization. Such being the case, the practice became the focal point of theological education, and it came

---

[11] For contemporary issues connected with theological education in universities, see David Ray Griffin – Joseph C. Hough Jr (eds.), *Theology and the University*, State University of New York Press, New York, 1991.

in conflict with the theory aspect. By then, the theory dimension too got narrowed down. Instead of teaching the pursuit of truth through research and study, it became a matter of imparting the conclusions of the researches done in different branches of theology like for example in the field of biblical studies. Practice was viewed as the application of the various principles and theories. With the passing of time, it was not clear what was theological about the practice, since, as I noted, it became more and more a matter of performing certain practical functions, and it lost sight of the spirit of search and enquiry. In other words, the practical turn to theological education has been so clericalized that it means in effect learning those skills and crafts which will enable a ministerial candidate to function effectively in his or her congregation.[12] We need to rediscover today a deeper sense of praxis,[13] and that leads me to the next point.

### Re-focusing Theological Education on Christian Communities

Instead of trying to solve what appears to be a pseudo-problem, namely, how to bridge theory and practice in theological education, we need to widen its perspectives. We need to begin from the Christian communities and its practices. Theological education itself is an important means for deepening of the faith of the community and its engagement with the world and society, its mission and witness. Theological education of the leaders or pastors is but a part of this larger project with which it should be constantly in dialogue.

Unfortunately, there exists a general view that the faith of a community is fostered by providing it with a good catechism or of Sunday school programme, and familiarizing it with the biblical story.[14] These traditional means are inadequate. It is often assumed that Christian communities are served through catechism and Sunday schools, whereas theological

---

[12] Cf. Edward Farley, *Theologia. The Fragmentation and Unity of Theological Education*, Fortress Press, Philadelphia, 1989, p. 133; Id., *Fragility of Knowledge*, Fortress Press, Philadelphia, 1989.

[13] For an excellent analysis of the understanding of praxis in tradition as well as in contemporary times, see Daniel Franklin Pilario, *Back to the Rough Grounds of Praxis. Exploring Theological Method with Pierre Bourdieu*, Louvain, 2002 (It is the Ph.D. dissertation of the author); see also Clodovis Boff, *Theology and Praxis. Epistemological Foundations*, Orbis Books, New York, 1987; Kathryn Tanner, *Theories of Culture. A New Agenda for Theology*, Fortress Press, Minneapolis, 1997.

[14] Underlying such a view is a particular understanding of Christian identity, as something well-defined and circumscribed.

education is meant for the training of ordained pastors or priests. In this situation we need to affirm first and foremost that theological education is for the entire community. In today's circumstances, every Christian needs to be enabled in his or her own way to engage in Christian praxis through the interpretation of the Gospel. In our country, the endemic poverty and oppression, marginalization of the weaker ones, casteism, nefarious effects of globalization, suppression and exploitation of women – all these call for responses from the local Christian communities. The catechism and Sunday school knowledge of Christian faith may not come to our aid in responding to these formidable challenges. The Christian communities need to be then accompanied by a theological education.

Given that the Christian communities are at different levels, theological education needs to follow sound pedagogies. New ways – structures and means - need to be devised, so that the Christian communities are nurtured and sustained through appropriate theological education. This will help the communities reflect critically on their present practices and engage themselves in new ones that will transform themselves and the society around. This larger perspective can be identified in an important statement of the Indian Theological Association:

> We see theological Education as the process by which the Church educates herself, builds herself up and equips herself to collaborate with the people in the common endeavour of liberation and creation of a new world. It involves the whole community at different levels of theologizing.[15]

In this sense, theological education can be viewed as a means that helps the Christian community expand its practices to new areas in response to the challenges and demands of the times. For, ultimately, every genuine theology starts with an option for practices that define being Christian as

---

[15] Statement of the Meeting, no. 21. For the text, see Felix Wilfred (ed.), *Theological Education in India Today, op.cit.,* The reflection on theological education by Indian Catholic theologians was a consequence to think through the nature, orientation of theology in India in contemporary times. This was done in a conference held in Pune in 1978. For the papers and proceedings of this conference, see M. Amaladoss – Gispert-Sauch – T.K. John (eds.), *Theologizing in India,* Theological Publications in India, Bangalore, 1981. For the various statements of the Indian Theological Association contributing to the development of a new conception of theology and theological education, see Jacob Parappally, *Theologizing in Context. Statements of the Indian Theological Association,* Dharmaram Publications, Bangalore, 2002.

the following of Jesus' path in listening and responding to God's Word for the good of the entire community and of humankind.

Theological education of the local Christian communities will contribute to overcome the divide and conflict between the centres of theological education and the expectation of the congregations. It often happens that ministers formed in theological institutions, faced with theologically uneducated Christian communities succumb to the wishes of the congregations and acquiesce to the existing order; or, the ministers impose their theological vision and views to unwilling congregations who rise in protest. There needs to be then a co-relation between the theological education of the communities and centres of theological education.

This focus on Christian communities would free us from the tendency to consider the various theologies, for example, Dalit theology or Feminist theology, as theological questions out of the mainline theological trajectory. Dalit theology, feminist theology, etc., are meant for the entire community, and are not to be relegated as a concern of one or other segment in the Christian community.

## Coming to Terms with Fragmentation

In the past, theological education paid great attention to create a point of unity and give a coherent basis to whatever was taught. This is true both of Protestant and Catholic traditions. The whole corpus of theological knowledge was brought under a common point of unity, as for example in the neo-scholastic tradition of Catholicism with its theological manuals.[16]

Let us view some of the reasons for the present state of fragmentation. First, the assumption that knowledge is furthered by atomization and increasing specialization has its impact also in the field of theology and biblical studies.[17] There is dispersion and fragmentation of knowledge in theological field as well. Second, the preoccupation to make theological education more complete has led to the practice of introducing new courses whose connections with other areas of studies are often not evident. The mélanges of subjects to which the students are introduced creates confusion in their minds, and they are not able to make sense of the maze of courses

---

[16] Cf. Patrick W. Carey – Earl C., Muller, *Theological Education in the Catholic Tradition*, The Crossroad Publishing Company, New York, 1997.

[17] Cf. Erik Borgman – Felix Wilfred (eds), "Theology in a World of Specialization", *Concilium* 2006/2.

they are exposed to. What already at the end of 1950s Richard Niebhur
and others foresaw has become even more serious today.

> The greatest defect in theological education today is that it is too much
> an affair of piecemeal transmission of knowledge and skills, and that,
> in consequence, it offers too little challenge to the students to develop
> his own resources and to become an independent, life-long inquirer,
> growing constantly while he is engaged in the work of ministry.[18]

Third, the view that much of theological education is centred on intellectual
input devoid of practical import and relevance, has created an ethos in
theological institutions to devise new courses and units that would make
up for this deficiency. It took the form of courses and programmes oriented
to field-studies, case-studies and imparting of ministerial and therapeutic
skills, etc.

In these circumstances, the students in our theological centres need
to be helped to integrate within themselves those insights and fragments
as they journey in a spirit of discovery to new frontiers and realms of
theology. It will need the able assistance of faculty members who foster
spirit of collegiality, cooperation and dialogue among themselves and with
the students. The tendency of viewing various disciplines as water-tight
compartments could be overcome through constant dialogical practice.
In particular, curriculum development needs to be a participative and
dialogical venture among the faculty members who will interact cutting
across disciplinary boundaries. These are but various means through which
the danger of dispersion and fragmentation could be overcome. But I think,
ultimately, the real point of unity is in the overarching purpose of
theological education which the teachers and students share. Creative
renewal of this purpose will prove the kind of unity which the unitary
doctrinal systems cannot anymore provide.[19]

### Re-thinking the Scientific Character

The academic approach to theological education suffers from a misguided
understanding of neutrality of science. Let me illustrate the point with

---

[18] Richard Niebhur – D.D. Williams – J.A. Gustafson , *The Advancement of
Theological Education*, Harper & Brothers, New York, 1957, p. 209.

[19] However, there are authors who think that the point of unity in theological
education needs to be Christian identity. And this identity is often conceived
in a static way. See for example: Joseph C. Hough Jr – John B. Cobb Jr., *Christian
Identity and Theological Education*, Scholar Press, Atlanta, 1985.

reference to biblical studies. The historic-critical method which, following scientific method, investigates text, could claim neutrality. This neutrality has meaning over against biblical fundamentalism, or the unwarranted and often unenlightened interpretation of the Scriptures by ecclesiastical authorities. But then, one cannot hold on to this neutrality in the face of oppressive human situation which requires a biblical interpretation that is carried out from the perspective of the poor and the marginalized. What is adopted here is the overall perspective of the Bible with regard to particular texts. It needs to take into account our concrete social location where the interpretation takes place.

Scientific character means also adopting a critical approach. One important area where critical approach needs to be deployed is the area of Christian tradition. Obviously truth is not identical with tradition. The entire Christian history, its development of doctrines, structures and institutions etc., need to be subjected to critical scrutiny and re-read and reconstructed through the lens of our experiences, questions and issues in India. Here is an instance where the hermeneutics of suspicion needs to be applied.

Moreover, the scientific character in theological education also means that it critically reflects upon the dominant practices, values, priorities of the Christian communities in Asia. This process will help reconstruct Christian identity anew and theological education needs to be seen as an important means for realizing this objective. This radical path needs to be followed if theological education is to be truly Asian and responding to our experiences and contexts.

The scientific character required for the study of theology calls for an inter-disciplinary approach as well. There is a growing realization that disciplinary boundaries, though have some value, are to be transcended in the pursuit of fuller truth.[20] This applies to theology and theological education in a deeper sense. Theology could be stultifying if it is done in isolation and without the support of other disciplines. Theology could prove to be even very dangerous if this isolation is combined with the claim of possessing totality of knowledge and truth. The inputs of these disciplines are necessary for theology to be able to understand and get enlightened on the complexity of the issues in the world and society. In particular, those studies and disciplines which throw light on the context

---

[20] Cf. Patrick Gnanapragasam – Elisabeth Schüssler Fiorenza (eds.), *Negotiating Borders. Theological Explorations in Global Era. Essays in Honour of Prof. Felix Wilfred*, ISPCK, Delhi, 2008.

are to be fostered. For example, theological education should relate to the disciplines of social sciences, literature, history of the country, of the particular state etc. Today, it is necessary to relate closely with natural sciences and technology as well. For, new ethical questions are raised in these fields which call for enlightened responses from faith and theology. As liberation theology has taught us through its methodology, the sciences, especially the social sciences, are crucial for theology for an analytical mediation of the message of the Gospel.

Finally, the scientific character calls for also a deeper examination, both in Christian communities as well as in centres of theological education, of how power is operative in the structures as well as in the content, methods and approaches to theology. A critical examination of the power and its movements in a theological institution will help fostering of a theological "communication without domination".

## A Public Role for Theology and Theological Education

Theology should be accountable to the people and be socially responsible. A concrete way in which this could happen is when we are able to see that theological education contributes to the common good. We live in a world and society in which there is a phenomenal growth of information and data. The inherent limits of any identification of knowledge with information has created the need for a shift from facts to values, which presuppose a horizon of wholeness, against which individual branches of knowledge could be assessed. Theological education could develop a sense of wholeness that could help solve some of the vexing problems affecting humankind.

The public role of theology comprises various aspects. Theological education should be sensitive, first of all, to the political implications of Christian faith, mission and witness. As history and experience testify, the credibility of Christianity was at its height, whenever it prophetically intervened to challenge the powers that be to defend the poor and the marginalized, minorities and other vulnerable groups. In contemporary times, the role played by the group around the *Kairos Document* in South Africa for the overthrow of apartheid is an inspiring example;[21] so too the

---

[21] Cf. *The Kairos Document: Challenge to the Church. A Theological Comment on the Political Crisis in South Africa*, Second Edition, Skotaville, Johannesburg, 1986; R.M. Brown (ed.), *Kairos: Three Prophetic Challenges to the Church*, Eerdmans, Grand Rapids, 1990.

role played by Bishop Tutu in that country;[22] Bishop Belo of East Timor in the midst of much social and political upheaval had a decisive influence on the political process.[23] It is the theology behind such involvement that theological education should mediate to the Christian communities and to its leaders. In these instances, faith, theology, mission and Christian witness have a different understanding and approach – different from the dominant paradigm.

## Theological Education as Education for Justice

Anyone who views empathetically the condition of the poor, the marginalized and the subaltern in Asian societies, cannot but question the kind of theology and theological education we promote. These have an accountability to society. How do theology and theological education express their social responsibility today? One very clear mode of doing it is to place the issue of justice at the centre of theological and biblical curriculum and study. This is something which perfectly dovetails with the scriptural orientation.

> So strongly do we believe that justice is the foundation of human life well lived that we understand the primary theological and educational task of the churches to be the work of justice in the world. This does not mean that all of us must be political activists in order to be involved in the work of justice. It does mean that no seminary teacher or student, regardless of his or her discipline, interests or skills, is excused from the accountability to human well-being. It means that the scholar who is indifferent to justice is not an excellent scholar.[24]

This calls for that we shape theological education in such a way that it is firmly based on critical solidarity with the victims. This will be the hallmark of the theological education in these times of globalization with increasing number of victims. Underlying many communal conflicts is the issue of

---

[22] Cf Shirley du Boulay, *Tutu. Voice of the Voiceless*, Eerdmans, Grand Rapids, 1988; John Allen, *Rabble-Rouser for Peace. The Authorised Biography of Desmond Tutu*, Rider Books, London-Johannesburg, 2007.

[23] Cf. Arnold Kohen, *From the Place of the Dead. The Epic Struggles of Bishop Belo of East Timor*, introduced by the Dalai Lama, St. Martin's Press, New York, 1999; Carlos Fiipe Ximenes Belo, "The Nobel Lecture", given by Nobel Peace Prize Laureate 1996, Carlos Filipe Ximenes Belo, Titular Bishop of Lorium and Apostolic Administrator of Dili (East Timor), Oslo, December 10, 1996.

[24] The Mud Flower Collective, *God's Fierce Whimsy: Christian Feminism and Theological Education*, The Pilgrim Press, New York, 1985, p. 33.

justice, which needs to be addressed by theology.[25] But unfortunately enough has not been done in this line.

## Inclusive Character of Theological Education

The poverty of theology and theological education is due, among other things, to the fact that they have exercised exclusion. The exclusion I am talking about refers to the experience of women, Dalits, tribals and other subaltern groups. The reformulation of theological education does not happen by simply adding courses on feminist, Dalit or tribal theologies. What is intended here is that the experiences represented by these traditionally excluded groups should be part of the texture of theology and an immanent discourse in theological education. Theological education becomes a process in which women and other traditionally excluded groups gain a voice and become subjects of theology and those who are able to critically contribute to the reformulation of the traditional theological education, its values, priorities, etc. Including the experiences of women and other silenced groups means that theological education should undergo a mutation both in its structure, scope and pedagogical approach. Feminist experiences, when analyzed through the help of growing feminist movements and studies, can help immensely in the re-conceptualization of theology as a whole. Elizabeth Schüssler Fiorenza spells out the importance of feminist studies for theological education:

> Feminist Studies have searched for educational processes that foster articulation and analysis of experience, critical thinking, interdisciplinary and transdiciplinary learning, cooperative work, and anti-hierarchical, democratic leadership. Any discussion of theological education that seriously insists on the inclusive character and global-political context of theological education must learn from Feminist Studies. It must stress both the theoretical re-conceptualization of the academic disciplines and the development of an egalitarian process and critical method for theological education.[26]

---

[25] Cf. Tissa Balasuriya, "Ethnic Conflict in Sri Lanka and the Responsibility of the Theologian", in R.S. Sugirtharajah (ed.), *Frontiers in Asian Christian Theology. Emerging Trends,* Orbis Books, New York, 1994.

[26] Elisabeth Schüssler Fiorenza, "Theological Education: Biblical Studies", in Don S. Browning – David Polk – Ian S. Evison (eds.), *The Education of the Practical Theologian. Responses to Joseph Hough and John Cobb's Christian Identity and Theological Education,* Scholars Press, Atlanta, 1989, p.11.

Similarly, the experience of Dalits and their struggles associated with Dalit movements and Dalit studies could bring in substantial changes and corrections to the prevailing theology and theological education.[27] The same is true also of tribal experience.[28]

There is another important reason for valuing the voices of the excluded groups as part of theology and theological education. For, in this way, biblical studies are challenged to break loose of the presumed neutral and positivist stand of their studies and become a critical and creative interpretation of God's Word in relation to the oppressed humanity. Similarly, theological studies will be freed from being a matter of learning doctrines and their meaningful interpretation to become a struggle with the larger community to address, in the light of faith, the questions and issues which affect people, especially the most vulnerable ones. As a result, the critical aspect of theology and theological education will move from being an intellectual exercise to become a matter of moral reason with its demands and implications.

The inclusive character serves also as a powerful resource for a critical approach. Generally the critical element is seen as a matter of conforming to the exigencies of reason and its procedures. The inclusion of the marginalized groups transforms the critical element from an epistemological question into an ontological issue of reality. The real critique to theology and theological education today are the voices from the margins.[29] The voice of Dalits, women, tribals and other discriminated groups help us refashion our theology at every step in close touch with reality.

### Conclusion

In conclusion, I would like to underline the importance of following the general principles of education also in the field of theological education, just as we should follow the general principles of hermeneutics in any theological or biblical interpretation. A good education is one in which the students are the active subjects, and the best in them is brought out. If the most effective pedagogy is one of learning by doing, this is what

---

[27] Cf. James Massey (ed.), *Indigenous People: Dalits. Dalit Issues in Today's Theological Debate*, ISPCK, Delhi, 1998.

[28] K. Thanzauva, *Transforming Theology. A Theological Basis for Social Transformation*, Asian Trading Corporation, Bangalore, 2002.

[29] Cf. Felix Wilfred, *Margins. The Site of Asian Theologies*, ISPCK, Delhi, 2008.

theological educational praxis needs to do, be it in relation to the Christian communities or in institutions meant for theological education of pastors and priests.

In his remarkable work "The Idea of a University" Cardinal John Henry Newman distinguished between useful knowledge and cultivation of the mind.[30] Theological education is not a "banking system" of depositing ideas and conclusions of researches in the minds of the students.[31] It is a matter of cultivating the minds of the students, so that they remain ever fresh springs of theology wherever they are. They will continuously learn from praxis, understood as transformative praxis. For, praxis is a stimulating source for knowledge-production in any field, including the field of theology.

To this we need to add the importance of commitment and motivation for engagement with the larger society and the world. Commitment is facilitated in any theological institution by the way it functions. Theological institutions are not a place; they need to become a milieu where theological mind and committed engagement are cultivated.

There is need also for a change in the environment of the Churches. One of the reasons for the increasing lack of interest in theological studies is the fact that the ecclesial policies and practices are often anti-theological. If in the life of the Church anti-theological elements are allowed to occupy positions of power and there is no "reward" for serious theological engagement, then it could be for many students quite discouraging, and theological education may not attract the best of talents.

The quality of theological education in an institution is to be judged by the extent it facilitates the emergence of more and more "organic theologians" who will be trail blazers, different from "traditional theologians" who will serve the maintenance of the system and its functioning. Fixing such clear objectives will help in the choice of faculty members and guide the process of theological formation. The present conditions in our Asian societies invite us to a radical transformation of theology and theological education for an engaging mission and Christian witness.

---

[30] John Henry Newman, *Idea of a University*, Longmans, Green and Co., London, 1907.

[31] Cf. Paolo Freire, *Pedagogy of the Oppressed*, Continuum, New York, 2007.

# Chapter 16
# Historiography of Asian Christianity

*"There is politics behind all writings of history, consciously or unconsciously pursued. What is often described and advocated as neutral history is a myth. But then the construction of history, whatever the interpretative structure, and despite the blurring of the disciplinary boundaries in social sciences, has necessarily to respect the fundamental tenets of the discipline in order to qualify for the status of history"* — K. N. Panikkar[1]

## A Basic Question

Historiography is the mode of writing history or the way of representing the past. The meaning we attribute to the past – events, personalities, institutions, movements, etc., – will depend upon the presentation we make and the approach we take. But before going into the historiography of Asian Christianity, let me begin with a fundamental question: To what extent could history be written from the perspective of the *religion* of a people or group? Is there any justification and legitimacy to write a historiography based on religion? Does not, for example, writing of an Asian History of Christianity, Buddhist history of Sri Lanka or History of Islam in Indonesia, History of Hinduism create division among a people? Moreover, if we take religion as the point of reference and make a history out of it, does not this enterprise isolate people from the complex texture of life made up of social, political, economic, cultural and regional realities? There is, then, a lot of truth in the apprehension about the history of any

---

[1] K.N.Panikkar, "Alternative Historiographies. Changing Paradigms of Power" in Felix Wilfred – Jose Maliekal (eds), *The Struggle for the Past. Historiography Today*, Department of Christian Studies, University of Madras, Chennai, 2002, pp.19-20.

group written from the viewpoint of their religious affiliation. And this applies as well to the Asian history of Christianity. Like in other cases, the way the Indian history of Christianity is narrated and presented can become, and indeed has become a point of debate and controversy.

In this chapter we want to confine ourselves to reflect on the problematic of an Indian Christian historiography. What is said of Indian Christianity applies to a large extent to other parts of Asia and could stimulate rethinking on the important question of historiography.

There can be legitimacy of and justification for an Indian Christian history only when it is narrated and viewed in the broader framework of the life of the people. To the extent it sheds light on the total life of the people in their particular context, the enterprise of an Indian history of Christianity could become meaningful. But, is this happening? Conventional history of Indian Christianity excludes in its narrations many aspects of the life of the people and in the process could turn out to be a distortion of facts and truth. There is then an urgent need to think of a historiography of Indian Christian history that would not isolate Indian Christians from the life they share with their neighbours on an everyday basis and from the life-world made up of many factors and forces. What is said is true also of other parts of Asia. This is not only for the purpose of representing the past in fairness, but given the inextricable link between politics and historiography in our Indian context, it is important that such an enterprise does not contribute to foment communal divide. The future orientation for a historiography of Indian Christianity, and Asian Christianity at large should begin from a critical view on the mainline approach. That leads us to our next consideration.

## Historiography and Critical Hermeneutics

What I am trying to say is that we approach the conventional historiography of Indian Christianity with the important critical tools offered to us by contemporary hermeneutics. One such tool is that of suspicion. Like in other areas, hermeneutics of suspicion needs to be applied also to the history of the Church in general, and to Asian history of Christianity in particular. For, the Church as part of the society is not exempt from the dynamics of power. "The ruling ideas of each age have ever been the ideas of its ruling class"[2] - so said Karl Marx. We may adopt this statement and say - 'The ruling interpretation of the history of each

---

[2] Karl Marx, *The Communist Manifesto*, Penguin Classics, Berlin, 1848, chapter 2.

age is the interpretation of its ruling class'. Like in other spheres of life, in reporting the past too, the dominant social position of a group or class determines the content and style of the narration. In the process truth becomes the victim.

Reconstruction of the past is basically a hermeneutical act in which the subject with his or her interests and values is implied. This hermeneutics challenges the empiricist approach characteristic of general approach to history which assumes that we arrive at things as they happened (*wie es eigentlich gewesen* – Leopold von Ranke). Hermeneutical approach takes seriously the involvement of the subject, the person in understanding the past. In the case of the Church, those occupying power are the members of hierarchy and consequently, it is the institutional interests of the Church and its concerns that have got reflected in the Asian historiography. Similarly, in mission history, the interests of the missionaries, their values, and priorities got reflected in reporting events and situations.

Let me illustrate the point with a contemporary example. One of the most striking things said about Africa is that it is becoming more and more Christian.[3] This could create a lot of enthusiasm among the Christian community and one may write the history of how this change has taken place as a history of successful mission. But one would miss really the other Africa in this Church history. For, Africa is today also the continent full of political fiascos and economic disasters, hunger and starvation, dictatorship and corruption. A history of Christianity in Africa without reference to these realities would be history of Christian triumph while a great majority of the people there live a life of penury and misfortune. These critical realities of the situation do not form part of the triumphant expansion of Christianity in that continent. This gives us also a clue as to how critically we need to look at the reports regarding mission and mission history. Very often they leave us in darkness with regard to the other side of reality. Today writing Asian Christian historiography has the challenging task of finding out the social, cultural and political aspects of history and integrates these with the story of Christian presence and engagement. Over the past few decades in Asia, there has been a lot of interest in relating Christianity to culture. But to write the history of Christianity with reference to its relationship to culture is too narrow and

---

[3] Cf. Philip Jenkins, *The Next Christendom. The Coming of Global Christianity*, Oxford University Press, New York, 2002.

limited, if it has the institutional interests of Christianity as its focus. But in reality the history of Asian Christianity would be written when it is viewed as part of the larger history of the people in their social, political and economic life.

Evidence from mission history shows two major constraints that also explain why the missionaries could not cover the larger canvas of the life of the country in its social, political and economic dimensions. Firstly, the dominant theology looked at these realities as not connected to its religious ends. Secondly, they were under pressure from the colonial authorities not to meddle with local politics for fear of the repercussion it could have on their governance. These factors among others contributed to the limit of the past Indian Christian historiography. A reconstruction of history in relation to the life of the people in its diverse dimensions is a challenging but a very rewarding task. This will bring about a history of Christianity in its context, and the context is much wider than the Church-context.

## From History of Transmission to History of Reception

Like in other realms, in writing history of Indian Christianity, what has prevailed is the conception of history as devised by the European Enlightenment.[4] It is obvious - and I need not belabour the point here - that the mainstream history of Indian Christianity is a story of how faith was transmitted, with missionaries playing the leading role. Within this story, what occupies a pride of place is the mission enterprise by the institutional Church and its agencies like the missionary societies and religious orders. The reconstruction of the past has not been simply done in the manner of historical empiricism. There was in the mainstream history of Indian Christianity a general explanatory framework. This was constituted by a particular understanding of mission supported by a specific theology. To this we should add the ignorance about the complexity of the life of the people and of the country on the part of the mission agents.

---

[4] This western enlightenment paradigm has been critiqued by G.C. Pande, Ashis Nandy and Vinay Lal. Cf. G.C. Pande, "Historiography of Civilizations and Cultural Presuppositions", in *Journal of Indian Council of Philosophical Research,* vol. 34 (1996), pp. 31-47; Ashis Nandy, "History's Forgotten Doubles", in *History and Theory,* 34 (1995), pp. 44-66; Vinay Lal, "History and the Possibilities of Emancipation – Some Lessons from India" in *Journal of Indian Council of Philosophical Research,* 34 (1996) , pp. 95–137.

What I am suggesting is that we need an Indian historiography that will investigate how the people of the land in their diverse historical and social backgrounds received and appropriated the faith that was transmitted to them, and the various expressions they themselves gave to faith. Moreover, one needs to investigate the Hindu, Buddhist, Muslim response to Christian faith in each historical period. These are not to be taken as simple elements to complete the history of Indian Christianity. There is more to it. This approach from the reception of the people and response of the neighbours will change the whole perspective on history, and bring into focus facts, events and personalities who have received hitherto no attention or only marginal reference.

What happens when one takes transmission of Christian faith as the general framework, is illustrated by the case of the well-known French missionary Abbé Dubois. After thirty-three years of preaching in India, the end-result for him was desperation. He did not conceal this but made it known through his famous three letters on the state of Christianity in India whose sub-title reads "The Conversion of the Hindoos [sic] is considered as Impracticable". There was little in the missionary effort that responded to the social, economic and cultural aspirations of the people to whom they preached. This part of history is covered even now in obscurity. In other words, we need to investigate what is that made a person like Dubois to despair? The people had their own ways of relating to Christianity, faith, etc. The missionaries followed their own path, while the people had their own way, and the two rarely crossed each other.  For example L'Abbé Dubois writes with a sense of bitterness:

> I do not remember any one who may be said to have embraced Christianity from conviction and through quite disinterested motives. Among these new converts many apostatized, and relapsed into Paganism, finding that the Christian religion did not afford them the temporal advantages they had looked for in embracing it; and I am verily ashamed that the resolution I have taken to declare the whole truth on this subject forces me to make the humiliating avowal, that those who continued Christians are the very worst among my flock.[5]

These words hide a situation of Christianity that needs to be investigated to gain a fuller understanding of people's response to the preaching of the

---

[5] Abbé J.A. Dubois, *Letters on the State of Christianity in India in Which the Conversion of the Hindoos Is Considered as Impracticable*, Longman, Hurst, Rees, Orme, Brown, and Green, London, 1823, pp. 134-135.

missionaries and their continued connection with their former religious universe. There is the whole untold story of relapse of Christians back to Hinduism after a brief encounter with Christianity. There are also on the other hand heroic stories of several Christians and native assistants of missionaries who were cast out of their homes and disowned by their dear ones. The struggles these men and women went through to live their faith were immense. They had to also face several court cases.

In writing history we need to go into the least known facts and situations. I would also say that the history of transmission is one-sided since it excludes the role played by the local agents like the catechists, interpreters and others in the process of the transmission of faith. The knowledge the missionaries could acquire about the country was very much dependent upon these local collaborators.[6] These agents were deeply rooted in their tradition and some of them were Hindus and remained as such even after long association with missionaries. Whereas in the field of trade the role of local middlemen are quite well-known and have been historically highlighted, in the case of the history of Christianity, the role of local assistants and others have not been explored. It would open up an entirely new perspective on the history of Christianity in the mission era. These native assistants were irreplaceable. It is high time that the Indian Christians tell their stories freed from the Eurocentric perspectives inherent in most missionary sources. This will serve a constructive dialogue with the historiography of the country. It will also be a story of how the Christian communities have responded to the Gospel through the social and political history of the different periods and regions.

In addition to these reasons, in the case of missionary reporting there have been other factors responsible for the distortion of the life and culture of the people. It is not uncommon to find in the missionary reporting about India, gross exaggerations and graphic depictions which altogether gave a dismal picture of the country and of its people. Let me adduce at least two important motives that coloured the narratives of mission. First of all the theology of the times viewed the world in terms of light and darkness, well demarcated. What the missionaries brought was light and for this

---

[6] Cf. Heike Liebau, "Country Priests, Catechists, and Schoolmasters and Cultural, Religious and Social Middlemen in the Context of the Tranquebar Mission", in Robert Eric Frykenberg (ed.), *Christians and Missionaries in India. Cross-Cultural Communication Since 1500*, William B. Eerdmans Publishing Company, Grand Rapids, 2003, pp. 70-92.

light to shine forth a dark background was necessary. Therefore, most often India and the people of the country, their culture, etc., were portrayed in the darkest colours. Secondly, the Indian Christian historiography needs to take into account also the national and class background of the missionaries and the social and political backgrounds in their own countries of origin, all of which colour their accounts, letters and reports constituting primary materials in most cases for writing Indian Christian History. For example, Pope Benedict XV referred to the influence of the nationality of the missionaries in their activities about which he lamented.

> We have been greatly grieved by certain publications on the subject of Missions, which have appeared in the last few years, in which less desire is apparent for the increase of the Kingdom of God than for the influence of the writer's own country; and we are amazed that these authors seem not to care how much these views alienate the minds of the heathen.[7]

### Christianity, Colonialism and the Politics of Representation

Besides the theological colouring, in the conventional mission history, we need to pay attention also to the traces of colonialism. Colonial historiography whether in India or elsewhere in the world was closely connected to the mode of production of knowledge about the colonized people in such a way that it  provided the ideological justification for domination over them. This included also the attitude towards history. We need to only recall here James Mill's *History of British India* – a standard history book for many generations.[8] For the colonizers, the colonized are a people without history, without culture and a civilization of their own. If many followed this path of denial of history to the subjugated people, others tried to denigrate even the small space of history they allowed to the subjugated. All this has led to a very stringent view of the history of Christianity in India by critical secular historians. For example, let us note what one of the great Indian historians, K.M. Panikkar, who in his well-known work *Asia and Western Dominance* observed:

> It may indeed be said that the most serious, persistent and planned effort of European nations in the nineteenth century was their missionary activities in India and China, where a large-scale attempt was made to

---

[7] Pope Benedict XV, *Maximum Illud*. English Translation, Catholic Truth Society, London, 1936, p. 12.

[8] James Mill, *The History of British India,* Baldwin, Cradock and Joy, London, 1818. This work saw several editions and reprints, and served for long as a standard reference work.

effect a mental and spiritual conquest as supplementing the political authority already enjoyed by Europe. Though the results were disappointing in the extreme from the missionary point of view, this assault on the spiritual foundations of Asian countries has had far-reaching consequences in the religious and social organization of the peoples.[9]

Let me illustrate the point further with an example. There is the greatly admired work of Samuel Hugh Moffett on *History of Christianity in Asia*. It is indeed a monumental work of two volumes comprising the entire history from the beginning to the end of 19th century.[10] The breadth of scholarship is admirable, just to think of 90 pages of bibliography and sources the author has consulted. The wealth of these materials unfortunately are ordered within a framework that views the Christian religion in terms of its advances and its recessions. The author enumerates thus five advances Christianity makes in Asia and the three recessions it has suffered during its history from the beginning to the 19th century. The framework is suggestive of a military expedition with advancement and retreat.[11] The lack of perspective undermines significantly the value of this painstakingly done labour. In these volumes, there is little we have of the people of Asia as subjects who respond to the Gospel in their unique ways and make a history of their own.

---

[9] K.M. Panikkar, *Asia and Western Dominance: A Survey of the Vasco Da Gama Epoch of Asian History 1498 – 1945*, George Allen & Unwin Ltd, London, 1953, p. 481.

[10] Cf. Samuel Hugh Moffett, *A History of Christianity in Asia*, vol. I & II, Orbis Books, New York, 1998 & 2005.

[11] We are reminded here of the *Ecclesiastical History* by Eusebius which was heavily under the influence of his theological conception and political theory. A friend of the emperor Constantine assisting him also at the Council of Nicea, Eusebius saw a direct relationship between the empire of Constantine and the Kingdom of God. Under the influence of Neo-Platonism, he saw the visible things as the symbols of the invisible; so was the Empire for him a symbol of the Kingdom of God. The Roman Empire itself was according to divine disposition a preparation for the spread of Christianity. Moreover, Eusebius admits that he speaks of only those things of the past history that contribute to the glory of Christianity and omit anything that could disgrace it. The same tendency could be observed in his work on the Life of Constantine which is an eulogy of the emperor. All this go to show how the writing of the history of Christianity is not exempt from many influences including ideological ones.

What is emerging more and more clearly is that the relationship of Christianity to colonial powers, for example, should be viewed in a much more complex fashion.[12] On the one hand, among the Christians themselves there was no one common view regarding the relationship to colonial powers, or to the national movement. While some supported colonial powers and opposed nationalist tendencies, other Christians critically challenged colonialism and made common cause with the nationalists.[13] On the other hand, it is not true that the relationship of Indian Christians, for example, to the colonial government was simply based on religion. The fact is that among Hindus, Muslims and others there were groups which supported the colonial regime no less than some of the Christians. Very often the relationship was on pragmatic grounds than on religious ones. As for as the relationship between missionaries and colonial administrative authorities, there were many strains and rifts and even opposition to the colonial imperialism.

Uma Chakravarti rightly cautions us with the reference to the case of Pandita Ramabai, that the reality was much more complex.

> There has been an easy conflation not only of nationalism with Hinduism but more importantly of Christianity with colonialism. There is a latent assumption that in opting for Christianity, Ramabai and others had accepted the religion of the rulers and had therefore become 'compradors', and were complicit with the colonial presence. Such an assumption is simplistic and motivated. The mere existence of a relationship between Christianity and colonialism is not enough to treat Christianity automatically as the handmaiden of colonialism. That there were some shared ideological positions is evident but it needs to be noted that there were also major moments and points of tension between the colonial administration and Christian missionaries.[14]

---

[12] In this connection the many contributions of Robert Eric Frykenberg on Indian History of Christianity are valuable. One could refer usefully also Susan Billington Harper, *In the Shadow of the Mahatma. Bishop V.S. Azariah and the Travails of Christianity in British India,* William B. Eerdmans Publishing Company, Grand Rapids, Michigan -Cambridge, 2000.

[13] Cf. Mary John, *"National Movement and Catholic Christianity in India 1857-1947. A Study Based on the Official Catholic Journals of the Period"* (Unpublished doctoral dissertation written under my guidance, University of Madras) Chennai, 2006.

[14] Uma Chakravarti, *Rewriting History. The Life and Times of Pandita Ramabai,* Kali for Women, 1998, pp. ix-x.

To clear the general misunderstanding it is important that Indian Christian history goes deeply into the intricacies that characterized the relationship of the Church to colonial powers. In this context, the struggle and conflict of the Syrian Christian Church in India -which traces its origins to the apostolic tradition of St. Thomas[15]- with the Latin Church missionaries of the Portuguese colonial times, is also pertinent. I think there is ample room for a critical historiographical investigation in this area. This will contribute to shape Indian Christian historiography of the colonial era.

The interconnection between colonialism and Christianity is so complex that any attempt to present a picture of complete compliance of missionaries with the colonial power would be equally naïve as the thesis that would declare them free from any complicity with the colonial rulers and administrators. But there is one instance where the missionaries were very close to the colonizers, and that is in their views about the Indian past. What the historian K.N. Panikkar says of the colonial rulers could be, *mutatis mutandis*, applied to missionaries in relation to Indian history.

> The growth of historiography in India, during the last two hundred years comprehends within it, the changing contours of power and politics in Indian society. The bulk of the early writings on India authored by the colonial administrators and ideologues were intertwined with the interests of the colonial rule. One of its aims was to delegitimise the precolonial. The familiar themes of colonial historiography, like the despotism of Indian rulers and the characterization of the pre-colonial era, as a dark age are integral to the structuring of power.[16]

It is remarkable that the power-interests of the colonizers converged with the theological interest of the missionaries for whom, as we noted earlier, it was important to paint all that preceded the arrival of the Gospel as dark and uncivilized. The idea of Divine Dispensation also played a role. As the early Church-historian Eusebius saw the Roman Empire as divinely ordained for the spread of Christianity, so also for some British Empire represented the preparation for the Gospel-mission in its colonies.

---

[15] Cf. George Nedungatt, *Quest for the Historical Thomas Apostle of India*, Theological Publications in India, Bangalore, 2008.

[16] K.N. Panikkar, "Alternative Historiographies: Changing Paradigms of Power", in Felix Wilfred – Jose Maliekal (eds.), *The Struggle for the Past. Historiography Today*, Department of Christian Studies, University of Madras, 2002, pp. 12-13.

## Nationalist Historiography and Christianity

As for the Indian Christians, they suffered from a nationalist historiography in which one sought to conflate nationalism with Hinduism. In this connection we need to distinguish between a nationalist historiography which turned out to be a revivalist religious nationalism, with the equation of Hinduism with nationalism, and the other which was secular with the vision of India as a composite culture of many peoples and tribes. In the nationalist historiography of the revivalist type, the animosity against the colonizers turned also against Christians as stooges of western colonial power. This perspective affected even more moderate representatives. It is unfortunate that the nationalist historiography has not found any place for a person like Bishop Azariah who is said to have been "enemy number one" of Gandhi. While both were immersed in uplifting the marginalized, the role of Azariah has been sidelined from Indian national historiography.

> At the time of his death, Gandhi dressed as an Indian peasant while living in a businessman's Delhi mansion; Azariah dressed as an Anglican bishop – complete with resplendent robes – while living in his rural village. Both men were preoccupied with the problems of poverty and untouchability and both men had devised entirely different strategies for alleviating its hardships...[17]

All this opens up an important avenue for the future. I suggest that there be greater dialogue and exchange between the efforts for an Indian Christian historiography and the historiography of the country. On the one hand, Indian Christian history needs to follow closely the general developments of the people, of the society, culture, etc., in order to situate itself. On the other hand, the historiography of the country needs to overcome its trend of excluding Indian Christian history from the mainline history of the nation. The calculated attempt to alienate Indian Christian history from the history of the nation is an attempt to brand Christians as aliens. The bond a shared history makes in the life of a people cannot be effected without a share in that history.

## History of Subalterns and the History of Indian Christianity

In history writing, empirical data need to be collected and evidences to be gathered. Whereas in natural sciences these empirical data are fitted into a general theory of explanation against which these facts could be verified and tested, in the case of history, the point of reference is the

---

[17] Susan Billington Harper, op.cit.

*interest* that commands the historian in relation to the data and evidences he or she is faced with.[18] To this we need to add also the ideology that is overtly or covertly espoused by the historian.

In the mainline history, people are not viewed as political subjects of history but objects of a history narrated by those who dominate over them with their explanatory frameworks and grand narratives. This imposed history that denies identity to the subalterns is an insult. Today, Indian history of Christianity needs to draw inspiration from the subaltern studies that try to re-read the Indian history in a different light and from a different perspective.[19] This approach interrogates the static picture of the mainstream history and highlights the dynamics within the society, and brings to the fore in this process, the peoples, events and forces that have been left in oblivion.

To cite the case of Indian national Independence, this subaltern approach will distance itself from the "grand narratives" centred on a single person like an idealized Gandhi to whom is attributed the liberation of the country from the foreign yoke. The narrative of the story is almost hagiographic. Such a simplistic picture is challenged by the whole ferment in the country among various segments of the people like the workers, peasants, Dalits and other groups whose sustained struggle, so to say, broke the back of the colonial power. Their agenda was anything national but local, intervening as they did in the questions and problems that afflicted them in day to day life or in times of crisis.[20] I propose that we move *towards a subaltern Asian Christian history*. This history will throw light on forces and factors that have not been brought to light and bring alive what is invisible, hidden or forgotten.

---

[18] Cf. Alun Munslow, *Deconstructing History*, Routledge, London-New York, 2001, p. 4.

[19] The collective venture of subaltern studies was inspired by Ranajit Guha who edited the first volumes of this series. Ranajit Guha, *Subaltern Studies. Writings on South Asian History and Society*, vols I – VII, Oxford University Press, Delhi, 1982. The volumes that followed were edited by other authors. Over the years there has also been a perspectival change on the nature of subaltern studies. See for example, Sumit Sarkar, *Writing Social History*, Oxford University Press, Delhi, 1997, "The Decline of Subaltern in *Subaltern Studies*" pp. 82–108.

[20] Cf. Ranajit Guha, *Elementary Aspects of Peasant Insurgency in Colonial India*, Oxford University Press, Delhi, 1983.

It would be naïve to explain the changes that happened and the changes that did not happen by referring to the intention of the dominant actors - in our case missionaries, bishops, the clergy, etc. We need to enlist in explaining the developments in Indian Christianity also the social, cultural, political and economic factors. If that is done, then we have the people as the real agents of change or non-change. It would then lead us to find out why certain events took place the way they did take place. To put it in more philosophical categories, history cannot be a matter of time alone; it has to include also spatiality. When the space inhabited by people and their life is ignored, and is centred merely on time, history would be simply a history of power that projects the dominators also as actors of history.[21] It creates an illusion of continuity, whereas in reality there are many discontinuities and gaps. History in terms of chronology, annals and diachronic flow of events need to be, then, challenged by a synchronic approach to history that is focused on spatiality where the uneventful life of the people would find voice and place.

All this calls for a critical re-examination of the historical sources and available  new evidences that will challenge the mainstream Christian historiography and its claims. A subaltern approach would imply a de-clericalization of Asian Christian history. The hierarchy and clerical-centred mainstream Indian Christian history would be the grand-narrative that needs to be de-mystified and exploded by investigating what happened to the people who believed and what are the struggles they went through and how they lived their faith. The faith of the people and the identity they created in their encounter with Christianity need to be investigated. In other words, how Asian Christians appropriated Christian message and responded to it remains a major area of historical research. This is part of a subaltern approach to history.

---

[21] Within the Western tradition of history, it was Ferdinand Braudel who highlighted the importance of *geography* in the writing of history with his monumental study on this question. See Ferdinand Braudel, *The Mediterranean and the Mediterranean World in the Age of Philip II*, University of California Press, Berkeley, 1996 (The original work in French appeared in 1949 and was revised several times subsequently). For an overview on historiography including contemporary theorizing,  the following work could be profitably consulted: Michael Bentley, *Companion to Historiography,* Routledge, London – New York, 1997; see also John Sturrock, *Structuralism,* Fontana Press, London, 1993 (second edition), pp. 56 ff.

Asian Christian history has to contend with the general problematic of the politics of representation. History is distorted when the people and groups about whom they report are mute and their voice is not heard. This could befall also the writing of History of Asian Christianity. In spite of its avowed intention to set a different orientation, the project of Church History Association of India (CHAI), for example, to produce a "History of Christianity in India", is still part of the mainline historical writing.[22] I do not want to undermine the authors who have made a remarkable contribution by pooling together a lot of scattered materials and evidences to formulate a coherent historical discourse. I find in these volumes by and large an empiricist reconstructionism rather than an interpretative constructionism.

An effectively different historiographic orientation, however, requires a lot of micro-studies like that of the subaltern series, which will bring out from different regions the interaction of the people, and the problems and questions they grappled with. In short, we need to hear the voice of the subalterns of Asian Christianity. The more we go into formation of indigenous Churches, the role of local assistants, catechists, etc., and the popular practices which people devised to live and give expression to faith, the more we create space for a different historiography closer to the soil.

## Theology and Historiography

In every writing of the history of the Church, there lurks a particular theological orientation, as in every administrative decision of the Church-authorities there is at work an implicit ecclesiology. To identify the underlying theology is an important task of critical historiography. We need at the same time a proper theological orientation to evaluate and assess the past. I think we need to take the following points into account. They are required, so that we could make sense of the past for our present, and learn from the past. For, history, as it is said, is *magistra vitae* – teacher of life.

First of all we need to enquire what is the conception of the Church behind the historical narratives, and more specifically the rationale behind the missionary enterprise. Here, probably a reconception of the Church and the nature of its mission, as we have for example in Vatican Council II of

---

[22] *History of Christianity in India* – a series of publication in progress and the very first volume was published in 1989.

the Roman Catholic Church, or in the various statements of the World Council of Churches, will provide us with a point of reference to analyze the past critically. Secondly, the historical sources and reporting imply a certain understanding of missionaries in regard to the cultures and religions of the people, regarding sin and salvation. The theology of the times prompted the presentation of Christian truths and life in what *distinguished* them from alternatives, which obviously conditioned the mode of writing history. We are in a better position today to analyze the sources from this angle. There is a double-process involved here. On the one hand, the documents of missionary era reveal to us the past Christian conceptions about the culture and religions of the people. On the other hand, knowledge of these conceptions help us understand why history has been written that way and not differently, and why certain persons and events got  highlighted and others left in oblivion.[23]

The relationship of theology and historiography needs to be explored also from another angle. Just as theological perspectives affect writing of history, so also historiography can greatly help the process of theologizing. Even more, our critical and analytical perspectives on the past of the Church is a significant force in doing theology that is true to the reality people are living through and experiencing. History in this way leads us "to drink from our own wells". The grounding of theology in the social and political historiography helps overcome the temptation of seeing Christian history, as is being done in recent times, as an encounter with a static and a-historical culture. Writing from the perspective of culture does not make Christian historiography Indian or Asian. How the Gospel and Christian communities are earthed in the social and political history of a people through the ages is a perspective that needs to be underlined. This will help also overcome the way of looking at Asian Christian history as part of someone else's history of mission.

---

[23] Furthermore, the theological analysis of the conception of the Church and the vision about other religions and cultures need to be in dialogue with a deeper understanding, from the sociological perspective, of the nexus of religion and power, and the insights from the sociology of knowledge, especially in reconstructing the past. Thus, a study of popular religions – both Christian and Hindu – written from the perspective of Christian orthodoxy will be very different from an approach that is refracted through anthropological prism or through ritual studies. See for example James Ponniah, "*Folk Religion and Ritual Power in Society. A Study on Chutalaimatan Cult*" (Unpublished doctoral dissertation written under my guidance, University of Madras), Chennai, 2005.

## Conclusion: A Model for Asian Christian Historiography

The Bible is a historiography from below. For example, the context of Exodus is that of Egypt, the most powerful empire and civilization of the times. But we do not find in Exodus a description of the glories of Egypt nor the power of its imperial life. It is a description of the story of a simple people, a people at the margins of the empire. It is their story which exodus highlights; it is their struggles against the empire it depicts and sees God's own association with this struggle.

Similarly, the events of the Gospel takes place in a colony of the Roman Empire. There is but little reference in the Gospels to the life of the empire, its impeccable organization and the resounding triumphs of its armies. Instead, the Gospel story is a history of those at the margins of this Roman Empire, at the periphery of a colonized territory. It speaks about the multitude – the peasants, the shepherds, fisher folk, about the widow, vineyard labourers, etc. In short, what we have in the Bible is a history that is about those who are excluded from the main narratives of the times. It is the experiences of these people and especially their history of struggles and suffering that require to be highlighted. To this effect, let me conclude with a quote from late Prof. Balasundaram which highlights the oppressed and their suffering as an important historical source.

> The need of the time is history written in such a way that it is relevant, relevant in reflecting the human experiences of suffering and bringing about a vision of social transformation. We need to come of age and recognize that we need the perspective of the oppressed people. That is to say, the collective experiences of the oppressed people must be recognized as legitimate historical source in a relevant reconstruction of history.[24]

---

[24] Franklyn Balasundaram, "The Contemporary Dalit Issues", in Prasanna Kumar (ed.), *Liberating Witness*, vol. I, Gurukul Lutheran College and Research Institute, Chennai, 1995, p. 411.

# Part IV

# Continuing
# Common Journey

# Chapter 17

# Asian Paths to Catholicity

*"And what should they know of England who only England know."*
– Rudyard Kipling[1]

*"And at this sound the multitude came together, and they were bewildered, because each one heard them speaking in his own language. And they were amazed and wondered saying 'Are not all these who are speaking Galileans? And how is it that we hear, each of us in his own native tongue?'"* – Acts 2:6-8

Should we characterize in one single word the distinguishing feature of Asian theology today, it is its spirit of catholicity. I underline here the spirit of catholicity because catholicity could be interpreted as a notion of totalizing and hegemonic universality. It is an attempt to make something present everywhere, and it is often an agenda of power and domination, that is unmindful of the diversity and plurality of varied contexts. Hegemonic universality breeds all forms of exclusion. Any form of exclusion is opposed to true catholicity. The development of Asian theology could be characterized as a path of continuous inclusion, and it makes sense, especially in the context of exclusions at various levels and areas in the contemporary world. I am using this inclusive notion of catholicity as the key to interpret the Asian theological contribution to global Christianity. For catholicity is a matter of wholeness which is not something already preordained and given, but a process and a project. In addressing issues of the larger society or public concerns, Asian theology exercises its catholicity.

---

[1] Rudyard Kipling, *The English Flag (1891)*.

### Catholicity in the Methods and Sources of Theology

Asian theology has tried to widen the horizon of theological method by attributing central importance to experience and by recognizing spatiality or context as an important locus of theologizing. Experience and context are inter-linked concepts. Experience can have a thin and thick description. By thin description of experience I mean the impression made on the subject through anything which the senses perceive, and it could become a means for understanding more closely the future perception of the senses.

Thick description of experience, on the other hand, would refer to the mediation of reality through the subject. It is an affirmation that the subject is deeply involved in the approach to reality which in its depth and expanse could never be fully grasped. The mediation by the subject gives rise to the discovering of more dimensions of reality, when what is perceived by senses is reflected upon. The vibration of reality on the subject through what the senses perceive is different in respect to diversity of spaces and contexts from where the senses draw. Diversity of space and context also elicit different responses. When texts, events, traditions etc. are viewed from different spaces, they all appear differently, and cannot have the same identity everywhere. The experience and knowledge accumulated through centuries and millennia in the different contexts of the world offer rich resources for the pursuit of theology. This awareness has led Asian theologies to draw from this plurality for a more integral understanding, interpretation and praxis of faith. This sense of inclusion, according to me, is the spirit of catholicity.

Of the two Kantian transcendental aesthetic, forming the *a priori* intuition of all sense experiences – time and space – the former, namely time has acquired great importance in the theological field, especially with the advent of historical consciousness. Through this impulse there came about not only the deployment of historico-critical method in Biblical studies, but also a renewal in theological hermeneutics.[2] Historical consciousness was deepened by the philosophical orientation set by the *Sein und Zeit* of Heidegger. However, the other primordial dimension of human experience – the space – and its implications in the process of perception and genesis of knowledge has remained unexplored. Space has been a rediscovery of contextual theologies, and it has been a major source of theological creativity in Asia.

---

[2] Cf. Werner Jeanrond, *Theological Hermeneutics. Development and Significance*, Crossroad, New York, 1991.

Spatiality is the matrix of culture and civilization, modes of thinking and ways of acting. From an epistemological point of view, the importance of context derives from the fact that our thoughts draw from experience. Space, at the primary level, is where the senses come in touch with reality to stimulate the human mind and to generate ideas. Space is also inextricably bound up with culture – the natural and social environment in which people live. Any theology that neglects spatiality will not only be incomplete but also can become a distortion of truth. For Christian identity, its praxis and meaning is never in the abstract, but always with reference to a particular situation, context or space. The highlighting of space and context in Asian theology can, in sum, be viewed as an expression of catholicity. It is a view diametrically opposed to the prevalent assumption in universalizing theologies that one arrives at truth by abstracting the reality from its context, its location.

These two theological sources – experience and space – shape Asian theology as a movement towards wholeness – a wholeness that is in the process of becoming. Both these sources invest Asian theology also with a deep spiritual character. The divorce between the theological and the spiritual, to the neglect of the latter due to theology's claim to be a scientific discipline,[3] gets now reunited in Asian theology, which defines itself as an understanding indissolubly tied up with spirituality and praxis of faith.

## A New Conception of Catholicity in Relation to Other Religions

Asian contribution to catholicity is most evident in its approach to other religious traditions. From the past five centuries of missionary expansion, Asia inherited a conception of salvation that excluded most of its children because they professed a religion other than Christianity. The contemporary Asian voices have tried to alter this situation by including everyone in the ambit of God's salvation.

> According to the new paradigm, creation itself is a self-communication of God, who is reaching out to all peoples through the Word and the Spirit in varied ways, at various times, and through the different religions. This ongoing divine-human encounter is salvific. However, God's plan is not merely to save individual souls, but to gather together all things in heaven and on earth. God is working out this plan in history through various sages and prophets. Jesus, the Word incarnate, has a specific role in this history of salvation. But Jesus' mission is at the service of

---

[3] Cf. Felix Wilfred – Erik Borgman (eds.), "Theology in a World of Specialization" *Concilium* 2006/2.

God's mission. It does not replace it. Taking a kenotic form, it collaborates with other divine self-manifestations in other religions as God's mission is moving towards its eschatological fulfillment. As disciples of Jesus we must witness to the Abba and his Kingdom of freedom, fellowship, love and justice.[4]

It is difficult to assess in what ways Asian theology of religions, universalistic in its spirit, has had an impact on the rest of the world. There are instances where we could hear the Asian voices resounding. For example, when Pope John Paul II acknowledges that other religions do have "participated forms of mediation of different kinds and degrees"[5] and recognizes the presence of the Spirit in other histories, religious traditions, etc.,[6] it appears to espouse the position long held by Asian theology.[7] Otherwise, it is difficult to explain how the position we find in *Evangelii Nuntiandi*, that other religions are simply human efforts, 'and arms stretched towards heaven'[8] could, within the span of few years, acquire a more radical stand as we find in the words of Pope John Paul II.

---

[4] Conclusions of the Research Seminar, "A Vision of Mission for the New Millennium", in Thomas Malipurathu – L. Stanislaus (eds.), *A Vision of Mission in the New Millennium*, St Paul's, Mumbai, 2000, p. 203.

[5] *Redemptoris Missio*, no. 5.

[6] "The Spirit's presence and activity affect not only the individuals but also society and history, peoples, cultures and religions. Indeed, the Spirit is at the origin of the noble ideals and undertakings which benefit humanity on its journey through history". *Redemptoris Missio*, no. 28.

[7] For example, already in 1974, the Asian Bishops in their First Plenary Assembly in Taipei showed their remarkable catholic spirit in relation to other religions when they stated: "In this dialogue we accept them [religions] as significant and positive elements in the economy of God's design of salvation. In them we recognize and respect profound spiritual and ethical meanings and values. For many centuries they have been the treasury of the religious experience of our ancestors, from which our contemporaries do not cease to draw light and strength...How then can we not give them reverence and honour? And how can we not acknowledge that God has drawn our peoples to Himself through them?" Statement of the Assembly no. 14. For text, see Gaudencio Rosales – C.G. Arevalo (eds.) *For All the Peoples of Asia (Federation of Asian Bishops Conferences Documents from 1970 – 1991)*, Orbis Books-Claretian Publications, New York – Manila, 1992, p. 14.

[8] "Even in the face of natural religious expressions most worthy of esteem, the Church finds support in the fact that the religion of Jesus, which she proclaims through evangelization, objectively places man in relation with the plan of God, with His living presence and with His action; she thus causes an

### Dialogue – A Path to Catholicity

If catholicity is "wholeness and fullness through exchange and communication",[9] then we see how important dialogue is as a way of life and praxis to nurture catholicity. Asian theology has been following this path of catholicity through a triple dialogue – with religions, cultures and the poor. This was something underlined repeatedly by the Federation of Asian Bishops' Conferences ever since its First Assembly in Taipei in 1974.[10] In this notion of catholicity, just as religions are viewed from the perspective of God and God's universal salvation offered to all human beings and to the entire creation, so too the cultures with their rich diversity reflect the creation of God. They are the hidden treasures of God, and without them there is no wholeness and salvation. Dialogue and exchange with cultures foster catholicity of God's creation and salvation.

The exclusion of the poor from dignity, power and community is something opposed to the spirit of catholicity, and hence the importance of bringing to the centre the poor who are marginalized. Without recognition of the poor as the Christ of today, there is no salvation (Mt 25: 31-46),[11] or as Jon Sobrino puts it *"extra pauperes nulla salus"*.[12] (outside the poor, there is no salvation). Dialogue with the poor is extremely important for the entire humanity to save it from the grave illness in which it has fallen. Contrary to the general attitude, the poor have so much to give to the present world, and without their contribution there is no fullness and wholeness. In a continent still marked by forced poverty affecting

---

encounter with the mystery of divine paternity that bends over towards humanity. In other words, our religion effectively establishes with God an authentic and living relationship which the other religions do not succeed in doing, even though they have, as it were, their arms stretched out towards heaven." *Evangelii Nuntiandi,* no. 53.

[9] Siegfried Wiedenhoffer, *Das katholische Kirchenverstaendnis,* Verlag Styria, Graz, 1992, p. 279.

[10] Statement of the First Plenary Assembly of the Federation of Asian Bishops' Conferences nos. 9–24. For the text, see Gaudencio Rosales – C.G. Arevalo (eds.), *op.cit,* pp. 14-16.

[11] That the poor are the *vicars of Christ* has been the conviction of the Christian Middle Ages. See Michel Mollat, *The Poor in the Middle Ages,* Yale University Press, New Haven – London, 1986.

[12] Jon Sobrino, "Extra Pauperes Nulla Salus, Pequeño Ensayo Utópico-Profético" in *Revista Latinoamericana de Teología* (UCA, San Salvador) September – December, 2006.

millions of people, Asian Christianity finds its catholicity not only by reaching out to the poor through bonds of inclusion and through acts of justice, but by receiving as well what they have to offer in the spirit of dialogue.

Asian theology believes in what I would call *reverse catholicity*, that is a process of becoming universal by receiving, and by learning from others – other religions, cultures, the poor, etc. From its very inception, Christianity allowed its sacred books to be translated into all languages, which is recognition of the catholicity of the human family. Secondly, Christianity sent out missionaries to the entire world – again recognition of the universality of humankind. But these two forms of catholicity are incomplete. Christianity needs to allow itself to be interpreted and reshaped by what these peoples with their cultures and religious traditions have to say about God and humanity; and what the poor have to tell us about their experience of our world. As long as this reverse catholicity or incoming universality, in contrast to outgoing catholicity, does not happen, Christianity is incomplete. The idea of Christianity as a mission spanning the entire world with the whole of humanity as recipients of its Good News, is a unilateral catholicity. Christianity to be more completely universal requires a multilateral catholicity which calls for the reception of the Gospel of Life from the people of diverse contexts. If the outgoing universality is from God; so is the incoming universality for which Christianity needs to make room. The incoming universality is the movement by which Christianity receives the ways of the Spirit from other religions.

The praxis of dialogue as fostering catholicity could be looked at also from another angle. Theology most often turns around questions and issues that speak to the Christian communities, and these issues are couched in a language which is understood within the limited Christian circles. The dialogue with religions, cultures and the poor widens the horizons, and the issues in theology become more catholic in spirit by addressing larger questions and issues which touch upon the people of a particular continent.

Catholicity needs to be interpreted as recognition of pluralism, which happens through a process of dialogue. The plurality and diversity we experience in every field and at all levels, may not be reduced to any one single reality. Any such reductionism would rob the particular of its unique specificity and concreteness. Universality is respectful of the otherness of every identity, of the other, and therefore is part of any centrifugal movement.

Dialogue makes us realize that catholicity is possible for the humans only in germ. For, the claim for totality as a possession has the proclivity for violence. The proclivity for violence is as much in misconstrued identity as in distorted universals, as is the case with "hegemonic universals" – epistemological, cultural, political, etc. The inchoative character of the universal which alone is available in our human condition tells us that in every encounter, in every pursuit of truth, there is the horizon of the not-yet.

Finally, the understanding and praxis of dialogue in Asia needs to be viewed against the background of the sense of mystery. It is based on the respect for the other and the otherness of the other. This is not to be confused with what is talked about today as discursive practices. These discursive practices, as in the discourse ethics of Juergen Habermas for example, are by nature rational and argumentative, claiming for validity of one's statements on the force of one's reasoning. This approach to theology is certainly a step ahead of deductive method, as it involves the other in conversation.[13] But the difference of this type of approach to dialogue in Asian theology is that, at a deeper level, there is the recognition of a mystery that envelops the world of the dialogue partners, and it can never be plumbed through rational tools and arguments alone.

### Appropriation of Faith – Catholicity as Inclusion of the Subject

We can speak of a catholicity of faith in regard to the manner in which it is approached. In the traditional practice of mission, faith was viewed as an object of communication. This was a 'non-catholic' approach, so to say. For, it failed to include the world of the subject in relation to the understanding and practice of her faith. The catholicity which Asian theology is bringing, invites us to overcome the paradigm of communication of faith and move towards appropriation of faith. This implies that faith is viewed and practiced from the horizon of the subject taking into serious account her agency.[14] In fact Asian tradition, by and

---

[13] Cf. Jürgen Habermas, *Erlaeuterungen zur Diskursethik*, Surkamp, Frankfurt, 1991; Donald Moon, "Practical Discourse and Communicative Ethics", in Stephen K.White (ed.), *The Cambridge Companion to Habermas*, Cambridge University Press, Cambridge, 1995, pp. 143-163.

[14] One speaks of the process of *"reception:"* by which is meant that a teaching or doctrine is not only imparted, but that it needs to be also received by the

large places greater emphasis on the inner experience and self-awareness
of the subject of cognition than on the object of this awareness. This is
particularly the case in regard to theology in which the object of enquiry,
the Divine, is not one object among many and outside of oneself, but a
mystery bound up intimately with the subject who enquires and
experiences.

Now, if we look at faith as an experience that touches ultimately the
self of the believer, ultimately he or she becomes the chief point of reference.
Faith understood as an experience confers on it a certain dynamism which
neither dogmas nor institutions could provide. Moreover, we need to take
into account the fact that the subject and her belief are very much affected
by other subjects and their beliefs. In this respect, we need to value the
faith of our neighbours and learn from them. The faith-experience already
there in our neighbours gets reflected in different measures when they
encounter with the Christian Gospel message. The formation of faith here
becomes a creative process of mutuality and less a result of effective
communication strategies. This is so because the formation of faith is not
only, much less exclusively, a rational process of getting into some system
of belief. It is a kind of emotional involvement nourished by various
cultural practices. Here is a rich realm for understanding and experiencing
the catholicity of faith.

## A Catholic Anthropology

The understanding of universality is deeply linked to the mode of identity-
conception. This is very evident in the case of conceptualizing the human
identity. The dominant western conception has been one in which the
identity of the human was viewed as that which distinguishes it from the
rest of reality. Even more, the modern conception of the human which
distinguishes human beings as those who rule the rest of creation, and as
"masters" are able to dominate and manipulate the nature and the world,
invoked Biblical roots. The consequent model of development is one in
which human beings continue to forge ahead realizing all that they can
in the world and in the universe, unmindful of its effects on nature and
on  human survival itself.

---

faithful. Thus one may speak of the "reception of Vatican Council II". But what
I mean by appropriation goes beyond the sphere of this concept which is by
and large confined to teachings and doctrines. Appropriation focuses attention
on the world of the subject and its interpretation of Christian life, message, etc.,
something that includes also a process of selection.

There is another approach to human identity which, while recognizing the distinctive character of the human, nevertheless views the human as deeply embedded in a web of relationships with the entire nature and the whole of universe. This is a vision that is dominant in the Asian world-view and way of life, and this relational approach offers a more catholic and wholesome path to the human. Human beings could be said to be the centre of the universe, provided we understand the centre as in a wheel with the responsibility to hold through its spokes the entire nature together and facilitate its uninterrupted movement. A truly catholic understanding of the human is the one which is sensitive to the cords that bind the human with the rest of reality, and it has deeper implications for the understanding of faith, salvation, and the evolution of humanity in its right relationship with the rest of creation.[15]

An understanding of the human as an independent individual cannot form the basis of any genuine theology that tends to the wholeness of reality. There is the dependence of the human on nature and universe. It is this wholistic and interdependent anthropological perspective that inspires Asian theologies. A recovery of this wholistic anthropology by Asian theology drawing from its rich civilizational and religious sources appears to be highly important when the survival of humanity is threatened more than ever before through exploitation and wanton destruction of nature.

### Open-endedness of Asian Spirituality

Religion and spirituality are distinct realities, not to be confused with each other. But as a matter of fact, religions have claimed control over the spiritual existence of its believers. This could not but have a stifling effect on the spiritual quest of people, which may go beyond the confines of one's religion or religious group. In the Asian religious traditions, what comes foremost is the spiritual seeking, and religion is subordinated to it as a means. This approach opens up immense possibilities for the growth of persons and communities. Spiritual quest may take a person across many religious traditions from which one may draw nourishment. There is then a legitimate space to speak about catholicity of spirituality, unbound by any particular tradition, institution, history, etc. Moreover, Asian traditions, especially the Indic tradition recognizes that a plurality of spiritual paths is required according to the nature and psychological make-up of different persons.

---

[15] For more on this point, see the chapter on Eco-theology.

Drawing from these resources, Asian Christian theology has attempted to develop a spirituality that is more open and inclusive. This could be seen from the fact that it has no difficulty to accept as part of one's spiritual growth methods like yoga, Zen, etc. These could be well-integrated within the understanding and practice of faith of the Asians, and could be a true contribution to global Christianity, its theology and spirituality as the Asian bishops suggest:

> The spirituality characteristic of the religions of our continent stresses a deeper awareness of God and the whole self in recollection, silence and prayer, flowering in openness to others, in compassion, non-violence, generosity. Through these and other gifts it can contribute much to our spirituality which, while remaining truly Christian can yet be greatly enriched. Sustained and reflective dialogue with them in prayer...will reveal to us what the Holy Spirit has taught others to express in a marvelous variety of ways. These are different perhaps from our own, but through them we too may hear His voice, calling us to lift our hearts to the Father.[16]

The possibilities of such open-ended spirituality have been, unfortunately, misunderstood. Such misunderstandings have not deterred Asians from continuing their spiritual quest across borders.

One of the reasons why Asian spirituality proves attractive is the fact that it tends to be integral, especially integrating the human mind, spirit and body as one single reality, and thus overcoming the dichotomous body-soul divide. Secondly, the belief that different individuals require different spiritual paths, defying all homogenization, allows a large space and choices for the spiritual flowering of individuals.[17] Asian theology draws from these traditions to reinterpret Christian spirituality and way of life in a more comprehensive fashion with due place given to human

---

[16] Final Statement of the II General Assembly of the Federation of Asian Bishops' Conferences, no. 35. For the text, see Gaudencio Rosales – C.G. Arevalo (eds.), *op.cit.* p. 35. What is striking in this statement is not only the open-ended spirituality it advocates drawing from other religious traditions, but the fact that it goes even to the point of advocating practice of prayer with peoples of other faiths. This was advocated by the Asian Bishops already in 1978 well before Pope John Paul II invited representatives of other religious traditions for prayer in Assisi in 1986.

[17] In the Hindu tradition, the spiritual canvas is large with many spiritual colours and hues with the *Vedic* on one extreme and the *Tantric* on the other.

body as is the case with yoga and Zen, and many such rich and variegated spiritual streams of Asia.

This kind of catholic or wholistic spirituality has proved attractive also to many Westerners. But often the search on the part of Westerners for the open-ended spirituality is interpreted as resulting from the crisis of values in Western society. This is a somewhat a myopic interpretation. The assumption here is that, left to itself, Western spiritual tradition is complete, and it does not require anything more. But the point is that many sincere seekers find themselves in a stifling atmosphere, and their aspirations do not find any vibration within the confines of a narrowly interpreted Christian faith, praxis and spirituality. The yearning for a truly inclusive spirituality calls for a deeper dialogue of Christianity with Asian religious traditions.

## Conclusion

Today certain approaches to truth, practice of faith and forms of spirituality are viewed as extraneous to Christianity and its assumptions, and are being characterized as post-Christian.[18] What Asia is telling is that, what is described as post-Christian can, in fact, be found within Christianity – in the Asian re-interpretation of it with a universal outlook and the spirit of inclusion. The Christianity one wants to leave behind, in fact, is one of its limited understandings within the Western history and tradition. Underlying the phenomenon of post-Christianity is the conviction that certain concerns so very important for today's life do not find a place in the traditionally interpreted Christianity. However, European post-Christianity need not mean the end of Christianity. Asian Christian theology moulded in a true catholic and inclusive spirit shows that the concerns of post-Christianity can be reconciled integrally with a fresh understanding of it, when seen and re-interpreted through Asian eyes and Asian experience and an Asian approach to reality and truth. They will find it in the Asian reconstruction of Christian identity.

The tragedy that happened to Western Christianity is that it got so entangled with the Western classical metaphysics as to make its survival depend upon it. When the new cultural developments took place through the last few centuries, metaphysics was slowly dissolved. But the point is that Christian understanding of God, the world and the entire reality was

---

[18] Cf. Gianni Vattimo, *After Christianity*, Columbia University Press, New York, 2002.

so bound up with metaphysics, that its dissolution became in effect also dissolution of Christianity. What Asian Christianity is telling is that Christianity is closer to its own self when it is interpreted in the spirit of catholicity, and its dynamism is such that it does not require for its survival and flourishing the Western classical or medieval metaphysical thought. The end of the era of metaphysics and foundationalism is not the end of Christianity. Here again is a point of convergence between Asian Christian theology and post-Christian concerns, and a genuine dialogue is possible in this regard. [19]

Finally, it is no exaggeration to say that the spirit of catholicity that the evolving Asian Christianity embodies in the life of its believers, theology, praxis, etc., augurs well for the transformation of global Christianity. Therefore much of what Asian Christian theology tries to interpret in the context of this continent has a wider significance. A deeper analysis of Asian theology tells us that it revolves around a refreshing and dynamic understanding of catholicity, which in its turn leads us to a creative interpretation of Christianity and its future. In sum, the most significant contribution Asian theology is making for the global Church is a new understanding of catholicity close to the vision of Jesus and his Good News to humanity.

---

[19] In fact, Gianni Vattimo attempts to disconnect classical metaphysics and Christianity when he proposes that the very Christian belief in incarnation as *kenosis* itself is a weakening of metaphysical thought. If such is the case, then, like in the case of secularization which is not really opposed to Christianity, but a product of it as Weber maintained, the challenge to metaphysics of presence is not something opposed to Christianity but in fact the result of it. Within the Western situation, Vattimo attempts to rediscover Christian faith by overcoming that type of Christianity which was object of severe critique and despise by Nietzsche and others. Vattimo's underlying attempt to find a different shape of Christianity not tied to an immobile tradition or *stasis* can be read in the ambiguous English title of his book. The "*After*" in the title could be interpreted in a chronological sense, as something that historically succeeds Christianity, but the "After" could be interpreted as well to mean the quest, search for Christianity.

# Chapter 18

# In Quest of Mystery
## Interreligious Journey in a
## Post-metaphysical World

*"The Ethiops say that their gods are flat-nosed and black, while the Thracians say that theirs have blue eyes and red hair. But if horses or oxen or lions had hands or could draw with their hands and accomplish such works as men, horses would draw the figures of the gods as similar to horses, and the oxen as similar to oxen, and they would make the bodies of the sort which each of them had."*

- Xenophanes[1]

In former times critical questions were raised about religious narration of God, because they were either anthropomorphic or served as helpful illusion to make sense of life, or to bear the oppressive conditions of life. But today the question has shifted to new grounds. The cultural shift from the metaphysical to the post-metaphysical has brought about perhaps the greatest challenge to the conventional ways of thinking. If there was one reality in the understanding of which metaphysics was crucial, it was the question of God. The traditional edifice of metaphysics with its penchant for essentializing every reality of experience has crumbled in the face of the recognition of language in the constitution of meaning and inter-subjectivity and communication in the discovery of truth.[2]

We need to relate this situation to the experience of a general crisis in the Semitic, and especially Christian conception of God. Crisis as it is

---

[1] Xenophanes of Colophon, *Fragments,* edited by H. Lesher, Toronto, 1992.
[2] Cf. Jürgen Habermas, *Postmetaphysical Thinking,* Polity Press, Cambridge, 1998.

said is also an opportunity – an opportunity to rethink. The crisis of the Christian conception of God, occasioned among other things is by the post-metaphysical shift. By the post-metaphysical is meant a way of thinking that abstains from the habit of defining everything by their essences, by their foundation, by their nature, by their origin, goal, etc. Post-metaphysical challenges the kind of "objectivism" which claims to grasp reality that comes to us with their metaphysical constitution from "nowhere", and all that we need to do is to record them in our knowledge. Rather for post-metaphysical thought what becomes important is the *communication and interaction* among various subjectivities and social actors which is crucial in creating understanding, consensus, and indeed in the construction of reality itself. The postmodern situation is one characterized by its departure from the metaphysical thinking. It does not claim any all-comprehending view. Instead it is focused on fragments, without reference to any centre that would hold everything together. Post-secular characterizes a situation in which one does not think that God, religion and mystery wane into oblivion as society modernizes itself, as was held by the thesis of secularization. The post-secular opens up a new conception of religion vis a vis society, and contrives a new role to it, without however falling back into old models of a religion that tries to control society and public life.

Given the convergence of Asian theology of praxis and the post-metaphysical situation, we raise the following questions: To what extent could interreligious dialogue and exchange respond to the post-metaphysical situation? How could religious traditions in dialogue with each other say more about God than each one of them singly? Is there a greater understanding of this mystery than if we were to struggle each one within our own traditions? Finally, what does interreligious dialogue on God mean in a postmodern, post-metaphysical and post-secular society? These are some of the questions and issues on which we want to reflect in this chapter.

## Crisis of the Christian Conception of God

If we begin with the Christian tradition, we observe that its conception of God is undergoing many a crisis. The first crisis relates to the question of the relationship of God to the world or the universe. In Christian understanding, God is a creator and originator of all that is. The world and God are related to each other in terms of cause and effect, and therefore different from each other. That is perfect metaphysics. But this way of conceiving God has been found too extrinsic and modeled after human action producing some effect. God and the world exist apart. For the majority of Hindu streams of thought, this appears to be dualistic. The mystery of God instead, is viewed by them as a reality lying deep in the world and not separated from it. For them, there is, so to say, a mutual indwelling and intertwining of both these realities. The mystery of God is in the world and the world is in God. Ultimately, the point is that of identity and difference. The Indic tradition of *advaita* takes a position of non-duality. According to it, Brahman or the Ultimate reality and the world are neither one nor two (*a-dvaita* or non-duality). Even the theistic branch of Hinduism connected with the *bhakti* movement, while admitting a personal God different from the devotee – which allows room for love and devotion – would not hold a total separation of the two.[3]

A second source of crisis is the insistence on the one-ness of God or *monotheism*. Many thinkers of religious studies and anthropologists expressed the view that monotheism is something that stands as the culmination in the narration of God, since it represents a purity that is obtained by discarding plurality of gods and goddesses. In the Semitic tradition, it is so central that anything that refers to plurality of gods and goddesses is viewed as the greatest of sins – the sin of idolatry. If there are consequences of the notion of God and its narration for the society and for the political order, it is clearly the case of monotheism. Since the world of the humans is viewed as the reflection of the invisible world of God, monotheism became the ideological justification for centralization, authoritarianism and for the destruction of plurality. Thus, ironically, that which has been defended – the monotheism as the purity in the narration of God - has had a tragic history of impurity and violence.[4] Monotheism, instead of solving problems has created more ones, making in the process polytheism more appealing. From a broader perspective, what it shows is that the religious conceptions have terribly serious social consequences – a reason why religious traditions need to come together in the narration of God, so that no one narration or image of God becomes a tool that contributes to violence.

---

[3] Cf. John B. Carman, *The Theology of Ramanuja. An Essay in Interreligious Understanding*, Yale University Press, New Haven – London, 1974; Id., "Hindu Bhakti as a Middle Way", in Peter Berger (ed.), *The Other Side of God*, Anchor Press, Doubleday – Garden City – New York, 1981, pp. 182-207.

[4] Cf. *Concilium* 1985/1. The entire issue is dedicated to the question of Monotheism.

One must recognise the intricate logic of the language which underlies both monotheism and polytheism. It is not a question of how many supernatural beings there are, though it has sometimes been misleadingly phrased in that way. It is a question of how one is going to interpret the experiences of spiritual realities which can come to men, and attempt to make them coherent with the general range of one's knowledge.[5]

If we take it that way, polytheism in the Indian tradition could be interpreted as an affirmation of the inexhaustible character of the divine mystery. The 330 million gods Hinduism believes in, wants to say that there are endless forms and expressions of the divine mystery that cannot be exhausted in any single form. Therefore, Hindus do not have difficulty to have in their temples along with a particular god, also other gods and goddesses. Hindu belief in God/gods/goddesses could be compared to "a diamond of innumerable facets; two very large and bright facets are Vishnu and Shiva, while the others represent all the gods that were ever worshipped. Some facets seem larger, brighter, and better polished than others, but in fact the devotee, whatever his/her sect, worships the whole diamond, which is in reality perfect."[6]

The admission and positive recognition that there are endless ways that lead us to the ineffable mystery of God is a contribution to tolerance, peace and harmony. In fact it is precisely because of the absence of belief in one exclusive God that Hinduism has nurtured tolerance and positive approach to the God-experience in other religious traditions. To admit a plurality of world views and God-views has even become indispensable not only for the sake of peace but also for enriching the life of humans and of nature. Historically, the various names used to refer to one God as *Deus, Elohim, Allah,* etc., in the monotheistic traditions reflect in their etymologies the names of particular gods in a polytheistic world, so much so it is not far from truth to say that monotheism itself is the progeny of polytheism.[7]

A third crisis relates to the contradictions in the Christian conception of God, especially in confronting the problem of evil – the so-called theodicy question. An exteriorized conception of God separate from the

---

[5] Keith Ward, *The Concept of God*, Basil Blackwell, Oxford, 1974, p. 101.

[6] A.L. Basham, *The Wonder That Was India*, Grove Press, New York, 1954, p. 309.

[7] Cf. Pierre Gibert, "The Philosophical, Political and Ethical Problems with Unity and Plurality/Monotheism and Polytheism – An Introductory Overview of the Discussions" in *Concilium* 2004/4.

world, cannot but call for the explanation of evil – *unde malum?* It is well known how the earthquake and tsunami of 1755 in Lisbon dealt a blow to the traditional Christian image of God. The experience of tragedy and unmerited torment did not square with the dominant narrations of God. Unfortunately, it did not lead to any significant revision and rethinking of God. But I think the encounter with other religious traditions and also a dialogue between faith and reason[8] could throw some light on this question, unresolved over centuries. [9]

A fourth crisis derives from the fact that a transformed life (which is more than the practice of ethics) does not necessarily postulate the existence of a transcendent God. The clear instance is that of Buddhism which is decisively ethical in orientation. In fact, the resurgence of Buddhism and its spread in the West shows only the appeal of the ethical understanding of right relationships and the waning of a metaphysics that founded the conceptions of God in terms of a dependent relationship. In this regard Stafford Betty notes, "It is clear to me that Buddhism is responding to a need that many sensitive Westerners feel keenly: a way of salvation that does not depend on an anachronistic deity that you have to flatter and abase yourself in front of in order to join the club".[10] The transformation of the self here is connected with an experience of a reality than elaboration of concepts, and this reality is referred to vaguely as the "great Reality" or "Luminosity" or "*Nirvana*" into which one enters and into which one is absorbed and by which one is enveloped. The experience of that great Reality becomes the source of wisdom and compassion. A personalist dimension to this ultimate reality is given in Mahayana Buddhism.

This challenging orientation of self-transformation without reference to transcendence is joined by many forms of ethics today such as utilitarian

---

[8] Cf. Francis X. Clooney, *Hindu God, Christian God. How Reason Helps Break Down the Boundaries between Religions*, Oxford University Press, New York, 2001.

[9] Cf. Felix Wilfred, "Prophetic Anger and Sapiential Compassion: Grappling with Evil Today", *Concilium* 2009/1, pp. 27-38; Dennis Gira, "A Buddhist Approach to the Question of Evil", *Ibid.*, pp. 100-107. See also H. Schwartz, *Evil. A Historical and Theological Perspective*, Fortress Press, Minneapolis 1995; Paul Ricoeur, "Evil" in *Encyclopedia of Religion*, vol. 5, Collier Macmillan, New York, 1987; Susan Neiman, *Evil in Modern Thought*, Princeton University Press, Princeton, 2002; Wendy Doniger O'Flaherty, *The Origin of Evil in Hindu Mythology*, University of California, Berkley, 1997.

[10] Stafford Betty, "What Buddhists and Christians Are Teaching Each Other About God" in *Cross Currents*, vol. 58, no. 1, pp. 115-116.

ethics and humanistic ethics all of which do not require God as their basis.
Also the modern literature in which the human predicament is narrated
in its fallibility and precariousness does not have recourse to God or
transcendence. Human life is depicted often as a drama in which one plays
one's part in the midst of agonies and ecstasies.

### The Role of Interreligious Dialogue

Interreligious dialogue has widened the horizons of understanding God-
quest. In the first place, it has led to a critical questioning by the believers
about the conventional conception and understanding of God in their own
religious traditions. It has evoked a desire to experience the divine mystery
beyond one's own tradition. An attempt to participate in the God-
experience of another religious tradition has brought to the fore also a
sense of plurality. Interreligious dialogue has led to realize the
innumerable ways in which the mystery of God could be approached.
There has come about the realization of the fragmentary aspect in
approaching and narrating God today. There is no claim that interreligious
dialogue will give us any comprehensive idea and narration of God. That
is not the goal of interreligious dialogue. What it does is, to provoke us
to seek with others, new and different paths, and discover the presence
and action of God even beyond the boundaries of religion. In other words,
all religions together can say a little more of the mystery of God than any
one single religion can, and even challenge people to go beyond them.
For this to happen, there needs to be the consciousness in each religion
about the limits of its God-narration or discourse. Metaphysics often goes
with the claim of final and absolute truth that renders any dialogue and
conversation superfluous. Interreligious approach to God is precisely post-
metaphysical in nature in so far as there is the openness to transcend one's
limits and to seek something that lies beyond.[11]

Globalisation has helped the communication of religious beliefs,
symbols and practices across religious traditions and has made the meeting

---

[11] This contrasts with the metaphysical approach. As J. Derrida notes, "The
history of metaphysics ... is the determination of Being as *presence* in all senses
of this word. It could be shown that all names related to fundamentals, to
principles, or to the center have always designated an invariable presence -
*eidos, arche, telos, energia, ousia, aletheia, transcendentality, consciousness, God, man,*
and so forth." J. Derrida "Structure, Sign, and Play in the Discourse of the
Human Sciences", *Writing and Difference*, University of Chicago Press, Chicago,
1978, p. 279.

of religions easier. Moreover, Globalisation with its wide network of communication, has enabled individuals in various religious traditions to share their personal experiences and encounters with God. It has also made available, not only narrations of God in classical religious traditions, but also in marginal and popular religious traditions, in the subaltern cultures and their ritualistic expressions, etc. It has widened the canvas of God-seekers by making available the experiences of people in different parts of the world and even along the margins of life.

## The Mystical Approach to God

The crisis of God-conception in general and of Christianity in particular leads us to reawaken the mystical tradition which is to be found in all major religions. It is utopian to believe that there are many people who will be convinced of the existence of God through the five ways of St Thomas, or other rational arguments. The mystical approach to God acknowledges that the mystery of God is something to be experienced and lived. There is a realm of experiential knowledge into which mysticism leads us. It is knowledge through union rather than through differentiation of the knower and the known. Religious traditions converge in this direction, especially if we take into account the experience of the founders of these traditions like in the case of Islam and Christianity and Buddhism and the experience of ancient seers in Hinduism and the prophets in Judaism. Speaking of mysticism, the Indian philosopher Dasgupta notes:

> Mysticism means a spiritual grasp of the aim and problems of life in a much more real and ultimate manner than is possible to mere reason. A developing life of mysticism means a gradual ascent in the scale of spiritual values, experience, and spiritual ideals. As such, it is many-sided in its development, and as rich and complete as life itself. Regarded from this point of view, mysticism is the basis of all religions – particularly of religion as it appears in the lives of truly religious men.[12]

The encounter of religions teaches us that comparing and contrasting of the different conceptions of God does not take us anywhere. It tells us about the importance of experience when we refer to the mystery of God. And that leads us to recognize the place of mysticism in the approach to the Divine. In the past, mysticism was thought as a peculiar experience that is accessible to a limited group of people known as mystics. But the crisis of God we experience today tells us that any approach to God needs

---

[12] S.N. Dasgupta, *Hindu Mysticism*, Motilal Banarsidass Publishers, Delhi, 1927 (reprint 2002), p. ix.

to be mystical and therefore mysticism is part of everyone's experience of God. The mystical approach in all religious traditions does not trust that the power of reason or the capacity of human mind could take us to the divine mystery. Here we have a point of reference to a forgotten aspect of Christian heritage.

The theology of Dionysius Areopagite, the classic *The Cloud of Unknowing*,[13] and medieval thinkers like Meister Eckert make us realize that we have in the Christian tradition an approach to God that could vibrate with what Hindus and Buddhists experience. They make us realize that when it comes to the ultimate reality, we may not speak in clear and distinct ideas but may have to enter into the "dark luminosity" to which Dionysius the Areopagite refers. Plato's allegory of the dark cave in his *Republic*, the Upanishad's approach to Brahman as *neti..neti* (not this..not this), and Dionysius the Areopagite's negative theology all point to the ineffable character of the Divine.[14]

Religious experiences of the Ultimate Mystery without venturing to name it could set everyone on a path of quest and discovery. It is important that God is not pre-defined to be known as an object but a mystery that is discovered by awakening[15] of the self to God's presence within and outside and through an inner journey of mindfulness. Especially in today's condition of an open-society, no one would follow a faith or belief in God because of social pressure. It would appear that there are no external circumstances warranting belief in God. If it is, it has to come out from within, from the "inner voice" – as Gandhi would say – to which one would respond.[16] In that sense, the post-metaphysical God is someone experienced within while recognizing that presence also outside. If such is the case, then the meeting of religions on the basis of their experience of the divine could help the individuals to listen to the inner voice. Then there would not be anymore questions of which religious belief or image of God is the right one, nor the question of having to choose between

---

[13] *The Cloud of Unknowing: And The Book of Privy Counselling*, edited by Phyllis Hodgson , Early English Text Society,  Oxford University Press, 1944.

[14] Pseudo-Dionysius, *The Complete Works*, translated by Colim Luibeiheid, Paulist Press, New York, 1987.

[15] It is interesting to note that Emmanuel Levinas too refers to the experience of the mystery of God through "awakening" (*réveil*). See Emmanuel Levinas, *Of God Who Comes to Mind*, Stanford University Press, Stanford, 1998, p. 63.

[16] Cf. Margaret Chatterjee, *Gandhi's Religious Thought*, Macmillan Press, London, 1983.

monotheism and polytheism. There will be convergence of all the religions in the task of helping people discover the divine. This task of helping the discovery of a post-metaphysical God, transcending the metaphysical mould in which each one of them have traditionally narrated the presence of the mystery, will bring the religious traditions more closely to each other. It also means then that interreligious dialogue will be first and foremost at the experiential level.

## Fluidity of Religious Borders

An interreligiously oriented post-metaphysical narration of God is made possible, thanks to the fluidity of religious borders today. Generally the quest for God is taken up within one's religious tradition with available sources in which the given image of God played an important role. But today along with the realization that the divine mystery can never be exhausted within the narration of any one single religious tradition, there is also the realization that the borders and boundaries cannot be so rigid and fixed. If the divine mystery cuts across all borders, religions need to open up their boundaries and reach across to other religious traditions and experiences. In fact, this has come about not as a move from the institutionalized religions, but from the experience of people themselves who seek the face of God.  They draw inspiration and resources from religious traditions other than their own, and even do not hesitate in some degree to participate in the religious rituals of other religious traditions. What stands out in this trend is the conviction that the reality of God and the sacred one is in search of, is much more important and these cannot be substituted by institutionalized religions. This is not something totally new, but has been in fact practiced in the religious traditions of India, China, Japan, etc., and now is becoming more and more convincing mode of religious existence also in the West. As Catherine Cornille notes,

> The erosion of religious territories formerly affixed by geography or politics seems now also to have come to affect the individual consciousness. A heightened and widespread awareness of religious pluralism has presently left the religious person with the choice not only of *which* religion but also of *how many* religions he or she might belong to. More and more individuals confess to being partly Jewish and partly Buddhist, or partly Christian and partly Hindu, or fully Christian and fully Buddhist... In the wider history of religion, multiple religious belonging may have been the rule rather than the exception at least on a popular level.[17]

---

[17] Catherine Cornille, *Many Mansions. Multiple Religious Belonging and Christian Identity*, Orbis Books, New York, 2002, p. 1.

In fact popular religious practices all over the world, and especially in Asia, show the ease with which people are able to enter into the symbolic and experiential world of neighbours of other faiths and undertake also pilgrimages to the holy shrines of other religious traditions. Similar trends could be observed in Afro-Brazilian rites. It is only in the context of institutional religions placing emphasis on an exclusive commitment and belonging that the possibility of the quest for the divine or the ultimate mystery across religious borders runs into difficulty. But then the commitment is to the experience of God which is a response to the unfolding mystery, and not to the religion as such. What is advocated here is not a total absence of any religious-belonging. One may well-belong to a particular religious tradition by birth, by choice or through other circumstances; but the point is that one does not limit the God-quest within the boundaries of that particular religion but is open to seek the mystery of God with peoples of other faiths. We have instances of deeply spiritual persons entering into the God-experience of other religious traditions. Here I would like to recall Jules Monchanin,[18] Swami Abhishiktananda (Henri Le Saux)[19] and Swami Dayananada ( Bede Griffiths)[20] all of whom, while being Christians enriched their Christian experience of God through Hindu experience of the Ultimate and the experience of *Saccidananda* – the divine mystery as truth, knowledge or logos and bliss. This was not a notional knowledge but experiential one.

### Post-Metaphysical God in Post-Secular Society

Interreligious dialogue, especially with Buddhism and Hinduism, shows us that it can vibrate with the character and orientation of the post-metaphysical world. In one sense, the encounter with Buddhism and Hinduism will help perceive the post-metaphysical not as a threat, rather

[18] J. Monchanin, *Mystique de l'Inde, Mystère Chrétien,* Fayard, Paris, 1974; *Ermites du Saccidananda*, Casterman, Tournai, 1956.

[19] Abhishiktananda, *Saccidananda – A Christian Approach to Advaitic Experience,* ISPCK, Delhi, 1974; *The Further Shore*, ISPCK, Delhi, 1975; *Guru and Disciple*, SPCK, London, 1974; *Prayer*, SPCK, London, 1972. See also Bettina Bäumer, "Abhishiktananda and the Upanishads" in *Vidyajyoti Journal of Theology*, 50 (1986), pp. 469 – 477.

[20] Bede Griffiths, *Return to the Centre,* Springfield, 1982;" The Advaitic Experience and the Personal God in the Upanishads and the Bhagavad Gita" in Indian Theological Studies, 15 (1978), pp. 71-86. See also the interpretation of Bede Griffiths' advaitic approach, Wayne Teasdale, *Towards a Christian Vedanta*, Asian Trading Corporation, Bangalore, 1987.

as an invitation to enter more deeply into the divine mystery.[21] In fact, unlike the Western and Semitic tradition, Indian tradition, especially the Buddhist tradition, has always emphasized the fluidity or the transience of reality in contrast to the solidification of it in a metaphysical mould. In this sense, much of Indian tradition has been post-metaphysical for over 3000 years!

The Western post-metaphysical society will find, as I noted earlier, resonance with the Hindu and Buddhist traditions which in turn will help to re-interpret the Christian understanding of God. But this needs to be tied to another important question. The secular, among other things, came into being as negation of a conception of God and of religion that claimed to explain the totality of life in all its dimensions. It is in reaction to this that the Western secular ideal was formed claiming the autonomy and independence of the world. In other words, secularization was a legitimate reaction to an order of the world based on a misrepresentation of the idea of God. The secular did not question the wrong idea of God, but what it questioned was the wrong order that was based on this idea. It resulted in exiling, without examining, the idea of God that created a particular order of the world. A revision of the process of secularization has made us aware of its pitfalls.

If the post-metaphysical set the individual on a journey of discovering the ultimate reality, the post-secular character tells us that this discovery has social and even political significance. I mean to say the post-secular approach to religion challenges the naive conception that it is something that belongs to the private realm and does not have public relevance and character. The post-metaphysical approach to God then needs to go hand in hand with the post-secular, challenging the validity of the process of the secular. In fact, in many countries of Asia, religion far from becoming a force of the past has found ways of entering into public life very intensely. Could the discovery of a post-metaphysical God remain as an experience of the individual without at the same time finding concrete social and political expressions in the post-secular situation? If so, what is the social and political significance of the post-metaphysical God? Could the post-metaphysical experience of God find a prophetic expression? What would it mean to integrate faith with justice? These are questions that all religious traditions need to grapple with. At the moment there does not seem to be any clear picture emerging.

---

[21] Cf. James L. Fredericks, *Buddhists and Christians. Through Comparative Theology to Solidarity*, Orbis Books, New York, 2004.

The great advantage of a post-metaphysical approach to God, which needs to take place in all religious traditions, is that it challenges the given narration of God or beliefs as the ultimate, beyond question and probe. For religions are caught up in the metaphysical myth when they are attached to a pre-given fixed image of God and belief-systems. An evolutionary world view and the realization of how much the subject is implicated in the construction of reality have great repercussions in the traditional narrations of God. These approaches, while challenging the narrations of God tied to metaphysical fixations could also have an influence on the public realm.

Anthropocentrism need not be a hindrance to God if it is understood that human beings can approach the divine mystery starting from their own experiences. It is natural that human beings use images and symbols that reflect themselves when they speak about God. There is room for anthropocentrism but the important thing is that one be aware of this basic human limitation in any human language in speaking of God. That is why there should be a conscious effort today to narrate God from the relationship of the humans to nature. Nature in a way mirrors the ultimate reality no less than the human beings. Therefore, the human language needs to incorporate also the language of nature, an eco-spirituality in narrating God.

Eurocentrism unfortunately confines the approach to God and the narration of God within the limited Western experience. For example, *person* has been a central category in the Western conceptualization of the Divine. On the other hand, Indian and other eastern traditions have conceptions of God that are not solely centred on person. They try to overcome the limits of this approach by taking a trans-personal approach in the narration of God.[22]

If the religious traditions do not revise critically the metaphysical foundations of their narrations of God, they could intervene in society and in the political realm in a way that threatens peace and harmony. On the other hand, if they reconsider their God-conceptions in the post-metaphysical spirit, their presence and engagement in public life could be very promising and constructive. This presupposes a post-secular environment. For in a secular environment the intervention of religion in the name of God would not be tolerated; rightly so if religions on the basis

---

[22] Cf. Piet Schoonenberg, *Auf Gott hin denken*, Herder, Wien, 1986.

of metaphysical certainties, assumptions and claims were to cause disruption and even violence in the society. The post-secular society will be one which will not be averse to the concrete expressions of a belief in post-metaphysical God, since the very tolerance that is required of religion will apply also to the secular society. In this regard we may note how differently the secular could be interpreted. France prohibited the use of scarves in schools for Muslim girls on the basis of the secular, which goes against manifestations of religious identity in public. Ironically, secular was the reason why in Mangalore, the demand was made that Muslim girls be allowed to wear scarf as a sign of their religious identity when they were forbidden to do so by the SVS College. The tolerance to the public practice of religion in its social and political expressions would make a society truly post-secular. The societies in the East and the West have to be both post-metaphysical and post-secular. This calls for a transformation on the part of religions about their traditional metaphysical narrations of God, and on the part of the secular societies a transformation into post-secular society, so as to permit the social and political expression of the post-metaphysical experience of God.

In a post-secular society we are able to discern that many of the ideals such as liberty, equality, fraternity, human rights, etc., professed by the secular ideologies have deep religious roots and even historically religious traditions have been instrumental in the secular flowering of these ideals. If such is the case, then the interreligious dialogue of religions in the post-secular society will allow the root-experiences behind what passes as secular ideals to have influence in the public realm. For this to happen, it is important that religious traditions do not get fixated with given narrations and images of God but are able to arrive at a more flexible and at the same time an interior image of God responding to the quest of genuine God-seekers.

Today we see how religions are increasingly wielding influence in public life, and this includes the United States too in such a way that the case of Europe as a secularized society has become more of an exception to this general trend and development than a norm. But then even within Europe itself, the consciousness of the religious presence in public life has become more and more evident, if we take into account particularly the presence of Islam in that continent.

The sad experience of religious strife led to a position that the constitutional state ensures that the citizens encounter each other not simply as members of any particular religious group but as citizens. This was an important reason for the waning of the public influence of religion. But today, in the developing societies as well in the post-secular societies, we recognize the role religion could play. A renewed interpretation of religion and image of God in the various religious traditions is crucial for a public and constructive role of religion in societies – East and West.

## Conclusion

Stamp-collectors could speak with each other most enthusiastically when each one shares what one has with others, and try to find out more about the stamps collected by other colleagues. This is an interesting form of exchange and it is understood best by the tribe of stamp-collectors, and may not excite others. When we speak of God interreligiously, it should not end up in the manner of stamp-collectors' sharing. Religions are not god-collectors. I am reminded of Thales of Miletus who said "The world is full of gods"! We need to move beyond and ask why it is necessary to seek together interreligiously the face of God. It cannot be simply to satisfy our intellectual curiosity by putting together the jigsaw puzzle of God with the help of others. *Deus semper major* - God remains ever more, and above all our efforts – individual and collective. Our common search for the Divine would acquire meaning if the very search for the mystery beyond all naming guides our relationship with each other and with the entire nature which I said is no less revelatory mirror of God.

In this interreligious dialogue, there is opportunity for each religion to critically examine in the light of the experience of the neighbours of other faiths. The spirit of the post-secular would be completely misunderstood if it were to be re-interpreted as reinstatement of religion or a vindication of its conventional conceptions and practices. Rather the post-secular situation needs to be taken as a learning process for the religions themselves, so that they begin to see God not as a metaphysically defined abstract conception, but as an invitation to re-imagine the God-narrative in such a way that the presence of this mystery is experienced more and more in the solidarity of the humans among themselves and with the entire universe.

## Chapter 19

# Towards an Interreligious Eco-theology

*"I said to the almond tree, "Sister, speak to me of God," and the almond tree blossomed".*                                              – Nikos Kazantzakis[1]

The crisis of the earth is also a crisis of God and a crisis of human beings when nature stops being a manifestation of the divine. If crisis is an opportunity for rethinking and change, then we need to look at the inter-relationship of religions vis-à-vis the unprecedented crisis that afflicts our earth. We require the concerted effort of all religious traditions to respond to the ecological crisis, each one drawing out the best of its resources. Construction of a common ecotheology by the various faiths could contribute to the transformation of consciousness, attitudes and a new praxis in relation to the earth. Here we have an opportunity to forget the past and forge unity. While the understanding of God and human beings continue to divide religions, it is less likely that the earth will divide them. On the contrary, today it is the earth that holds the prospect of bringing the religions together, and consequently leading them to a meaningful dialogue on God and humanity. The horizon of our understanding of human beings, of creation and God will get widened through a continuing dialogue focused on nature and environment.

### The Burden of the Past

In their rituals and symbolism, religions show a closeness to nature, its cycles and rhythms. The Bible and the Qu'ran praise the glory of God, the creator. Similar to the Biblical praise we hear in the verses of Qu'ran the

---

[1] Nikos Kazantzakis, *Report to El Greco*, Simon and Schuster, New York, 1965.

close relationship of God and creation. "And the earth We have spread out like a carpet; set thereon mountains firm and immobile; and produced therein all kinds of things in due balance" (Q.15:19). Hinduism, Buddhism and Daoism and especially primaeval religious traditions do have rich resources for promoting an ecologically sound way of life among the humans and help fostering of nature and its gifts. In this sense, religious traditions can play their role to overcome the ecological crisis. However religions do not come into the picture as unblemished contributors. For, they have been responsible in different ways for the negative attitude to nature and have been no less ideologically supporters of the exploitation of nature than science and technology.

Think of the very distinction in the Christian theological tradition of the natural and the supernatural which implies a devaluation of the natural as if salvation consists in moving away from what is natural. We cannot expect from this premise a positive outlook on nature or the earth, nor any impulse for overcoming the ecological crisis. On the whole, the same dualism of body/soul that created a prejudicial attitude and praxis towards women has been sanctioned by religions also in regard to nature.

The ascetic ideals and spirituality developed by religious traditions, each in its own way, was far from sympathetic to nature and its elements. Hinduism and Buddhism may not have taught dominion of human beings over the earth, but they have in them certain ascetic ideals which foster flight from the world and nature, causing a rift and dualism. Even well-meant efforts to interpret Christian faith in evolutionary framework (meaning a matter-spirit continuum) could not hide dualism and hierarchization as for example when spirit is said to be, in Karl Rahner's view as self-transcendence of matter.

> [W]e then must ...try to see man[sic] as the being in whom the basic tendency of matter to find itself in the spirit by self-transcendence arrives at the point where it definitely breaks through; thus in this way we may be in a position to regard man's being itself, from this view-point within the basic and total conception of the world. [2]

Matter has its own consistency, and its reality is not to be judged in what it is in relationship to the spirit as the teleological goal of matter itself. Is the future of the universe going to be a transformation of all matter into spirit? What will happen to our earth with all its materiality?

---

[2] Karl Rahner, *Theological Investigations*, vol. V, Darton Longman, Todd, London, 1966, p. 160.

## Evolution – a Common Point of Reference

The interreligious ecotheology we are envisaging is one that will be based on solid empirical data that science provides. For this we need to have a more dynamic understanding and approach to nature as provided by scientific facts. Of fundamental importance would be the development of a more complex and evolutionary understanding of nature. The interdependence and interconnectedness of reality gets concretized by adopting an evolutionary perspective. Biological evolution tells us that no species is independent or self-enclosed or static, but has undergone mutation and development. It helps us overcome the walls of separation between the various species in nature and see them sharing many things in common, including ancestry, genetic code and the process of germination of life, its growth and flourishing, decay and dissolution. The humans are no exceptions to these, but rather form part of these primordial realities of life-processes. In this way, biological science reinforces our understanding of relationality in the universe and helps us to view human beings themselves from this larger frame of reference.

Interdependence in terms of the "origins of species" and similarity in terms of life-processes, however, does not rule out the obvious presence of conflict in nature – about which many are scandalized - and any organic and holistic view without this would be too idyllic. Ultimately, the evolutionary perspective helps us overcome the nature-destructive anthropocentrism. For, it makes us aware that human beings are one species among many, and reinforces the interconnectedness of the entire creation, and the need for a holistic understanding. In particular, it makes us realize how much the humans are a part of an interlocking eco-system and how they depend for their very existence upon the elements of the universe – the earth, air, water, fire and the sky, what the Hindu tradition calls the *"panchabhuta"*.[3]

---

[3] Cf. Raimundo Panikkar, *The Vedic Experience. An Anthology of the Vedas for Modern Man and Contemporary Celebration*, All India Books, Pondicherry, 1977. About the earth we read in *Atharva Veda* XII. 1:
  Untrammeled in the midst of men, the Earth
  Adored with heights and gentle slopes and plains
  Bears plants and herbs of various haling powers
  May she spread wide for us, afford us joy.

  Bearer of all things, hoard of treasures rare
  Sustaining mother, Earth the golden-breasted
  Who bears the Sacred Universal Fire,
  Whose spouse is Indra – may she grant us wealth" as Quoted on p. 123.

What is special about the evolutionary perspective of nature is not that it is science, but that it is a *different science* from the mechanistic one, especially in its technological application. The evolutionary perspective seems to intersect with the fundamental *Weltanschauung* of Hinduism, Buddhism, Daoism, etc. For monotheistic religious traditions, reconciling themselves with this perspective has been problematic as could be seen from the long opposition to evolution in the Christian tradition, which even today has not come to cease.

## Ecotheology - An Interreligious Project

An evolutionary framework is very important for any interreligious ecotheology. In some of the religious traditions like Hinduism, Buddhism and Daoism evolutionary thought is interwoven into their beliefs and world views, while other traditions like Christianity, Judaism and Islam may have more of a static view of nature, the earth and the universe. Therefore, what is called for is a convergence of all religious traditions. In any case, scientific evolutionism challenges all religions, albeit in different grades, their attitudes towards the earth and all forms of life. As for indigenous and primeval religious traditions, more than doctrines and beliefs, they embody the relationship of peoples to the ecosystem in their day to day expressions, and they are repository also of the indigenous knowledge and classification of the biodiversity of the region.

The common responsibility of religions towards the earth would call for a re-examination and re-interpretation of some of their foundational conceptions regarding God, human beings and nature.

> As we confront the environmental crisis, all religious traditions, if they are to survive and continue to contribute to solutions, must undergo some degree, perhaps, a considerable degree of reconstruction. Such work cannot be undertaken without a thorough and courageous examination of foundations. To list, marshal, or even carefully orchestrate apparently ecofriendly elements of any religious traditions and then declare the whole tradition ecologically sound, without having critically examined the deeper context, will produce, short-lived inspiration at best.[4]

In recent times there have been attempts in the Christian tradition to interpret the mystery of God, of Christ, and faith in general from an evolutionary perspective, bringing thus Christian beliefs closer to nature

---

[4] Christopher Key Chapple – Mary Evelyn Tucker (eds.), *Hinduism and Ecology*, Harvard University Press, Harvard, 2000, p. 152.

and its processes. By way of example we may think of the reflections of Karl Rahner on Christology and of Schoonenberg on creation.[5] But now what is called for is that we think of our relationship to the earth in a more fundamental way from the evolutionary perspective as well as from what Hinduism, Buddhism, Daoism, Confucianism, etc., offer in this regard. They try to explicate the human starting from the universe and not the other way round as we find in anthropocentric approaches. This is important since our relationship to earth has serious practical implications. We cannot remain only at the level of explaining traditional doctrines from an evolutionary perspective, but we also need to see what kind of praxis and attitudes they imply.

An unenlightened labeling of traditions like Hinduism of being monistic and pantheistic prevented Christianity from taking up the deeper insights and challenges these traditions presented.[6] Christian tradition needs to develop more and more the immanent dimension of the Divine mystery which is a necessary prelude to a deeper and meaningful understanding of nature and the earth. Therefore, the experience of seeing God in everything which is also part of the Christian mystical tradition needs to be fostered. Here is a point of intersection with Hinduism, Buddhism, Daoism, etc. We need to reopen the question of salvation in dialogue with them, and indeed in a more radical and transformative way. That leads me to the next point.

### Partners for the Salvation of *Terra Mater* and of Human Species

Not long ago a question that seriously agitated many theological minds was whether non-Christians have elements of salvation for humanity. Today, we would respond saying that other religious traditions have crucial and indispensable vision and values for the salvation of the earth without which there will be no salvation and future for humanity. Therefore, the new question that we need to pose is: What can Christianity

---

[5] Cf. Karl Rahner, "Christology within an Evolutionary View", in *Theological Investigations*, vol. 5, Darton, Longman & Todd, London, 1966; Piet Schoonenberg, "Evolution – Hominisation – Geschichte" in his *Auf Gott hin denken*, Herder, Freiburg, 1986, pp. 129 ff.

[6] There is an effort today to absorb the Hindu heritage without acknowledging its contribution, when some Western authors want to speak of *panentheism*. See the various contributions in Philip Clayton – Arthur Peacoke (eds.), *In Whom We Live and Move and Have Our Being. Panentheistic Reflections on God's Presence in a Scientific World*, William B. Eerdmans Publishing Company, Grand Rapids, 2004.

learn in dialogue with other religious traditions for the salvation of the planet earth so that human salvation can happen? A deeper dialogue will lead to the evolving of an interreligious ecotheology.

The convergence of perspectives among religions and a common engagement for the cause of the environment and social justice will naturally lead them to challenge the present dominant economy. In this sense, religions have to necessarily become political for the salvation of humanity. For, greed and competition-based system of economy and an unbridled production and consumption pattern will stretch the earth beyond its regenerative capacity. Unchecked, this system and pattern of life will lead the human species to disaster and even extinction. That will be the revenge of nature which will go on even without the human species. If not here, where does the discourse of salvation begin about which all religions are so very concerned? The salvation of the humans as envisaged in traditional theology had a particular cosmology.

Where there is greed, there is also instrumentalization inevitably at work. Instrumentalization of the earth goes along with manipulation of human beings and negation of equity through a play of power and domination. These are diametrically opposed to salvation which is a reality beyond teleology. From this perspective the earth and nature are to be respected in themselves and not to be viewed simply as objects for the fulfillment of human greed. The earth has its own rhythm as a mother carrying all beings in its womb and caring for them.

Efforts like creation of Nature Park, animal conservation projects, etc., are technical solutions that do not measure up to the moral and spiritual crisis stemming from the greedy and wasteful use of natural resources. They seem to separate the realm of facts from those of values. We need to hold these together in responding to the ecological crisis. Greed is at the root of the ecological crisis. The radical solution would appear when we address the issue of greed interwoven with violence and aggression of all kinds, and it is again here that we need to look up to the religious traditions for their wisdom and insights, and especially when they develop jointly interreligious perspectives on such fundamental issues conjoining facts and values. Such a common engagement will only revitalize religions and their theologies. As Dalai Lama notes with reference to his Buddhist tradition,

> In Buddhist practice we get so used to this idea of nonviolence and the ending of all suffering that we become accustomed to not harming or destroying anything indiscriminately. Although one does not believe

that trees or flowers have minds, we treat them with respect. Thus, we share a sense of universal responsibility for both mankind and nature.[7]

The way of life we practice vis-à-vis the nature also tells whether we are violent or non-violent. A non-violent and compassionate bearing gets reflected in the way people go about in their relationship to nature and all the materials things of daily life - either by wantonly and aggressively destroying them, or by nurturing and caring for them. Interreligious ecotheology will try to imbue our approach to nature with a sense of sacredness (which is not to be confused with "sacralization of nature") and a sense of wonder and mystery. To put in Christian theological terminology, this could be called a sacramental approach to creation that will help correct and balance an overly anthropocentric approach with a lot of emphasis on time and history. The realization and experience of the immanent presence of the Spirit in all of creation helps us overcome the gulf that divides, in traditional understanding, the creator and the created universe.[8]

> Nature speaks a truth scarcely heard and, up until recent years, insufficiently formulated among theologians. In our minds, we have eliminated or excluded the role of created nature as central to the salvation of the world. I say "in our minds" advisedly, because if God is revealed in the created world, then God is present "in all things" (Col. 3:11). In other words, there is an invisible dimension to all things visible, a "beyond" to everything material. All creation is a palpable mystery, an immense "incarnation" of cosmic proportions.[9]

## Rediscovery of Sources

A second aspect we need to consider is that of the relationship between creation and the mystery of God. In the Semitic or monotheistic religious traditions (Judaism, Christianity and Islam) the relationship between the creation and the creature is viewed through causality. So the Psalmists could say, "The heavens tell the glory of God and the firmament proclaim God's handiwork" (Ps 19:1). Both are differentiated and clearly demarcated with God as the cause and creation as the marvelous effect. In the Hindu

---

[7] Dalai Lama in his preface to Julia Martin (ed.), *Ecological Responsibility. A Dialogue with Buddhism*, Tibetan House – Sri Satguru Publication, Delhi, 1997, p. vii.

[8] Cf. Roger S. Gottlieb (ed.), *The Oxford Handbook of Ecology and Religion*, *op.cit.*, pp. 96-97.

[9] *Ibid.*, p. 97.

tradition the world and God are not two different realities. From the perspective of *advaita* (non-dual) thought, God and world are viewed neither as a single reality nor as two separate entities. This has led to an outlook, attitude and praxis that sees the  immanent divine presence in nature, in its most soft version, and the whole universe as the body of God, in its strong version. These intuitions have found poetic, mythical, devotional and ritual expressions in the Hindu tradition through millennia.[10] Expressing the basic Hindu intuition in an aesthetic image, I would say that the relationship of the creator to creation is that of a dancer becoming the dance itself. In fact, in Hindu Saivite tradition, Siva creates the whole universe through his eternal dance. The motion and rhythm of the divine dance keeps the entire universe in movement.

Buddhism, on its part, would challenge the very category of causality at the basis of the differentiation between creator and creation. It speaks of "dependent co-origination" (*pratityasamutpada*) of the entire reality which allows no room to think of cause and effect categories. On the contrary, the cause is in the effect, as much as the effect is in the cause, something that helps us to interpret the divine immanence in a much more intense and deeper way than a perspective of hierarchization of cause and effect, as can be seen in the traditional interpretation of the relationship of creator and creation.

The close relationship with nature is very characteristic of the Chinese vision of Daoism too. It views virtue in the human realm as the reflection of the healthy principles of balance and systemic equilibrium at work in nature. The health of the human body itself is a situation of homeostasis in which the principle of *yin* and *yang* are correlated and balanced, and the body in turn is in tune with the environment.  Hence harmony with nature is commended as the way the humans need to follow for their general wellbeing of mind and body. How could one dismiss all this beautiful vision as simply "natural" and view human salvation as something supernatural? But does not, on the other hand, a deeper Christian intuition see the body itself as the hinge of salvation – *caro cardo salutis*?

### Is Christianity to Blame?
The well-known critique of Lynn White laying the blame at the door of Christianity for the ecological crisis is somewhat simplistic as it fails to

---

[10] For a very good selection of classical Hindu texts in this sense, see Raymond Panikkar, *Mantramanjari, The Vedic Experience*, All India Books, Pondicherry, 1977.

make necessary distinction and differentiation.[11] Provoked by this thesis, Biblical scholars tried to interpret dominion as stewardship, care, etc. I think these exegetical exercises do not take us far. For, there is the incontrovertible fact of the consequences of a certain praxis that shows actually, domination is the way how Biblical tradition was interpreted in praxis. But the point is that this domination and mastery is something for which the entire Christianity is not to blame. We have in the Oriental and Orthodox tradition much more earth-related understanding of faith and creation.

The real point is that the Christianity that is faulted is one that was interpreted through the Enlightenment anthropocentrism of the West, which fosters  disenchantment with nature as a mark of progress. As a matter of fact, Christianity and Christian heritage were one-sidedly interpreted for the project of the Western Enlightenment and was profoundly influenced by the same. It is the same Enlightenment which taught that the creatively human emerges by transcending through freedom the world of nature or the realm of necessity. A misinterpretation of Genesis 1:28 in favour of human sovereignty served the anthropocentric purposes of the Enlightenment. Therefore, the project of interreligious ecotheology which will bring Christianity in dialogue with other religious traditions may help it recover the hidden dimension of its ecological message, and provide an occasion to bring to light the ecological sensitivity we find in the Christian tradition as borne out in the life of St Francis of Assisi,[12] Hildegard of Bingen[13] and others.

## Reinterpreting the Christian Tradition

Speaking of the factors that are responsible for anti-ecological attitudes, we need to highlight also the role played by, what I would call, *an inflated historical consciousness* in Christian tradition.  The practice of domination goes hand in hand with an exaggerated historical consciousness with human beings as the master-interveners who re-create the world and the

---

[11] Cf. Lynn White Jr., "The Historical Roots of Our Ecological Crisis", in *Science* 155 (10 March, 1967), pp. 1203–1207. This article generated a lot of world-wide debate.

[12] Cf. Julien Green, *God's Fool. The Life and Times of Francis of Assisi*, Harper San Francisco, San Francisco, CA, 1987.

[13] Cf. Hildegard of Bingen, *Scivias*, Paulist Press, Mahwah-New York, 1990; Sabina Flanagan, *Hildegard of Bingen 1098-1179. A Visionary Life*, Routledge, London-New York, 1989.

order of the earth in their image through the exercise of their freedom. Concepts of millennium and apocalyptism are closely tied to this outlook and conception of history.

The projection of this perspective has overshadowed the Biblical conception of a cyclical renewal that is closer to the rhythm of nature. Six days of work is followed by a break or the leisure of the Sabbath, and it continues. Similarly every six year of cultivation is followed by a pause of leaving the land fallow to renew its energies. And then there is the cycle of Jubilee by which the relationship of humans to the land is re-ordered. It renews both the earth as well as the human society.

These are perspectives which help us forge closer relationship with Hinduism, Buddhism, Daoism, etc., and resonate their view of nature, land and human society. Therefore they require to be highlighted in Christian theological reflection which has unfortunately tended in the past two hundred years towards supporting human history and its domination as supreme values, forgetful of the responsibility towards the earth and of the respect we owe to the rhythm of the earth that continues to nourish us. This relationship to the earth facilitates the realization of the divine immanence, as when Paul says, "in him we live and move, and have our being" (Acts 17:28). This immanence is not only in relation to the humans but of the entire cosmos. We understand more closely what it means "God all in all" (cf. 1Cor 15: 28) when Dionysius the Areopagite in his typical mystical slant tells us that "while remaining within God's self, God is also in the world (*encosmic*), around the world (*pericosmic)* and above the world (*hypercosmic*), that God is above heaven, and above all being, that God is sun, star and fire, water, wind and dew, cloud, archetypal stone and rock, that God is all, that God is no thing".[14] Such a Christian reinterpretation of creator and the created in terms of immanence will interlock with the vision many of the other religious traditions of the world, especially with what Hinduism has to say. There is then a lot of scope for an appropriate interreligious ecotheology for today.

## Ecotheology in Praxis
In Gandhi one would not find any environmental rhetoric of contemporary times, nor any nature-romanticism. Unlike his contemporary, the poet

---

[14] Dionysius the Areopagite, *On Divine Names,* 1:6. See *Pseudo-Dionysius. The Complete Works*, Paulist Press, New York, 1987, p. 56. I have made some adaptations in the translation, especially to use inclusive language.

Tagore, Gandhi rarely speaks of trees, birds, animals, landscapes, rivers or mountains. Abstemious as he was, at first sight there is nothing that could qualify him as an environmentalist; nothing that could ecologically inspire us. But then we are mistaken. It is in his whole way of life that we find an *embedded ecotheology*. He was opposed to waste of nature's resources and anything that would upset the balance of the natural environment. To foster the resources of nature is by voluntarily restraining oneself from use of things beyond the minimum required.

Gandhi's entire life functioned much like an ecosystem. This is one life in which every minute act, emotion, or thought was not without its place: the brevity of Gandhi's enormous writings, his small meals of nuts and fruits, his morning ablution and everyday bodily practices, his periodic observance of silence, his morning walks, his cultivation of the small as much as of the big, his abhorrence of waste, his resort to fasting – all these point to the manner in which the symphony was orchestrated.[15]

The critical question that can be raised is how these individual practices could cause the kind of structural change that we require. But that does not undermine the value of restraint and renunciation translated in practice, meaning frugal use of natural resources. The point is we need to create an environment and structures that would encourage the espousal of similar practices by more and more people and groups. Like voluntary silence which conserves human energy, frugal use of the goods of the earth helps preserve the equilibrium of nature. It has its social implications in as much as it contributes to create equitable social relationships. Here we understand the implications of a theology that links inextricably the creator and the created and the bonds that bind human beings to the earth.

What many environmentalists fail to acknowledge is that there is a deep co-relation between our approach to nature and the kind of relationship prevailing in the society. The destruction of eco-system at the same time causes wounds of injustice in the body of society. Interreligious ecotheology then should lead us logically to joint engagement in the question of social justice. An equitable distribution of natural resources is the best guarantee against exploitative use of them causing present-day environmental crisis.

---

[15] Vinay Lal, "Too Deep for Deep Ecology: Gandhi and the Ecological Vision of Life", in Christopher Key Chapple – Mary Evelyn Tucker (eds.), *Hinduism and Ecology, op. cit.*, p. 206.

A religiously inspired approach to nature and its protection can achieve where appeal to reason seem to fail. In fact, in recent times the recovery of nature is taking place in the West by employing the religious symbolism of *Gaia* – the earth-goddess.[16] I would like to highlight here the *Chipko movement* of India - one of the largest ecological movements in the world - was religiously inspired, and it affirms the spiritual value of nature. Women of the Himalaya region in North India were involved in protecting the trees of their villages when economic interests wanted to do the logging and denude the forests, and they hugged these trees and let no commercial interests fell them. There are numerous such examples from indigenous peoples all over the world whose approach to nature offers a lot of insights for an ecotheology.[17]

## Conclusion

There is a growing realization that we need a change of paradigm in our relationship to nature which in turn will bring about a transformation also in the relationships among human beings. To achieve these interrelated goals, one may not simply rely on technical and managerial solutions, or on some cosmetic changes in the model of development being followed. Change of paradigm calls for a new vision, attitude and values which, religions in spite of their tainted history could still provide, especially by developing appropriate ecotheologies. For, as John Clammer notes in his this theology is still one discipline that tries to maintain an integral vision of reality.[18]

The direction and inspiration from an interreligious ecotheology we expect is one that will help humanity realize the primordial bonds that bind together all that is with each other. From the realization of interconnectedness and interdependence flows the attitude of empathetic compassion towards all creatures and a deep sense of solidarity among human beings. From an ecotheology we could expect that it will help us realize also the fluid and provisional sense of the borders separating various realms of reality – the human, the cosmic and the divine.

---

[16] Cf. Erich Neumann, *The Great Mother*, Pantheon Books, New York, 1955.

[17] Cf. John A. Grim, *Indigenous Traditions and Ecology*, Harvard University Press, Harvard, 2001.

[18] Cf. John Clammer, "Learning from the Earth: Reflections on Theological Education and the Ecological Crisis", in *Concilium* 2009/3, pp. 95-101.

The development of interreligious ecotheology would presuppose that each religious tradition critically examine its own belief-system, world views and values to see to what extent they have been responsible for the ecological crisis, particularly by promoting a short-sighted anthropocentrism. On the other hand, the same religious traditions could provide us today elements for overcoming the crisis and enter into a harmonious relationship with nature and the entire reality.

Interreligious ecotheology needs to challenge an insulated understanding of the individual placed above the community and nature and help stem the tide of competition and accumulation of wealth responsible for brining about the present ecological crisis. Ecotheology has also to face the challenge of bringing about radical changes in the present-day structures of economy and development, which means it has to become truly political in its praxis.

Finally, ecotheology, I think is one that can foster mysticism in the religious traditions today. The earth and nature bring the religions together to meet the ultimate divine mystery. Pursuing together an ecotheology, the religious traditions encounter each other the God who is deep in  all creation and in the entire universe. Let me conclude, as I began, with a quote from Niklas Kazatzakis showing the inimate connection between the divine mystery and the world of nature. .

> The seeds are calling out from inside the earth: God is calling out from inside the seeds. Set him free. A field awaits liberation from you, and a machine awaits its soul from you. And you can no longer be saved, if you don't save them...the value of this transient world is immense and immeasurable: it is from this world that God hangs on in order to reach us; it is in this world that God is nurtured and increased...matter is the bride of my God: together they struggle, they laugh and mourn, crying through the nuptial chamber of the flesh.[19]

---

[19] Nikos Kazantzakis, *Ascetic Exercises* (5th ed.,) Athens, 1971. As quoted in Roger S. Gottlieb (ed.), The *Oxford Handbook of Religion and Ecology*, Oxford, 2006, p. 113.

# Chapter 20

# Conclusion
## *The Public Significance of Religious Pluralism*

> *"That since wars begin in the minds of men, it is in the minds of men that the defences of peace must be constructed; That ignorance of each other's ways and lives has been a common cause, throughout the history of mankind, of that suspicion and mistrust between the peoples of the world through which their differences have all too often broken into war."*                   UNESCO[1]

The world is becoming, today, what Asia has always been – a multi religious society. Since millennia people of various religious traditions have co-existed and interacted not only in what concerns matters of belief, but also in mundane questions. Buddhism, for example, is not only a religion; it is a way of life that has profoundly influenced the Asian ethos, and it has been in dialogue with other religious traditions; while giving many things, it continued to also receive no less. It allowed itself to be shaped by cultures and religions of various regions of Asia. As a result, we could speak of a Chinese Buddhism or Japanese Buddhism, Thai Buddhism, etc. Islam too is not a monolithic religious entity. The Islam of Indonesia is not the same as in Arabia and the rest of West Asia. In Indonesia it has been shaped by the Hindu and Buddhist religion and culture, and therefore we could speak of an Indonesian Islam.

What history tells us is that religious encounter of peoples has been very enriching. In the case of Buddhism it provided the environment in its monasteries for higher education in ancient Asia. We remember the renowned universities of Nalanda and Takshila where higher education

---

[1] These memorable words are found in the Preamble of the UNESCO Constitution.

in various secular fields was promoted by Buddhism, and thousands of monks from China visited these centres of higher learning and carried precious Sanskrit manuscripts which are today, ironically, not available in original Sanskrit but in Chinese translation! In short, in Asia, to speak of religious pluralism is to recall its culture, its traditions, ways of life, modes of education, etc.; in short it is to recall the Asian civilization.

We need to be aware of the fact that in the present circumstances, religious identity conditions the lives of the people. People are often identified in relation to their religion in national politics. For example, to be Thai or to be Sinhalese amounts to being a Buddhist; to be a Malay means a Muslim and to be a Nepalese means to be a Hindu; to be a Filippina means Christian. Such religious identification has got its repercussions in all spheres – political, economic, cultural, educational, etc. That is another important reason why we need to take into serious account religious pluralism in Asia.

## Religious Pluralism – From Fact to Option

Religious diversity is a self-evident and observable fact. Recognition of this fact is not the same thing as acknowledgement of religious pluralism. Religious pluralism says that we are not simply in a factual situation of *religious* diversity, but that we opt consciously to relate ourselves to these traditions different from ours. There is the will to engage oneself with the religious beliefs and practices of one's neighbours; there is the desire to participate in some measure in the religious experience of others and to understand others as they would like to be understood.

There is something called phenomenology of religion. It means I study another religion as it appears to me  in its beliefs, institutions, practices, etc. What makes religious pluralism different from phenomenology of religion is that it is engaged with others, with what they hold as most precious – their religious world-view and convictions. In this way, religious pluralism cements deeply the relationships in society.

Religious pluralism is much deeper and wider in scope than religious tolerance. Religious tolerance could be motivated by the pragmatism of "live and let live". It could nurtured lest there should be harmful religious conflicts and violence. Religious pluralism takes us beyond religious tolerance. It positively recognizes the value of other religions and believes that each of the religion has a unique contribution to the welfare of humanity and its future. This is what the great emperor Ashoka, a convert to Buddhism and non-violence, after the shocking experience of a bloody war, tried to promote. He noted in one of his edicts the following:

> A man must not do reverence to his own religion [sect] or disparage that of another religion without reason. Deprecation should be for specific reason only, because the religions of other people all deserve reverence for one reason or another. By thus acting, a man exalts his own religion, and at the same time does services to the religions of other people. By acting contrariwise, a man hurts his own religion and does disservice to the religions of other peoples.[2]

In modern times we have several great spiritual leaders who have inspired us with high ideals that augur well for the future of humanity. One such figure who promoted very actively interreligious understanding is the Ajahn Buddhadasa Bhikkhu, the most influential Buddhist monk in twentieth century Thailand. He saw the role of all religions as the same, namely, to liberate human beings from selfishness and suffering. He was a person of religious pluralism, interreligious dialogue and harmony.

Religious pluralism is very important today to understand and practice religious freedom, which is a public issue and a matter of fundamental right. Here the respect is shown to our neighbours by recognizing their right to be different and to believe, practice and propagate their religious convictions. It is no exaggeration to say that the barometer of political and social standards of any society is constituted by its readiness to accept religious pluralism and religious freedom. Where this is present, there is assurance of peace and harmony in society. Where there is the culture of religious pluralism, the upholding of religious freedom becomes a matter of course.

Speaking of religious pluralism we should not limit ourselves only to major religious traditions. There are numerous primeval religions among the tribal and indigenous peoples of Asia. They are very important today, especially because of their close connection with nature and their cosmic vision. They teach us the importance of harmony with nature and the universe and our obligation to nurture the earth and not wantonly destroy its resources and cause environmental degradation and crisis.

---

[2] N.A. Nikam – Richard McKeon (eds.), *Edicts of Ashoka*, The University of Chicago Press, Chicago, 1978, Rock Edict XIII.

## Religions as Complex Symbolic Systems

There are certain experiences which defy our conventional language. Such is the case with religious experience. That is why in order to convey what lies behind such experiences, religions use myths and symbols. This is true of all religious traditions. For example, one may not explain through the power of reason the presence of evil in the world, especially evil as the suffering of the innocent. Hence, all religions have recourse to myths and symbols to throw some light on this mystery. We have the highly symbolized narration of the original fall (Adam and Eve), the theory of *karma* bound up with many myths and the belief in predestination which also has a certain mythical character.

Religions use also elaborate symbols in their ritual practices. Each religion can be characterized as a system of symbols and codes. Consequently, to know another religion cannot be simply a matter of notional knowledge. We need to get into the world of experience of our neighbours. It is like learning a new language which is also a system of codes. We understand peoples of other faiths when we try to enter into their world of experience and their symbolic system. Such an effort brings us closer to our neighbours. Because, in this way, we participate in something which they believe to be very intimate and sacred to them. On the other hand, we will do great harm if we do not respect the religious symbols of our neighbours, simply because they are not like our own. This could lead to violence.

## Identity and Dialogue

Does the acknowledging of religious pluralism and dialogue mean the dilution of one's identity as Christian, Buddhist, Hindu, etc.? No, on the contrary, we become more Christian and understand what we believe and practice more deeply when we see ourselves in relationship with peoples of other faiths. Any culture, in order to survive and flourish, needs to be constantly stimulated by other cultures; so it is with religions. Our religious identity is not watered down but is grasped in a new light when we reach out in dialogue with our neighbours of other faiths. If we go through the history of Christianity, we will note how all through the centuries, especially in its early period, it was influenced by other religious traditions – Greek, Roman, Germanic, Gallic, etc. The elements of these traditions have gone into the texture of Christian faith, worship and practice. The close association with another religious tradition can help purify our faith, and see what is more important and what is secondary in our religious practices. In this way, religious pluralism deepens our faith.

In recognizing the faith of our neighbours we acknowledge what God has done to them, especially when we meet Hindus, Buddhists and Muslims who give such an inspiring witness to selfless love, deep spirituality and live a life of commitment and dedication. This is what Bishop A.J. Appasamy had to say after trying to understand the faith of the Hindus:

> I for one cannot believe that such profound devotion to God, conviction of the utterly degraded nature of the devotee, sense of the need for complete surrender, radiant joy in God's presence which are found abundantly in Hindu religious literature can be achieved by human effort; they can only be regarded as God-given.[3]

## The Role of Religion in the Public Sphere and for Liberation

We recognize history has been scripted today with a new signature: Barrack Hussain Obama, whose ancestry goes back to the infamy of slavery, has emerged as the leader of his country. If such surprises could take place at much faster pace than projected, it is due to various reasons, not the least, through the influence of religiously inspired pioneers like Martin Luther King, who was a religious minister and yet was fully involved in the civil rights movement. We think of his renowned speech in Washington: "I have a dream" which today has become a reality. The dream of this minister was that the discriminated black people be given the same opportunity and be treated equally.

If apartheid was abolished in South Africa, it is due no less to the involvement of Bishop Desmond Tutu. In East Timor during the years of great convulsion and violence, the leadership of Bishop Belo contributed to peace and reconciliation. It is remarkable that none of them was defending their religion, or were primarily interested in religious rituals. They were men who were moved by the plight of the people without any consideration of religion, race or ethnicity. If in Korea and the Philippines dictatorships were brought to an end, it was again due to the important role played by religiously motivated people to act in the public sphere. Similarly we could cite the example of the role religion played in the breakdown of totalitarian system in Eastern Europe.

---

[3] A.J. Appasamy, "Religious Experience in India", in *The Pilgrim*, 2 (January 1943), p. 87.

Now the point to note is that the role religions are called upon to play in the public sphere could more effectively and fruitfully be done by *cooperation* among the various religious groups towards common good, and what pertains to the welfare of the community. In this way, the inter-relationship among religions have wider scope than coming to an understanding among themselves as religious entities. Religions enshrine resources, which when rightly interpreted, could be harnessed to the goal of liberation and humanization. This has been the crucial point in the interpretation of Christianity in Latin America, for example. This experience has given also a new impetus for religions to come together to respond to the plight of humanity and work towards its emancipation.

The interreligious dialogue and cooperation in Asia should be a contribution to Asia's struggle for greater humanization. It is this which calls for dialogue and understanding among religions, so that they could participate in the public space and join hands to build up the community. M.M. Thomas, one of the great 20th century Asian Christian thinkers put the matter in this way:

> Christianity, renascent religions, and secular faiths, are all involved in the struggle of man for the true meaning of his personal social existence – each on its own terms but together. It seems to me that the relations between Christian faith and other living religions and secular faiths is passing to a new stage, because they not only co-exist in the same society but also cooperate to build a secular society and culture. It is within such co-existence and cooperation that we can best enter into dialogue at the deepest level on the nature and destiny of man and on the nature of ultimate truth.[4]

To be able to understand the public role of religion, we could usefully distinguish, following Niklas Luhman, between two dimensions of religion: *Religion as function* and *religion as performance*. Through belief-system, rituals, sacred authority, etc., a religion continues to function and reproduce itself in society. Function would be what it does to its adherents in terms of providing meaning, celebrating rituals, etc. "Performance" means, on the other hand, "when religion is 'applied' to problems generated in other systems but not solved there, or simply not addressed elsewhere. Examples of such problems are economic poverty, political

---

[4] M.M. Thomas, "The World in which We Preach Christ" in Ronald K. Orchard (ed.), *Witness in Six Continents*. Records of the Meeting of the Commission on World Mission and Evangelis of the WCC.

oppression, familiar estrangement, environmental degradation, or personal identity. Through performance relations, religion establishes its importance for the 'profane' aspects of life."[5]

Religion as function means that it continues to repeat the beliefs, rituals and practices through the course of time. This helps the maintenance of religion and its status quo. On the other hand, religion becomes a performance, when it tries to respond to those questions and issues which the various systems in society have raised, but have left unanswered. Starting from a wholistic perspective, religion could intervene in various areas of life for greater humanization and for the creation of fellowship and true community. Traditional theology was catering to the 'function' of Christianity, whereas public theology is one that would support the 'performance' of Christianity.

In many Asian societies, religion and religious leaders hold the key for peace and amity in the society. If religiously committed people engage in dialogue and understanding, peace and harmony will reach the societies faster than through any other means. Therefore, the axiom that "there is no peace in the world without peace among religions" could be verified also at the micro level in the different societies of Asia.

### Influence of Religion in Various Areas of Public Life

Religious beliefs, convictions and practices have repercussion in various departments of human life – in political praxis, cultural configurations, formation of social mores etc. To what extent religion could influence and condition politics is well-known and does not require elaboration. What is less known is the fact that religions and religious beliefs could shape also economic activities. Let me cite two examples here. In his classical work on *"Protestant Ethics and the Spirit of Capitalism"*, Max Weber showed how Protestant ethics was responsible in creating a culture of work, frugality and how the belief in predestination spurred on people to produce wealth which was viewed as a clear sign of God's blessing and an assurance of eternal salvation. The other example is from Jainism. The belief in non-violence led the Jain community to shun agricultural profession and take up commercial professions.[6] Again we have the

---

[5] Peter Beyer, *Religion and Globalisation*, Sage Publications, London, 2000, p. 80; Niklas Luhmann, *Funktion der Religion*, Suhrkamp, Frankfurt a. M., 1977; Id., *The Differentiation of Society*, Columbia University, New York, 1982.

[6] Cf. P.S. Jaini, "Ecology, Economics and Development in Jainism", in C.K. Chapple (ed.), *Jainism and Ecology*, Harvard Universty Press, Boston, 2002,

example in Japan of the intimate connection of Zen Buddhism with the economy of frugality. Zen Buddhist monks played an important role in the commercial activities of Ashikaga Period in that country. During the Tokugawa period (1600-1868), religion was an important factor in the economic development of Japan.[7]

### Secularism and Religion

There is ample room to speak of the secular in Asian societies. For, secular thinking is not the monopoly of any one people or culture. There is an Asian secular approach to reality which has been reflected in its history, philosophy, tradition, etc. Buddhism was a secular movement that challenged the hegemony of religion and religious agents, and proclaimed the equality of all, and the possibility of every one reaching the ultimate goal. In all our nations we could find the emergence of secular movements.

However, Asian secularism does not want to banish religion from the public life of the people. No one knows the harmful effects of the dichotomy between the private and the public, as the feminists do. Religion cannot be relegated to the private realm in our Asian societies. The point of secularism in Asia is one that does not favour any one religion in preference to others. All religions are treated equally (*sarvadharma samabhava*). The Asian secularity is not a matter of the absence of religion from the public realm. The real secular question in Asia is that in every country all religions receive the same treatment. In this sense, several countries face the problem of the secular in their societies, especially in the relation of the state to religions. Secularism is not ignorance of religion, nor denial of the role of religion in public life. In Asia, secularism is a way of life that includes respect for all religions.

### Conclusion

There is enough reason to despair about religions, for their various omissions and commission through the centuries, for the violence they have engendered and the gender discrimination they have caused, and the justification they had given to caste, colonialism, etc. But then as all realities in human life, religion too is ambiguous. There is also a brighter side to religion. The most sublime things human beings are capable of

---

pp. 141-158; Atul K. Shah, "Corporate Governance and Business Ethics", in *Business Ethics: A European Review*, 5, 4 (1996), pp. 225-233.

[7] Cf. Robert Bellah, *Tokugawa Religion. The Cultural Roots of Modern Japan*, The Free Press, New York, 1985, p. 107.

have been done in the name of God and motivated by religious beliefs. In this regard we need to take note that science and technology too exhibit the ambiguous character. It could be employed to produce biological, chemical and nuclear weapons, to wantonly destroy nature, etc. Whether it is space technologies, chemical technologies or biotechnologies – all these could be abused. But that is no reason to write them off. In the case of religion, it is a question of drawing the resources for greater humanization, for change and transformation in society, for a culture of peace. Precisely, aware of the potential of religious traditions, the UNESCO organized a series of conference on "Religion and Culture of Peace".

Religious pluralism may not be of interest to a large number of people for the difference they manifest in doctrine, tradition, rituals, etc. The significance of religious pluralism today is to be seen more and more in the richness each religious tradition bears in itself to contribute to the public issues affecting society and humanity. The various public questions in Asia we dealt in this book have also shown the avenues for religious traditions to make their contributions. It is important then that public theologies be developed in the various religious traditions and there be continuing dialogue and exchange among these theologies. Christian theology is challenged to become truly a partner among the various public theologies of the continent sharing the same historical, social, political and cultural situation and turn into a force of transformation for justice and peace, and for harmony with the entire creation.

# Index

www.ingramcontent.com/pod-product-compliance
Lightning Source LLC
Chambersburg PA
CBHW060412030726
47495CB00003B/545